BUBBLES OF TIME

LORNA HOPKINS KEITH

DEDICATION

To Greg, my husband and partner in life

ACKNOWLEDGEMENTS

Many thanks again to the Wordsmiths, my critique group who have shown me the way to better writing.

LIST OF CHARACTERS

BORN ON EARTH

LIVING ON PEACE

Granlyn (Lyn Harlan), first matriarch and first with mind Talent

Grampa Bay, Lyn's second cousin, leader of the other branch of the clan

Grampa Larry (Larry Brock), her cousin and mate, only one without Talent

Gramps Bill, Lyn's nephew, man of all trades

Granli (Pauli), Lyn's niece and Bay's mate

Old Art, Bay's cousin, retired head of science department

Old Chad, Bay's cousin and head of construction

Old Maria, Bay's sister and Chad's mate and cousin. Bay's sister, and head medic

Papa Allen, Lyn's youngest nephew, an empath

LEFT ON HARMONY

Adam (killed by aliens), leader and Lyn's half-brother, raised on the world of Ruthor

Betty (taken by aliens), Old Art's mate, organizer

LIVING ON PEACE

Allen, Granlyn's nephew and Janni's father, explorer

Anne, head medic (Peter's mate)

Big Art, head scientist, Old Art's son

Artie, rising scientist, Big Art's son

Bay (Grampa Bay), construction leader retired, a loner (Granli's mate)

Beth, Bay's daughter and Gabe's mate, named after her grandmother on Earth, runs childcare

Brian, Willie's brother and Glori's mate, the smart one.

Carla, Anne's older daughter, good with crafts

Old Chad, Bay's cousin and current construction boss (Old Maria's mate)

Chad III, Chad's son, in construction

Charley, Bay's son, Perri's mate

Curtis, one of late arriving twins to Lyn and Larry

Dottie, creator of journals

Elli, Roroy's mate, an arrival from a later Earth

Freddie, Dottie's mate

Gabe (Adam's son), a recluse since lost touch with Bramite sister.

Glori, Janni's best friend, daughter of Susan, Marisa's best friend, born at same time as Janni

Jan (Janice, Janni) Perri's granddaughter, Marisa's daughter, her Talent led her to space

Jimmy, Joan's son, had a tendency to get in trouble

Joan, old Art's daughter, Susan's mother, totally against Sam's people coming to Peace

Mindy, Beth's daughter, practically lives in the big kitchen

Maria, Bay's sister and also against Sam's people

Marisa, Lyn's granddaughter and the acting matriarch, she found the quines and the world, Peace

Mary, Old Art's youngest daughter, never got over loss of her mother.

Megan, Mindy's twin, also works in the kitchen

Mick, Janni's brother, too smart for his own good

Nancy, Mary's daughter and violently opposed to the newcomers.

Noa, the Bramites' head medic and Lyn's friend

Old Beth, Lyn's sister, left on Earth

Old Maria (see Maria)

Pauli (Granli), Lyn's niece, now retired and sits with the children.

Perri, Lyn's daughter, who followed her twin to another world.

Peter, Perri's twin, kidnapped by aliens

Richard, the last of Janni's cohort, born Harry Richard

Ricky, Marisa's brother, too smart for his own good

Ruthie, Brian and Willie's mother, a scatterbrain but good mother

Steve, Janni's brother, a pest

Susan, Marisa's best friend, who keeps people under control

Uncle Art (also Artie), scientist, can see into machinery to see how it works.

Uncle Laurie, Marisa's brother

Uncle Peter (see Peter)

Will (Grampa Will) Beth's son

Willie, Will's son and Janni's mate.

ALIENS

Ambaak: humanoid, self-sufficient, Cityworld.
> Liia, showed Sam how to use plants
> Giil, her mate and leader
> Jone, who took in two abandoned children Brad found

Beast: From Roroy's world, big and black with a big heart

Bramites: humanoids whom Lyn and Larry lived with for two years and came with them to Harmony.

Centar: Golden giants who wanted Lyn's people for their own use.

Cray: humanoid, from world Peter taken to.

Felce: feline, intelligent, on Cityworld

Ghind: humanoid, live simply, Cityworld

Noreg: Humanoid, live off the land, Cityworld

Quine: equine, intelligent, have mind link, bonded with Marisa's people

Roroy: humanoid Marisa found on other world who came to live with her people, in crops and construction, with Beast

Volen: unknown, built City on Cityworld for the humans and others, and let it die.

Watchers: nonphysical entities who gave Lyn's family Talent that would allow her clan to become the New Watchers to take the place of the dying race.

Wati: brown furred humanoids (Judee) who rescued Lyn and found Harmony for all of them.

FROM STARVIEW

Samanda Lar, mayor

Brad Lar, her twin, in charge of communications

Emily, his wife, head of childcare

Del and Felicia, their children

Todd, her other brother, head of legal, with his father

Hal, her companion, man of all trades

Maxee, a Klocti, Sam's alien sister, very clever

Arlene, Sam's assistant and surrogate mother

Doug, watermaster

Evelyn, head medic, Hal's mother

Dirk, former counselor, Hal's father

Jan, Hal's crippled sister, and artist

Glenda, Sam's second assistant, and real head of construction
Gus, her mate, head of construction
Ben and Alex, their sons
Zilla, Medical department head
June, head of food processing and caffs
George, head of science department

BUBBLES OF TIME

PROLOGUE

PEACE

FOURTEEN-YEAR-OLD JANNI WHOOPED as she felt the beginnings of womanhood. Now she could be part of the clan council and, in time, become the matriarch. Granlyn, the current one, was old, and Gramma Perri, her daughter, had no interest in it. Mama, Gramma Perri's daughter, always said she'd had enough of leadership fourteen years ago.

Dangling the bag of vegetables she'd collected at the storehouse, Janni dashed across the stone paved plaza to her home. The first thing she'd do, after collecting her period rags, was tell her friend, Glori. Then she'd go tell Granlyn. The old woman always wanted to know everything.

'Glori, Glori,' she *sent* to the other girl in her mind as she ran into her house and dropped the bag on the wooden table. 'It's started.' She dug out the period rags and stuffed them in her pants as she *heard* Glori's squeal.

'About time,' Glori sent. Hers had started two months before.

Janni ran out to Granlyn's. It was easier to tell the matriarch in person; her mind Talent wasn't nearly as strong as the younger generations'.

In her rush, sudden dizziness overcame the girl. Janni's feet tangled, she tripped over a rock, and fell beyond reality into darkness dotted with tiny white lights. Stars. Although she perceived the stars, she could not sense her body.

Visiting the stars would be more exciting than exploring her world, Peace, her current goal.

•   •   •

Janni pushed up through the layers of consciousness to awareness and a sense of wonderment. The white globes of light and swathes of blues and purple she'd perceived were like nothing she'd ever experienced. Somehow, she knew she'd see them again.

The girl opened her eyes to a bouquet of square faces framed by dark curls that mirrored her own. Propped up on her own bed, words came out of her mouth. "What? How …"

"You're back." Mama hugged her. Janni *caught* her thought about becoming a woman too soon.

"Of course, I am." She looked around at the pale yellow walls peppered with her drawings, the shelves with Papa's carvings, and her narrow table under the window. Her home.

"We couldn't wake you," Medic Anne said with concern in her voice. Her curls were touched with gray. "Charley found you on the ground and carried you home." She checked the girl's pulse and respiration. "Normal," she added.

"You had us worried," Gramma Perri said. "What happened?" She tugged at her tunic.

Mama patted Janni's arm. The smell of purple purrflowers permeated the room.

Janni thought for a moment. *Grampa Charley. It would be him.*

"I was running home because my period started – oh." She clutched her abdomen. Still dazed, Janni closed her eyes and felt the rags between her legs. "Anyway, I tripped and fell. Then there was blackness with lights like stars and colors, then I woke up."

She blinked. She'd have to think about that.

"Stars?" Grampa Charley asked. He crossed his legs.

Deep within, Janni knew it had been real. She tried to hold onto the experience, but it faded away like a dream.

She shook her head. "I think so, it's going away. I don't know." She felt like she'd lost something precious.

"Do you suppose this could be something to do with a new Talent?" Mama looked at the others. Every generation had the original mind Talent, but each new one had a new Talent in addition to the previous ones.

"Could be," Grampa Charley replied. "Or some kind of hallucination."

Unable to put it in words, Janni thought, *No, it was real.*

"Janni, we know you have the Talent of mindlink that all of us have, and that you can move things and people without touching them," Gramma Perri said. "Have you bent time like your mama did?"

Janni's mind cleared. "Once, when I picked up Willie's cutter, and he got really mad at me. I put it back and closed my eyes. When I opened them, I was just reaching for the tool, like I'd gone back in time before I picked it up. I don't think he noticed; he never said anything." Janni shook her head. "Maybe this thing I saw is a new Talent?"

The others looked at each other and shrugged. The Harlan clan had mixed feelings about Talent. On one hand, it was quite useful, even saving lives; on the other hand, the mindlink generated a lack of privacy, as it became harder for those with stronger Talent to deal with it. And worst of all, it meant that clanspeople were becoming alien Watchers.

Janni found it was almost impossible to shut out other people's thoughts when she wanted privacy in her mind. It was fun when she was little and she could see what others were thinking, until Mama and the others clamped down on her. She still did it, but didn't tell anyone.

Medic Anne climbed to her feet. "Let's let her rest now and collect her thoughts. Maybe later she can tell us what she thought she saw."

Mama, Gramma Perri, and Grampa Charley all kissed Janni and followed the medic out.

"I'll be here in the house," Mama said as she left the room.

Janni sat back against the pale wall and stared at the cracks. She knew what she had perceived was real.

Why wouldn't they believe me?

1

PEACE

THREE YEARS LATER, in the spring, Janni was not happy. Although she was on the council, she had little say in things, she still lived at home with her parents and two younger brothers, and she had not seen the stars again. The clan village of Freedom was too small; she felt stifled. She was a woman with no mate, no place of her own, no purpose to her life.

The only people on the world of Peace, the clan just managed to produce a decent living, with everyone expected to perform their assigned tasks. The village lay between two rivers, and the air smelled fresh and sweet with masses of flowers everywhere.

Janni thought about going exploring, even though only certain people were allowed to go farther than a half day from the clanhome and, even then, not alone.

One day, she *heard* Granlyn's voice in her mind, *summoning* her to come by after she finished with the garment she was mending.

'Okay,' she *sent* back, glancing around the craft hall with its white walls and rows of worktables where people did everything from making clothing to painting clay pots.

Next to Janni, Glori said, "Did you hear that?"

"Granlyn?"

"Yes. You too?"

Glori nodded and put her mending away.

Janni finished sewing the last button on the tunic she was holding, stood up, and said, "Come on."

"Granlyn wants us," Glori said to Gramma Perri as the older woman looked their way.

She nodded, and the two young women left.

The two walked across the plaza and up the flower-lined path to Granlyn's house with the vines around the porch posts. The old woman welcomed them in, and they found Leona already there. She and her twin, Curtis, were Granlyn's late-middle-age miracle babies, born just before Janni and Glori. Leona had the same square face and black curls as the others in Granlyn's line, but blond Curtis took after his dad, Grampa Larry.

"Welcome," Granlyn said as Janni and Glori sat on the sagging brown couch next to Leona. "I've asked you here because it is time for you gals to set up your own households. Janni, you'll mate with Willie, and Glori, you with Brian."

About time, Janni thought. *Something was finally happening.*

Because the clan was so small, and she was the first born female and Willie the first born male of her generation, Janni always knew she would be mated with him.

"I guess that leaves Richard for me," Leona said, rolling her eyes.

"Unless you want to wait for one of the younger boys to grow up."

Leona shook her head. "I always figured it would be him."

Janni wondered what it would be like to mate with someone you loved, like Granlyn and Grampa Larry did. He and Granlyn had grown up with each other and always been together.

"There are several things we need to discuss," Granlyn began. "First, have any of you discovered any kind of new Talent?"

"No," said Glori.

Leona shook her head.

Janni thought of the stars she'd seen, but that wasn't a Talent. She shook her head.

"Okay. Let me know immediately when you do. Our Talents are creating a big problem. Some of the others in my generation, especially Maria, Chad, and Old Art, are afraid of your generation and want the Talents to go away."

"Do *you* want them to stop?" Janni demanded.

Granlyn smiled. "Yes and no. They do have their uses, the mindlink and teleportation. But Marisa's time thing, no. We don't want to turn into Watchers; we want to stay as we are and make a home here for humans for many generations to come."

"But what can we do?" Janni asked. "I don't want to give up the Talents I have, just not have any more." She thumped the couch.

"No, Janni," Granlyn said. "We need to pull back. The mind Talent would be safe to keep, but not the others." She rocked in her chair.

"But Granlyn ..." Janni began.

"How could we do that?" Leona asked.

"Try not to use them," Glori suggested.

"Glori," Janni cried.

'Calm down,' Glori *sent* on their private mindlink.

Granlyn moved around in her chair. "Janni, control yourself. Glori has a point. Leona, do you have anything to offer?"

"Okay. What if we three don't have babies, or maybe just boys, and the younger ones of our generation can have whatever they want." Leona rubbed the arm of the couch.

"What if the new Talent just goes to the firstborn girl, no matter when she comes?" Janni asked.

Granlyn shook her head. "I think we should simply use our Talents as little as possible. For right now, you three put off having babies for as long as you can. Think about it." Granlyn looked at Janni. "Second, have any of you started on your houses?"

"Willie and Brian have laid out our houses," Janni said. *A safe subject.*

"Good. Go ahead and get started on them." She paused and closed her eyes.

The young women waited.

When Granlyn opened her eyes and sat up, she said, "You do know the history of our people well, don't you?"

Three nods. Janni knew her great-grandfather, Grampa Larry, was Granlyn's cousin on her mother's side and so had no Talent. He was very good at telling what people were thinking by observing their body language.

"Good. We must never forget where we came from. And we must not forget there may be other human colonies on other worlds. Just because we were taken from Earth when men were barely to the moon, doesn't mean interplanetary spaceships weren't built, and people traveled to other planets later."

"Oh," said Janni. That had never occurred to her. She looked at the books on the shelf across from her. Old books brought from Old Earth. Some were about people on other worlds.

"Now. You are the first three girls of your generation," Granlyn said. "I expect you to become responsible adults and conduct yourselves as such. You will set an example by not using your Talents unless necessary."

"But ..." Janni began.

"No buts, Janni. It may be that our Talents will atrophy if not used. You three also be thinking of any possible ways to rid ourselves of these Talents."

No way. The thought came from deep within Janni. *I need my Talents.*

"One more thing," Granlyn said. "About your children ..."

Before she could say another word, a loud boom came from the plaza area and, at the same time, screams in their minds.

"Mick," Janni cried. "He's hurt."

Her thirteen-year-old brother worked with Big Art and his son, Uncle Artie, the clan's scientists. She *heard* her mama scream as the three girls ran out the door, followed by Granlyn.

Janni smelled the smoke first. The science lab on the east side of the plaza was on fire. People grabbed buckets and scooped water from the river to throw on the blaze. Uncle Artie and three boys sat on the ground nearby. Mick lay beside them.

She ran to Mick, already being treated by Medic Anne. He had a big gouge on his forehead, blood running into his closed eyes, and burns on his arms and chest. He bit on a stick and moaned.

"Mick," Mama cried. She dropped beside him.

"He'll be okay, Marisa," Medic Anne said. "Poor kid, he got the worst of it."

"You were using Talent, weren't you?" Janni said, *seeing* in his mind what he had been doing.

"Leave him alone," Mama said, holding his hand. "What happened?" she asked Uncle Artie.

"He tried to use a Talent he hadn't fully mastered, moving things without touching them."

Janni's younger brother, Steve, ran up. "What happened? Did he do something bad?"

"Steven, hush," Mama said. "Just be thankful he's still alive."

"Okay." He sat and watched.

Granlyn arrived. "Were you using Talent?" she asked.

"Yes," Janni said.

"Well, that does it." Granlyn sat down carefully. "We must stop this Talent."

"I agree, but how?" Mama asked.

"Or at least do a better job of training the youngsters. He said he knew how to use it." Uncle Artie rubbed his head. "Sometimes Talent's useful, but it takes time for a young one to learn to use it right. The other boys and I only have minor injuries." He ignored Marisa.

"Well, think about it," Granlyn said.

Papa arrived and carried Mick to the clinic, followed by Medic Anne. Before Marisa could go after them, an older woman and her daughter stepped out of the group that had gathered around.

"When are you going to control your brats, Marisa?" the younger one demanded. "Look at the mess."

"Nancy, children, especially boys, are going to make mistakes," Marisa said, balling her fists.

"Tell them not to use Talent until they're grown up and can handle it."

"Now, Nan," the older woman said.

"All right, Mama," Nancy said. "But this has got to stop."

"Don't tell me how to raise my children," Marisa snapped.

Janni had never heard that tone of voice from her mother before. "Go, Mama," she whispered. *About time those old snoops got slapped down.*

"Girls, girls," Granlyn said in her boss tone. "That's enough. You two go on about your business, and you, Marisa, see about your son."

"Yes, Granlyn," Marisa said, and left for the clinic.

Janni tried to follow, but Granlyn held her back. "He'll be taken care of. You need to look after Stevie."

"Okay." Janni added, "Come on, Squirt."

"Smartyass," he said, and followed her to childcare, behind the schoolhouse. "Why can't I go home?"

"Because your lesson starts soon so you need to be here."

Janni returned to her craft project.

2

STARVIEW

MAYOR SAMANDA LAR THREW HER STYLUS across her tiny office in the town of Starview, on Cityworld. "I've had it. Why do we have rules when half the people won't follow them?"

"For the other half who do."

Arlene, her assistant, reached down, picked up the stylus, and handed it back to Sam. Sam wiped her forehead with a small cloth. Even with the door open, stuffiness filled the office.

Starview consisted of long strings of apartment buildings down South, North, and West valleys, punctuated by caffs, medical clinics, and schools. Government buildings, labs, and a caff huddled together on the mesa by the river, plus the homes of the mayor and most department heads. Sam's house had the luxury of two trees on one side and one on the other.

Many people still wanted the amenities they'd had back in City, run by the Volen, a caretaker species. But the Volen and City were gone, and the citizens had to make do with what the caretakers had left them and their own skills and knowledge. Sam had to deal with those citizens, including those who thought they shouldn't have to work, and food shortages.

Why can't we go somewhere else and start over again? The thought came again as Sam picked up a piece of paper, put it down, and laid her head on her arms on the table.

Arlene rose, brushed aside Sam's long red hair, and rubbed her back.

"You need a vacation," she said.

"How? Where?" Sam propped her chin in her hands. "Arlene, I'm so tired of this, always having to fix problems, make decisions about things I know little of, being a leader. Just because I worked as an investigator, and somebody out there stuck me with being the leader." She paused. "And now something new and big is coming at us."

"What?"

"I can't tell yet. But it's going to change a lot of things around here, and I'll have to deal with that too." Sam's farseeing ability was not always welcome.

Arlene patted Sam's shoulder. "You've done enough. Finding this place, moving the people from dying City up here, and running the place for ten years. You need to retire."

"And do what?" *If I only could.*

"Nothing, for a while. Isn't there anything you'd like to do, that you've been thinking of but had no time for?"

Sam sighed. "I'd like to have time to sit all afternoon and watch the river go by. Not have to worry about having to get up and do things. Maybe visit with my brothers, Maxee, other friends. Maybe work with plants." *Don't tempt me.*

The thought popped up again. "Maybe find a new place where we could start all over again, with fewer people." Sam sighed.

"Sounds nice, but we'd probably mess it up again." Arlene sat down.

Sam nodded. She poked at the coming event her farseeing showed her, but could discover no details.

I just know it's not going to be anything good.

3

PEACE

That night, Janni dreamed of the stars. She'd often gone out to stare at the night sky. Big Art, the clan's science expert, said there was no way to tell which star was Earth's sun or Harmony's, since they'd come here through the Gates between worlds.

Once Janni and Willie, Glori and Brian had completed their houses, Granlyn announced it was time for the mating. Richard and Leona were still working on their home.

Janni and Glori sat in the latter's house with the pale pink walls, talking about their upcoming bondings. People had called it marriage on Old Earth, but Granlyn and Grampa Larry had learned to call it mating on the Bramite world. Granlyn, because she had few memories of Earth, and Grampa Larry, because Janni suspected he still had a tinge of the first cousins not marrying taboo. There had only been six humans among the Bramites, so they had assimilated the Bramites' customs. Granlyn and Grampa Larry were the only ones of the six left.

"I'm really looking forward to my own house," Janni said. "Not having Mama tell me what to do all the time, and no pestering little brothers."

She liked Willie, and being with him, but preferred Curtis, Leona's twin, who was a lot smarter. However, Granlyn said Willie; so Willie it was. Perhaps in a month or so, she could talk Willie into going exploring.

Glori smoothed her auburn hair back from her narrow face. "I do like Brian and being with him, and, of course, having my own house, but having to do all the housework is not what I want to be doing. I thought we'd have got over the Bramites' patriarchal nonsense by now."

Janni nodded. "I agree, but I guess that's part of the deal."

She had mixed emotions about the upcoming event. On the one hand, she'd have her own house, but on the other, she was also hesitant about sharing her bed with a man, even though she knew him well. She hoped he didn't snore.

"Two more days," Glori said. "Are you going to be ready?"

"I hope so."

"Has Granlyn talked to you about the ceremony?"

Janni sighed. "Yes. Doesn't she remember we've been to bondings before?'

"A long time ago, when we were little." Glori jumped up and grabbed a mug from the table in front of them. "It's hard to sit still."

Janni followed her into the tiny kitchen. "I know. It's time for my class. The little children will be waiting. Bye."

"Bye."

Janni trotted out the door to her classroom to teach little ones their numbers and letters. Thoughts boiled in her head. As she had grown up, the clan had seemed to shrink. Janni wanted more, to explore this world of Peace that her mama had come to, not long before Janni was born. She wanted to meet more people, find new ideas.

•　　•　　•

The community buzzed about the three new couples and the prospects of more babies. The last generation hadn't had as many children as the clan had hoped for in order to grow the clan.

Everyone, except the brides-to-be, were involved in preparing the feast for the new generation to come. Even those who thought Marisa and her children were above themselves, pitched in. A feast was a feast, and no one was going to miss one. A group of men hunted for longears, small animals with long ears, in the forest to the east, and another four fished in the great river to the west. Several young people went down to the beach to collect clams. Others prepared vegetables and made bread from the ever-present loovah roots.

The clan had brought the loovah plants from Harmony, where they had lived with the Bramites, who had had the original plants. Loovah grew everywhere and under all but the most extreme conditions. Their leaves provided food, and fibers for clothing and paper; fruit and roots were more food, and the stems made sturdy ropes.

A feeling of expectancy wafted through the community. Janni and Glori felt it as they hung pictures on Glori's walls. Through their private mental link, they were aware of each other's feelings and uppermost thoughts.

Janni's house, with pale green walls, stood next door, both constructed by the two couples, as was the custom for young people to build their houses before they were mated, with help from the builders. The houses were built with half logs, smooth side in, chinked with clay from the small river by the community.

"Are you excited?" Janni asked as they walked over to Marisa's house. "I am."

She was more excited about having her own place than being mated, although she did like Willie a lot. The small log cabins did not allow much room to get away from Mama and little brothers, Mick and Steve.

"Mostly." Glori *sent* Janni a picture in her mind of a large house and a small man. The two giggled.

At Marisa's house, Glori's mama, Susan, waited with Marisa to help them get ready for the bonding. Granlyn, the oldest female, would perform the ceremony. She had already reviewed with the couples how they were to proceed at the event. She and Leona showed up shortly after.

In Janni's room, the girls donned their long, pale pink tunics with lace edging and sat so their mamas could fix their hair.

Janni looked into the glass, a scratched relic of the *Emprisa*, the ship in which the clan and the Bramites had come to Harmony, at the pile of curls on top of her head surrounded by a narrow blue ribbon. The long blue tail hung down her back. *Only for today.*

"The girls are so lovely," Susan said. "I'm not sure I'm ready to be a grandmother yet."

Marisa studied Janni's hair. "Be thankful you will be, someday."

"I already am," Granlyn said, smiling at Marisa. "You remind me of my sister, Beth," she added to Leona. "You're blonde like she was." Leona's hair fell in long blonde curls.

Janni *sensed* how strange Leona felt, being mated at the same time as her niece's daughter. "We're all family," she said.

Susan patted Glori's hair, her narrow face and brown eyes glowing. "Oh, I know. Children are such a blessing."

Glori's dark auburn hair was done up the same as Janni's. "I hope I can lie down in this," Glori said, turning her head this way and that.

Tall and thin, like Janni, she had the same narrow face and brown eyes as her mother.

"You can, if you don't stand on your head." Marisa left briefly and brought back a long scarf of blue and green swirls. "This was Granlyn's father's scarf. It's been passed down through the family women, and now I'm giving it to you." She handed it to Janni.

 Granlyn nodded and smiled.

"Thank you, Mama." Janni ran the silky material through her hands and tied it around her waist. The scarf made it all real to her, the new house and the new mate. She shivered and tried not to cry.

Granlyn gave Leona a narrow purple scarf. "This was my mother's."

"Thank you, Mama." Leona draped it over her shoulders and a tear ran down her cheek.

Susan pulled a dark blue scarf out of her bag and gave it to Glori. "My grandmother brought this from Earth. It's yours now."

Glori smiled, brought the scarf to her cheek, and draped it around her shoulders.

"I'll treasure it forever."

"I must go now, to get prepared." Granlyn patted Leona's shoulder, picked up her bag, and trudged out.

"One last visit to the outhouse while I check my hair," Marisa told the girls, and they ran off.

When the three returned, the five females marched over to the meeting house, teased by a warm spring breeze, and peered in the side door. Janni clenched her fist. Most of the clan filled the seats. Janni saw Gramma Perri and Grampa Charley in the front row. The grooms waited at the back door, shifting from foot to foot. Willie and Brian, large young men with round faces, like their father, solemn and wide-eyed, sported dark curls hanging below their ears. They wore white tunics and pants. Richard, smaller, with light brown curls, grinned as the girls approached.

"Go on in," Marisa said with a half-smile.

Janni and Willie moved together, clasped hands, and stepped into the building. The crowd turned to view them. Head held high, clinging to Willie's clammy hand, Janni marched down the aisle to the platform at the front. The other two couples followed. Janni led the way up the center steps onto the platform and faced the audience, as Granlyn had instructed, Willie at her right. Glori stood beyond Willie, and Brian next to her, and Leona and Richard next to them.

Pink and blue ribbons decorated the windows and the back of the platform, with tubs of white flowers at the front corners. Sweetness of flowers and scent of clean bodies filled the room.

Janni sensed the expectancy and excitement in the room and felt a little nervous herself. Willie trembled beside her.

Granlyn climbed onto the platform, placed herself facing the side of the couples, and motioned for everyone to rise and sing the mating song.

> *Oneness, hold these young people in your hand.*
> *Give them life,*
> *Give them caring,*
> *Give them children.*
> *Be with them as they*
> *Grow our numbers, our land.*

After that, she gestured for the audience to sit, and turned to the couples.

"Here before us stand six young people who will begin the next generation. May they prosper and be prolific." She turned to the couples. "You must respect and care for your partners. Listen to them when they speak, and when they don't. Communication is the foundation for a long-lasting relationship."

Janni *sensed* Willie thinking, *Let's get this over with.* She caught Mama's eye as she sat in the front row next to Grampa Larry.

"May you grow together in harmony, have long and useful lives, and provide an abundance of new members of our clan. Now raise your hands and speak," Granlyn said.

The couples did so and recited after her, "Caring forever, sharing forever, and many children."

Janni winced inside at the 'many children'. That was something she was not ready for and would not happen for quite a while.

"You are now mated," Granlyn said. "You are excused until the feast."

Several women dabbed their eyes with hand cloths, and Janni noticed Grampa Larry and Papa blinking.

The couples kissed, and Granlyn gave each person a hug. Janni jumped off the platform, followed by the others, and ran down the aisle to cheers and tossing of flowers. Janni, Glori, Leona, and the men trotted off to their new houses.

•　　•　　•

Later, at the feast, as the three young women waited for people to uncover the roasting pits and bring out the longears and fish, they giggled together about their afternoon.

"I didn't realize he was going to be so big," Janni said.

"Took Brian three tries to get it in." Glori giggled again.

They, their mothers, and grandmothers had been raised to be unselfconscious about body functions.

Leona sat nearby, just smiling.

People bustled here and there, and children ran around with their new carved toy animals and dolls, created for the occasion. Cheerful conversation rang through the plaza, a squarish area paved with flat stones. The meeting hall, school, medical clinic, craft hall, and community kitchen surrounded it on three sides; the fourth open to the small, tree-lined river beside the science lab. Along the base of the brown and gray log buildings, a rainbow of flowers bloomed.

Women brought bowls of fruit and vegetables and platters of bread to the tables the men had set up. Finally, all the food was ready, and everyone settled into their seats. An aroma of flowers and food drifted about them.

Granlyn stood and raised her hands. "Thank you, Oneness, for this good food and our growing clan. Amen."

Janni added, in her mind, *Oneness, every being who has ever lived, is living, and will live, every creature, every part of nature, everywhere and everywhen in all of the universes.*

Granlyn sat, and people began to serve themselves. Instead of sitting at a table with her parents as usual, Janni and Willie sat with other young couples. Unused to being apart, she kept looking for her mama to tell her something, and she wasn't there.

Afterward, Janni, Glori, and Leona went to help with the cleanup.

Granlyn told them, "Go on home. Tonight, you are off duty. Have fun."

The three brides ran off, looking for their mates.

4

PEACE

THE FOLLOWING MORNING, as a faint dimness appears in the east, Janni wakes momentarily. The part of her being that is Janni leaves her physical body and drifts into the blackness with the lights that she perceived three years before. Stars. There is no time, only now. An entity gathers her into the folds of space, and she finds herself next to a bubble of light. A sphere in the center shines brightly, with smaller orbs circling the light.

Worlds, she thinks.

Janni proceeds from star to star with no sense of movement. One moment, she is at one, the next instant, she is at another. Each softly shining globe has a similar arrangement, although a few only have one or two large orbiting spheres. One has none. She knows her world's system has one small, rocky planet closer to the sun, and three gas giants farther out.

At a different star, something outside of her draws her into the system. She is aware of marks on a lesser orb. Zooming in toward mountains, plains, and a sea, she becomes aware of roads and groups of buildings. *People,* she thinks. Suddenly she is back outside the globe.

Her mind fills with confusion. This is not what she expects space to be like. *Where is the floating among the stars feeling? Where are the winds of space?* 'Mama,' she wails in her mind.

Now something other, not of herself or her world, makes itself known, but, before she can focus on it, she is back in her body.

•　　•　　•

Back in the world of time, Janni opened her eyes and tried to hang on to her experience. It was so utterly different from anything she'd previously experienced, she had nothing to compare it to. She knew it had been real; the reality thrummed throughout her body, emphasizing its importance to her and her clan. The otherness gave her an uneasy feeling. It was like a bad dream you couldn't quite remember, fading away.

She grasped the experience to her as she crept out of bed, trying not to disturb Willie. She would tell him later. After hurriedly dressing, she ran out back of her house, to sit on a low branch, her thinking place. She tucked the stars away in her memory and looked at the Other. That was like a bug bite you could barely see, but it itched a lot.

Janni's first question was how could she get out there again? She had no idea how she got there to begin with, but thought possibly something had been controlling her.

'Hey, Janni, what's up?' she *heard* in her mind from Glori.

'I am. I've seen stars and their worlds.' The words popped out on their own.

'Some wild dream.'

"It was not a dream; it was real." Janni spoke aloud as she jumped down from the branch and yanked at a leaf.

'Calm down. You know how vivid your dreams are sometimes.'

"Yes, and this wasn't one of them.' Janni cut the connection and turned toward the house.

Willie barged out the back door and yelled, "Janni, where are you?'

"I'm coming." She wasn't sure what to do now.

Willie ran and grabbed her in a hug, then led her back to the house. "I'm hungry, but first ..." He led her to the bedroom.

Afterwards, Willie demanded breakfast. Janni realized she was hungry, too, and went to the kitchen. She wasn't sure where Mama had put things, and hunted through her cupboards. She found a pan in the bottom cupboard of the three stacked in the left corner, eggs in the double lined cold box on the right, and bread on the shelf above. She turned on the cooker, which used solar power, provided by what Grampa Larry called a Goldberg contraption of assorted pieces of metal and wire. As she prepared their meal, she told him what she'd seen.

"That's a wild dream."

Janni whirled around to face him. "It was not a dream. It really happened. I was out in space, out of time."

Wille put his hands up. "Okay, if that's what you want to believe."

Janni made a face at him, dished eggs onto plates, and slammed them down on the table. They ate in silence, and Willie left for the plaza to find out what job he had that day.

Sighing, Janni put the dishes in the wash tub and looked around her own house. A feeling of *'this is all mine'* came over her as she wandered around, touching walls and doorways. She thought about what furniture she needed, what she was going to put where. And pictures and things on the wall. Then she could show Granlyn.

"Oh," she said aloud. Should she tell the matriarch about her experience? Granlyn always wanted to know what was happening.

Janni decided to tell her and trotted over to Granlyn's. She and Grampa Larry sat rocking on their porch, greeting passersby. Retired, they spent their time observing the others and giving advice. Pink flower vines circled the logs holding up the front corners of the porch roof.

"Well, good morning, Janni." Granlyn said. "You're out early. How are you?" Although her curls were silver, her face was unlined. She said it was part of the Talents.

"Sore." Janni caught her breath.

Granlyn smiled and glanced at Grampa, who chuckled. "That's to be expected. Was it good?"

"Would have been better if it didn't hurt so much." Janni paused for breath. "Granlyn, I went out to space, with the stars. Each had its own bubble and orbiting spheres. On one, I saw little groups of buildings and roads."

"Sounds like solar systems," Grampa said. "But that couldn't be real. Must have been a dream. You have some imagination."

"It was too real, Grampa." Janni stomped her foot. "And there was nothing between the stars. I was at one, and then I was at another. I was out in space." Although she knew it to be true, she could hardly believe it herself. "There were blue and purple patches in places too."

"Nebulae." Grampa looked up at the sky. "If Marisa could bend time, maybe you can go outside of time. But no, you couldn't possibly have been actually out in space, you couldn't survive out there."

"Not my body. Me." Janni couldn't find the words for what she meant.

"How does one go outside of time?" Granlyn asked. "I thought time was time."

Janni shook her head. This was all so confusing, unlike everyday life.

"Time is fluid, from what I read," Grampa said. "We knew in the seventies, when we left Earth, that time runs slower on fast spaceships than back on Earth. If they hadn't killed scientific research, imagine what they could have discovered by now."

"Okay, Larry. Janni, don't worry about it now."

"But Granlyn, if I wasn't out there, who put it in my mind that I was?"

Granlyn and Larry looked at each other.

Janni sensed the questions in their minds. She felt lost, that there was nothing for her to hold on to. If they didn't believe her ...

Granlyn shook her head and said, "It's your first day of wedded life. Go back to Willie. You belong with him now." She creaked to her feet and hugged the girl.

Janni trotted back to her house, wondering why they didn't believe her. It had been so real. Willie was gone, and she didn't know what to do at home, so she headed to the craft hall. There were always tasks to do.

Janni sighed. She still didn't understand how it happened, but she definitely wanted to go back. Something inside told her she must go back. The whole thing was disquieting and scary.

5

STARVIEW

HUNGER GONE, AND GRATIFIED with the company of her twin, Brad, Sam walked to her house after late meal at the caff where everyone ate. She enjoyed the evening breeze and the continuing pleasure of seeing her home.

The bland exterior opened to walls of swirled pink, a room with table, chairs and cabinets, and another room behind it with a wide window overlooking the river. After Sam took off her badge of office, a necklace of colorful wooden beads, she dropped it on the table and followed Brad out to the porch with a better view.

Sam sank into the chair beside him and gazed at the river below, trees beyond, and glimpsed of mountains in the distance. This was her special place, home.

"Is there anywhere else on this world like this we could move to?" Sam asked.

Brad raised his eyebrows. "Why? I thought you liked it here."

Sam stuck a toe on the solid wooden railing. "Not what it's become. It was great when we first came, with all the trees and bushes in the valley."

"I know." Brad tugged his moustache. "But we had to use the trees to build the houses."

"Could you fly around the world and look?"

Brad had a four-seater airship that flew in both atmosphere and space, courtesy of the Volen. Solar-powered, he didn't have to worry about fuel.

"I could, but she needs some maintenance, and I have to watch my credits, since we're not earning any, anymore."

"What will you do when you run out?"

"Fly her 'til she dies."

"What about the Itzas' land? It's empty since they were moved down to the southern continent. It was green in the hills."

Brad rose. "I can check that out. Gotta go collect the kids. Emily's working in the caff tonight. See you."

He brushed her hair with his hand and strode through the house. His home was next door.

Sam sat back. She was fortunate to have her brothers and alien sister Maxee, and friends like Arlene. Maxee, an alien brought to City as an infant, had been raised by Sam's father along with Brad and herself. The alien looked like an adult-sized gray teddy bear and had learned a lot more in City than she probably would not have on her home world. Yes, the coming event would involve Maxee, too.

6

PEACE

I T TOOK A FEW DAYS for the community to settle back into routine. Other than the spring and harvest feasts, the only other feast was at the mating of the first couples of a new generation. Janni and Glori returned to their tasks. Janni enjoyed teaching; her maternal forebears had all been teachers. Glori did fine stitchery with needles made from fish bones.

Janni adjusted to her new life and found she didn't have as much time as she used to for Glori and her other friends. She made sure she didn't get pregnant. All women with Talent could control their eggs.

She began to wonder whether she would go out into space again.

•   •   •

Two weeks after the bonding, at the beginning of dawn, Janni finds her being in space again. This time she tries to locate Peace, but has no idea from which direction she came. It can't be too far, but there is no reference. Mentally shrugging, she searches for Earth, the world in the picture on Grampa's wall. She'll ask Grampa about it when she gets back.

Janni is at the star system with four small inner planets and four large outer planets and finds herself hovering above Earth.

How did I get here?

It's not blue and green and white like the picture, but a grayish brownish blob with white smears at the top and bottom. There are a few greenish spots, and she makes a note of these. Small groups of people appear to live there.

She senses no attraction to this world and leaves. At a nearby star system, she finds another world with evidence of people. A voice *sends* the word, 'Watcher' to her.

Janni jerks around, but perceives nothing.

'Hello?' she *sends.*

No response.

A disconcerting knot in the wonder and pleasure of this place, something underneath tells her this is not right, not for humans. Uneasy, she returns to her body.

•　　•　　•

Later that morning, after Willie had gone off to his duties, Janni met with Granlyn and Grampa Larry. She'd decided not to say anything about the Watcher. Their house smelled of flowers, from a wooden vase of red blooms on the table, and old man. As she shared what she'd perceived about the home planet, Grampa grimaced.

"You have quite a vivid imagination, girl. What makes you think that was our Earth?"

"Grampa, it was. I asked for Earth, and that's where I went." Jenni turned to the old woman. "Granlyn, please believe me. It was real."

Granlyn closed her eyes. "Show me," she said.

Janni *sent* her vision of Earth to Granlyn's mind.

"I see." Granlyn opened her eyes and looked at Grampa. "I wish we could show you, Larry. I think she's right. To her, it is real. And that place was Earth. I remember the outlines of the continents from when we returned there, flying in on the shuttle."

"Jeezuz Christ. If it is, how did that happen? Did someone push the button?"

"Button?" Janni asked, relieved that at least Granlyn believed her.

"The red button to launch nuclear war." Grampa looked at Granlyn, who shook her head. "Janni, are you saying we're the only humans left?"

"I don't know. Were you the first to leave Old Earth?"

"Yes, and they were nowhere near having the capability to build a starship. Heck, they'd only just got to the moon."

"Janni, can you go out there whenever you want to?" Granlyn asked.

"No, it just happens, usually at dawn. When I started my periods and with Willie."

"Life changes," Granlyn said. "Have you ever asked your mama how she learned to bend time, or your grandma how she learned to move things?"

Janni shook her head. "I never thought to, it came so easily to me."

"You must figure out how to go out there when you want to. We need to be able to use your Talent if necessary." Granlyn sighed. "Go talk to your grandma and mama. Don't let yourself get pregnant; you don't want to be tied down with a child yet. We need to take care of this Talent thing first."

Grampa Larry continued to mutter about Earth as she departed.

"Go back to your duties." Granlyn rose. "We'll talk more later." The old woman gave her a hug, and Janni ran back to her house.

She felt drawn to space, but it also terrified her. It was what she'd always wanted; to go somewhere away from the clan, somewhere different, but this was a little too different. Too close to what she didn't want to become — especially after those worlds she'd perceived.

Humans weren't meant to be anything else.

Janni stepped into her home and sat down. The whole Talent business was wrong, even though she mostly liked having them. She had noticed that the others in Granlyn's generation who had come from Earth, except Papa Allen, were withdrawing from the younger generations, only interacting with their immediate relatives. Papa was thirty-something years older than Mama, but they were very happy together.

Janni cleaned up the breakfast dishes and tidied the place. Willie tended to leave his clothes wherever he took them off.

When she finished, she trotted down to the craft house on the plaza, full of hum of people working and aroma of freshly-dyed fabric and glue, and dropped into a seat next to Glori.

"I went out in space again this morning." Janni took her little loom and thread out of the cubbyhole in front of her, at the back of the table. She was making squares for a quilt.

'So that's where you were. Are you seeing things again?' Glori *sent.*

"Glori, it's real. I'd show you now, but we're supposed to be working." Janni unrolled the end of a spool of green thread. "I saw Earth, and it's dead."

"Oh, come on."

"Glori ..." Janni *shot* an image of Earth into the other woman's mind.

'No way.' Glori *sent* back mentally. "I mean, I saw it, but it doesn't make sense. Are you sure you just didn't dream it?" She looked skeptically at the belt she was working on.

"Yes, I'm sure. I know what I saw and heard." Janni rammed the needle into her square.

'Okay,' Glori *sent.* 'Brian keeps asking me when I'm going to get pregnant. He wants a son.'

'Willie, too. I tell him when I'm ready. You know Granlyn told us not to. Which is fine with me. I'm not ready to be a mother.' Janni tied her thread to the corner of the loom.

Gramma Perri came by a little later to see how they were doing. She oversaw the needlework.

"Having problems, Janni?" she asked.

Janni's threads were every which way. This was only the second square she had done. Gramma Perri took the loom, made several adjustments to the threads, and handed it back. "Remember, over, under, over, under."

Janni rolled her eyes. She knew how to do it; her fingers just wouldn't cooperate.

"Gramma, how did you learn to move people?" she asked.

Gramma Perri looked at her. "The first time scared me silly. A toddler was running down a trail and about to go off a cliff. I just grabbed him from way above and put him down by his mama. I never thought about it, I just did it automatically. It happened occasionally when someone was in danger. When Cray fell into a pit, I helped lift him out."

"Cray?" Janni asked. She noticed Glori was listening, too.

"A friendly alien who helped us get back to Harmony after I found Peter. He died on Harmony." Gramma Perri paused. "Anyway, one day, I realized I actually thought of it before I moved someone. After that, it was easier and easier."

"Okay, thanks."

Gramma Perri left, and Janni continued to work on her square.

Later, she ran into her mama, but Marisa didn't have time to talk. The next few days Gramma Perri and Mama kept Janni so busy with tasks, and Willie at home, she could hardly think.

Finally, Janni caught up with her mama and asked her how she learned to bend time.

"I don't know," Marisa said. "I just did it when it needed to be done without thinking about it."

"That's no help."

•　　　•　　　•

Once again, two weeks later, Janni finds her being in space. She seeks humans and finds globes where a few of them eke out an existence, including the remains of Earth. Close to her limit, she finds a world with a large human colony and several alien ones. As she leaves that system, the voice sends, 'You need more people on your world to replace those of you who become Watchers.'

'I'm not becoming a Watcher.'

No response.

Janni stores the location of the large colony world in her memory and returns to her body.

•　　　•　　　•

When Janni awoke, she recalled the words from the unseen entity.

How dare they assume we'll blindly become Watchers.

Willie stirred beside her, mumbled something, and turned over. She was getting used to a warm body next to her in bed. It was comforting.

Later, her brain fully awake, she thought, *That won't work. If Mama, Susan, Glori, a few others and I are going to be Watchers, the clan will fall apart. Old Maria's extended family and Big Art's will go their own ways, leaving Granli's family, Gabe's, and Gramma Perri, Grampa Charley and Uncle Peter and his family. The new people will keep to themselves, and soon the clan will be gone.*

I guess it's up to me to get rid of our Talent. But I want to keep mine.

Janni recalled the colony and realized she'd found out nothing about them, except they were human.

Oh, well, next time.

After Willie awoke, and they had breakfast, she reported to Granlyn and Grampa Larry about Earth and where the survivors were. She showed them on a map where a great crater in North America took out half a country.

"So Yellowstone finally went," Grampa said. "I guess it was a good thing we left when we did."

"What about Beth and her kids and all the cousins?" Granlyn demanded.

"It's been forty years here and on Harmony; it must be at least forty on Earth. Could be more." Grampa Larry shrugged. Beth was Granlyn's sister, not his. The three of them had grown up together, because his mother died not long after he was born.

"Some of them are in a valley in the southwest corner," Janni said. She pointed to the map.

Granlyn closed her eyes. "I choose to believe they are there. Now, Janni, do you have any idea why this happened this morning instead of some other day?"

"No. I wish I did. I wish I could go more often." She kept the words and her uneasiness about them to herself.

"I know. Keep working at it. Don't you have tasks to do?"

"Yes, Granlyn." Janni rose, went to the matriarch and kissed her, and trotted off to the plaza.

All day, as she went from one task to another, something about the Watcher's words, tucked into the back of her mind, niggled at her. When she tried to pin it down, it disappeared. Back home, with Willie, she forgot about it.

7

PEACE

G RANLYN CALLED A MEETING of the three young women. Janni, Leona, and Glori sat in a row on the couch again.

"Have you thought of a solution to our Talent problem?"

Three heads shook no.

"I don't think we can," Janni said. "It's too hard to not use them when we need or want to."

"I agree," Glori added. "I think we need something outside of ourselves to pull them out."

"How did we get them in the first place?" Leona asked.

Granlyn frowned. "Leona, I thought I taught you ..." She shook her head. "The Watchers, dying aliens, programmed my ancestors to become a new race to take their place. My paternal grandparents started the two lines, led by Bay and me. I first became aware of my Talent in my twenties, when we were trying to get away from the Centar on another world."

I know. "If the Watchers did this, then maybe they could take the Talents away," Janni said.

"Yes, but how are we going to find them and get them to do it?" Granlyn moved in her rocker. "Not even Bay has been able to *reach* them from here." Grampa Bay had the strongest mind Talent of his generation.

"What if we try all together, all of us?" Glori asked, rubbing her nose.

"I'd thought of that and have been talking to people. People in my and Bay's families don't want to lose their Talents, and some of the others are afraid if we contact the Watchers, they'll turn us all into Watchers overnight."

After a period of silence, Leona said, "Is there something we could do to attract their attention? Something they wouldn't want us to do, but not hurt anyone?"

Granlyn shook her head. "I have no idea what would change their minds about us. To change the subject, how are you gals enjoying bonded life?"

Glori and I looked at each other.

"Good," Leona said.

Glori nodded and added, "Except for housework."

"Okay." Janni couldn't add up the plusses and minuses. Her trips to space confused things. She needed a more ordinary, everyday life to be able to make a true assessment.

Granlyn looked at her, but didn't say anything. To the three of them, she said, "Keep thinking. If we don't get rid of the new Talents, it could tear our clan apart. Then everyone would lose. There's not that many of us, you know. There were only six couples to start with."

"Yes, Granlyn," the girls chorused.

"Janni, it's time for you to take your turn in the loovah fields. Glori, go back to what you were doing. Leona, stay a moment." The old woman rose and led them to the door. Giving each a hug, she added, "Keep your thinking caps on and work on your relationships with your mates. Take care."

"That didn't get us anywhere," Glori said as she and Janni walked back to the plaza.

Janni agreed mentally.

"See you."

Glori trotted over to the craft hall and Janni made her way to the store house to pick up a harvest basket and go over to the crop fields. Surely there couldn't be anything unpleasant there.

8

PEACE

A S JANNI SAT, removed, and checked the small leaves, she thought about these plants that grew like weeds. Outer, large leaves for fiber for paper and clothing, inner leaves, fruit and roots for food, stems for rope; this was an inheritance from the humanoid Bramites who had come to the world of Harmony with her clan and stayed there. Granlyn, Grampa Larry, and Granlyn's half-brother, Adam, had lived with the Bramites for over two years. Adam, Willie's great-grandfather, had died on Harmony.

Janni liked working outside on her free afternoons, if it wasn't too hot. She wondered how she was going to get back to space. She felt a need to go back that she didn't understand.

When she returned to the plaza, she ran into Willie.

"Where have you been," he demanded, grabbing her shoulders. "I've been looking all over for you. It's supper time." He pulled her toward their cabin.

"Working on the loovah harvest." Janni jerked away. "It was my turn."

"Why didn't you tell me this morning?" He took her arm.

"I didn't know this morning." She jerked away and ran ahead, past her mama's house, to Glori's. She'd always been able to run faster than Willie.

Glori, returning to her house, caught Janni.

"What's going on?" Glori asked as Willie came running. She stepped in front of the shaking Janni. "Leave her alone."

Willie stopped. "I want her to come home." He bunched his fists.

"Not yet." Glori led the young woman to her house.

What just happened? Why was he all of a sudden getting bossy? Why'd I respond like that? Now what do I have to deal with?

Janni followed Glori into her house.

Once inside, they collapsed on the couch. "Now tell," Glori demanded.

"He got all over me because he didn't know where I was, out in the loovah field." Janni twisted her fingers. She didn't like that attitude of Willie's. *Why does he always have to know where I am?*

"I know. Brian says when he was young, Willie always had to know where his mama and papa were. On the other hand, some of the boys say you're being too bossy." Glori looked out a window.

"Bossy? Yeah, maybe." Janni glanced at Glori. "Oh, sometimes I have to tell him what to do. His mama never taught him how to do things around the house."

"Yeah, I know. Brian neither, but Brian's a fast learner. Just take it easy on Willie for a bit."

Janni looked around at Glori's pink walls and wooden shelves. "He also wants me to get pregnant right now, which I don't want, and Granlyn said not to."

"Well, you know who's in charge of the eggs." They both giggled.

Men's voices came from outside. "That's Brian," Glori said. "Let's tune in."

The two young women tuned their mental links to the two men outdoors and made it one-way so the men wouldn't know they were listening.

'She's driving me nuts,' the pair *heard Wi*llie say.

'How so?' Brian asked.

'She won't get pregnant. I know she's doing it on purpose, but she won't tell me why. She's always telling me what to do. Some of the fellows are saying things behind my back.'

'I know, brother. Remember, she always bossed us when we were kids. She's not gonna change now. You shoulda let Richard pick her. Too late now. See you.'

Janni and Glori disconnected as Brian strode into the house. "Your mate wants you," he said to Janni.

'I wouldn't have Richard for anything,' Janni *sent* to Glori. 'He's too lazy, and you and Brian were already together. So who else was there? I didn't want to wait for a younger boy to grow up.'

"And you have a mate who needs his supper," Brian repeated, pulling Glori to her feet.

"Okay, Janni, see you later." Glori pushed him away. 'You're right, you had no choice,' she *sent* to Janni as she left.

I wish there'd been a better choice. Janni trudged home.

Willie sat on the porch. Janni stalked by him into the house and to the kitchen, where she banged the big pot on the cookstove. She had chopped carrots and potatoes, put them into the pot with water, and dug out a handful of small loovah leaves by the time Willie came in.

"Sorry," he said, as he stood and watched her.

"Okay, I'm sorry too," Janni said without turning. *Was this what mated life was going to be?*

She dumped in some leftover chicken. Chicken was everyday meat, fish once a week or so, and longears for special occasions.

Willie stomped back into the other room, and she heard the couch groan as he dropped onto it.

As they ate, they didn't say much. Janni didn't know what to say, how to deal with this situation. She decided she'd rather live by herself than be mated.

That night, she found herself in space again.

•　　　•　　　•

In the dawn, Janni's being hangs out in space. The stars have moved, and she searches for the human colony. The voice speaks in her mind.

'Would you like the human colony to join you on your world?'

'Who are you?' she demands.

'Watcher,' comes a whisper. 'Check them.'

'No. I don't want to be a Watcher, I won't.'

No answer. The entity is gone.

Well, it can't hurt to check out those other people.

She locates the solar system bubble and sinks down into the sphere, to the world. And onto it, in the mountains above the human colony. Time begins to move. She glides down a trail until she reaches a place where she can look out over a green valley divided by a tree lined river. Both sides hold buildings and pathways. And people. Many people. More than she can count easily.

Janni *reaches* with her mind. These people have no mindlink receivers. Except one. She scans the world and finds other beings: some like humans; others different, but aware. If she could go down there and meet them, that would be glorious. She hesitates and finds herself back out in space. After searching for and finding no other humans, she returns to her body.

•   •   •

When Janni came to, the word, 'Watcher' floated in the air.

"I'm not," she said aloud, sitting up.

"Not what?" Willie mumbled.

"Not a Watcher." She swung her legs over the side of the bed.

"Huh?"

"I'll tell you later."

She prepared for the day and ran to report her visit with the other human colony to the elders. The cool morning breeze tousled her curls as she darted along the grass-lined path.

"I found a big human colony on a world with several alien colonies," Janni told Granlyn after she caught her breath, "but they don't have mindlink. Except one who is different."

"Of course, they wouldn't have the mindlink. We're the only ones that do." Granlyn tugged a silver curl. "Come on inside."

"Hello, Grampa," Janni said as Grampa Larry rose from the sagging brown couch. One of the pictures on the wall behind it fell off.

"Another one of your stories?" he said, frowning, looking at the picture. He picked it up and dropped it on a little table nearby.

"Larry," Granlyn snapped. He shrugged and shuffled into the bedroom. "I'll talk to him later. What did you find out?"

Janni sat on the couch. "They have a lot more people than we do: hundreds and hundreds. I didn't try to contact the one with mindlink; everything was too strange. There's lots of long buildings, which I guess is where they live. There was a high place with larger buildings which I guess was like their meeting hall and things. People on both sides of a river and as far west as I could see. Big crop fields and orchards."

"Okay." Granlyn frowned. "Did you meet any of the humans?"

"No. I touched a few of their minds. They seem to be worried about having enough food. Seems all they have is vegetables and grains."

"Normally, we don't go into others' minds without their permission, but under the circumstances I'll let it pass."

Janni was reluctant to tell her about the Watcher, if indeed that was what the voice was. She didn't want to get anyone's hopes up. Besides, she had to figure out how to deal with it/them.

"I'd like to go back. I mostly sensed images and emotions from them. Some things, like carrots and squash, seemed to be similar to ours."

Granlyn sighed. "With your Talents. I'm sure you can find a way. Don't you have tasks?"

"Yes, Granlyn." Janni rose and paused. "Their world is different, too. All hills and valleys and mountains, with a river down the middle."

"That sounds nice." Granlyn sat back and closed her eyes.

"Bye." Janni ran off.

All that day, she thought about the people in the other colony and wondered what they were like. The voice haunted her, no matter how much she tried to push it away. If it was a Watcher, maybe she could get it to take their Talents away. And leave her hers.

Willie grabbed her in a hug as soon as she came in the door that evening. "I couldn't wake you this morning. Granlyn said not to worry. Were you out there?"

"Yes. I'm okay." She pulled away and headed for the kitchen.

He followed. She didn't want to talk about it, didn't know what to say, how to explain it to him.

"I don't like you doing it," Willie said, behind her.

"I have no choice; it's my new Talent." Janni peered into the food box. A loaf of bread and two elderly squashes looked back at her. "Oh, rats." She turned. "Did you bring any food?"

"No."

She *heard*, 'that's your job' in his mind. *At least he didn't say it out loud.* "There's nothing here but bread. Do you want more?"

"Of course. I've been working all day. Why didn't you get food when you were over there?"

Janni grabbed a couple of bags and ran out, down to the storehouse. It had a row of vegetables, fruits, and preserved foods along one aisle, clothing and fabrics on another, and assorted tools on the third. She found Gramma Perri also doing some food shopping.

"You work late again?" she asked the girl.

"No, I forgot again." Janni picked out a bunch of smaller loovah leaves and several fruits.

"You need to keep your mind on the here and now." Gramma picked her own bunch of leaves. "You have a household to run. How are you on doing laundry?"

"Mama made me do it the other day. I don't know how Willie gets his clothes so dirty."

"Men do. Just don't get too far behind."

Janni grabbed a bag of potatoes and a few other vegetables and ran off. Having her own house wasn't nearly as much fun as she'd thought it would be.

•　　　•　　　•

Two weeks later, Janni's being, the nonphysical part of her that is 'Janni', floats outside the globe that holds the other human colony. She notes a few other small colonies in other spheres and pinpoints the area where another entity hangs, one not the voice. She also finds another world with great patches of blackened areas where cities once stood. Looking closer, she perceives a single survivor, human male, trudging along a road with a bundle on his back.

Without thought, Janni flicks him to the other human colony through notime/nospace. She studies this destroyed world. Only the places where humans lived are burned out. Many beasts still roam the vast forests and the great seas. There is no sign of alien sentience, and the danger is gone from this place.

Who did this? Why only humans? There is no sign of new colonization, so that's not why it was done.

Now Janni is at the human colony, inside the solar globe.

Time begins to move.

Janni perceived that the human male is on the trail above the community. She must tell the people who live here, and searches for the one with mindlink. That one is not human, but lives among humans.

We need a better way to communicate, but how? If I could just get into their minds.

'I am Janni,' she *projected in pictures* with her mind to the alien. 'I am from another world. Who are you?'

She *sensed* the being jump.

No response.

Janni *sent* a picture of herself on one side and several outlines of people with question marks inside on the other.

"I am Maxee," the being said.

Janni understood her from her thoughts.

"I am Klocti. How you speak?"

'I communicate in the mind. It's an ability I have. We need to meet.' Janni *sent* a picture of two beings coming together.

"Why?"

'To get to know each other.' Arms around each other.

"How? Where?"

'I am at a place where I can see your river and valleys on each side.' Janni *sent* an image of her view of the river and a question mark. 'You know where?'

"Iss. Come now?"

'Yes. I wait.' She *sent* an image of herself.

"I will come, bring Mayor Sam."

9

STARVIEW

MAYOR SAM BREATHED A SIGH OF RELIEF as the last group of complainers left. Even though she had set up channels for complaints, most people wanted to come see her in person.

"Just say 'no'," Arlene, her assistant, said.

"Oh, sure." Sam hunched over her table in her tiny office, her head in her hands, wishing someone pleasant, such as Maxee, her alien sister, would show up next. Here open-door policy wasn't working the way she wanted.

As if she heard her name, Maxee trotted in. "Sammie, Sammie, someone in my head." The teddy bear-like alien stopped at the table and bounced on her toes, waving her gray furry arms about.

"What?" Sam stared at her. "Calm down and tell me."

"Someone send pictures in my head. Two worlds, one here, one away. Wants leader."

"Who? How?"

"Know not. You come to Overlook."

"No," said Arlene. "Sam's too tired. Get Brad." She touched a button on her comm.

"I'm not that tired." Sam sat up. "Who is this person? Where are they from?" *Is this part of the new trouble?*

"She Janni." Maxee shook her head.

Silence overtook the trio. *Something new, something strange. I have to find out.*

Brad, Sam's twin, strode in. "Somebody call me?" Tall and brown-haired, he crossed to Sam and touched her hair. "You're working too hard, sis. You need to take a break."

"Yeah, right." Sam leaned against him.

Maxee explained the newcomer to Brad.

"Wow," he said.

"We need to check this out. Can you go with us?" Sam asked him.

"Us? I'll go." Brad pulled Sam to her feet and gave her a hug. "Arlene, make her go rest."

Arlene snorted.

"I'm going." Sam shoved her papers in her drawer. "Come on, Maxee."

Arlene sighed. "I'll cover for you. Again."

Sam and the others left.

•   •   •

Sam perked up as they trotted down the trail from the top of the mesa to the river path. She had to walk fast to keep up with Brad as he strode down the tree-lined trail along the river. A few yellow leaves decorated the trees lining the gurgling water. A hint of fall filled the air.

"This policing work is never ending," Brad said. "Nobody listens. Too many people think the rules don't apply to them. We need to find a better way to keep the people in order."

"Well, that's what you wanted to do. Maybe we need a suggestion box."

Maxee held a finger at her throat and breathed deeply, inflating the air sacs in her legs, lengthening them so she could keep up with the others. A grin on her face, she bounced with every step.

"Maxee, tell me," Brad said as they neared the bridge to North Valley. "Do they use the same language as us?"

"No. All in pictures. Two worlds. No know what they want."

"This just come to you?"

"All sudden." Maxee waved her hand around. "First, square face smiling. Then two worlds. Then one circle above many others, with mark. Be leader."

"If you say so."

They passed the bridge and headed on up along the river.

"Let's go see what this is all about."

A faint trail led through the trees along the waterway, curving to their left as the river arced in that direction.

Sam sucked in the forest aroma and listened to the chittering and rustling of woodland critters. This was the environment she wanted, needed. *If I could only come here more often.*

When they reached the overlook, an open space by the river with a view of North Valley below and South valley in the distance, Sam saw someone at the uphill end.

A tall, slim young woman, with a square face, green eyes, and a mass of black curls tied behind her head, stood there. She wore a pale green tunic and matching trousers. Maxee marched over to her, and Sam and Brad followed.

She is the key, Sam thought. *The key to the future menace.*

"Hello. I Maxee. I hear you in head." Maxee pointed to her ear then her head. "This Mayor Sam and Brad, her brother."

The girl did not move.

"Janni," Maxee said, pointing to the girl. She cocked her head, listening.

This was like how she sometimes communicated with her kubs, Sam thought.

"Is man on trail above," Maxee said. A pause. She asked Brad, "How many of us?"

"About twenty thousand," he said. "Most in the valleys west of Starview."

Maxee looked at the girl, repeated Brad's words, and pointed to the west. After a few moments, the furry alien said, "Is colony healthy?"

"Mostly. The river's low." Brad looked at Maxee.

"No," Sam said. "Not enough food, many people sickly." As Maxee repeated their words, the girl began to shiver even though the air was warm.

Maxee communed with Janni again. "Here thousand years. Yes, many babies, I have four kubs," she held up four of her six fingers at her chest, "and he and mate also four." She pointed at Brad.

More communication. "She from smaller place," Maxee said. "Will come back."

Sam realized she could see the trees through Janni, and, as she watched, the girl became more and more transparent until she blinked out, vanished.

Sam gaped. "What?"

"She only picture. We go home now." Maxee turned and started back down the trail.

'So how were you talking to her?" Brad asked, following her.

"I hear in head, I think words as I say them, she hears them from my head."

Sam said, "Okay," and frowned. *What did this person want of us? Why didn't she say more about herself? How did she get here?*

Brad nodded. "So there are other colonies. Too bad we don't have our ship." The ship their ancestors had arrived in was long gone, stripped of everything the least bit useful.

"Who fly it?" Maxee asked. "Could you? You fly little ship."

"No way. It takes hundreds of people to fly a big ship like that." Brad nodded again.

They tramped down the trail, single file, Maxee in the lead. Bushes and tree branches brushed them now and then, and the burbling of the river followed as woodsy aroma enveloped them. A chirped conversation followed them in the tops of the trees.

After a while, Maxee said, "We need find man."

"What man," Sam said.

"Janni said man on trail." Maxee stopped and pointed up the trail.

"How far?" Brad asked.

Maxee shrugged.

"Okay, we can't do it now, it's getting late, and we'd have to go back for travelling packs if he's far enough up to have to camp over." Brad said. "Can you get off tomorrow, Sam?"

Sam stopped and stared at him. "What! You mean leave him sitting there all night?"

"Sam, what would we use for light? The old lightsticks are practically dead and the lanterns only last a couple of hours. The weather's nice and whatever's in the woods won't hurt him."

This can't be happening. Another new person.

Sam didn't like the way things were going, but had to agree with Brad. Hiking up a strange trail at night was not the smartest thing to do. If one of them got hurt …

She shook her head. "I'll manage tomorrow somehow. You?"

"I can't, maybe Todd can. We'll check when we get back."

"Okay." Sam wasn't looking forward to another trek so soon, but it was her place as mayor to be there to greet the newcomer.

Oneness knows what shape he's in.

•   •   •

That evening, Brad, Sam, Maxee, and Arlene sat around the table in the back room of Sam's house. The front room, with pink swirled walls, where Maxee's four kubs played, held Sam's bed platform and the big window overlooking the porch, the river, and the mountains beyond the north valley. Sam was still processing the idea that there were other humans out there who had the ability to come to her world without a ship.

"We need to discuss this person who invaded our world today," Sam began. "I don't understand how she got here. Also, apparently, she brought someone with her and he's up the trail somewhere. I and one of you will have to go up in the morning to find him." She looked at Brad.

"I can't. Back to the mystery girl. Her body wasn't here." Brad fingered his dark beard. "What we saw was a projection from wherever she was, and Maxee heard her in her mind. How she accomplished that, I have no idea. I believe she is a real person, somewhere. Possibly on a nearby ship."

"Does this mean there are more humans around than just us?" Arlene asked.

"Didn't you see any when you were in Space Patrol?" Sam asked.

"We didn't go to that many worlds. I saw several types of humanoids, but no real humans. I never thought to look. Everyone had always believed we were the only ones. But, sure, more ships could have been sent out from Old Earth after our ancestors' ships and gone to other worlds."

"Okay, Brad, so she's real, and there's more of her people somewhere. What do we do about it?"

"What can we do?" Arlene tugged her ear.

"Wait," Maxee said. "She be back in some days. Think of question to ask her." She bobbed up and down in her chair.

"Good idea," Brad said. "Do we want to tell anyone else?"

"No." Sam fisted the table. She still wasn't sure how she felt about the situation.

"Yes," Arlene said. "A few. Todd, Hal, Glenda, at least."

The others agreed. "Okay, go find them," Sam said.

Brad left and returned with the three of them. Hal, Sam's partner, Todd, her other brother, and Glenda, Sam's second assistant and head of construction joined the group.

"We have a situation," Sam said after everyone settled in their seats. She had extra chairs because she used her house for small meetings. "A young woman from another world showed up at the Outlook, by some means we haven't figured out. She asked some questions, via Maxee, in her mind, and then faded away. We don't know where she came from or what she wants. Maxee says she will return."

"Interesting," Todd said. "If there are others and they want to come here, we'll have to set up rules for dealing with them." He and his father ran the legal side of the government.

"Are they coming?" Hal grinned at Sam. "I'll go with you tomorrow."

Sam smiled at Hal and hoped they wouldn't. She had enough to deal with. "We don't know. What do you think, Glenda?" Sam looked at the tall woman with black hair.

"I think I'll take a wait and see option for now. We don't really know anything about them, do we?"

"Only that she definitely looked human," Brad said. "I would say they use some variation of Standard as their language. She was as almost as tall as I, so perhaps her world has a slightly lighter gravity than ours. Other than that ..." He shrugged.

"That's a start," Arlene said. "I'd say, let's wait and see what happens if she comes back."

Glenda nodded. "We can't plan anything until we know more."

"Okay, we'll do that," Sam said. "Thanks for coming."

After they all left, Sam went out to her chair on the porch and tried to sort out her feelings. She felt like she was on a pedestal surrounded by all manner of beings bombarding her with demands. Half the neighborhood leaders failed to check in when they were supposed to, and Hal had to spend too much of his time going after them. Too many people were complaining instead of pitching in to make the community run smoothly, and she didn't know what to do about it. They hadn't had rain in months, the river was so low the waterwheel barely ran, and there was never enough food.

And now this.

10

STARVIEW

S AM ROSE EARLY and caught Hal after first meal. "Are you ready
to go?"

"Sure, Cuddles." Close, but platonic partners, Cuddles was his
pet name for her.

They grabbed backpacks with food and medical supplies and
headed down the mesa and up along the river.

"What do you know about this new arrival?" Hal asked.

"Not much. Only that's he's a man and came from another
world. Janni brought him, don't ask me how. Up the trail aways."

"Okay." He did a skip and walked on.

At the bridge to North Valley, they stopped to rest. Tall trees
below the bridge screened the valley and more lined the narrow
trail along the river into the hills.

"How far up is he?" Hal asked.

"Maxee couldn't tell. We'll just have to keep going 'til we find
him." Sam leaned against him.

After her disastrous marriage and the painful aftermath, Sam
had sworn off marriage and men. Hal had lost his lover, Ross, in
the collapse of City, and they had turned to each other. It had taken

her almost a year to get totally comfortable with Hal, but now she loved him as a dear and close friend.

•   •   •

The sun hung low in the west when they trudged around a curve and saw a dark, shiny mound hunched by the trail. On an arc of grass under a group of trees, a large bundle sat beside it. Upon closer inspection, Sam saw it was a person. The cloak was made of some shiny stuff she had never seen. She shivered.

Was he human? she thought. *What are we going to do with him?*

Sam and Hal stopped some distance away.

"Hello," Sam said.

The top of the mound expanded upward, and a dark head popped out. Eyes blinked. The area of his face not covered by dark hair and beard appeared dusky. A half smile appeared below his wild mustache, and he nodded.

"I am Sam, and this is Hal. We're part of a large colony of humans here." Sam couldn't tell how much he understood.

"Sam, Hal. *Ich* Kirk." A hand appeared and he pointed to himself, but made no move to rise.

"Are you hungry?" Sam rubbed her tummy. "Thirsty?" She mimed taking a drink.

"*Ja.*" His dark brown eyes opened wider.

Sam had never seen eyes so dark.

She offered him a hunk of bread and an extra water pouch. He threw the cloak back and reached for them with long, thin, well-kept hands.

So he isn't a worker or a laborer. Who is he?

"*Danke.*" Kirk pulled out a small piece of cloth, wiped his lips, and sat back against a tree trunk, eyes half-closed.

"How did you get here?" Sam asked.

Kirk shook his head.

She couldn't tell whether that meant he didn't understand her question, or he didn't know.

So we'll have to teach him our language, Standard.

Kirk rattled off a couple of questions which neither Sam nor Hal could make sense of. Sam shook her head. Kirk frowned and screwed up his face. Sam tried to imagine what it must feel like, finding yourself on a different world and not being able to understand the locals. She had no inkling that she would discover that herself.

Hal pulled some blankets out of his pack. "It's getting dark, let's camp here." He gave one to Kirk, who studied it as Sam returned to Hal.

Kirk pulled his cloak around him, laid the blanket over his legs, and closed his eyes.

"Poor fellow," Hal said, as he and Sam settled at the far end of the grassy verge.

A thorny bush behind them between two stout trees protected them from any curious forest creatures. Sam could hear the river beyond the bushes on the other side of the trail. A cool breeze drifted over them, bringing a woodsy smell.

"Janni must have just moved him here without warning." Sam doffed her backpack. "However she did that."

"Some trick." Hal set out bread and turnips.

Sam and Hal ate and talked quietly. "What are we going to do with him?" she asked.

"Take him back, find out what he can do, and make him a citizen."

He pulled Sam down beside him. They lay and listened to the river gurgle, the whisper of the trees above, and sounds of animals moving in the forest.

"I love those sounds," Hal murmured.

"So do I. This is the world I thought I was getting when Brad and I first found the valley."

If I could just get out here, away from people, once in a while.

•   •   •

The next morning, they all had more bread, an apple-like red fruit, and water. Kirk got to his feet and went behind the trees. Sam noticed he was a little taller than herself.

When they were ready to go, Hal asked Kirk, "Is there anything I can help you carry?" He pointed to the bundle and motioned lifting.

"*Ja.*"

Kirk unrolled the bundle and pulled out a smaller bag. Out of that he took a cleaner shirt and changed into it. His chest was as dark as his face. Stuffing the dirty shirt back in, he handed the bag to Hal and rerolled his original bundle. The three started down the trail.

At the overlook, Sam showed Kirk the valleys.

"*Altstadt?*" Kirk asked.

Sam shook her head, and they continued on.

As they entered South Valley, Kirk received curious looks from the citizens the group passed, but no one said anything. Just beyond the bridge, under a trio of wide-leaved trees near the river, they stopped to take a break. A group of young people carrying large packs came by as Kirk unrolled his bundle on the grass and pulled out a long, tapered silver tube.

A lanky young man in front halted his group. "Is that a telescope?" he asked.

"*Fernrohr.*" Kirk held it out, and the fellow peered at it.

"I've seen pictures, but never a real one."

The others crowded around.

"Look at stars?" The young man pointed to the sky.

"*Ja.*"

"Could you show us sometime? We're all interested in the sky."

"I don't think he understands," Sam said. "He came from another world. Where are you going?" She peered at the instrument.

"Taking supplies to North Valley."

"Okay, you better get on your way," Sam said, waving a hand. "I'm sure they're sitting over there waiting for your loads."

"Sure. See you later." The group left.

Kirk held out his telescope to Hal, who peered through the large end.

"*Nein.*" Kirk took the scope and turned it around.

"Oh, I see." Hal peered into the small end and moved the tube back and forth. "Makes things seem closer." He handed it back and turned to Sam. "You know me. Never got into science. My family was always councilors."

"I know," Sam said. She peered into it and was fascinated by how close things appeared. The mesa seemed only a few minutes' walk away. "Amazing." She handed it back and rose. "We need to get going."

They walked down the path along the river. Kirk looked around at everything, the river on his right, low buildings on his left. He asked a question Sam didn't understand.

Kirk pointed at a low building and raised his hand so his finger aimed high.

"No," Sam said. "Only low." She raised her hand to the top of the building and stopped.

As they approached the mesa, they met several people, including Maxee. Kirk shrunk back from her. Maxee stopped and held out her hands, tan palms up.

Sam went to the alien, patted her shoulder, and said, "Maxee." To the others gathered around, Sam added, "This is Kirk. He's from another world and doesn't know Standard. He'll be living with us. Does anybody know, is there a room available in the guesthouse?"

"Yes." Arlene pushed her way through the crowd.

Sam introduced them. "Arlene, show him a room and bring him to midday meal. You can start teaching him Standard if you want."

Arlene snorted and beckoned Kirk to follow her. Hal accompanied them, carrying Kirk's other bag.

Something else to worry about, Sam thought, as she and Maxee went up to the meeting hall on the mesa.

"Need me?" Maxee asked.

"Yes. I want you to teach Kirk Standard. You're good at teaching children, now you get to teach a grownup. We need to be able to communicate with him and he with us."

"Okee. Now?"

"No. Tomorrow. Let him rest today. Then you can show him around."

"I teach as we go." Maxee teetered on her toes. "Okee."

"You can go now. I have to find out what's been going on." Sam patted the alien, and Maxee trotted out.

Sam turned to her agenda and groaned. Back to the same old grind. She kept the thought of Hal and herself camping by the river uppermost in her mind and the farseeing problem in the back.

11

PEACE

WHEN JANNI STIRRED, WILLIE GRABBED HER. Still bemused by her meeting with the other humans, she let him take her. Afterward, she dressed, prepared breakfast, and kissed him goodbye.

Even though she had her tasks, Janni dropped into her big chair to ponder her experience. This was what she'd wanted: to go somewhere else and meet new people — but somehow it wasn't totally satisfactory.

I suppose because I wasn't there in person.

She wondered why they didn't ask any questions.

Before she could decide whether or not to tell Granlyn about this latest episode, she *received* a summons from the old woman.

She met Glori on the way. "You too?"

"Yes." Glori sighed. They arrived and found Leona already there.

"Well, girls, any progress?" Granlyn asked after they were settled.

"No," said Leona. Glori shook her head.

Janni opened her mouth to say 'maybe', but 'no' came out.

Granlyn stared at Janni. "Have you tried contacting them when you are out in space?"

"No." It was the truth; the voice always contacted her.

"Do it. We have a problem. Someone's been going through the vegetable bins picking out the best ones. We all know we are to take what is on top. Mindy and the others turn them over each evening so the ones needed to be used first will be on top."

"Have someone stand watch," Glori said.

"Or have someone there to pick vegetables for each person who comes by." Leona smiled.

"We don't have enough people to do that. We don't have enough people to do what we need to do. Too many children are working because we need the hands. Children should be allowed to have their childhood for play."

"I know, Granlyn," Janni said.

Granlyn sighed. "We always knew we didn't have enough people, but this ... Never mind. Do any of you have anything to discuss?"

Glori shook her head and Leona asked, "When are we going to have more responsibilities?"

"When I decide you are ready. You are doing well, now." Granlyn leaned back and closed her eyes. "Back to your tasks, ladies."

Janni opened her mouth, then decided this wasn't the best time. Granlyn tired easily these days.

The three left and headed back to the plaza. As Janni settled into her chair in the craft hall, she decided she would have to go out as soon as possible. Every evening, she told herself she would go out in the morning. Five days later, she did.

•   •   •

Janni's being floats in space outside the solar system. She searches for the watcher and calls for him. Getting no response, she checks out her surroundings: stars here and there, and a bluish patch over yonder. Then she spots it: the other that bothered her before.

She inspects it from a distance, and perceives danger, undefined. Something else to deal with. Try as she might, she cannot pinpoint any details, not even of what kind of danger it is.

At the human colony, time began. Janni watches. Presently, she contacts Maxee.

'I need to talk to your Sam and another,' Janni *sent* to the alien.

"I here. I go find others," Maxee replied.

A pause. "Here is Sam and Arlene," Maxee announced.

Janni understood that two other people were with Maxee and saw them in the alien's mind.

'How long have you lived on this world?' she asked.

"Over a thousand years. Mostly in City."

I did hear right.

Janni was amazed. 'My people have mental Talents,' she continued. 'We can converse in our minds. That's how I can talk to you.'

"Okee," Maxee said uncertainly.

'Do your people have any special talents?'

A short conversation among them, then Maxee asked why she wanted to know.

'I think our colonies should get together and help each other.'

"Maybe." Maxee sounded defensive.

'We have so few people; it'll be nice to meet some new people. I've found other small human communities on other worlds, but you're the biggest so far. Granlyn says we need more people, and we have a whole world with nobody else on it. Do you have a ship?'

A hurried conference with Sam and Arlene. "No. Why?"

'To bring you to our world.'

"If you have fewer, why you not move here?"

'No. Won't work. We want to bring all humans to our world. I can only move one at a time. We need another way, like a ship. Do any aliens on your world have ships?'

"No," Maxee relayed from Sam. "Volen brought them."

'Volen?'

"They looked after this world and many worlds. We no see them. We had person to talk with them. They left ten years ago. City die. We come here."

Like Watchers, Janni thought. *I wonder* ...

She faded out.

•   •   •

On Peace, Janni woke to dawn peeking in the window. She lay still, unable to move, and replayed the visit to the other human world in her mind. They seemed to be on much the same level as her clan and did not fight her intrusion into their world. She would like to get to know them better. This was one of her desires: to meet people outside the clan.

Their Volen sounded a lot like Watchers. There's no reason why they could not have called themselves something different at different worlds.

How on Peace are we going to save them and the others? Something out there destroyed that world, and I don't want any others burned out. Now I can't destroy Talent because I need to use it for this.

She sat up, patted Willie's shoulder, and slipped out of bed. After her morning ablutions and a bite of bread, she headed for Granlyn's.

"I went out in space again," Janni said after greetings. "I went to the big colony and talked to the humans there. They're a lot like us, only there are a lot more of them. Twenty thousand, they said. And they've been on that world over a thousand years."

"If your story people came in a ship," Grampa said, "their earth must have had tech like the one I remember. It would have taken at least a couple of centuries or more for our Earth to get to the point of interstellar travel, plus the time it took them to get to their new world." He shook his head.

Janni *heard* him think, *What are those people really like? Are they real?*

"Perhaps they came from a different Earth than we did." Granlyn pulled a silver curl.

"Of course, time is different in space." Grampa looked at Granlyn. "Remember how much older Beth and Mom and Dad were when we got back to Earth?"

"True, but not a thousand years."

"There's no time at all out in space," Janni said. "I was doing everything at once, but my brain had to separate them into single events." This had just occurred to her. "The time it would take me to go to all the different places is a lot longer than the time I'm out of my body. Like I was outside of time, and each solar system is encased in a bubble of time."

"I'm sorry, I don't understand," Granlyn said. "Does that make any sense to you, Larry?"

"I remember something about space and time not set in stone, but this ... I don't know."

"I know because I was there, Grampa," Janni said. "There is a danger out there. I don't know what it is yet, or how it will affect us, but it's real."

"What what is?" Marisa stepped up onto the porch. "You need to get to your tasks, Janni."

"Yes, Mama." She told her mother about the other colony. "If we could get them to come, here, we wouldn't feel so vulnerable."

"No," Marisa said. "We're doing just fine. We don't need any strangers."

"Mama!" Janni was so appalled she couldn't find words.

"Just a minute, Marisa. Larry has something to say," Granlyn said.

"I'll talk to Art, see what he can come up with in his scientific mind," Grampa muttered. "I don't see how we can do anything now. Even if they are real. Maybe you can find a group who still has a ship."

"Okay, I'll look next time," Janni said. "I haven't noticed any other large colonies."

Again, she *heard* Grampa think, *We need to know a lot more about them before we bring them here. If they are real.*

"We'll talk later. Bye, Granlyn and Grampa."

Marisa led Janni away.

"I don't understand this space thing, and I wish you wouldn't go out there."

"I can't help it, Mama, any more than you could help bending time to save Roroy and Beast. And you went to other worlds without knowing anything about them."

"I know, but it's different when it's your child." Marisa sighed. "All right. Get to work on your quilt blocks."

As Janni settled in at the quilting table, she felt disoriented. This was her home, the only one she'd known, yet out in space she knew a freedom she'd never felt before. A freedom to be herself, to see other places and people. She ignored glares from some of the other women.

"Hi." Glori dropped into her chair. "Brian is at me to make a baby again. He wants us to have ours first so he can beat his big brother at something."

"What?" Janni came out her trance.

"Janni, where are you? Are you sure you're not pregnant? You've got your head in the clouds all the time lately. Is being mated really that good?"

"Sorry. No, it's not that." Janni looked at her friend. "I've met some people on another world." She selected a spool of thread.

"How? Oh, that space thing." Glori picked up her loom. "What are they like?"

"Like us, except for the alien with the mindlink. None of those humans have it."

"Poor things." She peered at the needle.

"Yes." Janni set up her threads on the wooden loom. "I only see and hear what I pick up from the alien's mind. I'd like to visit with them in person. And no, I can't take my body out there."

"How can you visit with someone in your imagination?"

"Glori! They're real people who can get hurt and die." Janni slammed her loom down.

"Calm down." Glori picked out another color of thread.

Gramma Perri appeared. "What's the problem?"

Glori rolled her eyes.

Janni took a breath. "Has Mama told you about my travels in space?"

"Yes. Your imaginary travels. I must say you have a wonderful imagination."

"Gramma! It's not imagination; it's real. Why won't anybody believe me? Mama went to another world without a Gate, why can't I?" Janni threw her loom across the room.

"That's enough," Gramma Perri said. "Go get your loom and bring it back here."

Janni tromped across the room and picked up her loom, ignoring the looks from the other workers. Back at her table, she set the loom on it and sat down.

Gramma Perri put a hand on the girl's shoulder. "All right. If you believe it's real, we'll say it's real. Do they know where we are?"

"No, I don't think so. They're good people, Gramma, and they could be in danger. We have to help them."

Gramma Perri sighed. "All right, dear. But right now, you have work to do. And so do I."

"Yes, Gramma."

Gramma Perri walked over to the next table. Janni watched her.

She still doesn't really believe. What am I going to do?

Janni thought about that as she worked on her square. She'd moved one person from one world to another. It didn't take any time to speak of, only the time to get him out of his bubble to space and from space into Sam's bubble, but it did take energy. She'd felt more tired after that trip than the others.

What if she only brought one person over? She couldn't bring Maxee because of her kubs; she didn't want to separate them, but what about Sam? If they were together physically, they could find a way to communicate. She would think about it. One person couldn't hurt.

12

STARVIEW

THE DAYS PASSED, and Sam saw little of Kirk or Maxee. Brad flew his small airship over to Ambaak, the next sector west, and dropped Hal off at Far West Valley on the way. Liia, one of the leaders of the Ambaak, a humanoid people, called to see how Sam was doing and why she hadn't come with Brad.

"We have a newcomer," Sam said. "From another world. Maxee is teaching him Standard. And I'm overwhelmed with work."

"Delegate more to others," Liia said. "I do."

"I have, as much as I can. But too many people still don't want to do anything. We had everything provided by the Volen, and we all got spoiled."

"We, too, at first," Liia said. "Someone found a plant growing in a crack between solar panels on roof and watched it multiply. She was one of leaders in food prep, saved seeds and planted them. They grew, she planted more and eventually we grew our own food. Found they would grow inside with skylights."

"You were fortunate. Our early farmers were glad to have someone else do the work. I've been meaning to call you. A young woman from another world came and asked us questions. Brad and Maxee and me. She said she would be back. I don't know how she got here, but she communicated with Maxee in her mind. She also brought our newcomer, a man like us. I understand his world was destroyed." Sam paused. "She appears to be human, like us, but has technology way beyond us."

"Interesting. Keep me in the know."

"I will. I'll try to get over one of these days."

"Be aware. Farewell."

"Bye." Sam disconnected.

She still didn't know how this device worked. Brad had said the alien Volen had some advanced way to use solar power. The devices were one of the few things the Volen caretakers had left for them.

Brad returned two days later, but Hal walked back, visiting the other communities on the way. It was almost a week before Sam saw him again. Maxee told her when he was coming, and Sam went to meet him.

Hal greeted her with a hug. "I missed you."

"Me, too. Did you get things done over there?"

"Mostly. I overheard people talking about cutting ties with Starview and making their own town, but no one said anything to me."

"Oh, crud." Sam pulled back. "Should we let them?"

"I've been thinking about it." He took her hand, and they walked back to Starview. "I would like to have a meeting with us five to discuss it. Brad, Todd, and Arlene along with you and me."

"Good idea. Just have to figure out when."

•   •   •

That evening, Maxee and Kirk ate with Sam and Hal in the mesa caff. Brad joined them later.

"I *sprechen* Standard," Kirk said.

"I speak Standard," Maxee corrected.

"*Ja.* I know words." He grinned.

Sam noticed his hair and beard had been trimmed, and he was wearing regular pants and tunic. "How do you like this world?" she asked.

"World?"

"Place," Maxee said.

"Good," Kirk said. "People friendly."

"Most of time," Maxee added.

"I *astronom.* I see stars. I show you. With telescope." He sounded out each syllable of the last word separately.

"Great." Sam smiled at him.

Pleased that he was settling in and getting along in the community, Sam turned her attention to the meeting about Far West.

•   •   •

Sam, Hal, Brad, Arlene, and Todd all got together at her house.

Sam looked at Hal. "So, Hal, tell us what all you heard about this breaking away."

"They have a new leader who thinks they can make it on their own and don't want us telling them what to do. I couldn't find out any details — even Jon, the fellow I stayed with, wouldn't talk about it. But I think they're serious."

"Okay." Sam twisted in her seat. "Do you think we should let them do it?" She sensed that this was part of the upcoming upheaval.

"If we do," Todd said, "we'll have to create a trade agreement, and they'll have to pay in some form for whatever we send them."

Trust Todd to see the legal side, Sam sighed.

"We would have to figure out how much we could give them, and they would have to take care of the rest," Arlene said.

"We could charge them for shipping," Brad remarked.

"How would it affect us?" Sam wanted to know. *In the short term.*

"Very little." Arlene wrote something on her notepad. "They only have a couple of items we need, and that can go in the trade agreement."

"Okay, let's wait and see what they do." Sam picked at a fingernail.

"Okay by me," Brad said. "I see you're about to drop. We'll see you tomorrow."

The four left and Sam dropped into her big chair. She decided not to think about anything tonight.

13

PEACE

A FEW DAYS LATER, Sam left her office and stepped into nothingness. After an unknown time, she became aware of herself. She lay on something spongy with hardness beneath and felt warmth, but no emotions. She breathed refreshing air. A question arose. *Where was she?* Sound. Murmur of voices and a background whisper she couldn't identify.

She opened her eyes, saw a blue green sky, and closed them again. *No, this could not be.*

She rolled over onto her side and opened her eyes again. Now she saw a green slope and distant sea. A hint of fear drifted over her.

No, Sam thought again, unable to comprehend her surroundings.

Something touched her shoulder and she jumped. A young woman with reddish-brown hair and brown eyes knelt beside her. Tall people hovered above. Sam's mind went blank as the woman said something. An aroma of grass mixed with people, but not like in Starview, stole over her.

Why couldn't she understand the woman? Only one word, 'Janni', made sense. *Was this Janni's world? Was this the beginning of the menace?*

Two women approached. They had Janni's square face and black curls. One asked a question Sam could not comprehend. She could only see, hear, feel with her body. She could not process what she perceived. Panic hit her. Sam began to shake, her fists clenched, and she gasped for breath. *Where was she? What happened?*

The older woman, who could have been the mother of the younger, knelt beside Sam and patted her shoulder, murmuring soft words. Soon Sam began to relax. At least, she sensed no danger. She dropped her face into her hands and drew in deep breaths. The woman continued to pat her shoulder. Presently, Sam felt safe and looked up. This woman also had green eyes.

Like Janni.

"Janni?" Sam said.

The woman nodded, and the panic was gone.

Somehow, Sam was on Janni's world. She was still unable to process thought.

A man with brown hair stood beside them. He reached down for her, and the young woman said, "No, Allen."

Sam understood 'no,' as the man pulled back.

Allen must be his name.

The young woman pointed to herself. "Marisa." Then to the girl and said, "Glori". The older woman was Gramma Perri.

Sam nodded, but could not speak. Words would not come. The sun felt warm, and a pleasant breeze danced around her, teasing her hair. This was not a dream, but not real, either.

I can't sit here all day.

She made a move to get to her knees. Marisa helped her up.

Sam clung to her, dizzy. Marisa was several inches taller than her own five six. Her legs felt like they had no bones.

"Where? Janni?" she got out.

"Sleeping," Glori said, her hands folded under her cheek.

The older woman nodded. She took Sam's other arm. The five of them walked up the grassy slope, through a line of narrow trees, past log cabins surrounded by red and yellow flowers, to a large stone-paved open area. Even though it was uphill, Sam barely noticed the incline. The women led her to a wooden bench and bade her sit. Sam collapsed onto it. Allen touched her shoulder and wandered off.

What on City is going on?

She had no trouble breathing. The air was fresh and clean, and the log buildings reminded her of Starview.

Marisa swept her arm around and said, "Hom."

Home, Sam thought. *Need language.*

She pulled the warmth of a pleasant breeze about her and inhaled the flowery aroma of the clear air. Gramma Perri said something and headed for one of the buildings. Marisa shooed Glori off and sat beside Sam.

Sam's mind began to clear as she looked around at the log buildings surrounding the paved area. A pair of long wooden tables with benches sat at one side.

This is what we need on our world: a central place to gather, she thought.

Two women came out of a nearby building, stared at her, and walked away.

In the quietness, she heard a faint murmur of voices from one of the buildings, rustling in the trees, and a faint gurgle of water. A distorted aroma of flowers told her she was on a different world.

Sam began to feel annoyed at being brought here out of the blue, which grew into a full-fledged mad.

"How dare you bring me here without my permission? Brad, Hal, Maxee, my people back home won't know what happened and they'll be scared stiff."

She tried to rise, but Marisa held her down and put a hand on Sam's head. Sam shook it off.

Marisa said what sounded like, "Please," and put her hand back. A picture of a person between worlds with a question mark came into her mind.

Sam only sensed it vaguely and said, "Damn right."

Marisa sighed.

At least she understands, Sam thought. She had no idea how she got there but felt sure this was Janni's world. *If Janni brought me here, she could send me back,* Sam hoped. First, she must learn how to talk to these people. Being unable to communicate was as disconcerting as being lost in the gray corridors of City.

Sam felt sure this was the beginning of the problem her future sight saw, but not even the bare outlines were clear yet.

How was she going to get out of this?

Marisa said something that sounded like 'okay?' and rose.

Sam, tongue-tied because she could not talk to her, just nodded.

Marisa led her past a row of cabins, all with their flowers, to a little cabin, indicated that this was for Sam, and motioned that she would return.

Sam looked around. A big, stuffed chair in green in one front corner, a small wooden table with two chairs in the other, and, behind a curtain in the rear, sat a narrow bed and a chest of drawers with a basin and pitcher of water on it.

Where's the outhouse?

Through a window, she saw a shed and went out to check it out. It was an outhouse.

After she used it, she returned to the cabin and sat in the one comfortable chair. Although she knew where she was, and had a place to stay, fear fought with her anger.

Sam leaned back and put thoughts together.

Okay, I'm on Janni's world, and if they gave me a place to stay, certainly they'll feed me. I have to learn how to communicate with them and find out how to get home. Whatever's happening, I must get back to Starview. And why was it morning here when it was late afternoon on my world?

Home. A great emptiness surrounded her. All the people she knew — Maxee, Hal, Brad, Todd, Arlene, all the others — were on another world far away. She worried about them being concerned for her, especially Maxee.

Sam stared out the window at trees. She became aware that she didn't have to jump up and go do things. She could just sit and do nothing. This was the break, the getaway she needed. Brad and Arlene could handle things. For a while.

And then she wondered why Janni had brought her here. She resolved she would find out and get things straightened out with that young woman.

Slowly Sam relaxed and slipped into a doze.

Later, a strange noise awoke her, and she sat up.

So I'm still here, it wasn't a dream. Since I'm here, I might as well explore this world.

Sam went out and looked around. This place was neater, more efficiently laid out, with paths clearly outlined with stones. The differences warred with the familiar. Flowerbeds with red and orange blooms dancing in the breeze lined the front and one side of the cabin. A tree stood in back, shading the place from the afternoon sun.

She listened, followed sound, and found a small river that didn't seem adequate for this colony. She followed the water, searching for something she could not name.

A tall man with straight, brown hair down to his shoulders and a cropped beard came around a tree, stopped her, and said something she didn't understand. Then, "I Roroy." He pointed to his chest and repeated the name.

He's another part of this menace.

"Roroy," Sam echoed. He was different from the others, but she wasn't sure how. "I Samanda." She also indicated herself.

"Samanda." He nodded and asked a question. She caught the word, 'you'.

"Other world," she said. "Janni."

"Ah." Roroy nodded.

Before he could say more, a huge black beast barged out of the bushes.

Sam gasped and backed away.

"Okay," Roroy said, a hand on the beast's back. The animal lowered its head. He said something to the beast, and Sam heard her name.

Was he introducing me to it?

He beckoned her over, gently took her hand, and held it out in front of the animal's nose. The creature sniffed and nodded. The man let her hand go, and she touched the black curls on the side of the animal's shoulder.

"Good," Roroy said. "Oo eh Bees."

'You met Beast,' Sam translated.

Maybe it wouldn't be too hard to learn their language. Theirs seemed similar to hers.

Sam studied the animal. It was not like any she'd seen pictures of on her screen in City. Barrel-shaped and wide, with sturdy legs and a stringy tail, the creature impressed Sam. The oblong head with small round ears on top held beady black eyes.

"Come," the man said, gesturing with his hand, and added something else.

Sam understood 'come', but nothing else. Since she felt no threat from him, she followed him away from the river, between rows of cabins, to a series of groves of trees to the west. The sun was setting in front of her.

Did I really slept so long?

Here, she found more animals. These were smaller in body, sleeker, brown with pale hair down the back of the long neck and long, pale tails. They looked at her, curiously, she thought, out of large, brown eyes.

"Quines," Roroy said, as Beast trotted off to one side.

"Quines," Sam repeated, studying the creatures.

One young one pranced up to her. Sam held out her hand. The quine sniffed delicately and nodded. Another, larger quine approached and nudged the first one out of the way.

"Hello," Sam said, delighted to meet real animals. The second one nosed Sam's hand and hair and gave a neigh of approval.

These creatures are also part of the menace.

"Oh, there you are," Marisa said, trotting up beside her.

"Roroy," Sam said. "Beast."

"Oh. This Qilla." She patted the smaller one's shoulders. "Janni. And Qione." She patted the larger animal and pointed to herself.

Sam gathered that each person had their own quine.

This place was becoming more interesting every moment. Even so, I would have preferred to have been invited and able to tell the others where I was going.

"We ride them," Marisa said, and jumped on Qione's back.

The quine trotted around, and Sam saw that the woman held the neck hair loosely.

It must be fun to ride like that, she thought. *'Ride'. That was the word she used.*

The quine pulled up and Marisa jumped off. "Now we go home for supper. Eat." She mined eating.

Sam realized she was very hungry, nodded, and wondered what their food was like.

14

PEACE / STARVIEW

S AM FOLLOWED MARISA TO HER HOUSE. Much larger than her little place, the living room held a pale green couch with two matching padded chairs, two small tables, and a large table with six chairs. Three doors at one side must lead to bedrooms, and a small area of shelves and cabinets at the rear indicated a food area.

"Sit," Marisa said. She motioned to a chair and headed back to the kitchen.

Sam sat and viewed the room. Smooth, pale yellow walls held rows of pictures of places, people, objects. A parade of old books sat on a shelf that matched the walls. A wooden vase of red flowers decorated the large table. Homey smells surrounded her, food, flowers, and something she couldn't define but made her feel protected.

A medium-sized boy with dark brown hair burst in and stopped. "Who are you?" he demanded of Sam.

"Steven!" Marisa called from the kitchen and came out. "Sam, this is my younger son, Steven, sometimes known as Steviepot. Steve, this is Miss Sam, a visitor who will be staying with us, in Janni's old room. Mind your manners."

"Hi." He glared at his mama and ran into the middle room.

Sam gathered the boy was hers and his name was Steve. He reminded her of Brad's Del, and she winced. "My brother son, Del, same age." She held her hand at height of the boy's top of head.

Marisa nodded. Whether she understood, Sam couldn't tell.

She strolled over to look at the books. She'd never seen a real one. The very old ones Todd had found had crumbled to bits as he copied them.

Allen, the man with the women when she first came, arrived with a larger boy. He smiled when he saw Sam. "Hello. Doing well?"

Sam nodded and smiled.

Allen indicated the boy and said, "Mick."

"Hello, Mick," Sam said.

Mick stared at her. Marisa came out and embraced Allen. "All here. All ready. Sit."

Allen sat at one end of the table, the boys on one side. Sam took a seat on the other side as Marisa brought in a large steaming bowl. Allen picked up a long loaf of dark bread, broke pieces off and handed them around. Sam liked the bread; the stew not so much. Something chewy had an odd taste.

As the family conversed, Sam picked up words here and there, and, by the end of the meal, was able to follow the exchanges. The boys went into their room and Allen settled himself in his chair with a small block of wood and a carving knife.

When Marisa finished cleaning up in the kitchen, she showed Sam to the front bedroom. Sam dropped her bag on the narrow bed. This room was pale green, with more shelves and roughly bound books.

"Come," Marisa said, and led Sam back to the third room which was not a bedroom. It contained a bathing tub, a chest with a basin and water pitcher and a pile of cloths.

Good, I could use a bath.

At the kitchen, Sam saw that there was another bedroom behind the main room. Marisa showed her how to access water. A hand pump brought water up from a holding tank outside and into a large basin. She handed Sam a slightly misshapen pinkish mug.

"Yours."

After getting a drink of water from the tap, they returned to the living room. Marisa took down a battered ABC book and Sam began her lessons.

When it got too dark to read by the lantern light, Marisa said, "Time to go to bed."

Sam prepared for bed, but was unable to sleep. A picture of Hal's face formed in her mind, followed by Brad and Maxee. "Please, Oneness, let them know I'm safe," she whispered.

•　　　•　　　•

After a breakfast of bread and some gooey yellow stuff which tasted pleasant, Allen and the boys left. Sam insisted on helping with cleanup.

Afterward, Marisa said, "Come. We go to Granlyn."

Sam grabbed her bag and they left.

Outside, they met Janni, coming from the plaza. Sam smiled at a familiar face. Janni managed half a smile as they went next door. This house had a little porch with a roof, and pink flowery vines around the porch posts.

Marisa knocked and an old woman with the same square face and green eyes opened the door.

"Granlyn, this is Samanda, from another world. Sam, meet Granlyn, our matriarch."

Sam smiled and nodded.

"Come on in." Granlyn beckoned. "Welcome," she said to Sam.

The three women sat on the old brown couch. Sam looked around. Smaller than Marisa's house, with more pictures and shelves on the walls, it had one small table with chairs for two under a window.

"Ah," Granlyn said, "we have a visitor. Janni, did you bring her?"

Sam understood most of what the old woman said. She'd picked up quite a bit at supper the night before.

"Yes, Granlyn," Janni whispered, ducking her head.

"Do you know why that was wrong?"

Janni shook her head. "I thought ..."

Marisa opened her mouth and Granlyn put a hand up.

"Janni, did you inform Samanda of what you were about to do? Did you give her a chance to tell someone there where she was going? Did you give her a chance to collect whatever she might like to bring?"

"No." Janni looked down at her hands.

"So we have this woman waking on a strange world, not knowing where she is and not being able to understand the locals. How do you think she must have felt?"

A tiny 'oh' escaped the young woman.

Sam felt sorry for Janni. "It's okay. I send message to my people?" She touched her chest.

"No," Marisa said.

"Cannot." Granlyn glared at the other woman.

"Go home?" Sam asked.

"When Janni go out." Granlyn pointed up. "How soon?" she asked Janni.

Janni shrugged. "Maybe a week, maybe two."

Sam didn't get the word and shook her head.

Marisa said, "Week," and held up one hand and two fingers on her other hand.

"Oh." Sam shrank back. She assumed the fingers meant days.

"Okay, ladies, we have a guest." Granlyn looked at all of them. "We must treat her as such. Samanda, you may stay in the little cabin. We will provide you with a few changes of clothes and anything else you need. In exchange, you will be required to do some work here. What did you do in your community?"

"I was the mayor, in charge of everything," Sam said before she realized she understood the old woman. Something in her mind ... She shook her head and continued. "Planning and seeing that everything went smoothly."

At their puzzled looks, she added, "Boss lady. Like you. Of course, I'll work."

Granlyn nodded. "Marisa, you will see that Samanda is fed. Janni, you will have to work harder to make up for the extra food."

Janni made a face.

"Samanda, you are welcome here, in spite of the method of your arrival. Enjoy your stay. Now, Marisa, you show Samanda around and get her a few changes of clothes and things. Whatever she needs."

"Yes, Granlyn." Marisa rose. "Come, Sam."

Janni sat up. "I wanted to …"

"No," said Granlyn, leaning back in her rocker and closing her eyes. "Stay."

Sam and Marisa left.

"All these flowers," Sam said, sweeping her arm around.

"Yes." Marisa smiled. "You have flowers?"

"Some." Sam wanted to say more, but didn't have the words.

At the plaza, Marisa led Sam to a large log building. "Storehouse," she said.

Inside, Sam saw rows of shelves, stretching from front to back. One row had what looked like food; another displayed clothing. Marisa took her down this aisle and stopped at a shelf with a pile of tunics. She picked out a pale pink tunic and held it up to Sam, then selected two more: a pale blue and a pale yellow.

Further down the aisle, Marisa did the same with pants. She showed Sam a pocket at the crotch she mimed stuffing rags in.

"No, two weeks." Sam said.

She had her comb and brush with her in her bag, but she needed a tooth cleaner, soap, and towels. These she put in her bag, and Marisa carried the clothes in another. They went to the meeting hall, which seemed much larger than Starview's hall, until Sam realized it had no offices along the sides, just groups of tables and seats.

At the clan kitchen, Sam saw how neat and organized it was, with prepared food available.

"This is nice," Sam said. "Better than ours." She would have to tell June about it when she got back.

At the clinic, she looked around. It was similar to Evelyn's, without the waiting room in front; just a row of chairs by the front wall. The schoolhouse was well laid out, as was the craft hall.

That's an idea. Her people all worked at home.

Marisa took her to a table near the back where an untidy pile of clothing lay. She picked up a tunic, inspected it, pointed to a tear and laid it aside. Another had missing buttons and she laid it in another place. She handed a third to Sam, who found a tear and put it on the other one with a tear.

Marisa nodded, smiled, and pointed to the pile and Sam. "I come back."

"Okay," Sam said and smiled also.

Marisa left and Sam began sorting the clothes to be mended.

This is certainly something different.

She was glad she could do something useful and was pleased that it was nothing like her usual tasks.

Marisa returned after a while and kept Sam busy.

That evening at Marisa's house, while waiting for supper, Janni came by.

"Hi, Sam," she said, twitching on her feet with her hands behind her back. "I came to apologize for bringing you here the way I did." She waved her hand. "I should have told you first."

Sam nodded. Somehow, she understood what the young woman said. "I accept your apology. But I need to go home, my brothers and friends will be worried about me."

"When I am ready. Takes lot of energy, I need time to recover. I'll let you know when I can."

"Okay." Sam sighed. All she could do was pray and worry.

"I've gotta go, gotta fix supper for Willie."

"Thanks for coming, Janni," Marisa said from the kitchen.

"Bye, Mama, Sam." Janni trotted out the door.

•　　•　　•

For the next week, Sam lived a different life. She got used to her little cabin, did whatever tasks Marisa assigned her, and met several of the people. She saw Roroy and Beast every so often, and learned about the quines. She had long talks with Granlyn, sharing their worlds. The more she learned, the more she wanted to bring her people here and use some of these people's methods.

Although she worried about Brad, Maxee, and Hal, she still enjoyed her new, leisurely life. A sense of belonging and wanting to stay there fought with her need to go home. Sam felt the beginning of a definition of the menace forming in her mind, that it would be here on Peace.

Finally, one day as they were cleaning up after a meal, Janni told Sam, "I'll send you back tonight. Sleep as usual, when you wake, you'll be on your world. Hold your bag." She gave Sam a packet of loovah roots and small leaves.

"Okay."

Although Sam wanted to return home, she was loath to leave this world, learning a new language and helping out wherever she was needed. No hordes of people demanding things they could not get, no complaints about shortages of food and other things, no one saying just this one more thing. But she did miss her brothers and friends.

That night, Sam lay sleepless until she sank into an uneasy doze. She felt something pick her up, but her mind wouldn't focus. Her whole body tingled, and then nothing.

•   •   •

When Sam came to, she was lying on the ground in a grove of trees. She opened her eyes and saw sunlight trickling down through the branches. She breathed deeply. The air told her she was home.

Sam ached all over. Now she knew how Kirk had felt. How long had he been sitting there before she and Hal found him?

She managed to prop herself against a tree and look around. Skinny trees with long needle-like leaves that she'd never seen before surrounded her.

She grabbed her comm and called Brad. Nothing.

"Oh, shit."

Was the device not working or was she too far away? Sam slammed it into her bag. She didn't need this now. *Calm down,* she told herself. Maxee would see that she was back and have someone come here; wherever here was. But that could take days. Marisa had given her a loaf of bread, but that wouldn't last very long.

Sam had a hard time putting two thoughts together but managed to get to her feet. She had to pee, anyway.

After that, she picked up her bag and tottered through an opening in the trees and down a trace of a trail. At least, it was downhill. Finding it noticeably harder to breathe, she thought she must be higher on the mountain. *And where was the river?* Fear tickled her spine.

After what seemed like several hours of pushing through bushes and between trees, Sam thought she heard the river and found the main trail. The sun hung low in the west. She collapsed onto a downed tree trunk and took a sip of water. Her hands and arms were scratched, and her tunic torn in places. Her hair, which she had pinned up on her head, hung down over her ears.

Sam dug out her comm. This time, when she tried to call Brad, she reached him.

"Yeah," he said.

"Is that any way to greet your sister?" Sam's fatigue and soreness disappeared at the sound of his voice.

"Sammie! Where are you? Where have you been? We've been worried sick."

"Janni took me to Peace. I'm up on the trail."

"Peace, eh. That's what Maxee thought. How far up are you?"

"I don't know. Still hard to breathe."

"You have food?"

"Some."

"Okay, I'll send someone up in the morning to meet you. You take it easy, find a nice place to camp out. Do you have any kind of wrap?"

"A minicloak in my bag."

"Good. See you soon, sis. Take care."

Sam felt much relieved. She rested for a bit, ate a little bread, and continued on. When the sun set, she found a place to curl up in some bushes. She was a long way from home.

15

PEACE

J ANNI'S BEING HANGS IN SPACE. After she sends Sam home, the
voice comes to her.

'Very good. But you can only move one at a time. Your world
has a Gate. You need to make a Gate to their world.'

'How? And can you make us stop being Watchers?'

'Not now. This is for your head scientist, to make a Gate.' A
mental packet invades her being.

'No!'

The voice is gone. Janni finds herself focusing on the
otherness, and something stings her. Sting is the only word for
what she feels. She jerks back into her body.

•　　　•　　　•

When Janni came to, she remembered the words and the
sting. She lay in her bed and checked her mind. Everything was as
it was supposed to be, but something had been added, something
new. She tried to open the thing. A faint echo of another mind
remained for a moment, then it, too, was gone. *Another mind,* she
thought. *Could those beings control others with their minds?*

Suddenly terrified, Janni jumped out of bed. She had to tell Granlyn and the others. Willie was gone, probably off to work.

Janni ran to Granlyn's, only to find her mother on the porch.

"You can't go in. Grampa had another stroke. He's okay, but Granlyn doesn't want to see anyone right now."

"But I've got to tell them, I think I know what the other is."

"Go find one of the other grampas. Gabe or Bay."

"But, Mama ..."

"Go." Marisa raised her hand.

Janni went. She *sensed* her mother's anguish and knew there was no point in staying. She went to Granli first. Grampa Bay's mate told her that he was over in the forest.

So, he was out. She looked for Grampa Gabe, but no one had seen him. He was one of the heads of the clan. He was also half-Bramite and had never gotten over the death of his human father, Adam.

Janni hesitated to tell him; he was so stand-offish. But she had to tell someone. She ran to the plaza and found Grampa Charley by running into him.

"Whoa, there, what's the hurry?"

"Oh, Grampa, I found the danger out there."

"What danger?"

"In space." She pointed at the sky.

"Okay, come sit down and tell me." Grampa Charley led her to one of the benches.

"You know I can go out into space." Janni wiped her forehead with her sleeve.

"Yeah, I heard that."

"This time I focused on the danger, and an alien mind touched mine. If they can go into other minds and control them ..." Janni clenched her fists.

"That doesn't sound good." Grampa Charley crossed his legs.

"I know. We can protect ourselves with our Talent, but Sam's people don't have it, so we have to bring them here so we can protect them too. It may take all of us."

"Sam. That was the gal who was visiting."

"Yes. But I can only bring one at a time every other week. We've got to find a better way." A memory tickled her mind, but she couldn't grasp it.

"Calm down, we'll find a way. Now run along. I'm sure you have tasks."

"Oooh!" Janni screamed under her breath as she ran to the craft hall.

Why won't anyone believe me?

•　　　•　　　•

That afternoon, Janni *received* a message from Grampa Charley that there would be a minor meeting at his house that evening and he wanted her to be there.

Meetings, always meetings. But that how things got done around here.

When Janni arrived, Gramma Perri, Grampa Charley, Mama, Papa, Big Art, Uncle Artie, and Uncle Peter were already there. Grampa Charley pulled chairs from the table into the main area and people sat. Gramma and Grampa sat in the two big chairs where Granlyn and Grampa Larry usually parked themselves. Mama, Papa, and Uncle Peter sat on the couch.

"Janni, tell them what you told me," Grampa Charley said.

"Okay." She told about the mind touch and added, "Besides Sam's, there is one world with people who don't have tech, and several smaller colonies. Another world was destroyed, all the cities and human places burned. I sent one survivor to Sam's world. None of them have mind Talent."

"Of course not," Gramma Perri said. "We're the only ones who do."

"I know, but that means they can't protect themselves. I couldn't sense what the danger actually was until this last time. There's something big out there, I'm not sure if it's a ship or what, but the sting came from it. It touched my mind but didn't hurt anything."

"No," Gramma Perri said.

"No," Marisa echoed, standing. "That's it. You are not to go out there anymore."

"Mama, I have no choice. Something pulls me out there. I can't stop it." Janni waved her hand.

"Allen, do something." Marisa wrung her hands.

"Marisa, there's nothing we can do. You heard the girl." Allen crossed his legs.

"If there is danger out there, we need to know about it so we can deal with it," Grampa Charley said. "I suppose the Watchers could have started more than one new race." He leaned back on the couch.

"Is this real?" Uncle Peter asked.

"Oh yes. I felt it." Janni gulped. "How are we going to save Sam's people?"

"If we had a Gate," Marisa said.

"We're not gatekeepers," Gramma Perri replied. "How could we make a Gate?"

That was it.

Janni sat up. "The Watcher gave me some information on making a Gate."

"Oh, really," Uncle Artie said. "Sam's people don't have a ship?"

Big Art grimaced.

"I don't know. But they've been there over a thousand years." Janni twisted a curl.

"So even if they had one, it probably wouldn't be operable," Uncle Artie said. "Would this danger thing get to them before us?"

"I can't tell." Janni's stomach knotted. She needed to know so much more.

"But the Gates," Marisa said. "Uncle Peter, didn't you say you looked into one?"

"Yes." He smiled. "I saw the basic workings. Push the button, and a signal opens the door, a sensor that closes the door after everyone stops moving over the threshold, and another one that opens the door to an empty room. But the actual mechanism of the transfer itself was hidden. I couldn't *reach* that."

"A physical block?" Uncle Artie asked.

"No, I don't think so."

Uncle Artie asked Janni, "Can you send that info to me?"

Janni nodded and did. Everyone watched Uncle Artie as he closed his eyes and mumbled.

"I think I've got it." Uncle Artie opened his eyes and grinned. "Want to see it, Pop?"

Big Art grunted and shook his head.

"I'm willing to go try it." Uncle Artie said.

"No," Big Art shouted. "Don't mess with the Gate. I've had it." He jumped up and left.

Uncle Artie shrugged. "It's time the Gate should be checked. I'll take Brian. I have to finish up a project in the morning, then we'll go," he said. "Maybe these younger minds can get through."

"Okay," Grampa Charley said.

"Can I go?" Janni asked.

"No!" Marisa said.

"Why not?" Allen grinned. "She's the brightest. Maybe she could figure it out."

"Allen." Marisa twisted her hands together.

"She'll be all right, honey. Janni, will Willie want to go?"

"He can't, he and Chad have to mend that broken pipe. I'll be all right." *I won't miss him.*

"Okay," Grampa Charley said. "Artie, you and your helpers work on the Gate, and you, Janni, check those other colonies to see if any of them have a ship." He pushed himself to his feet.

Gramma saw everyone off.

"What else?' Marisa asked as they walked back to their houses. "I saw something else worrying you."

"No," Janni said automatically. She had to figure out how to do it first. Then she said, "Mama, that Watcher out there wants me to move Sam's people here, so we'll have enough people after the ones of us who become watchers leave."

"Oh." Marisa stopped and looked at Janni. "But can it undo our Talents?'

"I asked, and it said, 'not now'. So, I don't know."

"We can't do it by ourselves, and since they gave it to us in the first place, they can undo it. Keep asking."

"Okay, Mama." Janni pushed the thought to the back of her mind.

16

STARVIEW

TODD VOLUNTEERED TO GO GET SAM in the morning, along with Maxee. She needed to know how her kubs would behave when she wasn't there. Several people said they'd keep an eye on the little ones.

Todd grabbed a backpack of supplies, and he and Maxee headed out.

"Going somewhere?" Arlene asked, stopping them.

"Sammie's back," Maxee said. "Up the trail."

"Hold on, I'll go with you." She corralled her assistant and collected a backpack.

Maxee trotted on ahead. Todd kept up with his long legs, but Arlene, not as young, dropped back.

"Slow down," she called.

Todd stopped. "Are you sure you want to come? It's all uphill."

"Yes, if I don't have to go fast. At least, it's not too warm."

Arlene looked at the clouds overhead. A breeze followed them down the trail.

"Okay. Maxee, slow down."

"Okee." She stuck her bottom lip out for a second, then complied.

At the bridge, they met Lucy from North Valley and told her Sam was back.

"Great. I'll let people know."

They continued up the tree-lined trail, the river gurgling on their left. Arlene insisted on brief stops to rest and drink water. Maxee remarked on how certain trees and bushes had changed since her older kubs' walkabout a few years before.

"Down trees on trail gone," she said. The skeleton of one lay along the edge of the trail.

A few bushes had red berries, and Todd collected some to take back and test. They continued on until sunset, yet no one wanted to stop.

When it got too dark to see easily, Todd halted. "Stay here." He went up around a bend and hollered, "Sam!"

He thought he heard an answer and returned to the others. "I think I heard her. Arlene, check your pack for a lightstick." He checked his and found an old, half-used one.

"Here's one." Arlene held up the thin stick. "I don't know how much juice it has in it." The lightsticks had been left behind by the Volen.

"Do you want to keep going?"

"Yes." Maxee bounced up and down.

"I'm good." Arlene sighed as she climbed to her feet.

They continued up along the river, using the ambient light from the stars and the light sticks in the deep forest.

Every so often, Todd hollered, and, after the third try, they all heard a return call. Arlene tripped over a root and fell.

"You hurt?" Maxee asked, helping her up.

"No, I don't think so."

Maxee held her arm. "I see good in dark. I show you where to go." She knew her night vision was much better than the humans'.

Presently, they reached Sam huddled under a tree. Arlene dropped down beside her, and Maxee sat on the other side.

"Good to see you. Where were you?" Arlene asked between puffs of breath.

"Janni's world, called Peace. It was peaceful." Sam was so tired and sleepy after another day of hiking she could hardly talk. Her internal time clock was way out of joint. "Tell you about it later. Sleep now." Sam fell asleep and the others settled themselves and joined her.

•   •   •

In the morning, refreshed, they headed down the trail to Starview.

"Although I'm glad to see you, I'm also surprised." Sam felt life coming back into her bones and muscles.

"I had to get away before I started screaming." Arlene grinned.

"That bad?" *How much worse could it have gotten?*

"You wouldn't believe." Arlene paused to smell a purple flower on a tree. "Not much scent."

"Todd, how's your department?" Sam asked.

"People keep disputing who owns what." He kicked a rock. "I've set up a board of arbitration, but even that doesn't always satisfy them."

"What do these people want?" Sam grumbled. *Yes, I'm back home.*

"Whatever they had back in City. Some people still don't get it that we can't go back, that we can't get the things we had before." Todd tugged at his backpack.

"After all this time?" Sam asked.

"Yes. Mostly the ones who were forced to leave before it got very bad." Todd humphed. "Those who are running the community work so hard, and the others don't appreciate what they've got."

"I know," Sam said. "Everyone on Peace did their share, even the little children had tasks to do. Of course, they'd been living there for seventeen years, and over twenty on the other place. And there's not nearly as many of them as there are of us."

"That makes a difference." Todd paused and glanced down at the river. "Papa took me down to the port once when I was about seven. The port master had some problem with one of the ship owners. I watched as they unloaded a grain ship into carts, and men would pull them up to a building on the backside of City. We went out on the dock, and I saw the sea. It went on forever." He paused. "It was the most amazing thing I'd ever seen, and still is."

"I know," Sam said. "That's how I felt the day Janni took me down to the beach. Unbelievable."

At the next rest break, on a grassy area overlooking the river, Arlene told Sam about a situation where a woman had started throwing her food in a caff and demanding a dish they were no longer able to make because they no longer had the ingredients.

"A couple of men subdued her and took her to the main clinic. I understand she's tied down to a bed now."

"Oh, no. Why can't they accept this new place?"

"Zilla said there are some people who are unable to accept a situation where something traumatic has happened. You know there are people who can never accept the fact that their spouse or child has died, and never move on."

"Yes, I'd heard that. What can we do?"

"I don't know. We certainly can't remake City for them."

"What about her family?" Sam picked a tiny purple flower out of the grass.

"A sister took in her children, and her husband ignores the situation. I think it's because he doesn't know how to handle it and won't ask for help."

"We could do a lot more if people would just ask if they needed something." Sam pushed her hair back.

"All right, ladies, time to get moving." Todd rose.

Maxee had found a five-pointed yellow flower and showed it around. Sam and Arlene climbed to their feet. Sam felt her normal self, but tired.

Even though the way was downhill, light was fading when they reached the mesa and went to late meal in the mesa caff. Brad and Hal met them there.

As they sat down in the long room filled with people at square tables, Sam was hit by a barrage of questions and demands.

"Where have you been?" a man called.

"Why haven't you got the oven in the big caff fixed?" came from the rear.

"You can't just go leave us like that," screeched a woman with whom Sam was not familiar.

Brad stood and yelled until there was quiet. "Sam just got home and is very tired. Let her eat and retire to her house. Tomorrow is time enough for questions. Leave her alone now."

There were grumbles, but Sam was able to eat in peace.

After the meal, at her house, Sam told Hal, Brad, Maxee, and Todd about her experience on Peace. "Once I figured out where I was, all my stress just disappeared like that." She snapped her fingers. "Everyone was so friendly and helpful. And the quines."

"Quines?" Todd asked.

"Animals they ride. Four legs and a tail. Brown with blonde hair on their necks and tails. Big brown eyes. They are intelligent and communicate with the humans some way I don't understand. Janni talked to hers and somehow received an answer. Their world has a lighter gravity than ours and it's easier to walk and run."

"Goody," Maxee bobbed in her chair.

"You'll have to watch that your kubs don't float away." Sam paused. "One more thing. The menace I saw is beginning to come into focus. It's going to happen mostly on Janni's world, but involves all of us."

"Wonderful," Brad said sarcastically. "I see it now, too. How lucky we are, Sam, that we can see the future."

"Thank Mother and her ancestors, and the Volen for removing the veil that kept us from seeing it before."

Sam barely remembered her mother's face. Her red hair matched Sam's.

17

PEACE

WHEN THE GROUP MET AT THE PLAZA to go to the Gate, Janni was surprised to see Big Art with Uncle Artie. He'd always resented Gramma Perri and her family because she hadn't saved his mother from the alien, even though Gramma had done everything she could.

"I've got to keep an eye on this," Big Art said.

Janni saw that he didn't want to miss anything.

Janni and Glori rode with Big Art, Uncle Artie, and Brian to the glade by the Gate, which was surrounded by trees and held a bubbling spring and stream. When Glori found out Brian and Janni were going, she insisted on going, too. The group found nothing in the glade to indicate anyone or anything had come through.

"Good," said Big Art.

He ordered Uncle Artie to *call* Grampa Charley with his mind to let him know they were at the Gate, and they camped for the night.

•   •   •

In the morning, Big Art opened the door in the side of the huge tree, and they all entered the Gate, leaving the quines outside.

Janni, Glori, and Brian gaped at the multisided room studded with doors, much larger than the tree. Only a few were marked. Both Arts had been through the Gate, on the way from Harmony. They headed for the control console with the screen.

Uncle Artie moved toward the seat, but Big Art pushed him out of the way.

"Pop. This is my project."

"Now, son, let's just see what we have."

Janni felt Uncle Artie's fury as he looked over his papa's shoulder. Big Art still treated him like a boy, even though Uncle Artie had a family of five. Janni's mind followed them in as they were using their mind Talent to look into the control system to see how the Gate functioned. She couldn't see much, could Big Art see anything at all?

After studying the system for a while, Big Art carefully removed the outer cover. The touch buttons stuck out of the front half of a curved gray box that had assorted wires and other protrusions on it. The two together could not penetrate the gray box.

"Janni, Glori, come here," Big Art said. "See this here?" He pointed to the gray box. "Can you two see what's inside?"

Their minds linked, Janni and Glori penetrated the block and jerked back. Janni saw a swirling mass of small items of every color, and some that were no-color, in a space that seemed much larger than the box. She saw from Glori's mind multicolored boxes growing and shrinking, popping up and disappearing. They *sent* what they saw to Uncle Artie.

He yelped and his eyes widened. Big Art looked blank.

Janni shook her head. The image stayed. An area at one side coalesced into a dark line that stayed still. "What do you see?" she asked Glori.

"One column of boxes freezing to a line. You two okay?" Glori asked the Arts.

"Weirdest thing I ever saw." Uncle Artie shook his head.

"Just a blur." Big Art looked at his son. "Do you see anything useful?"

"There's a vertical line on the left side," Artie said. "Let me put what Janni sent over it. Ah. I think we can do this."

He was still seeing the image too. This was almost weirder than being in space.

Janni didn't know how much more she could handle. Her gut was in turmoil.

"Can you touch or move it?" Big Art closed his eyes.

They could and did. Janni *sensed* Artie beginning to understand how Gate mechanics worked, and kept the others updated.

"This goes to the main control, I think." Uncle Artie looked up.

"That would be under here," Big Art said, opening his eyes and touching the base of the table. "Trace it down into the cabinet if you can."

Janni followed it down to a mass of colors, shapes, and things she didn't have a name for. To her brain, it was a muddled mess with no definite outline. A black line came out of the mess toward the back of the Gate, down into the floor at the edges of the cabinet. A few others left the side, and another short line came out of the front.

She pointed them out to Uncle Artie.

"Ah." He sat up. "That must go to the Gate to Harmony, and this will be the connection to the new Gate. To create a wormhole, the Gatekeepers must have gone to the new world in a ship to mark a target. Janni, you will need to go to the other world to be the target."

"Target?" Now Janni was confused.

"So we know where to send the other end of the wormhole. You do know what a wormhole is, don't you?" Uncle Artie asked.

Janni snorted. "A fold in space." *Does he think I'm an idiot?*

Big Art nodded. "We'll look at the one from here to Harmony." Uncle Artie ignored him.

"Any particular place?" Janni asked. *How could he tell where I am? How was I supposed to do that?*

"Somewhere partially enclosed, like a cave. Is there some way you can leave a trail so we can find you? Can you get Glori go with you to space to be the connection between us?" Uncle Artie was taking charge.

"It may take me a few days to find a place once I get there," Janni said. She paused and looked at her hands. "I think, if Glori comes with me, we can make a trail that she can bring back here. Okay, Glori?"

"Sure." Glori grinned. "Not too far from where the people live. A two-day trip is long enough."

"Okay, we'll do that, and let you know when we go out." Janni nodded. *It'll be nice to see Sam and Maxee again.*

Uncle Artie shooed the others away and pored over the Gate mechanism. He had the information from the Watcher now, and Janni hoped he would be able to use it.

The three young people wandered around the room, looking at the marks on the doors. Janni wished she could see what was on the other side of them. She could still see in her mind, faintly over her real vision, all the mechanisms in the cabinet, various shapes floating and changing, but in a certain order.

After a while, Uncle Artie called them back. "I think we've got this figured out. You three go on back home. We'll stay here."

"Okay."

Janni wanted to stay, but Glori *sent,* 'Let's go.'

"The door marked 'Exit'," Big Art added, as Janni hesitated.

Janni found it, and she, Brian and Glori went through.

He didn't have to be so snarly about it, she thought. She knew Big Art's sisters, except Medic Anne, resented her family's greater Talent.

The quines waited.

'About time,' Qilla *sent* to Janni's mind.

'Where are the others?' *asked* Big Art's quine.

"They'll be out in a bit," Janni said.

The quine flipped his head and snorted.

The trio mounted and headed down to the beach.

Since it was only mid-morning, they spent some time splashing in the sea, especially the quines. White puffs of clouds dotted the sky.

They took their time going home, looking for any interesting new plants along the top of the beach. The clan needed more variety in their food.

•   •   •

Back at Freedom, Janni and Glori reported to Grampa Charley. Grampa Larry was better, but Granlyn didn't want him disturbed. She sat in on the report at Grampa Charley's house.

"If they do get this Gate built and working properly, how long will it take to get her people over here, and where are we going to put them?" she asked.

"Plenty of room north of us, and they'll have the big river, too," Grampa Charley said.

"I know Sam was very polite and obliging, but what about the rest of her people? Don't they have a lot more people than we do?"

"Yes, Granlyn," Janni said. She was getting tired of saying that all the time.

"Do you know how many?"

"Not exactly. Sam said there'd be some who wouldn't want to come, but she didn't know how many. They're still asking who wants to come."

"We'll need to plan for that: how we can control our settlement." Grampa Charley stroked his gray-streaked beard.

"Agreed." Granlyn tugged a silver curl. "You menfolk get together and see what you can come up with. We women will plan how to deal with the women. We must keep Freedom to ourselves."

The next few days, Janni fell behind in her tasks. Granlyn called small groups of women to her to discuss the situation of the other colony arriving, often with Janni at her side. Those from Old Art's and Old Maria's families didn't want them to come at all, and most of the others, except Susan, were hesitant to let other people on their world.

Janni was pestered by questions — most of which she couldn't answer — and she had a hard time concentrating on her tasks. Some in Gramma Perri's age group wanted to know if they'd be like the Bramites.

"This is different," Granlyn said. "Only six of us were rescued by the Bramites, who didn't have mind talent, which scared them eventually. Here, this is our world, and Sam's people will have their own colonies away from ours."

"As long as they don't try to hurt us, like the Bramites did to my Jimmy," Joan said, shuddering.

On Harmony, her extended family, Old Maria's, had been chased out of North Point to the new human colony.

"We'll see that they don't."

Janni shivered. She'd heard the story more than once.

What had she gotten herself into?

She'd always been so sure of herself, knew she was the leader of her group, felt she could do anything. And now? A tiny knot deep within her told her of beginnings of a change.

"I liked Sam," Glori told Janni later. "It'll be fun to have more new people."

They overheard Chad III tell Uncle Peter, "I'm going to take a 'wait and see' stance."

"Fine. Just keep your mind open."

· · ·

Grampa Bay, the oldest of Granlyn's cousins, met with Granlyn and Janni to discuss the situation. He had basically retired from being in charge of construction and spent a lot of time in the forest. He had never been able to block out the mass of thoughts in a crowd and had always sought solitude.

They met at his house, away from the others. His mate, Granli, Granlyn's niece, still worked in childcare a few days a week. Her seats and chairs were all a dark pink.

As Granlyn and Janni settled in, Granlyn said, "I still remember your pink bedroom back on Earth."

Granli smiled. Her gray curls were bound up in back of her head. "That was so long ago."

"Yes. Janni, tell them what you have experienced." Granlyn sat back.

Janni told them how she'd found herself in space, how she'd found Earth and the other colony, and about the Otherness which held a sense of danger. "We need to bring Sam's people to our world to protect them."

"I see." Bay settled in his chair. "This Talent of ours has gone too far. I thought it was neat at first, when I was young, but not since the next generation came along. Are you sure about bringing them here?"

"Yes." Janni twisted her tunic. She was sure it was necessary, but she didn't know how to explain it to the others.

"Our clan is still very small," Granlyn said. "Even though we are protected by the Watchers cleaning up our genes when they gave my grandparents the Talent. I think it would be good for us to have another group of people on our world."

"Perhaps. Genes can mutate." Bay tugged his beard. "I know there's masses of open land north of us; that's not a problem. We'll have to keep our two groups apart at first, until we get to know them better."

Granli sat forward. "I agree with Aunt Lyn. We need more and different people on our world. We older folk have become stultified with only the few of us to interact with. And look at bondings. Even in Janni's generation she really didn't have much choice of whom to bond with."

"Anything like that would be in the future. However, it would probably be a good idea to have a larger population on this world. We would need to make plans. You two have any ideas?" Grampa Bay scratched his bearded chin.

"We would need to plan for extra food until they can get their crops going," Granli said.

"We could let some of our construction men help them build their houses, since our men don't have enough work now. But we will need to get them up there as fast as possible," Grampa Bay said.

"Right. There's not room here for a lot of people besides us." Granli looked around her tidy home.

"We need to arrange places for them to stay while they build their houses," Granlyn said. "What do we have in the way of tents and blankets?"

"I'll check," Janni said.

"Anything else?" Granlyn asked.

Silence.

"This has been very interesting. I'll have some of the men put up one room cabins up above Freedom. Keep us posted." Grampa Bay nodded.

Granlyn rose, and she and Janni left. The young woman walked the older woman back to her house.

"Can you come in for a moment?" Granlyn asked.

"Sure," Janni smiled. She felt better, knowing Granlyn and the others believed her. Inside, she found Grampa Larry propped up on the couch. He looked frailer than ever, but he had a big grin on his face.

"'bout time you came to see me," he mock-growled.

Janni ran over and kissed him. "You're looking good. How are you feeling?"

"I can still make it to the outhouse on my own."

Janni saw the two walking sticks propped at the end of the couch. For the first time, she *sensed* Granlyn's hidden terror of losing him. And she knew that when he went, Granlyn wouldn't last long. Not the way the two of them had been together all their lives.

"Gotta go," Janni said. As she left, she prayed to Oneness to keep them healthy as long as possible.

The next day, at the plaza, Janni tried to ignore the looks and mutterings of the older people. She knew that Glori, Willie, and Brian would stick by her side. After meeting Sam, they knew she was real, although the men didn't understand how Janni had brought her there.

•   •   •

The time comes for Janni's being to go out in space. She links with Glori's being as she leaves her body, and the two hang among the stars.

'This is so cool,' Glori *sends* to Janni.

'Isn't it?' Janni *sends* back.

The danger, the Other, is no closer, to Janni's relief. She finds Sam's world and moves her body there, to search for a place to put a Gate, leaving a mental trail to Glori.

18

STARVIEW

THE DAY AFTER SHE RETURNED, Sam woke to rain.

Good, we need this.

By the end of the day, the downpour showed no signs of stopping. On top of everything else, Sam had to worry about the rising river. She'd never seen a rain like this. Was this the World being's doing, to get her and her people to leave? It had never been happy with them out on its surface.

When Sam could not see the end of the rain, she became concerned. She'd always been able to see the end of a weather event. Was this part of the coming menace?

At her office, Sam found more complaints from neighborhood managers via Hal. He had a regular route around the neighborhoods to check in with the managers, since the only other way for them to connect with government was to walk to the mesa.

Top of most lists was lack of food.

"I tell them you can always grow your own," Hal told Sam.

Next on this day's list was rain.

"I say, we don't control the weather, you'll just have to live with it." He grinned. "Don't worry, it'll stop tonight."

•　　　•　　　•

Late that evening, unable to sleep, Sam sat watching the rain outside her window, as if she were looking though a waterfall.

Will things ever change?

Everyone had been in their own little rut until the Volen left City to collapse. She'd thought when they moved out here, people would bloom and create a lively new community. But no, most of them are still in their ruts, although slightly different ones.

And now this menace. As hard as Sam tried, she couldn't sense any more about it than she already knew.

Was it something from space? Then why there and not here. Was there another community on Peace that would attack Janni's community? Then why are we involved. Natural disaster? Again, why us. What else was there?

Sam's thoughts turned back to Starview. Troublemakers. So far, no real problem; although one, a janitor for the first big caff, had showed up at her office demanding better food and information screens. Some people still couldn't accept that City amenities were gone for good.

"He probably gets more food than some others," Arlene had said when she told Sam about him. "After all, he cleans up after them."

"What did he say about the possible move?"

"He didn't believe it, said the whole idea of another world was nonsense."

Sam rolled her eyes. "How can people ignore the evidence of their eyes and ears?"

Arlene shrugged. "People from Below only received basic education, very little science. Who knows what they believe."

Below, the below ground area of City, had been home to the factory workers and other less educated people.

Why haven't we given them more education? Maybe they didn't want to learn.

•　　　•　　　•

The next day, it was still raining, and the river was very close to the top of its banks.

At first meal at the mesa caff, Maxee said to Sam, "Too much rain. We stay up here." Her two oldest, smaller versions of herself, Brax and Toki, were with her.

"No problem. How are the kubs?"

"Okee. Ask too many questions."

"All children do that." Hal took a bite of bread. "My sister drove me crazy asking questions constantly. Why, why, why. What have you learned lately, Brax?"

"Stars be suns like ours."

"Very true." Hal nodded.

"Other suns have worlds." Brax bobbed in his chair.

"Yes." Hal smiled. Maxee beamed at her ten-year-old kub.

"Maybe worlds have people." Brax added.

"Some do," Sam said, "and maybe we'll go to another world someday."

Both kubs squealed with excitement, bobbing like leaves on the river.

"Sam," Brad said. "We don't know yet."

Sam sighed.

"Let's wait until we have more information." Todd drained his mug.

Sam was accosted only twice on her way to her office, after returning to her house to clean her teeth. First by one of Arlene's assistants, who pointed out the river was creeping over the edge, and then by a dripping wet errand boy who wanted to know when the rain was going to stop.

At her office, Arlene greeted Sam with, "Doug wants to know if he can get more helpers to deal with the deluge, and June needs people to clean up the mud everyone tracks into her caff."

"Have Brad tell his assistant, Cleon, to go ask around. He's good at that. There's always people complaining they have nothing to do."

Sam sat at her table. *It's going to be one of those days.*

She looked at a plan from accounting for a better way of keeping track of supplies, a half dozen requests to move to different neighborhoods, and a long list of demands from Far West.

•　　　•　　　•

The next day, it continued to rain. Sam donned her thickest soled footwear. A year after they'd all moved here, the Noreg, the humanoid people who lived in the next sector to the east, had shown Brad a tree whose sap could be made into a waterproof substance. Sam and many of the others owned capes and footwear with soles made from the material.

Looking out at the water running off the roof unnerved Sam, even though she knew now it wasn't part of the menace.

What if it never stopped?

She wanted to curl up in a ball in the corner, to call Janni to come take her to Peace, to go somewhere, anywhere, it wasn't raining.

Sam grabbed her waterproof cloak and marched out into the rain.

She went to several places in the valley to check on how people fared. At one clinic, Sam found Evelyn, Hal's mother, and his sister, Jan, who had lost her feet in an accident when she was young. Evelyn was instructing one of the aides with a bandage on an older woman's leg as Jan sat dozing near her in her wheeled chair.

"Is Jan okay?" Sam asked, after Evelyn finished with the patient.

"Oh, yes." Evelyn said as she put down the patient's chart. "I brought Jan over yesterday morning when the paths started getting mucky. There's no way we could get her in her chair through this mud. We're getting a lot of injuries from falls, everything's so slippery."

"How do you get to the caff?"

"We don't. They bring food. I understand they're delivering to a number of older people nearby. I'll be glad when this is over."

"Me, too. I think I've got permanent wet feet, even with the sap soles on my shoes. Anyway, keep up the good work."

Sam sloshed to the next place she needed to visit. When she got home, her feet looked like shriveled-up squash.

•　　•　　•

At evening meal, Brad said, "Mac, over in North Valley, says the crop fields closest to the river are being flooded. That land's lower over there and floods more easily. That's why crops grow better over there. He'll have to make higher levees for next time."

"Yes." Sam rubbed her eyes.

There wasn't a lot they could do until the rain stopped and the river receded. A vision of Peace popped into her head.

They have it made over there.

But the downpour didn't stop.

Once, the rain tapered to a drizzle, and Sam thought, *Oh good, it's finally stopping.*

Then the rain started up again. The river rose over its banks and crept inland. When Sam went home for her midday break, water was up to the bottom of the mesa and curled around the side.

Back at the meeting hall, people tracked in mud faster than anyone could clean it up. Sam took her footwear off and left it outside her office. Someone had left her a list of all the neighborhoods' reported problems. She wanted to crumple and pitch it in the waste receptacle, but she smoothed it out and stared at the handful of papers.

Hal appeared in her doorway. "The apartments along the river are being flooded. I've been talking to people in apartments farther away, to see if they will take in people who were flooded out. A few won't leave, and I've had to talk to three to find one person who will take someone in."

"They are small apartments," Sam said. "But still, we need to help each other."

"I agree. Anything else you want me to do, boss lady?" Hal grinned.

"Not at the moment. Just keep checking on situations."

"Okay, Cuddles." He blew her a kiss, turned and left.

Sam smiled, savoring the warmth of his words.

Then she sighed and attempted to deal with whatever presented itself the rest of the day, while worrying about the damage the rain was doing, why people weren't adapting more to this community, wondering whether she was doing a good enough job.

It was still pouring when she returned to her house after late meal. And, in the morning, everything was so gray, she thought she was back in City.

Oneness, please, please stop this rain, Sam prayed.

She slogged through another day, repeating her prayer.

When she left the caff after midday meal, only a light drizzle greeted her.

Maybe Oneness heard me.

She sloshed to her house with a smile.

That evening, the rain stopped. Although the thunder of rain on the roof was gone, the roar of the river gave Sam the shivers.

•   •   •

Sam woke to sunshine flooding though her window. She rose, stretched, and grinned at the bubbling river below.

At first meal, there was an air of jubilee, dampened by the thoughts of cleanup.

"Hal, you get to go around and make lists of what needs to be done as far as cleanup and repair," Sam said. "Brad, can you fly over the western section and check damage there?"

"Sure."

"Arlene, would you ..." Sam began.

"I've already talked to Lucy in North Valley. The main damage was to the grain fields. They can take care of their problems."

"Good." Sam took a bite of bread.

Maxee, sitting next to Sam, touched her arm. "Janni here."

19

STARVIEW

"JANNI? WHERE?" Sam looked around.

"At your house. In person."

"Oh."

Now what? What was she doing here? I don't need this on top of everything else.

Sam put down her napkin. "Excuse me." She didn't want to leave, but thought she better find out what the girl wanted.

Sam rose and trotted off to meet her. "Janni, what brings you here?" she asked as she entered her house. But Sam knew. This was another part of the menace.

The tall girl stood at the window looking out over the river. "Nice view you have here."

Sam joined her and sensed Janni wasn't sure how to go about telling her what she came for.

"What is it?" She could only think of the flood as she gazed at the raging river below.

Janni turned. "There's a danger out in space, a danger to all humans. I don't know what it is yet, but we need to get you and your people to our world so we can protect you.

"What danger? How?"

"Some beings out there can use their minds to make others do things, like destroying their worlds." Janni opened her hands.

That's nonsense. Sam refused to believe it.

Janni glanced at Sam. "If you are on our world, we can protect you with our mind Talents."

"What? What are you talking about?" *The girl made no sense at all.*

"Something out there can control people's minds and make them do what the controller wants," Janni repeated.

"Like you?"

Sam stared at a branch bobbing along below. Although she knew Janni's world and her people were real and honest, she could not accept the girl's statement. Confusion roiled her thoughts.

"No. We can send a thought to someone else, but we can't make them do anything if they don't want to. This thing is making others destroy their worlds." Janni shook her head.

Oh, come on. That's nonsense. "How do you know this?"

"I have seen it."

"How? Where? Show me." *How could she possibly know something like that?*

"In space. I cannot explain it, but I know it to be true. Please, Sam, you must listen."

Sam sensed the girl's sincerity and fear. "Okay, so if this happens, how are you going to get all of us from our world to yours? Do you have a ship?" *Her world did look more promising.*

"No. that's where the Gates come in. They are a way to get from one world to another. That's how my mama found Roroy and our Peace: going through Gates."

"Oh. So how did you find these gates in the first place?" Sam sat on the bed and beckoned Janni to sit beside her.

"Gramma Perri found them and had to go through a Gate when the aliens took Uncle Peter, her twin. He doesn't like being called Grampa, so we call him Uncle. But we need to make a Gate on this world so your people can come through to ours. Do you know anywhere there are caves?"

"Caves?"

The Felce sector came to Sam's mind, but that was on the other side of the world. *The Ghind sector also has caves, but it's not much closer. Maybe the Noreg ...*

"I don't know offhand. I'll ask our explorers. Why caves?" She paused. "Why are you doing this, really?"

"We are a small community. We need more people on our world. Your people." Janni seemed puzzled at Sam's question.

Sam realized she didn't know these people very well at all.

"Gate must be inside a structure," Janni continued. "Natural is best. You find one. I will stay here. Is it all right?"

Sam thought for a moment. *Do I leave her in my house or take her with and let people see her? If I say no, will it stop the menace?* Somehow, she didn't think so.

"I can't go looking for caves right now. I have to get back to work. I'll check around to see if anyone knows anything. You can stay here. I'll be back later." Sam stopped. "Do you have any food?"

Janni patted one of the pockets of the vest she wore over her tunic. "Yes. I'll watch the river."

Sam had no difficulty accepting the idea of going to Janni's world, but she couldn't understand how the Gates worked. And then there was the problem of getting people to go.

Trying to get them to leave City for a two-day trek here was bad enough, how on City could she get them to go through this magic gate? It would be like pushing cooked cereal up a hill.

Sam went to the meeting hall first, people were always coming and going there. She found two men who had explored in the mountains, but neither of them had seen anything like a cave.

Maxee greeted her at her office. "Looking for me?" Sam asked.

"Maybe."

"When you went on your walkabout with your kubs, did you see any kind of cave anywhere?" Sam asked.

"Iss. We stay in big cave the night big storm come and trees fall on trail."

"Do you remember where it was?"

Maxee nodded and jumped up. "I show you."

"Not right now. Maybe tomorrow. What do you think of this so-called danger?"

"Janni see something. She feel something she think bad. Could be real."

"Okay." Sam was still doubtful.

"Is better with more people, if room and food," Maxee noted.

"True." *That made sense. They have fewer people than one of our neighborhoods, and we don't have enough room for all our people.* "I've got to go back to work now. See you at late meal."

"I check on kubs."

Maxee bustled off, and Sam settled at her table.

•　　　•　　　•

After late meal, Sam and Maxee went to Sam's house.

When they entered, Janni turned and stared at the grey, teddy bear-like alien. "You have mind link?"

"Yes." She bounced on her toes. "I Maxee. I Klocti."

"Pleased to meet you," Janni said, a look of consternation on her face.

"She was brought here as an infant, raised with Brad and me, and learned our language and our culture." Sam patted Maxee. "She knows where there's a cave."

"I see." Janni nodded.

Sam wasn't sure the girl really understood. "How far up, Maxee?"

"One day." Maxee sat in the chair by the window.

Sam plopped down on her bed.

"We need to go to your cave tomorrow." Janni stayed on her feet.

"Why?" Sam asked, curious and uneasy. *This whole event was unreal.*

"Time," Janni said. "We don't know how long before danger comes, and it will take time to get all your people though."

"I don't know. I have a meeting and piles of paperwork to deal with. Maybe in three or four days." Sam looked at the window. *Is this all for real, or does she have some other motive?* "What do you think, Maxee?"

"I go when you want. I bring kubs."

"Must you?"

"Time for walkabout for Haki. No problem."

Not for you, Sam thought. "Her children," she said to Janni.

"Are they well-behaved?" Janni shook her head.

"Maxee will take care of them." Sam stared at Maxee, who nodded.

"We really should go tomorrow, Miss Sam. Trust me. I don't know how long it will take them to build a Gate, and we need to find a place for it right away." Janni held her hands out.

"I can't tomorrow. The day after?"

Sam's thoughts were in a muddle. She felt the girl was sincere, but a little voice kept telling her to be careful, and her futureseeing told her this needed to be done.

Janni sighed. "Next morning early. You know where the cave is?"

"Iss." Maxee looked at Janni, then Sam.

20

STARVIEW

A FTER A HECTIC DAY, Sam retired early and was up with the sun the next morning. She and Janni had a quick bite and collected Maxee and her brood.

As they headed down the mesa, Sam said, "Okay, Let's go find a cave." *Anything to get away from here. Someone else is going to have to take over as boss after this is all over. I'm fed up with this same old crap over and over.*

The group headed for the trail up the river. They had to go around the back end of the mesa as the river trail was flooded in front of it. Sam and Maxee reveled in the warm sunshine, even though trees still dripped on the muddy trail. Ten-year-old Brax held the youngest kub's hand, and the other two kubs kept wandering off to look at trees, bushes, and rocks.

Sam sensed Janni's impatience as the long-legged girl walked ahead, then had to wait for Maxee and the kubs. When they reached the bridge to North Valley, Janni stopped.

"We've got to go faster. If you carry the baby, I'll carry the little one."

"No." Maxee pulled herself up to her full height. "I take care of kubs. If you want fast, go fast. We come after. Is trail by big rock with tree on top."

Janni looked at Sam.

"Maxee knows what she's doing," Sam said. "I'm sure she'll be all right."

"Iss. Did it before by myself." Maxee sniffed.

"Okay. But if you don't show up after a while, I'll come looking for you."

Janni and Sam took off, leaving the little ones to explore all the exciting new sights, sounds, and smells.

After a couple of false tries, Sam found the rock and the trail to the cavern.

"This will do nicely," Janni said, as Sam dropped her pack. "Over here, I think. Uncle Artie says to build a room here with a small one walled off in back against the backside of the cave, with a door at the side, and one door in front, big enough to get anything through you want to bring."

"Uncle Artie?" Sam raised her eyebrows.

"His papa is our master scientist. Old Art, his grandfather, came from Earth, but he's retired. Uncle Artie is working on the Gate from the other end. His papa, Big Art, doesn't have enough Talent."

"Okay, I guess we can do that." Sam glanced at the entrance. Now that everyone had houses or apartments, Construction wasn't as busy as it used to be. But it would be fun getting the materials up here.

Was this really necessary? Was there any other way to deflect the menace? Why was she so anxious to get us over there?

"Nothing fancy, just boards and fasteners." Janni picked up some stones and marked the corners. "No roof.'

Sam watched her and found a front corner in the cavern for her bag.

After a while, Maxee and her family showed up. She led them around the cavern to a back corner. "Here before," she said. "Remember?"

Brax looked around and nodded. "Me there," said Toki.

"Haki, you too little to remember."

Haki peered at the wall. "Me," the kub said.

Maxee settled in the corner with them. Little Deki tried to climb into her pouch, but Maxee gently pushed the baby kub away. "No, you too big now."

Maxee looked at Janni. "How this Gate work?"

"I don't know exactly. Uncle Artie says there's a way to make two places that are far apart in space come together so you can step from one to another without having to spend years in a spaceship, and that's what Gates are."

"Okee," Maxee said, nodding her head.

Sam wasn't quite sure she understood. *In a way it makes sense, but how can you bend space?* She looked out the entrance. "It's getting dark. Let's camp in here." She didn't trust that it would not start raining again.

Janni paced the floor, but Maxee and her brood settled in their corner, and Sam made herself comfortable, settled into her spot, and pulled out a hunk of bread.

Maxee asked Janni questions about her world, but Sam was satisfied to just sit back and doze. A black, roundish shape wandered through her thoughts. The menace.

·   ·   ·

In the morning, Janni said, "I talked to my friend in space, and she'll go back and tell my people I've found a place. They'll build the Gate. I'll stay here so they know where to put it. You need to get your people to come up and build the room."

"Are you sure you'll be all right?" Sam repacked her backbag.

"Yes." Janni smiled.

Sam looked around the rough-walled place. "Be careful. There's beasts in these woods. Not nice like Roroy's."

Janni nodded.

Sam and Maxee left, trailed by the kubs, and trotted down the trail on another sunny morning.

When they arrived at the mesa, Sam returned the backpack. She found Glenda, her second assistant, and Gus, the head of Construction, in their office. Craggy Gus and tall Glenda had come from Below, the below ground levels, in City as trained carpenters. The light brown walls were lined with pictures of animals on one side and boats on the other.

They must have brought the images from City.

"I have a building project for you." Sam described it and added, "Janni will give you actual specs when you get there. About eight by eight, she said."

"Why?" Gus asked.

"For the Gate, so we can go to their world," Sam explained.

"Why?" he asked again. "What's wrong with ours?"

"Well, we're always short of food, and we almost got washed away," Sam said. She felt uncomfortable talking about an unknown threat. Few of the people knew about her futureseeing ability.

"There's more to it than that," Glenda said. "Is it going to get worse here?"

"It might." Sam looked at the wall behind Glenda.

"To tell you the truth, I'm getting bored here. Too many people in too small a space." Glenda wrinkled her nose. "With no new families, we're running out of things to build."

"Janni's world has tons of room for building houses."

"So?" Gus said.

"Gus," Glenda said pointedly. "We can do it. Let's sit down and plan this."

Gus shrugged. "Go ahead and plan it if you want. No guarantee we'll go."

Glenda made a face at him and pulled out a large piece of paper. "When does she need us up there?" she asked.

"Day after tomorrow. I told her you needed a little time to figure out materials and people to carry them."

"That's not much time." She brushed back her long, black hair.

"I know. Do the best you can."

Sam rounded up her other assistants and told them what was going on.

"So how is this going to work?" Brad asked. "Do we have a place to go to over there?"

"Yes. Janni said her people are preparing a place for us, north of their settlement. There's tons of room there, and that huge river for water. They have a waterwheel, so we probably could make one, too."

"I want to see that," Doug, the watermaster, said.

"You will," Sam said. "Do you want to go through soon?"

"Yes, if I can. My assistants can cover things here."

•　　•　　•

In the morning, Sam sent Hal around to all the neighborhood managers with the information about the proposed move. They were to tell their people and relay any questions through Hal.

His message was: 'We can stay here and deal with drought and floods, or we can move to a new world.'

"How do you know we won't have that there?" someone asked him.

"They haven't for the seventeen years they've been there."

That evening, as Sam sat in her chair and watched the river, thoughts of her ex popped into her mind. She knew he was responsible for her father's death, even though he was only tried for the attempted kidnapping of baby Max. Sam never forgot how he'd treated her; a secret she'd kept to herself. She wished she could completely forget him, but her mind wouldn't let her forget any memory.

•　　•　　•

The next day, Glenda and Gus led a procession down the river path to the mountain trail. Gus carried a bag of tools and fasteners along with his backpack. Glenda carried food. One fellow toted a large bundle of wire, and a dozen carried boards. Sam watched the group march away, pleased that at least some of the citizens were willing to work.

Why couldn't they all be like that?

•　　•　　•

Three days later, the crew returned. Gus marched into Sam's office. She put down the paper she was brooding over and looked up. "How did it go?"

"Room's done except for a couple of things. Took longer than we planned, had to keep going outside to charge the solar tools." These had been left them by the Volen. "Janni wants you and anyone you want to bring to come up day after tomorrow. My son, Ben, will go with you and finish it. Anything I need to know?"

"No. Ben has a couple of new jobs. The place is in an uproar, as usual."

"Okay. Later." He left.

Sam tried to go back to work but couldn't concentrate. The thought of being able to go up to the cavern, step through a door, and find herself on Janni's world consumed her. Excited and scared, anything to get out of where she was. Maybe if she left this world for good, she could leave her ex behind.

●　　　●　　　●

Brad and Ben went with Sam to the cavern. Ben fixed the two problem spots on the room. At least that was complete. Janni sent a note through.

A little while later, Janni said, "Oh, crud."

Sam turned. The girl was holding a handful of purple stuff.

"This was supposed to be a squash. Something we knew you didn't have here."

"It looks more like mush than squash," Sam said.

"Yeah." She went out, dropped the stuff in the bushes and wiped her hands on some leaves. "Anyway, this means Uncle Artie will be sending a rock through."

After a moment, the room hummed again, the door opened, and a mass of gravel poured out.

"This isn't working right." Janni frowned.

"Good thing that wasn't a person," Brad remarked.

Sam and Janni glared at him. Janni ran outside and returned with a large branch. She laid it on the floor of the room, closed the door and pushed the button beside it. When the door opened a little later, the room was empty.

"Now what?" Sam asked.

"We wait. I know what Uncle Artie will do."

They all waited and stared at the room. About ten minutes later, the room hummed, and the door opened. Bits of paper lay scattered on the floor. Janni collected them, and she and Brad pieced them together.

The message said, 'try again in two days, same time'

"I guess they need to work on it some more," Janni said.

"Two days," Sam said. *Oh, no. Another trek up here and another two days missed.*

Janni looked around in short jerks here and there.

"Janni, you can't stay here. Come home with us. You can stay at my house."

"Well." Janni looked at her. "Okay." They packed up and left.

The journey back to Starview produced no new surprises.

21

STARVIEW

WHEN THEY ARRIVED AT SAM'S HOUSE, Sam asked Janni if she wanted to come eat with them.

The people need to see her if they are going to believe they have to move.

"Okay. I'd like to see what you eat."

Maxee dropped her kubs off at childcare, where the younger children ate, and the four adults went to the caff.

"Do you always eat here?" Janni asked as they approached the counter.

"Yes, we have food preparers who only do that. We had them in City, because it was easier than having everyone prepare meals in their apartments."

"City? Where?"

"It's gone. That's why we're living out here."

They received their meals and went to join Brad, Todd, and Hal.

"Hi, Janni." Brad smiled. "What brings you here?"

"This is Todd, my other brother, and Hal. This is Janni from Peace," Sam said.

"Welcome." Hal smiled.

Todd nodded.

Janni took a few bites and pushed her dish away.

"I'm sorry our food isn't as good as yours," Sam said.

"Not your fault." Janni took a food bar out of a pocket. She looked at the men. "Todd, what do you do?"

"My father and I run the legal department."

"Legal?"

"When you have as many people as we do, we need to have laws and regulations. What's your population size?"

"About two hundred, including the quines. Of course, we all know each other; we're all related, except Roroy and Elli. He's from another world. Humanoid. Mama found him when she went looking for a new world. Elli just showed up one day when a Gate on her world, a later Old Earth, malfunctioned. We were unable to send her back. The quines take care of themselves, eat leaves and plants."

"Quines?" Todd asked.

"The creatures they ride," Sam said.

"Alien, too," Maxee said, bouncing in her seat.

"Are you planning to send people here?" Todd asked.

"No. You are to come to my world, Peace."

"That's a good name for a world," Sam said, pushing away conflicting feelings about moving her people again.

"We like it." Janni smiled and took a bite of her bar.

They continued to ask questions about each other's worlds. At the end of the meal, Sam felt a little less doubtful about going to another world.

Maxee asked Sam to come see her after she took Janni back to her room.

Sam found Maxee curled up in one of two chairs outside her home. "Hi. What did you want to talk about?"

"Janni. She scared. Project too big for her. She still young."

"How do you know?"

"I see in her head."

"Maxee, are you snooping?"

The alien's eyes widened. "Just want to know her. She not sure if Gate will work."

"Oh. So if it doesn't work, we'd be left here to face this unknown danger with no weapons." Sam sighed. She didn't know whether she wanted to go or stay. She had a thought. *Are the Ambaak, Noreg and Ghind enough different so that they won't be affected? From what I can see, Liia and Jone can pass for human. So can the Noreg and Ghind. I need to call them. When I know more about the Gate.*

"She miss her people. She want go home."

"She doesn't show it."

"Iss. Hides fear good."

"Thanks, Maxee."

Sam returned to her house.

Should we really trust a young, scared girl, even if she has some amazing talents? How much did she know about the menace?

She chatted with Janni a bit, watching her carefully, and wondering what was going on in her mind.

Later, Sam prepared for bed, and Janni curled up in a blanket in the big chair.

22

STARVIEW

T HE NEXT DAY, Sam showed Janni around Starview, introducing her to whomever they met.

After midday meal, Sam and Janni returned to Sam's house. Sam couldn't relax with the girl there, so she went to her office and put the 'Do Not Disturb' sign up on the door.

Unable to concentrate on anything, a half hour later Sam went out and walked around the top of the mesa.

As Sam approached the point where Kirk had set up his telescope on a stand, she saw him fussing with it.

"Seen anything interesting?"

He looked around. "*Hallo*, Sam. No, not really. Something odd in that sector." He pointed southeast. "I think it only a different kind of nebula. I not worry about it. I'm learning."

"Good. You're speaking Standard better. Keep at it."

Sam continued on her walk. When she came around to the path to the meeting hall, she paused. *Home or work?* She headed for her office. Janni would be at her house. *Oh. I didn't tell her she had to stay there. What if she went exploring?*

At the meeting house, she ran into one of the errand boys and asked him to see if anyone was at her house. Sam dropped into her chair and stared at the new pile of papers. She picked one up. A request for a new bed to replace the one damaged in the flood.

Sam sighed and reached for the next paper.

•　　　•　　　•

The following day, Sam and Janni returned to the cavern with the Gate. Todd went with them; he wanted to see it. A pleasant, warm breeze accompanied the trio.

"This is nice, to be out like this," Todd remarked. He flung his arms around.

"Yes," Janni said. "I like this, all these hills nearby."

"I just don't understand how people cannot enjoy this." Sam took a deep breath.

When they arrived at the cavern, Janni checked the room. It was empty.

Sam and Todd peered in. Bounded by bare board walls, a circle in the center of the dirt floor was covered with some shiny substance. Another circle on the back wall flickered so that it was impossible to focus on it. A black button to the right of the circle sat below a small blank screen.

"I guess it's not quite time yet for Uncle Artie's first trial," Janni said.

Todd prowled around the place, checking the side and back of the room, and Sam leaned against a wall and watched him.

"The back of the room is mostly against the wall of the cave," he reported.

Sam nodded. She was thinking about the piles of papers on her desk that wouldn't go away while she was gone. Tired from the three hikes in four days, she just wanted to sit and watch.

Presently, Sam heard a low hum, the door opened, and a round stone rolled out— with a crack halfway around it.

Janni sighed. She wrote a note on a piece of paper, stuck it in the crack, and sent the stone back.

After a while, another stone appeared, whole.

Janni sent it back. "It appears to be working now. Uncle Artie will send more things to test it before we send people through."

"I'm not going through that until I'm sure it works right every time." Todd returned to Sam's side.

Presently a soiled tunic arrived. Janni checked it carefully. "Looks all right. The dirt can be washed out, and this hole was there before. Uncle Artie marked it."

"How do you know all this?" Todd asked.

"Uncle Artie sat me down and went through all the possible outcomes and what to do for each of them. I'll send this back and he'll send something else."

Todd nodded and frowned.

All? Sam thought. *More likely, all the most probable. But at least they are testing the Gate.* "When someone goes through, are they right in your community?"

"No." Janni glanced at Sam. "The Gate on our world opens into a glade that's a two-day walk along the beach to the little river and up to our place."

"Oh." *Two days. Like coming up here and back. But maybe the beach will make it okay.*

"A beach," Todd echoed. "What's it like?"

"Wide, with forest along the top. There's a camp halfway along."

"That sounds nice."

Sam almost heard his thought, *... if we get there in one piece.*

The room hummed. The door opened, and a plant bounced out. Sam went over to look at it. Long, thin leaves surrounded several stems of orange, cup-like flowers, with roots hanging out the bottom.

Janni picked up the plant, turned it in her hands, and scrutinized it. "Looks normal."

"It's beautiful," Sam said, thinking of Liia's flowers.

"Uncle Artie will replant the flowers to see how they behave." Janni looked at Sam, then sent the plant back.

Sam wandered around, thinking about the requests for replacement items from people whose places had been flooded. Another problem. Furniture and clothes could be replaced, but not a lot of personal items.

The room hummed again.

The door opened, and a red and black creature with a small head fluttered out.

"A chicken."

Janni chased it down and scooped it up.

"I didn't think he'd send one through yet."

"Chicken?" Todd said.

"A bird. We eat them." She petted the creature's back.

Todd's eyebrows rose and Sam stammered, "What?"

"You remember, Sam. They were running around on the plaza."

"Oh, yes, now I do. I didn't realize you ate them."

Janni grinned at Todd. "Of course, we have to kill them and remove all the feathers first." She held a long, red leaf-like object up.

"Feathers," Todd said.

"Anyway, this is all for today." Janni made a nest with an old tunic by a wall and set the chicken down in it. The hen cackled. "Tomorrow, Uncle Artie will do more testing."

"That makes sense," Todd said. "Come on, Sam."

The two of them went outside and up the trail. The sun was low, weaving long shadows through the trees. He found a log overlooking the river, and they sat.

"I don't like caves," Todd said. "They remind me too much of City. What do you think of the Gate?"

"I wish I knew how it works." Sam picked up a red leaf. It reminded her of the feather.

"I've talked to Kirk, and he says the theory of bending space is solid. However, wormholes don't stay in one place. They wander around, disappear, and reappear. Whoever created the Gates must have found a way to keep the wormholes pinned to a certain spot."

"Okay, so how does that affect us?" Sam asked.

"I get the basic idea, but I still want to know how the Gate knows where to send items."

"What do we do?" Sam glanced around her.

"Tonight, relax. See what happens in the morning."

"Janni thinks it works." Sam leaned back, forearms on the log behind her.

"Of course. From what she says, it always has for her people. But those Gates were created by those other people, who were much more technologically advanced than we ever were." Todd stretched out his legs. "This one is being made by her people. No guarantee it'll work like the others." Todd smiled at her. "Don't worry, Sam, we'll make it through whatever happens."

Sam returned his smile. At one time, back in City, he had wanted to marry her, but she could only love him as a brother. He'd given up asking her, but they were still close friends. She wished she could believe that things would work out. She wished she didn't have the menace looming in her thoughts all the time. She wished she knew what it was and how to deal with it.

After the sun set, they moseyed back to the cavern for the night.

•　　　•　　　•

In the morning, Janni told them it would be a couple of their hours before anything happened. Sam and Todd went outside. Todd sat on a log and perused a stack of papers he'd brought.

"A case someone dropped off the other day that I hadn't had a chance to look at."

"You were smart to bring some work."

Sam poked through bushes to look at the river. It was much narrower up here but rushing just as fast. She felt the presence of World.

"I'm doing the best I can," she said.

Still, a bush swished in disapproval.

They returned to the cavern.

Soon the room produced its deep hum, the door opened, and a small loovah plant lay there. Janni picked it up, turned the plant over, and felt the leaves.

"Seems all right." She sent it back.

The chicken clucked. Janni went over to it, reached down and held up an egg. "Breakfast," she said.

She unfolded a flat pan out of her pocket, took a gadget out of another. Scooping some brush into a pile, she touched the gadget to it, and a flame sprung up. She laid the pan on the ground, cracked the egg on the rim, and white and yellow liquid ran into the cooking vessel.

Sam and Todd watched as Janni held the pan over the fire and the liquid slowly coalesced.

So that's where that came from.

Sam remembered eating it for first meal. She didn't think she'd ever eat it again.

After Janni ate, she wrote a note and tied it around the chicken's neck. Then she carried the bird into the room and sent it back.

Soon a square wooden box came through. Janni brought it out and opened it. She pulled out a ceramic bowl full of water. Reaching into the bowl, she held up a long, scaly creature. "A fish." After a quick check of the dripping and gasping animal, she dropped it back into the bowl.

Sam asked, "Why is it in water?"

"It has to stay in water to breathe."

Janni returned the bowl to the box and scribbled on the box. Then she set the latter on the circle in the room and sent it back.

This was followed by another chicken, which Janni sent back after a brief check.

During a longer wait, Sam thought about what she'd seen.

No immediate damage but who knows what would happen long term. And how does this fit in with the big menace? Why do I feel uneasy about the Gate?

The room hummed, and a boy rolled out and sat up.

"Stevie? They sent you?" Janni gaped, then turned to Sam and Todd. "This is my little brother."

The boy looked at Sam. "You came to visit," he said.

"Yes." Sam was stunned.

But the boy appeared to be unharmed. He ran to the cave entrance and looked out.

"Stevie, stay here. I'll be right back," Janni stepped into the room and disappeared. After what seemed like an hour to Sam, Janni reappeared. "Good, it works. Who of you wants to go through first? Sam?"

"No, I need to stay here until things get going."

"For your information, whoever goes through will come out in a glade. There may someone to meet them, also a spring and a stream. Follow the stream down to the beach. Go west on the beach. There will be streams and a camp area for the first night. Keep going the same way the next day, and when you come to a river past the end of the forest, follow the trail inland. There will be someone to meet you."

"Okay," Sam said.

"Send two people first, tomorrow, just after your sunset. Tell them to go into the room and push the button on the wall. We will be waiting. Come on, Stevie."

"I want to go outside," he complained, but followed her into the room.

"I can't," Sam began. But Janni and the boy were gone.

"Oh." Sam knuckled her mouth. "Let's go home."

Todd took one last look at the room, gathered his stuff, and headed for the entrance. Sam followed.

"No way we can do that," Todd said. "No one's going through until I see her in person again, alive and well. If she wants us, she'll have to come and get us."

"Right," Sam agreed. The Gate seemed to work, but … She tried to push the thought to the back of her mind. They had to be sure, because it appeared that the menace was coming from beyond their worlds.

23

PEACE

JANNI CAME TO IN THE GLADE ON PEACE, her quine, Qilla, nosing her. She sat up. "How'd you get here?" she asked the creature.

'Came with Artie.' Qilla sent to the girl's mind.

Joy swept over Janni as the realization she was home hit her. Steve was already poking around in the bushes.

Janni mounted Qilla and looked around for her brother. "Come on, Stevie, we're going home."

"Don't we have to wait for those people coming through tomorrow?" the boy asked.

Just then, Uncle Artie came out the tree door. "People coming through?"

Janni sighed. "Yes. Two. About this time tomorrow." What a letdown. She so wanted to ride through the waves and get home to Willie and her family.

"How are you feeling?" Uncle Artie asked.

"Fine, until little bigears here reminded me I have to stay here tonight."

"We have plenty of time before dark, let's go down to the beach," Uncle Artie said, mounting his quine. "I'll stay, too."

Down at the beach, Janni stretched her arms and let out an *'aaah'*. "It's so good to be back here. Uncle Artie, I was walking up and down mountain trails all the time I was there. They don't have anything or anyone to ride. All they can do is walk."

"That's all we had until your mama found the quines."

"I know." Janni had a hard time imagining living without the quines.

She yanked off her boots and ran into the sea, where the quines were splashing.

Uncle Artie *called* his papa, Big Art, by mindlink, and relayed Janni's message. 'She's fine,' he added.

Janni wrinkled her nose. Of course, she was fine.

At sunset, they returned to the glade. Janni *called* Marisa. 'Glad to be home, but I have to wait until the first couple comes through tomorrow.'

'I'm glad, too. Are you all right?'

"Yes, Mama. Both of us are. Steve behaved pretty well. You won't believe how many people there are over there. Houses and apartment buildings up and down the valley as far as I could see. And the food; I actually missed loovah. They're nice people, though, the ones I met.'

'Well, good. Take care and I'll see you in a couple of days.'

'Bye, Mama.'

Next, Janni *called* Glori. 'I'm back on Peace, but won't get back home for another couple days. Have to wait for some people to come through tomorrow.'

'Okay. I'll tell Brian to tell Willie. He's having six kinds of fits because you're gone.'

'Tough. I'll call him.' Janni sighed.

'Hi, Willie, I'm back."

'About time. You have no business going out there. I missed you.'

Janni *sensed* his misery. 'You know I have to. See you soon.'

She sat back against the big tree in the glade. Disappointed that she had to wait another day to go home, she thought about what she'd do when she got there. Uncle Artie had gone back into the Gate, and the quines wandered about, grazing here and there.

Later, Uncle Artie came out and sat beside her. "If no one shows up tomorrow, we'll go home," he said.

"Why wouldn't they?" Janni picked a white flower and played with the long, narrow petals.

"Look, from what you said about the time, Sam'll be getting home late. When do you think she'll have time to find a couple willing to go, who can pack up, go in the morning?"

"Sam'll do it. I told her." Janni flicked a petal away.

Uncle Artie sighed. "Look at it this way. Suppose someone suddenly shows up here from another world, and he marches into the plaza and says, 'Your sun is going nova and you have to move to our world right now.' What do you think Charley would say?"

"He'd want to know more."

"Right. I think Gramps would ask him to prove it. Unlikely he could. Who would volunteer to go? Would you?" Artie tossed a stone into the forest.

"But this is different. This is us."

Artie shook his head. "No, Janni, there is no difference. In both cases, a stranger comes and says your world will be destroyed and you must come to our world. You know us, but they don't. And the people you met may be nice, but how do you know they're not the only nice people there? Think about it."

"Oh, Uncle Artie." She had a glimmering of what he meant.

That night she slept uneasily.

●   ●   ●

The next day, nobody came through, and even though the sun was setting, Artie said, "Let's go." He *called* his papa to let him know they were coming, and they left.

No splashing, just hard riding. At the camp, they fell off their quines and dropped into sleep. When they woke, they found Marisa and Charley waiting for them.

"Mama, I told Sam to send two people through, but nobody came."

"The Gate is working; I checked." Uncle Artie said.

"Maybe she couldn't find anyone willing to go. Maybe she didn't have time to ask very many people. How much time did you give her?'

"Oh." Janni blinked. "I just wanted her to get started."

"I know. We'll keep watch on the Gate, so we'll know when someone comes through."

They took it slower and allowed the quines to splash.

"You go on home. We'll talk tomorrow," Marisa said when they reached the plaza and dismounted.

Willie, Glori and Brian were there waiting for her.

Janni ran into her mate's arms. "Don't ever leave me like that again," he said. "I missed you so."

"He had to fix his own food," Glori said, next to them. "No, Ruthie, his mama, and I took turns feeding him."

"Over at our place," Brian said. "I thought he'd never leave so Glori and I could be alone."

"You two," Janni said, and hugged Glori. "All right, I'll cook tonight."

Everyone grinned.

That evening, Janni told them about Sam's world. Later, in bed, she wondered when Sam would send someone through.

24

STARVIEW

S AM WAS TOO TIRED when she got home to deal with Janni's request. When she told Brad and Maxee, they said no way would they go through that thing.

•　　　•　　　•

In the morning, Sam remembered what Janni wanted.

How can I ask someone else to go through when I'm not ready to go myself?

She had Arlene round up the department heads and they met in the big meeting room. Sam told them what she'd seen at the Gate.

Glenda asked, "Are you sure it's safe?"

"For them, yes. I saw Steve come out, Janni leave and come back, and the both of them leave. She thinks it's safe. But I don't know whether it will be for us. And she wants me to start sending people through."

"From what I can see of the coming menace, we'll be safer over there," Brad said.

"It's getting there that's the problem," Todd remarked.

"What will happen if we stay here?" Glenda asked.

The women looked at each other.

"If the menace doesn't get us, we'll be on short rations until enough of us die off so the place can support the population," Brad said.

"And when the younger girls grow up and start having babies?" Glenda asked.

"Peace sounds better and better." Sam pulled her hair back. "So how do we select who goes first?"

"Ask for volunteers," Brad said.

"How? Go around and tell people about Peace and the Gate and ask them if they'd like to go? Who has time for that?" Sam slapped the table.

Silence.

"We'll go." Glenda sat up straight.

"Glennie," Gus barked. "No."

"Gus, think. We'd be first to colonize a new world." She paused. "I'd like to be first at something. Sam, you've been there. Would you be willing to go through first?"

"No," Brad and Hal said together.

Sam thought. She'd been there. Whatever was in Janni's people that kept them safe was in her now. "Yes, but I can't leave right now."

"I mean just go over and come back." Glenda picked at a fingernail.

"Oh. I guess. If I can get two more days off." Sam patted her tunic over her thigh.

"How do you know they didn't just hide in the back room?" Gus asked. "The kid could have come some other way when you weren't there."

"She was really surprised when she saw him. She didn't know he was coming. Besides, there's no way to get from one to the other except going outside the whole room. You should know, you built it."

Gus grunted. "They could have changed something later somehow so you couldn't see it."

"Gus, enough. Sam, if you will go through and come back safely, we'll go. We can look the place over, see where we can put our colony, and, if it's good, get started laying it out." Glenda grinned.

Gus looked at her as if he'd never seen her before.

"We'll get Ben and Alex to take over for us here. Our boys can do it." Glenda waved her hand.

"Are you sure you want to go?" Todd asked.

"Yes." Glenda nodded sharply. Sam knew that when Glenda decided on something, no one could change her mind.

"I suppose we could go." Gus frowned. "There's not that much work here, except for repairs, right now. Could we come back if we wanted?"

"Yes," Sam said. "I'm sure they'd let you."

"When would we have to leave?" Glenda asked.

"When will you be ready?"

"At least three days," Gus muttered.

"Three days?" Sam was dismayed. Janni had been such an optimist.

"Yeah. Gotta check all the neighborhoods' projects." Gus looked away.

"Yes, he's right," Glenda said. "He has to make sure everything's under control here before we can leave. Ben and Alex are good, but we don't want to leave them with any messes."

"Of course. Okay, on the fourth day after today, we will meet at my office right after first meal. All right?"

"Okay." Glenda nodded.

"This is what you'll need to bring. Food for at least a week and whatever else you'll need over there. We can eat most of their food, and they'll give you some clothes. I don't know what tools they have. Once you go through, it'll be two days before you reach their place, so take your best footwear. Anything else you want to have with you. They have plenty of wood available. Someone, Marisa or Janni, will contact you and show you where our new place will be. Remember, while they can communicate with each other in their minds, they won't be trying to peek into yours." Sam looked around. "Anyone have anything to say?"

"I wish you two the best of luck," Arlene said. "If that's settled, we need to get back to work." Everyone rose and went on their way.

Back in her office, Sam and Arlene went through a pile of replacement requests. "I didn't think this many people got flooded," Sam said.

"I think some people just want new furniture and things. I'm checking addresses against the list Hal made of those who were flooded, and when I get a request not on that list, I'm putting it aside."

"Good." Sam smiled at Arlene. "Would you like to take over my job?"

"Never." She rolled her eyes. "I might be willing to help whoever replaces you, but I'm not doing it. In fact, I'm thinking of retiring."

"Retiring? You?"

"Sam, I worked for thirty years in City and ten here. I'm ready to have a life."

"What would you do?"

"Relax," Arlene said wryly. "I might dabble in art. I was pretty good at drawing in school."

"Art as in painting?" Sam was surprised. She'd never seen this side of Arlene.

Arlene nodded smugly and picked up a pile of complaints papers.

They continued to work.

•   •   •

The day came, Sam packed and met Glenda and Gus. "Where are your bags?"

"Something came up. We can't go." Gus looked at his feet.

"Part of the roof of one of the clinics collapsed, and Gus has to oversee the repair." Glenda scrunched up her face.

"What would have happened if that had happened after you left?" Sam asked, annoyance fighting with disappointment.

"Ben would have taken care of it," Glenda said. "But we're still here so Gus has to do it."

"Okay." Sam sighed. "How long will it take?"

"If nothing else happens, about three days," Gus muttered.

"Was anyone hurt?"

"No. It happened last night."

Sam nodded. "Okay. Three days, then. No matter what happens. This'll give me more time to teach you their language. It's a lot like ours; a form of Standard."

She returned to her office and dumped her bag.

"They can't go yet, he has to fix a roof," she muttered to Arlene's raised eyebrows. "Pencil me in for three days from now."

This was like a step backwards.

•   •   •

Three days later, Sam, Glenda, and Gus left for the Gate. The couple each carried two huge bags. A cool breeze accompanied them. The closer they got to the cavern, the more nervous Sam felt. Brad and Hal had been very unhappy about what she was going to do, but neither of them nor Todd could go with her.

Since it was late when the three of them got there, Sam said, "Let's wait 'til morning. Either you camp here, or over there when you go through."

"You're going first." Gus sat down.

"Of course, but I'll be coming right back." *I hope.*

"I'd rather start fresh over there," Glenda said as she spread out her blanket. "I haven't hiked like this since we moved here." She flopped down on it.

"Different exercise from what I usually do." Gus dug out his blanket.

They all were too tired to talk much and retired early.

•   •   •

Light glimmered through the trees when Sam awoke. The other two still slept. She walked over to the main trail and across to the river. Some creature snapped a branch in the distance, and another tweeted from high in the trees. As always, the gurgle of the river. A flowery aroma drifted by, mingling with the forest smells.

It's so peaceful, I wish I could stay here forever.

"No, Sam, don't even think about it," she said aloud. She tore herself away and returned to the camp in front of the cavern.

The others stirred, and Glenda sat up.

"Oh, my back," she said.

Sam helped her to her feet. "You can go over here." She showed the older woman a place in the trees.

When she returned, Gus had his eyes open.

"Where's Glennie?" he asked. As if his voice brought her, Glenda stepped out of the forest. She sat beside him, leaned over and kissed him.

"I'm ready," she said. "Are you?"

"You're not going without me."

"Okay. Let's grab a bite and go."

Sam pulled some bread out of her pack. They all ate and went into the cave. The room door was open, and a piece of paper sat on the floor. Sam picked it up. 'Still waiting,' she read, crumpled the paper, and stuffed it in a pocket.

"You two ready?"

They nodded.

"Come in here. When you're ready to go, press this black button. Everything will go dark, and you will wake up in the glade on Peace. Okay."

They nodded.

"You still want me to go first?"

"Yes, please," Glenda said.

She and Gus stepped out of the room.

Sam gulped and pushed the button.

She came to in the glade, hearing voices.

"Hey, Sam, you came through. What's going on?"

Janni and her mate stood at her feet.

She sat up and shook the fuzziness out of her head. "Hi, Janni. First couple wanted me to come through and go back to show them it's safe."

"Okay." The girl didn't sound pleased.

"Quines." Sam saw a group grazing by the stream.

"Yes. We came two days ago with Uncle Artie, he checked the Gate and left. We stayed."

"Time alone together," Willie said.

Away from in-laws and relatives, Sam thought. She got to her feet and stretched. "Does going back and forth a lot hurt anything?"

"No." Janni swung her arms and Willie put his arms around her from behind. "Gramma Perri went through Gates four or five times when she was pregnant with Mama. Mama went through a lot, looking for worlds, then back and forth from Harmony to here many times. They're fine. I was born here."

"Okay." Sam walked around.

The glade was beautiful. Something large crashed through the woods and she jumped.

"We hear them a lot, but no one ever sees one." Willie grinned.

"When you feel rested, you can go back." Janni smiled.

"Okay. They'll be wondering. What do I do here?"

"I'll show you."

Janni touched something on the side of the widest tree Sam had ever seen, and a door slid open. The two women went in.

A large, many-sided room, much larger than the tree, with doors all around, held a table with machines and a screen in the middle.

Janni led her to a door marked with a big 'S' and opened it. "In here. I'll push the button out there."

Again, everything went black, and this time Sam awoke in the cavern.

"Oh, thank goodness," Glenda said.

Sam opened her eyes. "I'm back." She sat up, rubbing her forehead. "You two are in luck. Janni and Willie are in the glade and they have animals you can ride."

"Ride? Really?" Glenda's eyes widened.

"They're waiting for you. You may feel a little dizzy when you first wake up, but it goes away quickly. Good luck."

She rose and hugged Glenda. "Take care."

"Thank you, Sam."

Gus and Glenda went into the room, Sam heard the hum, and they were gone.

Please, Oneness, let them be safe.

Sam packed up her bag and called Brad to tell him she was leaving for home.

25

PEACE

BLINKING, SHE SAT UP. Strange trees. Long leaves. Gus lay next to her.

Must be the new world.

Excitement grew within her.

"Gus, wake up." She nudged him. They were in a glade with a trickle of a stream.

"Wha?" He opened his eyes.

"Gus, we're here. On another world." Glenda grinned.

Gus sat up and looked around. "Trees," he said.

A young couple came out of the woods. "Hi," the girl said. "I'm Janni, and this is my mate, Willie."

Willie nodded.

"We're Glenda and Gus, from Starview." She looked around. "This is Peace, right?"

"Yes. We'll show you to our community. Come on, when you're ready."

Glenda had a little trouble adjusting to her speech, even after Sam's lessons. She stretched and helped Gus to his feet.

"What are those?" Gus demanded, pointing to the quines.

They turned their long heads to look at him.

"Quines," Janni said. "We'll ride them later. Now we walk down to the beach."

Glenda stared at the beautiful, four-legged creatures. Sam had told her about them. She couldn't wait to ride one.

Janni said something to the quines and led the other couple down a trail beside a stream that came out onto a beach. The quines followed and trotted past them to the sea.

"Oh," Glenda said, as she saw the ocean. "It's so big." And then she saw the blue green sky. "Oh, wow. Gus, look at this."

Gus took one look and turned away to face the trees at the back of the beach. "Too much," he said.

"Okay." Glenda patted his shoulder.

At Janni's puzzlement, Glenda explained, "On our world, we all grew up in City, in small apartments with no windows. We never saw outside until we left for the valley. A lot of people couldn't handle the wide-open spaces. Gus had more problems than I did. This is more open than our valley. It's almost scary."

"Oh dear," Janni said, and looked at Willie.

"Nothing we can do about it unless you want to run around in a blindfold," Willie said.

"I'll be all right." Gus moved along with his head turned toward the trees.

Glenda watched the quines splashing in the sea. "They like the water."

"Can't keep them out of it. Come on, Qilla, time to go."

The big, brown creatures sloshed up to them.

"Qilla, this is Glenda and Gus, from another world. They'll need to ride."

Qilla nodded her head and moved up to a log at the top of the beach. Janni stepped up on the log and swung up onto the animal's back.

Willie mounted the largest one. Another nudged Glenda to the log and positioned herself next to it.

"Put your bags in the panniers," Willie said, pointing to the bags hanging over the animals' backs.

"You want me to ride you?" Glenda asked. She had never expected anything like this.

Gingerly, she climbed on the animal's back. Glenda felt the quine adjust herself underneath her bottom to a comfortable position.

"Oh, this is nice."

Gus refused to mount the other quine. "I'll walk." He did let the animal carry his bags.

"It's fine, Gus. Come on." Glenda waved at him.

He shook his head and started walking down the beach. Willie galloped on ahead, but Janni on Qilla kept to a walk, alongside Glenda. Gus plodded along beside them.

"Sam told us about these animals, but I didn't realize they'd be so big. Were they here all along?" Glenda asked.

"No. Qione, Qilla's mother, and five others came through the Mountain Gate on our other world. My mama and her friends found them and brought them home. They're very intelligent and understand our speech. Mama and I and some others hear them talk in our minds."

"How weird."

"Not for us. We've always heard others in our minds."

"Isn't that distracting?"

"Sometimes, but we learn to shut it out at an early age."

Glenda couldn't imagine what it would be like hear people talk to her in her mind.

A breeze teased her hair, bringing a salty aroma. Bushes of red and yellow flowers lined the top of the beach in front of the forest.

After a while, they stopped at a stream. Her quine knelt so she could get off. "Oh, my butt."

"You'll get used to it."

Gus came up and sat facing the trees. "Not like ours," he said. "We'll have to find out what is good wood and what isn't."

"I know, dear." Glenda took a big drink of water from the stream, in a cup Janni provided. "How much farther is it?" she asked.

"We'll camp tonight and get home tomorrow."

At the camp that night, Willie gave Gus and Glenda extra blankets and showed them the grass under the semicircle of trees at the back of the beach. Janni brought out food, and they ate around the campfire. Gus sat with his back to the ocean. Glenda couldn't stop watching the waves. Something hooted in the forest.

Janni and Glenda were cleaning up after the meal when two people rode up on quines from the direction their group was heading.

"Mama," Janni cried. "Uncle Laurie."

Glenda watched as the two dropped off their mounts and hugged Janni.

"Mama, this is Gus and Glenda from Starview. They build houses. This is my mama, Marisa, and my Uncle Laurie."

"Glad to meet you," Glenda said. She noticed how much Janni looked like her mother: same square face and green eyes surrounded by black curls. Laurie's curls weren't quite as black, and his eyes were brown.

"Everything go all right?" Marisa asked as they sat around the dying fire.

"Yes." Janni beamed.

"Not quite," Glenda said. "Gus has trouble looking out at the sea. Did Sam tell you about City and how some people couldn't adapt to outdoors?"

"Yes." Marisa smiled. "I can't imagine that. You'll get used to it, Gus. You two must be tired, go ahead and turn in if you want."

Gus rose. "Goodnight." He slogged over to the pike of blankets and picked one.

"I'm not that tired, I rode." Glenda looked around.

The sun had long since set, and masses of stars studded the sky. Although still warm, a cool breeze picked up.

"But even walking feels easier. This is a beautiful world. You can't imagine how much better this is than where I grew up. A tiny box of a place with no windows, long gray hall to go to the caff or work. I never saw the outside until we left to go to the valley ten years ago."

"How could they keep you in?" Janni asked.

"Oh, no." Marisa put her hands to her face.

"There was no way out except the portals to the sectors on either side, or the exit to the dock which only food prep people were allowed to use. We got our grain and vegetables from places in the other sectors. Everyone had screens where we could see pictures of trees and flowers and mountains. We didn't miss what we didn't know about."

"Didn't you want to see other places?" Laurie asked. "I always did."

"Mama and Papa couldn't keep him home." Marisa grinned at him. He grinned back.

Something trilled in the forest. "What's that?" Glenda asked.

"Some kind of flying creature. We hear it often, but nobody's got a good look at it." Laurie rose. "I'm going to turn in." He grabbed his pack and walked down the beach.

"We probably should too," Marisa said. "We can get an early start in the morning."

"Okay." Glenda saw the quines together at the edge of the trees, sitting down. One lay on his side. Happier than she had been for a long time, she didn't know whether she could sleep. Starview's people must come here.

• • •

In the morning, Glenda found Gus peering at a stump of a downed tree. "Looks like good wood," he said, straightening.

"Great," she said, hugging him. "How did you sleep?"

"Not bad."

They returned to the others, ate, and packed up. Laurie and Willie lifted Gus up onto his quine, and they moved on.

"They won't go fast unless you want them to," Willie said.

The quines splashed in the edge of the water, but still made good time.

The sun was little more than halfway down when they reached the little river. Several families and their quines were splashing in the water.

"They do like the water, don't they," Glenda repeated.

"Oh, yes. That was one thing Qione insisted on when we came here." Marisa jumped off so her quine could go out farther into the water.

Marisa introduced them to Susan, her best friend, and Susan's children, Glori and her younger brothers and sisters.

Glori ran to Janni and hugged her.

Glenda observed the others. All the young people were taller than the older ones. Everyone appeared to be well-fed and healthy.

An older woman called everyone out of the sea, and they all mounted quines. The group moved up the hill, across a bridge to a plaza surrounded by buildings. Glenda was impressed by the community. Gus had to examine one of the buildings to see how it had been erected.

Glenda and Gus were shown around and to a cabin for them, above the community, near the big river. "You will have to prepare your own meals most of the time," Marisa said. "I'll show you where to get food."

"We always ate prepared meals in caffs," Glenda said. "I don't know how to make my own."

"We'll show you. Janni, see if you can get them to send people from their food processing units next time." Marisa looked at the girl.

"Okay." Janni peered at her feet.

Marisa led them to her house where they had a meal. The two met Janni's father and her little brothers.

After the meal, Marisa took Glenda and Gus back to their cabin and showed them how to heat porridge for breakfast. She also showed them where and how to get water, and some clothes for them in the wardrobe.

"Thank you so much," Glenda said.

She slept well.

•   •   •

In the morning, Marisa's father, Charley, took Gus and Glenda up and showed them where his people had laid out the beginnings of a new community. "We'll work together on getting you set up." A pile of cut logs and other materials lay nearby. "Do you need any tools?"

"I brought most of mine," Gus said, dumping his pack and bag on the ground. "I'll let you know if we need anything else."

"Good. Here's some bread. Come to our house for late meal, at sundown." He gave them directions.

They surveyed the area, and Glenda picked out sites near the big river for her house, Sam's and Brad's. Together, they decided on where to place their plaza and the main buildings. The day was warm, and floral aromas drifted over from the white flowers under the trees along the river.

"We need to get some builders over here soon," Gus said.

"And people from the water department." Glenda looked around, pleased with what she saw. She would miss her little house in Starview, but not much else.

26

STARVIEW

BACK IN STARVIEW, in brief moments of respite, Sam wondered how Glenda was doing. She had her own hands full. She had returned to find that Far West had seceded. The agent they'd sent to announce this to Starview had arrived with a long list of demands for food and other items. Several couples accompanied him, wanting to move to Starview.

Todd told her, "I said I accepted their secession, but that meant that if they wanted anything from us, they'd have to pay for it. I asked him, 'What do you produce that we can use?' He gaped and gabbled and said, 'But we need this'. So I repeated my question."

"Serves them right," Sam said.

"He had no idea. I had Brad fly him back with a few things we could spare. There Brad looked around and found a tree that had a kind of fruit we don't have here and took a bunch. There was also some clayey type soil along the river there and Brad collected some of that."

"Clay?" Sam remembered the pottery on Peace. "Did someone try to use it?"

"Yes. A gal called Elsie. A friend of Jan's. Apparently, it didn't go very well. She's still working on it."

"What happened to the people who came with him?"

"Arlene took care of them. She said we could handle those few, but didn't know how many more."

Sam sighed. *No more, please.*

Sam also found food shortages growing. June, the head of food prep, said her people thought some were taking extra and stockpiling it. It was impossible to check everyone's pockets as they left the caff.

"Is there any way you can tighten control on the servings, maybe keep the bread behind the counter and give it out only when someone asks? Maybe limit one loaf per family or group?"

"I'll think about that. Thanks."

The food growers told her they were approaching the end of the summer crops, and the winter crops wouldn't be ready for a while yet. The loovah seedlings she'd brought were doing well, but were still small. The fall grains were doing fine, so there would be bread.

Sam returned to June. "Would you please choose a couple to go through to Peace? One who's knowledgeable about all different kinds of foods, who can go up tomorrow."

"Tomorrow?"

"Yes. I understand there will be someone waiting for them then."

"All right. Let me see if I can find someone who's willing to go."

She selected a couple whom Brad took up to the Gate the next day. They went through with no problem.

Three days later, Janni contacted Maxee and told her both couples were doing fine. She sent through more loovah plants.

Sam, Brad, Todd, Arlene, and Hal held a meeting to discuss a possible move.

"Even if this danger never materializes, I think we should move over there, as long as they let us," Sam said. "The Noreg are having food problems too, and, if we leave, they can have our land."

"I agree," Arlene said. "This place was nice for a small population, but we've got way too many people now, even with the western communities."

"True." Todd nodded. "But we have to plan this right. First, get people over there from each department, so they can start getting things set up. Then a small group from each neighborhood. We need lists to keep track of who's here and who's over there."

"What about people who won't go?" Sam asked. After the exodus from City, she knew there would be some.

"We'll worry about that later," Todd said. "Sam, you will need to go over occasionally to see how things are going. When can we send more through? Doug has been asking me."

"He and a couple helpers can go up tomorrow. I just told him that." Sam brushed her hair back.

"I have lists of the department people, and noted in what order they should go," Arlene said.

"Good." Todd touched his moustache.

"I hope those people know what they're doing," Arlene said.

"I think they do." Sam twisted in her seat. "How can we say no?"

"We can't." Todd grimaced. "You've already been there and made arrangements with them. We can't stay here, and where else would we go?"

As if to reply, the world shook. Sam and the others felt it, up on the mesa.

"Oh no," Sam groaned. "I guess we have to go now. I guess we'll just have to make sure our people will do their best to get along with Marisa's people." Sam sighed. "Well, let's get to work. What's next, Arlene?"

Not earthquakes, too.

•　　　•　　　•

The next day, Sam sent Doug and a pair of helpers up to the bridge, where Lucy's brother and his wife met them. The group headed on up to the Gate.

Late that afternoon, Sam got a call from him. "We're at the cavern. I'm going to leave my phone here for anyone who might want to use it. We're going through now."

27

PEACE

WHEN THE NEXT GROUP came through the Gate, Janni volunteered to go meet them.

"Only to the camp," Marisa said. "Who are you taking with you?"

"I thought I'd go by myself."

"Janni, you know better than that. Mick is old enough; he'll go."

"Mama." Not her little brothers.

In the morning, she and Mick rode off on their quines. Mick was taller than the other boys his age. When they reached the camp, Janni didn't see anyone at first.

"Under the trees," Mick said.

Three people reclined against their bags. The older man sat up.

"Hello, there," Janni called as she dismounted. "I'm Janni, and this is my brother, Mick."

The man got to his feet. A large man with gray in his dark hair, he gave her a big smile.

"I'm Doug, the watermaster, and these are my helpers, Jerry and Denise." The other two sat up but did not rise. "We're kinda tired, not used to this hiking."

"Okay, we'll stay here tonight, and you can ride tomorrow." She pointed to the quines splashing in the sea.

"Sam told us about those." Doug sat, followed by Janni. Mick poked around in the edge of the forest.

"How is Sam?" Janni asked.

"Frazzled as usual." Doug looked around. "This place is great. I'm looking forward to seeing that river."

"You said watermaster? We'll get someone to show you our waterwheel. And what do you two do?" Janni asked the couple.

"Everything," Denise said. "We help with the water system when Doug needs us. I work in the caff sometimes, make clothing, and do stitchery. Jerry does everything from bringing up the grain carts to construction, to helping George in the chem lab when he needs another hand."

"There are huge grain fields beyond the next sector and, when the Noreg harvest it, they ship it to a dock below City," Jerry explained. "Since City's gone, we have to pull them clear up to Starview. We grow some in North Valley, too."

"Oh, my," Janni said. "I thought with all your people, everyone would have her own specific job."

"Most are like that, but sometimes one or another will get real busy and need extra hands," Denise said.

Janni nodded. "You people must want to rest. We'll fix some food around sundown."

"I haven't hiked like this since we left City for Starview," Denise said. "Our children didn't want us to go. I told them we didn't have much choice, June chose us. I said, you have your own families to look after now, and we'll be fine."

"And they'll be here one of these days." Janni smiled.

She watched the others settle down and she and Mick joined the quines in the sea.

· · ·

In the morning, as they ate and prepared to leave, Janni asked Doug, "Do you have a mate?"

Doug looked down. "My wife died in childbirth many years ago." He shook his head. "Now, tell me about the layout of this place."

"You'll see when we get there."

All of them rode quines the next day and reached the plaza in good time. Marisa and Grampa Charley met them there.

"Welcome," Marisa said. "Mick, your papa is in the north field."

"Okay," the boy said, and ran off.

Janni introduced the new people. "Mama, this is Doug, the watermaster, and his helpers, Denise and Jerry. This is my mama, Marisa, and my Grampa Charley."

"This has been a pleasant, if tiring, trip," Doug said. "I'd like to see this big river of yours."

"I'll show you," Grampa Charley said, and the two men left.

"Janni, we're eating here tonight. You need to help in the kitchen. Come on. You, too."

The four made their way over to the kitchen. Jerry slumped down on a bench outside.

"If you'd like to rest, there are beds in the clinic over there," Marisa said.

"That's all right," Denise said. Inside, she found a chair near the end of a long table. "I'll sit here and watch. I worked in our caffs at Starview."

The couple who had come earlier were there, and Denise asked the woman questions. Her husband helped the men set up the tables in the plaza.

Janni sat at the table with a big pot and a pile of potatoes to cut up. "So what do you think of our place?"

"Very nice," the woman, Vannie, said. "A lot like our big caffs. The smaller ones aren't so organized."

"Some of the smaller ones only have shelves, not cupboards," Denise added. The three conversed as Janni worked on her potatoes and Vannie sorted loovah leaves.

At supper, Janni sat with the Starview people. "That river is something else," Doug said. "It could power a mess of cities. I'm itching to start on ours, but first I have to find a location."

"We'll take you up tomorrow," Glenda said.

"Good." Doug turned to Denise and Jerry. "What do you think of this setup?" he asked them.

"Different," said Denise. "Their kitchen here is a smaller version of ours, and they keep stores of food in the warehouse for people to take home. Two women, on a rotating basis, prepare food for people who choose to eat here. They have to sign up so the women know how much to prepare."

"Interesting." Doug tapped the table. "Guess I'm going to have to learn to cook."

A pair of grandmothers came out of the kitchen carrying bowls, followed by several young people with platters of bread and fruit.

"Come and get it!" one of the women called.

Doug lined up with the others, including a handful who had come to meet the new people.

After his first bite of the stew, Doug said, "This is quite good."

"Yes, isn't it." Denise took a bite of bread.

A grandmotherly woman across from them said, "Welcome. I'm Mary, and this is my daughter, Nancy. Where are you from and what are you planning to do here?"

Nancy demanded, "Why are you letting them eat our food?"

"We have plenty," one of the kitchen women said. "I'm Mindy."

"For one meal, not forever."

"We have masses of loovah," the other one, Megan, said.

"Now, Nan," Mary cooed.

"What is this 'loovah'?" Doug asked.

Three people tried to explain it at once.

"Well, I don't want to spend the rest of my life eating nothing but loovah." Nancy jumped up and stalked off.

Mary apologized profusely for her daughter. "She was always stubborn."

"Don't worry, we'll be able to take care of ourselves." Denise smiled at the older woman.

"She was ten when we came here, and the first winter was bad. Most of us had nothing but loovah. The pregnant and nursing women had whatever other food we had." Mary wrung her hands.

"I understand. We had a similar problem when we had to move out of City and up to the valley. But we didn't have a ubiquitous plant like your loovah. We had a lot of grain, so we mostly had bread." Denise smiled.

Mary nodded.

"We'll have our own community up north of yours, but maybe we can come down and visit from time to time."

"That would be nice."

28

PEACE

LATER THAT DAY, Megan reported the incident to Granlyn. She always wanted to know everything that was going on.

"Is there a problem with food?" Granlyn asked.

"No, we have plenty. Nancy works in the warehouse, but doesn't realize we have a lot of food prepared for later in the kitchen." Megan shrugged. "After each meal we serve, we prepare enough more to keep the cupboards full. I think she's complaining because her mother won't."

"Let's see. That's Mary, I believe. Betty's daughter. She was still young when Betty was taken by the alien, and Anne and Joan, her older sisters, were too interested in boys to pay much attention to her." Granlyn nodded. "And she's always been so timid. Let me know if anyone else fusses about the newcomers. There will be a lot of them. I told Janni to tell them to bring as much food as they can."

"Very well, Aunt Lyn." Megan left.

·　　·　　·

Over the next week, Janni noted that six more people from Starview showed up. One couple were farmers; another, medics; and the third pair, legal people. They all brought a week's worth of food; all they could carry along with their other belongings.

"You people need carts," Jenni said to the third couple, noting their bundles.

"Carts?" the man asked.

"Like that." Janni pointed to a large, two-wheeled cart parked by the storehouse.

"How would we pull them?" He cocked his head.

"Oh." *That's right; they don't have quines.*

Janni found someone to take the couples up to the new community and returned to her tasks. She thought about the new people and tried to sort her feelings. On one hand, they seemed pleasant enough and, except for Doug, the water man, were all young. On the other, they were strangers, and she sensed the unease in her older relations. And Sam was hiding something that scared her.

•   •   •

In the dawn, Janni's being leaves her body and searches space for other human colonies. She finds several that are no longer occupied, but none that were burned. And no sign of ships.

Janni becomes aware of the Other and tries to stay away from it. She isn't ready to deal with that yet. The Watcher voice *tells* her the Other are also pre-Watchers. 'Let them have it and leave us alone,' she *sends*.

'They are not ready yet,' the voice *tells her*.

At Sam's world, before she can contact them, she is jerked back to her body.

•   •   •

Janni returned to herself, heart pounding and head muddled. "What?" she mumbled.

Willie was kissing and stroking her. "Mmm?"

"I'm back." Janni opened her eyes. The crack on the ceiling was still there. "Willie? What that?" she lifted her hand to point up.

"Dunno. Check it later." He cupped her breast.

"No." Janni pushed at him.

"Come on." He kissed and caressed her.

She pushed harder, and with her mind, and rolled away from him. "Gotta think. Something happened."

Willie sat up. "What? What's more important than taking care of your mate?'

"Saving a world of people."

"Not that again." Willie cursed, grabbed clothes, and stomped out into the other room.

"Willie ..." Janni began.

He would never understand. He only believed in things that were real, right in front of his face. He accepted that air existed because he breathed it, but not much else.

Janni relaxed and tuned into her mind, to the area where she kept her contacts with Other. There was something new. Two messages: *Stop becoming. We not harm you,* partially overwritten by, *Must kill all others.*

Stunned, Janni's mind went blank for a second. A thought came: *How am I understanding them?* and then, *Watchers gave them Standard, too.*

She couldn't *reach* them from Peace. She'd have to wait 'til she went out again to try to contact them.

"Breakfast," Willie yelled from the other room.

"Coming." Janni swung her legs over the side of the bed and got up.

She dressed, ran a comb through her hair, and went out to the kitchen.

After they ate, glaring at each other, Janni and Willie went their separate ways. Janni wanted to go to Granlyn's, but was afraid to because of Grampa Larry. Maybe she could find Grampa Charley. Her first task was to help with inventory in the storehouse, and she did not see him on the way.

She *called* him, but got no response. If he was very busy, he'd just shut down his mind link.

Janni reported for duty, but couldn't concentrate on her tasks. Apparently, there were two Other and they didn't agree. But what could she do about it?

29

STARVIEW

S AM WAS PORING OVER A LIST OF REQUESTS when she heard a commotion.

Arlene went out and returned. "A young couple wants to ask you something. I think you should hear them."

Sam looked up and tried on a smile. "Okay. Come on in." *They were young,* she thought. *Must have been children when they came up.* "Have a seat.

Arlene left and the girl sat in the only other chair in Sam's tiny office. The boy stood behind her, hands on her shoulders. Some things never changed.

"How can I help you?" Sam asked.

The two looked at each other. The girl, dark hair and brown eyes, stuck her chin out and asked, "Please, Miss Sam, do you know of any way to reverse birth control?"

"Do what?" Sam dredged her memory. *Oh, that's right.*

The girl reached for the boy's hand. "I'm Beverly and he's Mark. We just got married. I had my birth control put in just before we left City. Now I want to have children."

Sam sighed. All they needed was more people. She had counted birth control as a blessing. "Actually, I'd never thought of it. I'd just had mine made permanent."

"Lots of us who had had it put in right before we knew we had to leave are now getting married and want children. The youngest children now are about ten, the ones born as we came, and a few babies for the ones too young to have birth control before we left. I'm a teacher. There are no children between five and ten."

Sam stared at her. She'd occasionally wondered why there were no school age children, but never really thought about it. But it made sense.

Back in City, when a girl had her first period, her parents took her to a Mediclinic and a procedure was done, provided by the Volen overseers. When she married, she was given a test to see if she would be a suitable mother, and if she passed, the temporary birth control was turned off. It was turned back on after the baby was born. They were allowed two children. At age thirty, the birth control was made permanent.

Sam recalled the moment she had got her notice that she needed to have a baby now before her birth control became permanent. Which led to thoughts of her ex-husband and his attempt to kidnap her ... She shook her head. She didn't want those memories.

"I have no idea how to go about that," she said. "That was a Volen thing." Their faces fell. "I'll talk to Zilla, the head medic, and see if she has any ideas." Something Janni had said about her eggs popped into her mind. "Here's a faint possibility. Have you heard about the visitor to our world?"

Bev nodded. "We never saw her, though."

"She has a talent of dealing with her eggs so she can control when she gets pregnant. Possibly she or her people could do something."

"Would we have to go there?" Mark asked.

"Well, you know they have built a Gate, and she wants our people to go through to her world. Would you be interested?"

They looked at each other. "Could we come back if we didn't like it?" Mark asked.

"I don't see why not."

"Yes," Bev grinned. "When?"

"Bev," Mark said.

"I have to warn you, there's no guarantee the Gate will work or that they can remove your birth control. Several people have gone through and seem to be all right, but we don't know about long-term effects. It's possible you could be changed or hurt in some way, or even die."

"Do we go together?" Mark asked. "I don't want to lose you, Bev."

"Yes. Other couples have gone through together."

"Okay," he said. "Bev, do you really want to?"

"Oh yes." She grinned and bounced in her seat. "Don't you, darling? If it means we could have children?"

"Well," he said, and smiled. "I guess so."

"You will have to tell your folks. I'll go with you if you want. And your bosses."

"Oh." Mark frowned. "I guess Ben won't mind; there's not that much to keep us busy. But Dad will have a fit."

"My folks too, but Mother will be thrilled to have grandchildren. My brother's wife was turned down, so they can't have any. I don't know why."

That evening, Sam met the couple at the girl's parents' house.

"Welcome," said the mother, dark like her daughter.

"What is this all about?" Father asked.

"Miss Sam, tell them," Bev said.

"There is a possibility that Janni, our visitor from another world, and her people, could reverse our birth control so that your daughter can have a child."

Bev's mother's eyes lit up. "Really? Could they?"

"I don't know for sure, but they can manage their eggs to manage their pregnancies."

"That would be wonderful."

"Do they have to go to this other world? How?" Dad asked.

"I believe so." Sam pushed her hair back.

"How? Is it safe?" Dad demanded.

"Several couples have gone through and are fine." Sam had to explain the Gate.

"Do you really think it would work?" Mother looked hopeful.

"I talked to Zilla yesterday, and she said the device they used was Volen, and they are gone. This looks like the only chance Beverly and the other girls have of having children."

"Can they come back?" Dad asked.

"Yes, if they want to."

"When are you planning to go?"

Bev and Mark looked at Sam. "You can go tomorrow if you wish."

"Yes!"

"Now, Bev."

"It's all right, Daddy, it'll work, I know it'll work."

Mother moved her hand around. "What will they need to take?"

"At least three days' worth of clothes, food for a week, personal items. Mark, any tools you might want to take. I know they have some there, but yours may be different. When I was there, some of the older people weren't too happy about my presence, but there was no problem with the young people."

"What's the land like?" Mark asked.

"A lot flatter. Low hills, mountains, and forest in the distance. But there is a beach, where the sea meets the land. And they have a moon."

"Moon?"

"A big rock orbiting the planet. Janni says it's like a big light in the sky. It was behind the world when I was there, so I didn't see it."

"Can I tell people?"

"Of course. Meet me at the base of the mesa path at second hour in the morning. I'll take you up to the Gate. It'll be an all-day hike, so wear your best footwear and bring water."

"Okay." Bev grinned.

"Now we have to talk to my father," Mark said as they left.

At Mark's father's apartment, the old man said, "Absolutely not."

"I have to agree with your father." Mark's mother played with the frills on her chair.

Nothing Mark or Bev could say would change the old man's mind.

"I have a grandson, I don't need any more," he said.

"I'm going and not alone," Beverly announced.

"Not with my son." The old man picked up a hunk of wood and a carving knife.

"He's my husband."

"And I won't let her go alone," Mark finished.

"Mark, must you?" His mother twisted a ribbon on the chair.

"Yes, Mother. We'll be all right. Come on, Bev."

"Don't bother coming back here," the old man growled.

They left as his mother pleaded with her husband.

"She always gives in to him," Mark said. "Your head teacher is closest. Let's go there first."

The teacher Bev worked with had just been married when they left City and had been unable to have a baby. She was thrilled to hear of Bev's trip.

"If it works, let me know," she said. "Good luck."

Ben, Mark's boss, was out somewhere, but his brother, Alex, greeted them in his office. Sam met them there and told Alex what was going on.

"Mark, do you really want to go?" Alex asked.

"Yes. If we can have a child."

"Good. Sam, do you know where they want us to build?

"Yes. Gus will be laying it out, above Marisa's community and by the big river. He'll show you what you need to do."

Alex nodded. "Mark, you check out the ground and the layout. Make a drawing. I expect a report when you return."

"Okay, boss."

Sam thought she heard a sarcastic tinge to his reply.

"Sam, did you hear, old Mrs. Travors died. That house is a mess. Ben is working on fixing it up for the next couple who needs one." Alex leaned back in his chair.

"No, I hadn't."

That was something else Sam had to deal with. Back in City, when someone died, the body disappeared in the night to be replace with an urn of ashes, done by the Volen as the citizens slept. In the following days, the family would have a memorial service.

Sam recalled her father's service. Little Maxee, known then as Max, curled up in her lap, and Brad sat next to her. She was unable to weep, but something inside her kept shivering. She'd refused to allow her soon-to-be ex-husband to sit with her. She knew he had caused her father's death.

Now Starview had a graveyard up in the corner where the hills curved toward the river.

"Okay, Mark, you and Alex go over what to take and do over there," Sam said, brisk again. "Bev, you get with your mother on what to take. Memories for one thing. Now I need to get back to work. See you in the morning."

Sam returned to her office and tried to figure out what was most important to take care of that afternoon. Later, she told Maxee where she was going, and asked if she wanted to come.

"No. Helping little child with broken arm. Someone go through?'

"Yes. Bev and Mark. We think maybe Marisa's people can help them have a baby."

Maxee nodded. "Good. Many young can't have."

"Right."

•   •   •

In the morning, Sam found the young couple both had backbags and another bundle. The day was warm, almost too warm, and they kept in the shade as much as possible. As they walked along the river trail, the trees whispering overhead, Sam thought of Todd's reaction.

"I don't like you going up there by yourself." He paced the floor of her office. "It's not safe."

"Todd, I have my comm. I've told them of the risks, and they want to go anyway. It's a woman thing. Women who want children will do anything to have them. Mark won't let her go alone."

Todd sighed. "Okay, Sam. But if anything goes wrong, you'll have to live with it the rest of your life."

"I know."

As they started up the mountain trail past the bridge to North Valley, a sense of uneasiness infiltrated Sam. She had gotten the message that Janni had sent that Gus and Glenda were fine. Doug called it to her from the cavern when he found the note in the Gate.

Will they make it through, and will Marisa and her people accept them? What if they won't let them come back?

"This is wonderful," Bev exclaimed, skipping along. "I never knew it was like this up here. All these trees and bushes and flowers and the river." Even Mark beamed.

"Enjoy it while you can," Sam said. "There's only small groups of trees other than the ones along the river over there."

"Will there be enough to build all the houses we'll need?" Mark asked.

"There is the forest, but you'd have to rig something to carry logs from there to where you build. It's not like here where you can just roll logs down the slope."

"Okay." He shrugged.

They reached the cave and went in. "Where's the Gate?" Mark asked.

"In the room." Sam gestured.

"How does this work?"

Sam pushed the outside button and the door opened. "See that black button on the back wall? Go in, stand on the circle, and push the button. You'll come out in a glade with a spring. Follow the stream that comes out of it down to the beach. Turn right. Head down the beach. You will see a cliff sticking out into the sea way far down. Partway along the beach you will find a camp area. You camp there the first night. Someone may meet you there, if not at the glade. The next day, as you get close to the cliff, you will see a small river and a trail along it. That will take you up to Marisa's community."

Sam could see Mark counting off the steps on his fingers. "Do not eat anything except your food, except from the loovah plant. Not everything there agreed with me. You'll have to work with them to see what you can and cannot eat."

"Okay. Let's go," Bev danced into the little room.

The door closed, the room hummed, and when Sam opened the door, the couple were gone. She crossed her fingers.

"We'll find out the next time Janni contacts us," Sam said aloud.

She camped inside the cavern, to be there just in case something went wrong and the two came back. She prayed to Oneness for their safety and tried to settle down.

I've been praying a lot lately.

Unable to sleep because of worrying about the couple, the community, and the menace, Sam rose before dawn and left. She felt she knew the trail well enough by now, and it was just beginning to get light.

She called Brad from the bridge. "I'm fine, they've gone, and I'll see you soon."

30

PEACE

J ANNI WAS ON HER WAY to work on quilt squares when she *sensed* something come through the Gate. She stopped and focused. *Two humans.*

Now she sends them, when there's nobody up there to meet them. I hope she told them how to get here.

'Mama, Gramma Perri, Papa, someone. Two people just came through the Gate and we need to send someone to meet them. I'd like to go.' Janni *sent* with her mind Talent to the others.

'No, you've been gone too much,' Marisa *replied.* 'I'll send Roroy and two quines for them to ride.'

'Mama.' *When was I ever not going to be bossed around?*

'Enough. Go to your task. Thank you for letting us know.'

'Okay.' Janni shrugged and turned back to her quilt square. To Glori, next to her in the craft hall, she said, "We have visitors."

"I know. I heard you." Glori picked up a baby shirt. "Do you really think this is going to work, having all these strangers here?"

"They won't all be strangers, and we'll get to know them over time." Janni didn't want to think about masses of people coming through yet. She still had to deal with the Watcher voice and the

Other. She wondered who Sam had sent, whether it was someone she'd met, and what they were going to be like.

A little later, Roroy walked in and loomed over the girls. "Is there anything you want me to tell these people before we get back?" he asked Janni. "Elli is going with me."

Elli had come through the Gate from 1990s Earth several years before. She had been drawn to Roroy as the only other offworlder, and he had 'found his angel', as he repeated to anyone who would listen.

"Some of us will meet them at the beach tomorrow afternoon. Tell them to enjoy the beach and watch out for the quines going in the water." Janni grinned.

"I will," Roroy left.

"Have a good trip," Janni called after him.

"Us?" Glori asked.

"Sure. Want to come?"

"Yes. Let's get the fellows too. They need a break."

The day snailed by. At supper at Marisa's house, Mama heard from Qione that Roroy and Elli had reached the halfway camp and the others were approaching. Quines had their own talents and Qione kept in touch with Elli's quine.

Later, they heard that the newcomers were quite excited about the place and the quines there accepted them.

The next day was even longer. Sometime after midday meal, Janni, Marisa, Grampa Charley, Glori, Willie, and Brian mounted their quines and rode down to the sea.

They all splashed in the sea, and the younger men collected a bagful of clams. Janni kept looking down the beach to the east, but Qilla saw them first. She told Janni, who mounted her, and they rode to meet them.

Willie grabbed his quine and followed her. The others stayed behind, Mama and Grampa Charley standing by their quines. Glori and Brian mounted and followed slowly.

"There they are," Janni exclaimed.

'Can't miss Beast,' Qilla *sent.*

"Hello," Janni called as the two groups approached each other. "I'm Janni, and this is Willie, my mate."

"This is Mark and Beverly," Roroy said, keeping himself and Beast a little away from the newcomers. The quines had no problem with the big black creature, but he could be frightening to newcomers.

"Hi," Bev said. "This is fabulous. I've never seen anything like this beach and being able to ride is heavenly."

"Yes, this is great," Mark echoed. "These creatures we're riding are very smart."

"Aren't they? They are people in their own right; people who live very simply." Janni beamed. "Oh, here's Glori and Brian. Willie and Brian are brothers."

"Glad to meet you," Mark said.

Qilla turned and headed back, the others following.

"And this is Marisa, my mama, and Grampa Charley."

"Welcome," said Marisa. "You must be tired. Let's ride up to Freedom and we'll show you a place where you can stay."

The group headed up the hill. At the plaza, they stopped.

"This is where we get off," Marisa said, doing so. "The quines live over there in those trees."

The others dismounted and the quines and Beast trotted off. Roroy headed for his house.

"See you later." Grampa Charley headed for the big kitchen to look for something to eat. Snacking there was not unusual.

The rest followed Marisa as she led them to a small log cabin above Freedom. "You may stay here for a while. There are clothes, and food which is safe for you. A few things didn't agree with Sam when she was here. Are any others coming through soon?"

"I don't know." Bev looked around at the place. "I don't think so. Sam didn't say anything about anyone else."

"Very well. We'll keep a lookout." Marisa left, but the two couples stayed. Janni showed Bev the outhouse, how the bathroom worked, and how to work the food heater.

"What did you do on Starview?" Janni asked.

"I was a teacher," Bev said.

"That's one of my tasks." Janni said. "Mark?"

"I work in construction. I would like to see where you want us to build."

"I do too," Brian said. "We'll go up tomorrow."

"Let's let these people rest. Eat what you want, and tomorrow morning we'll be back," Janni said.

Like the others who had come through, Sam had taught them the language, noting that the letters were the same but pronounced differently.

•   •   •

The next morning, Janni found that Bev had arranged their few belongings and had drawn the yellow flowers by the front door in her sketchbook.

"That's nice," Janni said.

"Do you have colors? We only have a few. I'd like to do color drawings."

"Oh yes. We've found lots of plants and rocks we can get colors from. Come on, we're having first meal at Granlyn's." She led the way to a cabin with pink flowers on the porch posts.

"Welcome, Beverly and Mark," Granlyn said after they were introduced. "How do you like our little world?"

"It's wonderful," Bev said. "I love the beach. Do you go down there often?"

"I don't, but the young people do. Once every two weeks they have a beach day and anyone who wants to can go down for the afternoon."

"Where did you get these animals you ride?" Mark asked. "They're magnificent."

"They came through a Gate on Harmony, the world we lived on before we moved here to Peace. They helped us move here." Granlyn indicated her table. "Sit down. Janni, help me with the food."

Bev and Mark looked around the cabin. The pale tan walls held pictures of beaches and mountains, and shelves of items ranging from books to carved figurines to colorful pots. One door at the side led to what looked like a sleeping room, another at the back to a small room. Bev watched the two women barely fit into the miniscule kitchen at the rear.

"One bedroom?" Bev asked as Janni and Granlyn brought plates of a yellow mass and bread.

"Yes. That's all we need and all we can handle now," Granlyn said. There were five places set. "Larry, breakfast is ready," she called.

An old man hobbled out of the bedroom and sat in the chair at the end of the table.

"My mate, Larry. He prefers to be called Grampa Larry. Not great grampa." He grinned. "This is Mark and Beverly, from Sam's world."

Grampa leaned over and touched Bev's arm. "I guess they are real after all." He chuckled.

"Grampa," Janni exclaimed.

Granlyn sat and bowed her head. "Thank you, Oneness, for this good food, for letting us live another day, and for seeing these young people safely to us."

"We have Oneness," Bev said, puzzled. "How is it you do too?"

"Oneness is everyone and everything who has ever existed, now exists and will exist, everywhere in all the universes. So both of our peoples have found Oneness. We obey the golden rule, treat others as you would like to be treated, and the Oneness takes care of us."

"I see. Too many of our people don't seem to understand that."

"That is sad," Granlyn said.

Janni *sensed* her displeasure.

Granlyn talked about the clan and their community.

After the meal, Granlyn *called* Grampa Charley, and he took Mark and Brian up where the river turned west and showed them where the new colony would go.

"Janni, take Miss Beverly down and show her the plaza buildings." Granlyn settled in her chair. "Tell whoever's in the kitchen that there will be a meal on the plaza tonight. You and your family, including Perri and Charley, and whoever else wants to come. Tomorrow, she can go on up to her place."

At the plaza, Janni showed Beverly around. At the schoolhouse, they peeked in. Five-, six-, seven-year old children sat around a table counting stones.

"We don't have children that age." Bev said.

"Why not?" Janni was appalled. "What happened?"

Bev explained how birth control worked in City. "So unless we can find a way to turn it off, we won't have any more children until the younger girls get married."

"Oh, dear." Janni shook her head.

"That's one thing I wanted to ask you. I had mine done just before I left City, and I really want to have children. Is there anything you or your people can do?" She scuffed the toe of her footwear in the dirt.

The whole thing didn't make any sense. "You mean you can't control your eggs?" Janni asked.

Bev stared. "How would we do that?"

"Oh. I guess it's part of our Talents." Janni turned away. "Come on."

"Talents?"

"We have mental Talents that we can use to talk to each other in our heads and move things around without touching them. Don't worry, we have strict rules about going into anyone else's mind without their permission."

"Oh." Bev still looked puzzled.

At the medical clinic, Bev met Medic Anne, who was Janni's great-aunt. Janni told her about Bev's problem. Bev blushed.

"Was something put in your body to block your eggs, or was it something to keep them from ripening?" Medic Anne asked.

"I don't know."

"Tell me about the procedure. Did you have to undress? What did they actually do?"

"I went to the clinic, took my pants off and lay down. They put a screen over my upper body and head so I couldn't see or hear anything. The medics went away, and the room went dark. Something touched me down there, then the next thing I remember is waking up with one of the medics watching me. Some of us think the Volen came and did something to us. The medics just said they didn't know anything."

A boy cried behind curtains drawn around a bed in the rear.

Medic Anne glanced in that direction. "Look, I have a patient now. If you would like, I will check your body and see if there is anything we can do, Come back in the morning. I'll be free then, if no one else falls out of a tree."

"Okay."

They left as Medic Anne turned to her patient.

Janni wondered what else would happen this day.

31

PEACE

JOAN, GLORI'S GRANDMOTHER, met them as Janni and Bev approached the kitchen. Lean and twisted with arthritis, her wavy brown hair was pulled back and tied in a ribbon. She frowned at the girls.

"Who's this?" she demanded.

"Hi, Granny," Janni said. "This is Glori's grandmama. This is Beverly. She and her mate from Sam's world came through yesterday."

"Why? We have enough people."

"Grampa Larry doesn't think so. Is there anything you need done?"

"Stop bringing strangers here."

"I have to. Their world is dying. They won't live with us, but way up north past where the river turns west."

Joan snorted, and limped away.

Janni looked at Bev's face about to crumple. "It's too bad, but the older generations are like that. Don't worry, we younger people will help when you need it."

Bev nodded and took a breath. "It's just that I've never been treated like that. There are people like that in Starview, but not near where I live and work."

"One reason I think they're like that is because when Granlyn's generation came to Harmony, they came with people called Bramites who don't have Talent. When Gramma Perri's generation came along, it wasn't too bad, but Granlyn said even then the Bramites began to fear our Talents."

Bev nodded.

"When Mama came along, and she could see where people were hiding in hide and seek, the Bramites rose up and told us to leave. So we moved to another place on Harmony, but it was still too close. When Mama grew up and found the quines, she went off looking for other worlds to move to. She found Roroy and Beast. Beast may look scary, but he's a real sweetheart and getting old. Roroy's had him forever."

Janni paused as they walked across the plaza.

"Go on. This is fascinating."

"Well, Mama and Roroy found Peace, and we had to move everyone and everything through the Gates to get here. But Granlyn says the older people who remember the Bramites are afraid that any new people will want to take over and we'll have to move again."

Bev nodded. "Moving's not fun. I remember when we moved out of City. I was thirteen, and for my friends and me it was a huge adventure, but I know the adults were all upset over it. Miss Sam and her friends were real good at keeping things going. Of course, we had duties, mainly looking after the little ones to see that they didn't get into trouble."

"What exactly happened to your city?"

Janni sat on a wooden bench and Bev joined her. The Volen, who made it out of some special material, told Miss Sam and people from the other sectors that they could no longer look after our world, and the Volen material would gradually dissolve and disappear. The bottom layers went first so City kept sinking. We had to walk all the way across it and climb hills to get to the valley. Mark got put to work on construction, building apartment buildings, and I learned to be a teacher."

"Oh wow. And you had to carry all your stuff?"

"Yes. We didn't have much. Miss Sam's brother has an airship, and he flew up the heaviest stuff."

"An airship? How far does it fly?"

"It can fly from one sector to the next, and up to the spaceport."

Janni sat up. "You have a spaceport? Why didn't she tell me? Can you fly your people up there? We could get a ship there."

"Brad's ship is little. I think it only holds four, including the pilot."

"Can he fly to your port and get a ship for your people?"

"I don't know. I'd have to ask Miss Sam."

"Do it."

They ate lunch at Janni's. She gave Bev an ABC book, took her to her cabin, and went to the craft hall. She *sent* a message to Mindy in the big kitchen about supper on the plaza.

Janni sat down and reached for a quilt block. These two people were very pleasant and smart.

If they are all like that, it'll be nice to have them as neighbors. I need to let Sam know they came through okay.

At dinner, about half of the clan showed up, mostly the younger people, just curious about the new arrivals. Janni and her parents and grandparents kept the couple from being overwhelmed. A group of older women at another table glared at them until Marisa had Mark and Bev trade places with Janni and Willie so that the newcomers' backs were to the women. Janni traded glare for glare.

•   •   •

At dawn, Janni finds her being in space, even though it is too soon after the last time. First, she goes to Starview, connects with Maxee, and lets her know Bev and Mark are fine.

'Bev said you have a spaceport at your world.'

"Iss. Big ships there, not planet. Sam says smaller ships for rent, but we no have credits."

'Oh.' She locates a few other colonies, but no ships. Then she looks for the Otherness.

The Watcher tells her, 'good start.'

The Other finds her first. Something touches her being. She jerks and clamps down. Something burns. Janni squeezes and lets go. Thoughts swirl in her mind and even the stars disappear.

•　　•　　•

As she rose toward awareness, something held her back. Words in her mind. No, not words: impressions. Impressions of another people with a mind Talent similar to hers. Not human; not like her people.

Janni fought her way to awakening. As usual, she lay on her bed, in her house. She tried to sit up, but her body refused to move. She tried her right hand, then her left. Nothing. Dismay crept over her, turning to dread as her feet refused to move. Water sloshing in the bathroom told her Willie was still here.

'Willie,' she *sent.* 'Come here.'

"Just a minute," he called.

'Now!'

"All right, all right." The sloshing stopped and he appeared at the door, holding a dripping cloth. "You're awake. Get up."

'I can't. I can't even talk. I can't *reach* anyone but you. Get Mama.'

Willie stalked over to the bed, grabbed her hand, and tried to pull her up. "Geez, you weigh a ton."

'Get Mama, Gramma Perri, or someone. Now.'

"Why can't you get up?"

'I don't know, but I can't fix breakfast until someone helps me.'

"Okay."

Janni saw the puzzled look on his face and felt for him. He'd inherited his father's Talents, but his mother's brains. She always thought of her mother-in-law as poor Ruthie. She had never been very bright.

After a while, during which she kept trying to move, and the dread edged toward terror, Mama and Gramma Perri arrived.

"Were you out there?" Mama demanded.

Janni tried to nod, but could only blink.

"We need Anne," Gramma Perri said. They *called* the medic.

When Medic Anne came, she put her hand on Janni's head. "There's something in there. Help me."

The other two also placed their hands on the girl's head.

"Use your Talent too, Janni."

The girl felt them in her head, surrounding the Otherness. They couldn't get inside it, but she could and did. The Otherness

— or what it had put in her head — fled. Janni poked around in the remains and found the key to unlock her body. She stretched her fingers and her hands.

"I found it," Janni said.

"What on Peace was that?" Mama demanded.

"The Otherness." Janni sat up and leaned back to catch her breath. "They are way different from us, but they have a mind talent like ours."

"Oh, dear," Gramma Perri said.

"I need to think about this," Janni said. "I'm all right now."

"Are you sure?" Mama asked.

"She is, dear," Gramma Perri said. "Come on, let's leave her alone."

"I'm staying." Marisa moved to a chair.

Janni got to her feet. Still wobbly, the young woman tottered out to the outhouse.

When she returned, Gramma Perri was gone, but Mama crouched in a chair in the main room. Janni sat down hard on the couch. There'd been no pain, but her legs felt like they'd forgotten how to walk.

"Are you sure you're all right?" Marisa asked. "I don't like the way you were walking."

"Yes, Mama. I need to think."

Janni found the place where the Otherness had been in her mind, but there was nothing there, only a few bits and pieces she could not put together. She opened her eyes.

"Okay, Mama, everything's gone. I'm all right."

She toddled out to the kitchen and scraped together some food.

Marisa rose and hugged her daughter. "Are you sure?"

Janni nodded. Marisa left, but Janni sensed the link from her mother. Then she dressed and went to the schoolhouse, where the little ones were waiting.

During the day, a few bits about the Otherness drifted through her mind, but she was unable to capture them. She plunged back into her everyday life, but the Other continued to haunt her.

32

STARVIEW

RELIEF WASHED OVER SAM when she heard Bev and Mark had made it through okay. One less thing to worry about. Janni had said to send another couple through. Sam had trouble finding anyone who wanted to go, even after they heard Bev and Mark were okay.

More people were showing up from the west, wanting to be in Starview rather than Far West. Arlene's assistants tried to find places for them, but already some had to camp out. Sam had written up a sheet about the other world, Peace, the people who lived there and why they wanted us to come, and about the Gate and how it worked. The only benefit of going now she could list was getting a good location for their houses.

Sam took a break and took her paper down to a group who had come from the west. Most just said no; a few indicated she was nuts; and one couple who said they were interested. Dale worked in food prep and Jay in crop management. They asked her many questions.

"Yes, you will be able to return, but if you do, you will be put at the end of the list. You will have to learn to live with Marisa's people, mainly staying out of their way. Some of the older ones aren't happy with a new set of people coming onto their world."

"Do you really think this danger they mentioned is real?" Jay asked.

"Janni thinks it is, so I'm paying attention." Sam wasn't going to tell a stranger about her farseeing.

"We need to talk about this. Can we get back to you tomorrow?"

"Sure. Come to my office in the morning."

•　　•　　•

The next day, they agreed to go. Sam told them what to pack and take, and she would meet them in the morning at the base of the mesa.

"Two more," Sam said to Arlene after they left. "This is going to take forever."

"We do what we have to."

•　　•　　•

In the morning, Dale and Jay appeared with back bags and a small carry bag.

"Is that all you're taking?" Sam asked. "Do you have food for a week like I told you? Do you have all your important items, clothes, necessaries?"

They looked at each other.

"I thought ..." Dale began.

"Remember, it's an all-day trip to the Gate here, and two days from the Gate there to their colony. You'll need food for that. Also, they don't have unlimited supplies of food and other things. They insist that you bring at least a week's worth of food, and three or four days' worth of clothing. And your own period rags, Dale. And blankets." Sam began to walk toward the living area. "Where are you staying?"

They showed her. They didn't have many more belongings there, so Sam led them to the nearest caff where they collected more food. "What food they give you is safe for you to eat, but don't try to eat anything else growing there, no matter how good it looks." She told them the story of the boys and the berries.

"Big beautiful blue berries, but I tested them, and they were iffy, so I told people not to eat them. Well, two boys did and got very sick. Fortunately, they survived. Remember, it's a different world, and fruits and vegetables have different compositions. They may have elements that are poison to us or they may not have the nutrients we need. Dale, you will need to work with their food people to find out what we can and cannot eat."

"Okay. That makes sense. Oh, something I thought of last night. Will our birth control work over there?"

"I have no idea. Talk to Marisa over there and their medics. They might know."

They walked over to the river path, now dotted with orange leaves. Since Todd insisted someone go to accompany Sam home, her friend, Susan, met them there. Susan had been one of Brad's assistants back in City.

"How's your leg?" Sam asked as they tromped along the river side trail.

"Okay," Susan said. She'd broken it in a freak accident six months before, but she wasn't limping. "It's sure nice to get out here in the woods."

"Yes, isn't it. Do you need any help with settling people?"

"No. Actually, most of them are stopping on the other side of the hills. They're building more apartment buildings over there, but the biggest problem is food."

"Always food," Sam said. Susan was in charge of residency, seeing that everyone had a decent home.

At the bridge, Lucy from North Valley met them with more bad news. The grain fields that hadn't been drowned had been attacked by some kind of bug, killing the plants.

Sam groaned. *Not another problem.*

Lucy said she called Brad and he was going to bring someone to look at it.

"Good." For the first time, Sam felt thankful they had another world to escape to.

Lucy gave her a little envelope with one of the bugs in it.

Sam passed it to Jay. "Take this and ask Janni's people if they've seen anything like this. If they haven't, kill it." She grimaced. "Thanks, Lucy."

Lucy nodded and went back across the bridge. Sam and her group moved on. Sam and Susan had a lot of catching up to do. It had been a while since they'd seen each other.

When the group reached the cavern, Sam showed them how the Gate worked.

"You go on through. We'll camp here tonight."

The couple stepped into the room and pushed the button.

Sam and Susan looked at each other and left the cave.

"Nice kids," Susan said. "Hope they make it."

They found a place under the trees overlooking the river to camp. Susan had overseen the last groups out of City and had been there when Sam and her group had been buried in the landside as the last ones to leave City. They had become firm friends.

"You and Hal seem to be getting along," Susan said.

"Yes. He's just what I needed. After what my ex did, I could never have a normal relationship with a man. I still don't talk about it, or his return that got me into this mess."

"My Rob was a good man, but I was never really in love with him. I wasn't allowed to have children, I don't know why, they wouldn't tell you why you were turned down." Susan sighed.

"I heard that sometimes when they put in the birth control that they accidently set it to permanent, but the woman wouldn't find out until she went to get approval to have children."

"I heard that too. It doesn't matter now. What are we going to do about all the girls who had it put in before we left City and now there's no way to turn it off?"

Sam pushed her hair back. "I told Beverly to ask Marisa's medics if there was anything they could do. They can look inside their bodies, at least the younger ones can. Maybe they'll find a way."

"I hope so. We're already missing part of a generation."

•　　•　　•

The next day, they returned to Starview to find that two boys had fought over a loaf of bread, and both were in clinics with injuries. The mother was slim to the point of gauntness.

"I get them as much as I can, even some of my own meals, and still they're always hungry. I don't know what to do," she said. "They've always been quarrelsome. The older one always wants everything for himself, and the younger teases him."

"Where's their father?"

"Dead, in the Level One drop."

"I'm so sorry." Level One had been the lowest level in the above ground section of City.

"Everyone is. Everyone I deal with has lost someone."

"I know. I lost my husband." Sam didn't know why she said that. The woman shook her head.

•   •   •

The next day, Sam went around to the caffs and interviewed the bosses. She asked how they were dealing with the food, where did they get it, how did they decide how much each citizen got. They found a few things they could correct, making sure no food was wasted, but with the problem in the grain fields that meant less bread.

Later, Maxee told Sam Janni had sent through a big bunch of loovah plants and left them in the cavern. "Our people doing well. Gus and Mark marking where buildings go. Beverly sit in classes to see how they teach school."

Sam sent a couple of assistants to fetch the plants. They were good sized and had root sprouts. These were planted along with some of the big plants, and Sam tried to remember what was what. The roots, along with the local root plants, made a satisfactory, filling mash. The young leaves made a tasty addition to other vegetables, and the fruits were doled out carefully.

A few days later, a pair of medics came to her office and asked to go through. Zilla wanted them to study the Peace procedures to see what was different and what was the same.

"Fine," Sam said.

The next day Brad took them up to the Gate and sent them through.

It was beginning.

I wonder how they all are doing over there.

Sam still had no idea what the menace was. "I need to know so I can prepare for it," she said aloud. There was no answer.

33

PEACE

JANNI WELCOMED THE NEWCOMERS, but her elders were not as appreciative. Grampa Charley brought Janni's family together for a meeting at his house. Gramma Perri had covered her couch and chairs in a dark green fabric to go with the pale green walls.

"Now that Sam's people are beginning to come through regularly, we need to set up some processes," Grampa Charley said. "We can't have people running down to the camp every day. We need to set up signs and markers to show them where to go, and they'll have to walk. We can't wear out the quines."

"But Grampa ..." Janni began.

"If their people who are already here want to meet them, on foot, that's fine. But we can't afford to have so much time taken away from vital work. I know you want to meet them all, Janni, but that's just not possible."

Gramma Perri nodded. She picked up a spork left on the table and took it to the kitchen.

"The first few days we'll let them get oriented and show them what they can and cannot eat and do. Then they must move on up to their area. We'll help with food at first. Some of the fellows planted a patch of loovah up their way, so they'll have that until their own crops get started." Grampa Charlie crossed his legs.

"We need to have someone show them how to use the loovah plant," Mama said.

"Right."

"And set up their own water wheel," Papa added.

A knock on the door and Grampa Chad III stomped in. "What's this I hear about new people coming to build here?" he demanded. His shaggy beard and hair belied a fresh tunic and pants.

"Where have you been?" Grampa Charley asked. "These are humans Janni found on another world that she is bringing here."

"Why?" Grampa Chad put his hands on his hips.

"Their world is dying, we need more people, and we humans should stick together," Janni said.

"I found my son and a couple others up there helping them build. Is that going to be the new normal?"

"Only until they get more people over here." Grampa Charley grinned.

"How many?" Grampa Chad demanded.

"I don't know. Janni?"

She shrugged. "Brad said twenty thousand, but I don't expect all of them will come, from what Sam said."

"And who is this Sam?"

"She's the mayor of Starview, her community, and Brad is her twin brother. Sam came for a visit a while back."

"They have a ship?" Grampa Chad let his hands drop.

"No. I brought her."

"You're getting too big for your britches, girl."

Marisa stood up. "Don't you talk to my daughter like that. She's a bonded woman."

"All right, all right." Grampa Chad looked around at everyone. Grampa Charley stared at him.

"I was over in the forest with Uncle Bay checking out various trees. Okay?"

"Fine. What did you find?" Grampa Charley asked.

"Sit down," Gramma Perri said.

Grampa Chad relaxed and sat. "North, about where the big river turns, we found some hard wood trees that don't grow down here. I brought a branch back to have Papa check it to see if it would be useful."

"Good." Grampa Charley nodded. "Since you're here, do you have any ideas for getting these people through Freedom into homes up north? Any way to build faster?"

"Make a checkpoint and list anyone who goes through, like we do with our materials."

"Yes," Janni bounced in her seat. "We will need a list of all of them, names, who's mated to whom, what they are best at doing, age, and so forth."

"Good idea." Gramma Perri returned and sat at the table. "Go ahead and set it up."

"Me?" Janni's eyes widened.

"You suggested it." Gramma Perri smiled. "I'll help you."

Janni sat back.

I should have kept my big mouth shut. Around here, if you suggest something new, you get to set it up.

"It's not going to be fun, Janni," Grampa Chad said. "The adults will most likely behave, but we'll have to watch for children sneaking down here. Or ours up there. Remember what happened with my Jimmy."

Janni knew the story. Old Medic Maria and Chad Junior and their children, including Chad III and Joan, and their children, had lived up at North Point on Harmony. Eight-year-old Jimmy had got into mischief and annoyed the Bramites, who locked him up and told the Terrans to get out. Old Art had gone up there and rescued them.

"We don't want that happening here." Grampa Charley said. "We will have to let them know of our Talents, and make sure none of us uses them against Sam's people."

"I think it's time we have a general meeting and let everyone know what's going on," Gramma Perri said.

"If there's no way to stop it," Grampa Charley said. "Is there?"

"No. They know about the Gate."

"It can be closed."

"I know. But they can't grow good food on their world. Everyone I saw there was so thin. I sent them some loovah plants. We can't just leave them there to die." Janni shook her fist.

"True." Gramma Perri sighed. "Along with this Talent, we have the responsibility to use it to help others. How soon do you think more will be coming through?"

"I don't know. Sam said no one was thrilled about it. Bev and Mark want to go back for a little while. He said something about tools. Maybe if they tell them good things, especially if Bev can get pregnant, more will want to come. I guess, expect a few at a time, but plan for more." Janni shrugged.

"All right," Gramma Perri said.

"I agree about the meeting," Grampa Charley added. "Perri, will you ask your mama to call one?"

"Certainly." Gramma Perri smiled at him.

Grampa Chad rose, said, "See you around," and left.

"Well," Marisa said. "Now look what you've gotten us into."

"Mama." Janni doubled her fists.

"It's all right, honey. You did what you felt you had to do. This Talent business is overwhelming at times. I thought Arisam from the parallel world said it wouldn't go past what I have, but obviously she was wrong."

The parallel world had tried to take over Peace when Janni was a new baby, and Marisa had saved her clan.

"That was when you all rode up and pushed the mist," Janni dared. Her grandmother had told her about it briefly, but Mama would never talk about it.

"Yes," Marisa sat on the couch next to Janni. "You were a tiny baby in a snuggy on my chest. Your tiny Talent helped, yours and Glori's, with Susan. All you babies were very good, no fussing or crying. You two, Ruthie's boys who were older, and Dottie's Richard."

"And Granlyn's twins, although they don't have much Talent beyond the mind. Willie doesn't remember anything about it."

"He was almost three, he should have some kind of memory. Anyway, the mist disappeared, the worlds separated, and we all collapsed, even the quines. Your Qilla was there, just getting used to her legs."

"She remembers a mass of quines and people and waking up to her mama nuzzling her."

"Yes, we had to stay there two nights and a day before the young quines were able to go back." Marisa twiddled her fingers. "It was rather a letdown, going home."

"I imagine."

Marisa rose. "I need to get home and you, Janni, need to go home to Willie." She kissed her mother on the cheek. "Bye, Mama, Papa." The two left.

At home, Janni told Willie there was going to be a general meeting.

"When?"

"When Granlyn sets it up."

Willie took her in a hug and began kissing her in various places. "Oh, Willie."

They adjourned to the bedroom. Janni forgot about other people.

34

STARVIEW

SAM WAS GOING OVER A LIST of names and supplies with Arlene when Maxee trotted into her office.

"Sammie, two come through Gate."

Sam looked up. "Who? Can you tell?"

"Not Janni."

Oh, great. Are they starting to come here? Sam pushed her hair back. "Okay, thanks. Arlene, who have we got who can go up and meet them?"

"Let's see. There's Phil, he needs a change, he's driving everyone crazy. And Sylvia. She'll go anywhere he does. The way is well enough marked, isn't it?"

"I think so. Brad put up a sign at the path to the cavern, and the trail's pretty obvious."

Arlene rose. "I'll go find them. Be right back."

There's no way everybody is going to get everything they want.

Sam sighed as she stared at the papers. She desperately wanted to go, but knew she couldn't take any more time off.

A little later, Arlene reappeared. "They are on the way. Now where were we?"

•   •   •

The next afternoon Phil and Sylvia returned with Beverly and Mark.

"Hi," Bev said as they entered Sam's office. "We're back,"

"Temporarily," Mark added.

Sam smiled. "So how was it?"

"Great. Janni, her mom and her friends are really nice, and they have everything so well-organized. And their food. They have this plant that grows everywhere, and you can use all of it. They gave us some to plant up in our crop field.

"Loovah," Sam said. Arlene's brows rose.

"Yes, that's it. Janni also gave me some to bring here."

"Good." *Now we have to teach people here how to use it.*

"And the best part is, their head medic, Anne, looked at me and did something so I might be able to have a baby." Bev grinned, matched by Mark.

"Great." Sam grinned back.

"We came back to tell people about that place, and to get some tools and things to take back," Mark said. "We got to ride the quines to the Gate. That was wild."

"They kept splashing in the water. Janni said it felt good on their feet. Did you see them when you were there?" Bev asked.

"Yes. They are beautiful creatures, aren't they?"

"People, not creatures," Bev said. "But it was scary at first, up on her back. The females have female riders and vice versa."

"Okay, you two go rest. Eat with us, and after late meal we will have a meeting of however many I can get to come, in the meeting hall."

They nodded and left.

Phil asked, "When can we go?"

"Not for a while yet. We need you here for now," Arlene told them. "Now what were you doing?"

"Okay." Phil rolled his eyes and he and Sylvia left.

Sam sent as many people as she could find to spread the work about the meeting.

•   •   •

At late meal, Bev and Mark sat with Sam and her group and told them all about Peace and their people, human and quines.

"Did you meet Beast?" Mark asked Sam.

"Oh, yes. I jumped two feet back. But Roroy said he's just a big sweetheart."

"Beast?" Todd asked.

"I told you, he's big and black and furry. Four legs; his head as tall as mine."

"Native?" Hal asked.

"No, he and Roroy came from another world that Marisa found." Sam took a bite of stew. "His mate came from a later Earth."

"I go see Beast and quines," Maxee demanded.

"Not yet," Sam said.

So far, the Gate had worked fine, but she was still a little leery about it, as was Todd. Brad wanted to go for a few days just to see it and was working on finding the time. Hal said he'd go when Sam did.

After they finished eating and bussed their dishes, Sam led them to the meeting hall. A few people were already sitting there in rear seats.

Arlene excused herself for a few minutes. "I'll be right back."

More people followed them in. Sam and Brad lit the vegetable oil lamps and settled on the dais. The sweetish smell of the oil mixed with the odor of people at the end of the workday.

When the trickle stopped, the room was almost full. Sam waited for a few more minutes, then stood.

"Welcome, citizens. Some of you may have already heard about the visitor from another world, and the possibility of us moving there. Here's what it's all about. That world is wide open. It has a very large river not likely to flood, all the space we could possibly use, and a beach. The gravity is lighter, meaning it will be easier to walk up the slope. And there is a moon, a rock in the sky that reflects light at night. Each family will have their own house."

Sam took a breath. "Why we would want to leave here. First, we all know about the shortage of food. That will not improve in the foreseeable future. We can't use part of our valley because the river floods." She looked at Brad.

He stood. "The nutrients in the soil here are being used up, so the food grown in it isn't as nutritious. We have too many people and too little space for crops to leave sections unused to regenerate. Sam says the world of Peace has much more room for both our houses and our crops. I think we should seriously consider moving there as long as the people there will allow us." He sat.

"Thank you, Brad. Moving itself means carrying our belongings up the river trail to the Gate, passing through the Gate, and walking two days to their settlement, called Freedom. If we're lucky, we may meet someone with quines so we can ride part of the way. Quines are large, brown, four-legged people who allow us two-legs to ride them, when they feel like it, which is most of the time. Our new colony will be north of their place. There are trees along the river and a forest well to the east. Todd?"

Todd rose. "From what Sam says, there is plenty of room for our homes, so we can lay out the town in an orderly manner, and everyone will own his own home. We can have more community buildings, with more space between them. And we can have a large plaza, a gathering place among the buildings."

He sat and Hal stood. "We would need to be careful dealing with their people. Their older people had trouble with another race that lived with them for a while and are wary of us coming into their world. Also, they are able to communicate in their minds and levitate people and objects. Plus, they are our hosts. We need to be polite and helpful when dealing with them. We can set up a complaint bureau where you can bring any problems you have in dealing with them, and Sam or Brad can then speak to their leaders."

Emily, Brad's wife, rose from a front row seat. "We would have to train our children to behave around the other group. Especially the older ones." Her oldest was nine. Her birth control had not functioned, so her children were some of the few under age ten.

"Very good," Sam said. "I wouldn't have thought of that. Bev, you have something to share?"

"Yes." Bev got up from her seat next to Emily and turned to face the audience. "For all of you gals who want children, but are stuck with permanent birth control, the people on Peace may have a solution." A buzz ran through the crowd. "I've had the procedure done; I'm just waiting to see if it works."

A thought flitted through Sam's mind, *But, no, I'm too old.* "Any questions?" she asked.

"How much can we take?" a fellow asked.

"As much as you can carry. It's uphill here, level over there."

"When can we go?" a breathless young woman asked.

"We'll start making a list and a schedule. I'll have someone make copies of my list of what to take and wear. You will need to take enough food for at least five days."

"Are they like us?" a young man asked.

"Yes, they are human like us. Many of the young people are taller than we are, because their world is lighter. Most of them have dark, curly hair."

Sam answered several more questions and dismissed the meeting.

A group of young women lined up in front of her. She started a list of those who wanted to go to Peace.

What have we got ourselves into?

Sam dropped the list off in her office and headed for home.

35

STARVIEW

THE NEXT MORNING, while Sam worked on a schedule, a young woman knocked and peered in. "Miss Sam, Medic Evelyn would like for you to come over to her clinic when you have a moment."

Sam smiled. "Tell her about a half hour."

"Okay." The girl darted off.

Now what?

When Sam entered Evelyn's clinic, the woman at the desk in the waiting area, a long narrow room with a brown bench along the wall, said, "Go on in."

Sam passed through the doorway to the clinic proper and to Evelyn's office just to the right. Her daughter, Jan, sat in her wheeled chair in the main room as there was not enough room for it in her mother's tiny office.

"Hi," Jan said.

"Hi, how are you doing?"

"I'm living here now. Too hard to manage this," she patted the big wheel at her side, "on those muddy paths."

Evelyn came out of her tiny office, patting her gray hair. "Glad to see you came. First of all, it's past time for your physical."

Sam groaned. "I don't have time ..."

"How much time do you have to be sick or worse? Come along."

Impatiently, Sam followed her to an examining area and sat on the chair by the little table. Jan followed, rolling her chair. Besides the table, there were three beds that could be curtained off. Sam couldn't describe the aroma except that it was common to medical clinics.

"Blood pressure first," Evelyn directed.

Jan pulled up beside Sam and said, "Put your hand out."

Sam laid her hand and arm on the table. Jan put her forefinger on Sam's pulse, shut her eye and counted. Sam watched her lips move.

"A little high, but not bad."

Evelyn nodded.

Jan took out a disk with a dial and two reeds attached. She stuck the ends of the reeds in her ears. She wrapped a band around Sam's upper arm, pulled it tight, and inserted a twisting stick. She placed the disk inside Sam's elbow just above the crease and connected a tube between them. Jan twisted the stick until Sam could no longer feel her pulse. Slowly, she loosened the band until the needle started moving, and when it stopped, she stopped.

"One forty-five over ninety," Jan said. "A little high."

"Too high," Evelyn said. "You need to slow down. Get more help if you have to."

"I can't," Sam said. "There's so much to do and everyone else is so busy. And with this move ..."

"Yes. I've been thinking about that." Evelyn frowned. "How are we going to get Jan up to the Gate? I hear it's a rough trail."

"Oh." That had not occurred to Sam. "Carried, I guess. Except there are a few places where there's barely room for two abreast. I'll have to think about it."

"Is there anywhere up there Brad could land his ship?" Jan asked.

"Not now, but maybe we can make one. I'll ask Brad how much room he needs."

"Okay. Jan, check her breathing."

Sam moved to a stool and Jan listened to her back with the cup.

"Sounds fine."

"Good. Any shortness of breath?" Evelyn asked.

"Only after I run up the mesa trail."

"Well, if you must. But try not to. Any pains or spots?"

"Only the usual aches after a long day. Are you training Jan to be a medic?"

"Yes. Not too many people are interested in doing it anymore. I don't know why."

"Is there a shortage?" Sam asked. *Another problem?*

"A few clinics only have one. We're all supposed to have at least two fully trained medics; one with at least three years' experience. One head of clinic told me she didn't see why, since they sit around with nothing to do half the time."

"But the other half ..."

"Right. Troubles seem to come in bunches. Well, you appear to be healthy, just see what you can do to keep your stress level down. I want to see you in two weeks."

"Evelyn ..."

"Come on, Sam, we need you healthy. What do you think would happen if you got really sick and had to watch others take over?"

Sam closed her eyes. "I don't want to think about it."

"Right."

"Okay, medic." Sam rose and left.

•　　　•　　　•

After the people at the meeting signed up, there was a lull. Brad flew Hal and a male assistant to Far West, and Hal and Ken would walk back to spread the word about the new world. He carried copies of information about it and what to take and where to go.

The second day, he called Sam. "Far West said no thanks, and other leaders were skeptical. One female leader said, 'We've been pushed out of City, pushed out of where we settled so many times, we're not going to be pushed anymore. We're making it just fine right here.'"

"I told her it was her decision and asked if her people agreed. 'Of course, they do.' I shrugged and walked away."

Sam asked, "How are we going to get through to those people?"

"We're not," Hal said. "If they want to stay here, let them. The only way to get them out is knock them out and carry them, and I'm not going to do that."

"But they could all die,"

"So, let them. We've dealt with this before. You have to realize, there is no way to save everyone, no matter how much you want to."

Sam knew he was right, but it still hurt her to think of all the people she'd let die in City because she couldn't get them all out, even though she knew it was physically impossible.

Meanwhile, Brad had taken two couples up and brought back a box he'd found in the Gate room.

"What's in it?" Sam asked.

"Don't know. Haven't opened it. Had your name on it."

Sam opened the long, narrow box made of woven reeds and found a copy of the ABC book and a bundle wrapped in loovah leaves. It held plants, loovah and others, with directions for planting. Also, there was a letter.

'Sam, you need to tell your people to follow the signs and ask the person at the bridge for directions, so they get counted. Tell them to stay out of our community. If they follow the way up to your place, there'll be no problems. Tell them, if problems, go to Glenda and she will tell me or Mama. And bring lots of food. Janni'

The next day, a whole line of people wanted to go to Peace.

Sam and Arlene set up a class that everyone who wanted to go through was required to take. The instructor gave explicit directions on what to take, what to do, how to act, and, most of all, what not to do. Then, when a person's day came to go through, Sam, Brad, or Arlene would test them to make sure they remembered their instructions, had everything they needed, and how to work the Gate.

"Remember, we are guests on another people's world. Treat them with respect and follow their wishes," one of the three would say.

At first, a couple would take people up to the Gate and usher them through. Soon, with people going every day, they were sent up alone. The trail and Gate cavern were clearly marked. Too many were going for other people to take two days off to escort them.

One day Sam awoke to see that at least part of the coming menace would happen on Peace. And that all her people needed to be there to survive.

"Oh, my Oneness," she said aloud.
Now they would have to make their warnings much stronger.
She shivered. She felt like the world was closing in around her.

36

PEACE

Janni, Glori, and Brian made and set up signs. At the bridge over the little river, there would be someone who would take Sam's people's information and tell them what to do next. Back home, Janni and Glori collapsed on Janni's blue couch.

"This is getting to be too much," Janni said.

Glori crossed her ankles. "I know, but we do what we have to. We certainly don't want them running around in our place."

"So true."

"And now we have to fix supper." Glori sighed. "Always something else to do."

"Yeah, I know."

Willie and Brian arrived. "Where's supper?" Willie demanded. Brian echoed him.

The two young women looked at each other and *sent* a private message to the other. 'Men.'

•　　　•　　　•

In the beginning of dawn, Janni's being is out in space again. She finds the Otherness. She shields her Talent and only uses a fine stream to search. She finds something that appears to be a ship, but not a long smooth cylinder. Although longer in one direction, there are many odd pieces stuck on it, no real definable shape. There are sentient beings in it.

Janni touches one as lightly as she can. She perceives a jerk and withdrawal.

'No,' comes the Watcher voice.

Janni ignores it and tries again.

This time, she captures something that feels threatening. She backs off. The bubbles of time sparkle around her. Then the connection to her body is broken.

Lights fade. She is lost. She is ... not.

•　　　•　　　•

Back on Peace, her body slept. After a time much too long, Marisa came to see why her daughter was not at her tasks. She went into Janni's mind, only to find nothing there. Marisa panicked and *called* Medic Anne and Gramma Perri.

"No," she screamed as Medic Anne stumped in the front door.

"What is it?" Medic Anne asked, trotting into Janni's room.

Marisa could only sob and point at her daughter's head.

Medic Anne tried to *enter* Janni's mind and gasped. "Her mind's gone."

"What?" said Gramma Perri, arriving. She gathered Marisa into her arms and rocked her.

"Janni's mind is gone," Medic Anne said shakily, automatically checking her pulse. "It didn't come back from out there."

"I knew it," Grampa Charley said, stomping in, followed by several others who had heard Marisa's scream in their minds.

Allen, Mick, and Steve ran in.

"Where's Janni?" Steve asked, looking scared.

Allen went to Marisa and gently took her from her mother.

"We'll find her, love," he murmured.

Glori arrived, terror and grim determination on her face. "Let me look." She went to Janni and placed her hands on the girl's head. She closed her eyes and *searched.* "There are traces," she murmured, dropped to kneel by the bed, and leaned her head against Janni's. The others *went in* with her.

The traces led her to space and the thing that held Janni's mind. Glori pulled and the others with her. Suddenly they all dropped to the floor. Glori sat up and shook her head, then looked up at the bed.

"She's back," she exclaimed.

They all hauled themselves to their feet, and Marisa turned to her daughter.

"Oh, she is." She began to weep, as did Gramma Perri.

Allen gathered them both into his arms, hiding his face in his mate's hair. Mick and Steve hugged everyone. The others dropped into chairs, in Janni's room and in the main room.

No one left, all waiting for Janni to wake.

•　　　•　　　•

Janni drifted slowly through layers of consciousness. There was something wrong in her mind. As she became aware of her surroundings, she tucked the wrongness in a private spot in the back of her mind.

When she opened her eyes, she saw several people-shapes in her room and sensed more in the other room.

"Mama?" Janni whispered, as the people-shapes resolved into her friends and relations.

"Janni, you're back," Marisa cried, and hugged her. She'd been sitting next to the bed.

"Why ..." Janni could go no further.

"You lost your mind," Glori said, grinning, "We got it back for you." She *sent* Janni a picture of herself putting a brain back into an empty skull, on their private link.

Janni tried to comprehend what had happened. Her mama propped her up and she looked around. There was Papa and her grandparents, Glori, Medic Anne. Others stuck their heads in the doors.

The front door banged, and Willie ran in.

"Janni," he yelled. Allen caught him as he rushed to her bed.

"Calm down. She's okay. Just took her longer to come back this time."

Janni smiled at Willie and reached out a hand. He grabbed it. His face went through a series of contortions from fear to puzzlement to relief. Now she had something to hang on to. Marisa moved away so he could sit beside her.

Papa Allen went to the other room and spoke. Janni heard the front door open and close as people left.

Medic Anne checked her once more and departed. "Keep an eye on her," she told Marisa.

"I better be going back to my sewing," Glori said. She *sent* Janni an image of a gold star in a field of silver stars.

"Thanks," Janni whispered. Although she felt fully awake, her mind still didn't feel right. Too many things she couldn't pin down. Fuzzy around the edges. "I'm all right," she said loudly, but it came out not much better than a whisper.

Willie kissed her. "You will be home tonight, won't you?" he asked.

"I hope so."

"We'll see," Gramma Perri said. "You go on, Charley, I know you've lots of things to do. I'll see you tonight."

Grampa Charley nodded, patted Janni's shoulder, and left.

"Marisa, you need to get to your classes," Gramma Perri said. "I'll stay here with her until you get back."

After a while, Janni sat up and swung her legs over the side of the bed. At least her body worked. "Outhouse," she said.

Gramma helped her to her feet and walked with her to the shed.

Back in the house, Janni collapsed on the couch. She sat back and breathed. This room was fuzzy too. It wasn't her eyes; when she looked directly at something, she saw it clearly. Gramma Perri sat in the big chair. Mama had already left for the schoolhouse.

"Well, Janni, do you want to talk about what happened?" Gramma asked.

Janni shook her head. Her mind was still too muddled.

Granlyn stumped in the door and demanded, "What happened?"

"I don't know," Janni said.

"Something took her mind out there and we all had to pull it back," Gramma Perri said, "Her body was here, heart beating and breathing, but there was nothing in her mind. Poor Marisa had hysterics. She's okay now that Janni's back. She went to her class."

"Do you feel any different?" Granlyn asked.

"My mind. I can't think."

'Can you hear this?' Granlyn *sent.*

"I felt something, not words."

Granlyn sat back. "Had any of you tried to *reach* her?"

"I heard Glori." A memory fluttered back into Janni's mind.

"Glori, of course." Granlyn said. "Marisa told me how you two linked right after you were born. The only time we needed two birthing chairs at the same time."

"What am I going to do, Granlyn?" Janni asked.

The old woman held up her hand. "Perri, you try."

"It almost sounds like words," Janni said. She *sent* 'Hello' to both of them.

"I heard you," Gramma Perri said with a half-smile. She looked at her mother.

Granlyn shook her head. "A faint noise. How are you feeling, Janni? Up to doing your tasks?"

Janni raised her right hand and watched it tremble. "No, I don't think I'd be very good at sewing today."

"Okay, you take the day off and relax." Granlyn got to her feet. "Perri, you stay with her until Marisa or Willie comes back." She rose and trudged out the door.

"Willie," Janni said. "His breakfast ..."

"Marisa fed him." Gramma Perri pulled some mending out of her bag.

Janni tried to contact Glori in her mind and got nothing. She lay back on the couch and tried to figure out what was going on. She wasn't able to feel much of any emotion; only a little fear and concern. Her memories were still there. Her life and Sam's world. People coming through — well someone else would have to deal with that.

She could still remember how to do things, like cooking and sewing. She wasn't sure about teaching. Her knowledge of her world was still there. The thing in her mind didn't want to let her think about space.

After a while, Janni rose, picked up Willie's clothes, and put them away.

"Feeling better?" Gramma Perri asked.

"Yes. I can do stuff like this. Maybe I can do some laundry."

Willie came home for lunch and gave her a big hug. "You okay now?" he asked.

"Pretty much."

• • •

That night, Janni lay next to Willie, after he had been satisfied and was snoring, and probed at the thing in her mind. She found an image of a being. It had a long body, two short legs, four arms, two from the top corners of the body and two smaller ones in front. And no head. The top of the body had a slight convex curve to it. Several markings just below it she took to be sense organs. She shivered.

What kind of people were they?

She wished she didn't have to find out.

What did they want?

They wanted to be the next Watchers.

Well, they can have it, Janni said to herself. *If I could just get the Watcher-voice to stop my talent and let them have it.*

She tried to sleep but dreamed of those weird creatures. She ran and hid from them, heard them talking, saying they were the only ones who would become Watchers. The only way to stop this other puny race was to obliterate them. In the dream, Janni tries to reach her mother and the others, but could not. Her Talent was gone.

Janni woke up gasping. Willie stirred, but didn't wake. He rolled over away from her. She *reached out.* Yes, her talent was still there. *So it was just a dream. Or was it?*

She could not get back to sleep, and, when she did get up, she decided not to tell anyone about it. They would all say it was just a dream. She knew it wasn't but didn't know how to deal with it. She also couldn't deal with getting rid of Talent; she needed hers too much.

• • •

Between her tasks and dealing with Sam's people, Janni had little time to think. She tended to her body automatically, hunger and full bladders do make themselves known. Every night, after she took care of Willie's needs, Janni wondered whether she would return to space next dawn.

Let others handle the mess. It would only become worse.

37

PEACE

JANNI WOULD WAKE TO WILLIE'S STRONG ARMS and forget for a while. In her class of little children, she wondered where the Sam's world's children were.

Were Sam's people still hesitant about the Gate? Or were they coming later?

Mama and Gramma Perri both gave her orders. "Janni, I need you to go get ... Janni, Anne needs you at the clinic, Janni, you need to oversee the girls sewing tunics."

In spare moments, between tasks, she checked on newcomers. At least they allowed her a few minutes to sit down and eat a bit of bread and fruit.

One night, Janni prayed. "Oneness, please send me out so I can rest."

Oneness, everyone who has ever lived, is living, and will live; every living thing, flora and fauna, rock and mountain and sea in all the universes.

•   •   •

Janni's being drifts in space. The Otherness is still there, in a different place, but no closer. She makes a note of the location; when she returns to her body and brain, she will check the locations. One world that had a small colony has been wiped out. In her body, she would feel furious and sad, but here, she only perceives the damage and cannot feel.

'You do well,' the Watcher-voice says.

'I'd do better if I knew my people weren't going to become Watchers. The Other want it; give it to them.'

'They are not ready.'

'Neither are we. Some of them want to kill all us humans so they can be Watchers.'

'Yes.' The voice is gone.

Janni goes to Sam's world and watches a stream of people laden with bags trudge up the mountain trail to the Gate. There are still many in the valleys below. She searches and finds Maxee.

'Hi. This is Janni. Please tell Sam to make sure her people understand the rules and that they must follow them. Too many are not. Test them. If they do not heed, do not let them come. We do not like what they are doing to our world.'

'Okee.'

Janni returns to her body and sleeps.

• • •

When Janni woke, Willie was stirring. He reached for her. Their mental link turned on automatically and she was only aware of him. Afterward, she went through the motions of fixing breakfast, and they ate. Only when he left for the crop fields did the link break.

Janni shook her head and prepared for the day. Mama *called* her to tell her to meet her at the plaza.

Now what? she thought. *I seem to be thinking that a lot.*

"You were out," she said as they met at the long tables.

Janni blinked. She'd never shown any signs of knowing this before. "How do you know?"

"I set up a checker in my mind to touch yours every morning at dawn. It woke me to let me know you were out. I've been calling, but you were with Willie and not receiving. What did you find?"

"Another wiped-out world. Left a message on Sam's world about making sure her people know what to do when they get here."

"Good. Artie is taking a pair of troublemakers to the Gate and sending them back. Now go work on your quilt squares."

"Yes, Mama."

When was I going to be able to make my own schedule? When was I going to be able to do what I needed to on my own? When was I going to be able to live my own life?

38

STARVIEW

S AM WAS HALFWAY HOME on her midday break when she ran into Maxee.

"Sammie, Janni not happy with our people. They not following rules, they in clanhome."

"Oh, shit," Sam muttered. "Thank you for telling me."

When she returned to her office, she told Arlene about it. "I'll call Lucy to stop the ones going up there and send someone up to retest them."

"I'll send Carolyn. She's good. I'll have her tell the groups she passes to return to the mesa." She tapped her comm.

"Okay. I guess I'll have to go out and re-educate them." Sam looked at Arlene. "Anything I really need to know about right now?"

"Nothing that can't wait a half hour. Go ahead and go."

Sam went down to the northeast corner of the mesa, where the town path split off from the river trail. Carolyn strode down the trail away from her and caught up with a group just leaving. Sam watched her talk to them, and they turned and came back.

"Hello," Sam said as they reached her. "Sorry for the delay, but they've been having problems over there. I need to recheck people." She ran down the list and they agreed. "Now, remember, stick to the pathways and go straight up to our place. There'll be signs and people to show you the way."

"Okay," said one young man.

"Can we go now?" asked a dark-haired girl.

"Yes." They took off, mumbling.

Sam didn't see any more coming and stepped over to the edge of the river. Frustrated and annoyed, she stared down at the river. It looked tired, too, just creeping along.

I'll try to hang on until I get everyone over there, but that's it. Someone else will have to be mayor over there.

She returned to the trail and waited for another group.

On her way back to her office, Sam ran into Brad.

"What's up?" he asked.

"Another message from Peace that our people are getting into trouble. We had the ones before the bridge return, and I had to go over everything with them again."

"Oh, crud. I guess I'll have to go around and make sure the instructors are doing their job." He began walking toward her office. "Also, I'm thinking of going over there."

"No," Sam cried. "You can't."

"Sammie, I'll be all right. Quite a few people have gone through. I'll have to go sometime, and so will you. We need someone in authority over there. Do you want to go?"

"Yes, but I can't." She clenched her fists, stopped and turned to him. "I need you here."

He took her hand. "We've been apart before. Don't worry, sis, I'll be fine. Time to get back to work." He squeezed her hand and trotted back down the trail.

Sam returned to her office battling fear. Why does Brad's going through the Gate scare me so? She couldn't bear to think of them being a world apart. Of course, they had been when he was in the Space Service, but that was different. She knew where he was and that he'd come home. The Gate still spooked her.

"You may be all right, but I won't be," she muttered as she approached the hall.

Sam had just settled at her table when Maxee trotted in and announced, "I go through with kubs."

"No," Sam yelped.

Maxee jumped and backed away.

"I'm sorry, but Brad just told me he wants to go." She stretched out her hand to her alien sister and Maxee took it. "I didn't mean to yell at you. I need you here. Don't worry, you'll get your turn."

Maxee stared at her with an unfathomable gaze. "Okee." She trotted out.

"Oh, my." Sam put her head in her hands. "Oneness, help me."

A young woman wearing a long bib tapped on the open doorway. "Excuse me, Miss Sam, but Medic Evelyn wants to see you in her clinic."

"Has it been two weeks?" The woman had left.

Sam heaved herself up out of her chair, left a note for Arlene, and went to Evelyn's clinic.

The medic had Jan take her blood pressure, and asked, "Have you figured out how we are going to get Jan up to the Gate?"

"Brad and Hal are working on an idea for it. I'll let you know when I know."

"Okay. Your blood pressure is down a little, but not enough."

Sam shrugged and left.

•   •   •

The next morning, Sam was shaken awake.

Earthquake.

She sat up as the shaking stopped. If she could feel it here, what was it like in Ambaak? Hurriedly dressing, she ran out and found others wandering around. She went to Maxee's house.

"We okee," Maxee said. "Kubs scared." She had her furry arms around them, all huddled on the big seat. "You okee?"

"Yes. Just a little shook up."

"I go now, iss," Maxee demanded. "No more shakes." She bounced Deki under her chin.

"No one's going right now. We have to see what the damage is."

"Okee. Soon." She wrinkled her nose.

"Next group, I promise."

Sam hoped she could keep that promise. She found there was little damage in Starview and North Valley, more in western valleys.

Sam called Liia, her Ambaak contact.

"We're in your Midwest," Liia said. "Many buildings down. Not built well. My people ..." she gulped. "Many with me. Many behind. Some of your people help, some not. We all are moving east. Where is future?"

"I don't know." Sam pushed her hair back. "We're sending as many through to the other world as possible, but we had to stop because some were making trouble over there. But you keep coming."

"I will." Liia sighed.

Sam and Todd went down to the valley. Minor damage, a few things broken. More people clamoring to go. Sam added them to her list and told them about the wait.

"You need to go to the classes to learn the rules and what you need to take. You will be notified when it's your turn."

Sam amended her list to let Maxee and her kubs go in a couple of weeks. Too many others had been waiting for a longer time.

That evening, as she sat on her porch, listened to the river and watched the cloud shadows on the mountains, Sam wondered whether she was doing the right thing by moving her people to Janni's world.

An aftershock gave her the answer: yes. No doubt about it now.

•　　•　　•

Five days later, Sam gave the go-ahead to Maxee and her kubs. Klocti can be very insistent when they want to be. With her, she sent two of Ben's most reliable builders, Carlos and Vern. The two men carried huge back bags and shoulder bags. Sam went with them to the bridge, telling Maxee everything she could think of about Peace.

At the bridge, Sam hugged her and told her to be safe. "I'll miss you."

"Iss. But I be good and kubs be good."

Sam watched as the little group headed up the river trail, then turned and trudged home.

Please, Oneness, keep her and the little ones safe.

39

STARVIEW / PEACE

MAXEE FELT THE BEGINNING OF IMPATIENCE, but was smart enough to understand the value of being fresh when they went through to a new world. She slept well, the kubs curled up with her.

When she came to on Peace, her lap was empty. She sat up and counted her kubs. "Where Deki?" she said. Brax sat up and looked around. "Find Deki."

Brax and Toki jumped up and looked around. "Deki," Maxee called, aloud and in her mind.

Haki jumped up.

Nothing.

For the first time since the kubs' walkabout three years before, Maxee felt a clutch of panic. She looked around, saw the door in the tree and pounded on it.

"Give me Deki," she howled.

Carlos sat up. "What is it?"

"My kub not here."

Carlos staggered over and pushed a button. The door opened and a small gray furry ball rolled out. Brax saw it first and picked it up.

"Maa?" Brax said.

Maxee took the ball and put it to her face. "Deki," she said, "Deki, we at new place. Come out now."

No response.

After two more tries, she tucked Deki in her pouch. She sensed e was still alive in there, but why wouldn't e come out? Her pouch bulged uncomfortably.

"You got him? Good." Carlos said.

Vern rose and dusted himself off. "Let's get going."

It was late in the afternoon, and they hurried down the trail. Maxee kept part of her mind on her youngest and the rest on taking in her surroundings. The glade had been pleasing, but she wanted to see more. Little yellow flowers in the bushes along the trickle of a stream lifted her spirits. They came out onto the beach, and she stopped, grabbing her young.

A wide stretch of tan sand led to a never-ending mass of water.

Maxee stared at it. *How could there be so much water in such a large place?*

"What is?" Brax asked. The younger two hid behind her.

"Is real beach," Maxee said. "Is where ocean meets land." Although she'd seen pictures, it took her a little while to fully process the reality.

"Wow," Carlos added.

"A lot nicer than City's." Vern stretched.

Brax ran down to the edge of blue and stuck a toe in. "Water," he said. "Nice."

"Come on, we don't have all day."

Carlos strode down the beach toward the out cropping in the distance. Kubs exploring slowed them down until Carlos picked up Toki and Vern took Haki. After that, Maxee had to extend her legs by inflating air sacs within them to keep up with the long-legged men, Brax running alongside.

At dusk, they came to a stream and stopped.

"Rest here," Maxee said. The men put down the kubs. "Go play," she added.

They ate and watched the youngsters dart in and out of the waves. Little Haki got knocked down and let out a howl.

Maxee told him in her mind, 'Be careful, this world not like ours.'

It was getting dark. "Up to going on?" Carlos asked.

"We go."

They had been walking for a while when Maxee noticed a light over her shoulder.

She stopped and turned. "What that?" She pointed to a misshaped globe in the sky above the water that painted bright streaks on the sea.

"I believe that's a moon," Vern said. "I learned about them in space school."

"Moon," Maxee tasted the word. "What moon?" She made sure her young were listening.

"It's a satellite that orbits this planet. It's bright now because the sun is shining on it."

"Okee." *Something else new and wonderful about this world.*

They camped at the second stream. When they reached the halfway camp the next morning, they stopped to rest. A sign said 'Halfway Camp'.

"You mean we've got twice as far to go?" Vern muttered.

"Nice place to walk," Maxee said, trying to keep track of the kubs.

Baby Deki still curled in a ball, unresponsive to her efforts. She felt sure e was alive and safe in her pouch.

•   •   •

The next day, they were resting at the last stream before the end of the forest when Maxee heard something. She looked up from a shell Haki was showing her and saw, in the far distance, something moving this way.

"Something come," she said, pointing

"Where?" Carlos said.

"I don't see anything," Vern added.

"Wait and see. I see farther than humans." Maxee grinned and went back to Haki.

Ten minutes later, Carlos said, "I think I see something."

"People," Maxee said. "On beasts."

"How can you tell?" Vern asked.

Maxee shrugged.

Soon Janni and Allen, her papa, rode up on their quines, with three extra.

Janni jumped off and ran to Maxee. "It is you," she said. "When I saw little ones, I thought maybe. I saw you had problem with baby. Is he all right?"

"Not he. Child no gender 'til grown and female, like me. Deki sleep deep. Maybe your people wake?"

"We'll have our medics look at it."

"Welcome," said Allen as he dismounted. "We thought you would camp in the glade."

"I'm Carlos and this is Vern. We're builders. I see you know Maxee."

"Yes. Janni communicated with her on your world."

Qilla, Janni's quine, had come to meet Maxee. 'Pretty fur,' Qilla sent as she sniffed the Klocti.

Maxee touched the quine. "Beautiful."

'Wait 'til you meet Beast.' The quine made a chuckling sound.

Allen's quine brought another over to Carlos. "You ride," Allen said. He helped Carlos on.

"Wow," Carlos said.

Another took Vern, and a third, Maxee. Brax rode with her, Toki with Carlos, and Haki with Allen. She kept little Deki in her pouch.

Maxee wanted to show Janni her baby, but decided it was best to wait until they got to the community.

At the river where they turned north, more people met them. Glori, Brian and Willie introduced themselves. A sign pointed up the hill.

At the bridge, Maxee saw another sign. *Good, People not get lost.* She took in the wide plain and the forest in the distance. More trees to the west. Trees were good.

When they arrived at the community, Maxee was pleased to see lots of flowers.

We need more flowers.

After they all dismounted at the plaza and the quines ran off, Janni led Maxee and her kubs to the clinic.

They will wake my Deki.

"What have we here?" Medic Anne asked.

"I Klocti. My kubs." She pulled her baby out of her pouch. "Deki in there, need help to get out." She held out the ball of fur.

Medic Anne took it gingerly. "Yes, there's something alive in there. Come here, Janni."

They sat with Maxee holding the ball, and the two Peace women *sent* their minds into the ball.

"Oh, there you are."

"I see it," Janni said. "Come along and open up. Your mama wants you."

Soon the ball began to lengthen, and a tiny tan foot stuck out.

"Come now," Maxee said. "It safe here."

The ball continued to grow longer and, with a pop, Deki appeared, looked around, and howled.

"Hush," Maxee cuddled the kub to her and rubbed its fur. Deki quieted.

The other three kubs huddled together and watched with big eyes.

"I have a room for them, if you'd like," Medic Anne said.

"Go rest," Janni told Maxee. "We'll bring you food later."

Medic Anne led them to a private room where they all curled up on the bed and slept.

Later, Janni brought food. "Tomorrow, I'll show you around and you'll meet Granlyn, our elder."

"Meet Beast?" Maxee asked.

"Maybe."

•　　　•　　　•

Maxee woke in the morning, feeling happy. All her kubs were safe and they were on a world without shakes. *If Sam were only here ...*

It was just getting light. Maxee rose and went out, leaving the kubs asleep. The sound of the river drew her, and she sat and watched it as the day brightened. This was a new world, and Maxee wanted to become part of it.

Finally, she returned to the clinic and found the young ones awake, listening to Medic Anne tell a story.

"Maa," the kubs cried as Maxee entered.

She gathered them up.

"Getting to know this world," Maxee said. "Come."

She led them out to the plaza.

"Our new world."

They wandered around looking at the buildings. When an older woman came by, Maxee said, "Hello," using their pronunciation.

The woman looked at her and ran away.

"Maa. She no nice," Brax said.

"She never see us before. Maybe scared."

"Of us? We not scary."

Maxee tried to ask another woman where she could find food or Janni, but she ignored the alien and hurried off.

Some of the happiness went away.

"Hello there."

Maxee turned to see Medic Anne. Anne was older too, but she did not turn away.

"Are you hungry? Do you eat what Sam eats?"

"Iss and iss."

"Come with me." Medic Anne took them to the kitchen and fed them.

Haki refused to eat anything except the bread. "Food, Maa."

"I don't have any. Eat what they give you." Maxee patted Haki's head.

Janni came in. "Oh, there you are. How are you doing?"

"We learning new world. What we do now?"

Janni sat down. "After you finish eating, we go see Granlyn. She is the oldest woman in our clan."

"Okee." Maxee took a cloth from the table and wiped little Deki's face.

Janni rose. "Are you ready? Let's go."

They passed through the plaza and headed north. After a short time, they came to a cabin with pink flowers on the porch posts. Maxee felt happy again.

"Welcome," said a much older woman.

"This is Maxee and her babies," Janni said. "This is Granlyn."

The old woman with silver curls welcomed them. She greeted each of the kubs and said, "They're so precious."

Maxee nodded and smiled wide. She liked this old woman, a good matriarch of this clan.

Granlyn asked many questions, and Maxee told her how Sam's father had found her as an infant and raised her with his own children.

"You are the only one of your kind?" Granlyn asked. "How do you have young?"

"Only one in City. Maybe others rescued by other people." Maxee shrugged and explained how Klocti reproduced. "Born no gender, adult what you call female, have kubs, then oldster, no gender." She watched as the others tried to comprehend this.

Granlyn tugged a curl. "Strange, but not impossible. Do you have any memory of your home world?"

Maxee shook her head. "Only trees important."

After more conversation, Granlyn asked Janni to show her around.

"Where quines?" Maxee asked. Her kubs stayed close in this new place.

"Over here." Janni led them to the trees. Several quines watched them approach.

"Hello, quines," Maxee said.

Janni giggled.

'Who are you?' Maxee heard in her mind.

"I Maxee, a Klocti. These my offspring." The younger three hid behind her. Brax stood close by her side.

"This is Qione, Mama's quine. Where's Qilla?" Janni introduced the large animal in front.

'Off with other young ones.'

Janni nodded, so Maxee understood that the girl had also heard the quine.

Qione nudged up a smaller quine and sent, 'Ride.'

"Me," Brax demanded.

Maxee and Janni boosted him up onto the quine.

'Quorn, this is Brax.' Qione *sent.* 'Behave.'

The quine walked around, Brax bouncing on his back, yelling, "Whoohee."

Toki watched with wide eyes. "Me next."

Maxee heard Qione say 'Enough,' and Quorn stopped.

"I want one," Brax said as his mother helped him off.

Maxee looked at Qione, who nodded. Maxee boosted Toki up. She heard the other quines murmuring among themselves.

After Toki's ride, Maxee looked at Haki. He nodded. She picked him up and put him on the quine.

Haki looked around as Quorn began walking.

"No," he screamed. "Too high."

The quine stopped and Maxee took him off and into her arms. "Haki too young," she said.

Qione nodded.

"We need to move on," Janni said.

"Where Beast?" Maxee demanded.

"They're out somewhere. I want to show you our plaza."

At the plaza, Janni pointed out the different buildings. Two or three people looked at them and turned away.

One of a pair of older women said, "What's that?" and pointed to Maxee. The other muttered something about that woman's offspring.

Janni snorted and tossed her head. "Don't mind them. Now I'm going to show you where you'll be staying tonight. Tomorrow, someone will take you up to your place."

"Okee." Maxee had expected some reaction at her alienness, but refused to let it bother her. She also wanted to see the new community, find a place to make her new home. "Food?"

"Yes. We'll get some already prepared from the kitchen."

They toted an armload of provisions up to one of the small cabins above the settlement. Janni dumped the food on the little table and showed Maxee how things worked.

"You can go straight over to the little river or the other way to the big river, but please stay out of our clanhome for now. It's just because some of our older people are not happy about you people moving here."

Maxee looked at her. "We different, too."

"Well, yes." Janni looked at the wall. "It's just having all you people here is new to all of us."

Maxee nodded. "We keep out of your way."

"Okay. Tomorrow morning I'll come and take you to Granlyn's for breakfast. She wants to talk to you some more." She left abruptly.

"Okee," Maxee said to her back.

"Maa, we find river?" Brax asked.

"Yes."

Maxee looked around the little place, packed a loaf of bread, and led her offspring to the little river. They found an open space between trees, and Maxee settled there. She watched the older three explore the area and dip their toes in the river. Deki sat in her lap and took in the surroundings with wide eyes.

"Cold," Brax said.

Maxee also watched the river, and a tiny black bug creep up the stem of a blue flower. When the kubs got hungry, she passed out pieces of bread. She dozed in the afternoon sun along with all but Brax. He built a structure out of twigs. As the sun set, they returned to their cabin.

•   •   •

In the morning, Janni arrived as the kubs complained of hunger. She took Maxee and her kubs back to Granlyn for breakfast.

"How did you sleep?" the old woman asked.

"Good." Maxee smiled. "Hard to wake kubs."

"Probably worn out from the last few days."

Maxee nodded.

"How was your tour of the clanhome?" Granlyn asked.

"Okee. Some people look at us funny."

"You've got to expect that. They've never seen anything like you."

After the meal, Granlyn *called* Marisa to find someone to take Maxee up to their place. Marisa's brother, Ricky, arrived shortly. He goggled when he saw her.

"Marisa not tell you about me?" Maxee asked, a twinkle in her eye.

"Oh, yes. I didn't think you'd look like that. Come on. Bye, Granlyn."

"Find yourself a nice home, and come back and visit," Granlyn said.

"We will."

Ricky showed Maxee the big river.

"You kubs stay away from that, now."

Maxee stared at the rushing water, much more than the river at Starview. They walked up along the river, resting now and then. Late afternoon, just below the new place, she found a copse that would make her a fine home. The trees grew around a tall rock with ledges and hollows, places for each kub. Mossy and comfy.

Ricky told her Carlos and Vern had already gone up.

After she staked out her place, Ricky took her on up to Glenda. Maxee was curious to see what the new place looked like.

Would it be better than Starview?

40

STARVIEW

TWO DAYS AFTER MAXEE LEFT, Brad and several construction people went up to the Gate and through. Sam could not dissuade him.

She trudged back to her office and plunked into her chair.

"He'll be all right. He can take care of himself," Arlene said. "Best to keep busy."

Sam had no choice except to work as fast as she could. At night, she ached for him. They had been separated when he was in the Space Force, but that was different. She knew he was on a spaceship and would come back to Spaceport. The Gate was something else.

The days crept by, and more people went, but Sam's list continued to grow. Bev had become pregnant, and every woman who wanted children demanded to go. Sam was very pleased to hear the former; not so much the latter. In the evenings, she spent time with Emily, who was as worried as she was.

Sam had lost track of the days when Brad called on the comm in the cavern.

"Brad!" she exclaimed.

"I'm back. Just a little tired. Just wanted to let you know I'm here. See you soon, sis."

Sam heaved a sigh of relief and grinned. "Brad's back."

"Now maybe you can pay attention to what you're supposed to be doing," Arlene said.

"Oh, hush." Sam giggled and Arlene grinned. Sam sent someone to tell Emily he was back.

•   •   •

That evening, when Brad walked into the caff with Emily, Sam jumped up and ran to him.

He gathered her into a hug and sighed. "Home again. Although that place over there isn't bad at all." He let her go. "I'm starving. Let us go get some food."

"Okay." Sam grinned at him and returned to her seat. Emily sat with the group.

When Brad came with two plates of food and sat down, Todd nodded at him.

"About time." Todd waved his bread.

"How was it over there?" Sam asked. "How's Maxee?" She grinned from ear to ear. One worry off her back.

"Maxee's fine. She found a neat little hidey hole for her family. She likes the quines, but had a fit when she first saw Beast. I guess he looked like whatever was the bad guy on her mom's world. She and the old lady, Granlyn, get along like twins."

"Good." Sam relaxed.

"I have messages from her, and Janni. The new place looks good, not as many trees as we have here, but the river is humungous. They're having trouble keeping our people moving through to our area; they keep wanting to look at everything. I put a few of our people down the way to direct traffic, along with Janni's people."

"How's the food situation?"

"Okay so far. The caff people who went through have it set up, and Janni's people bring us loovah almost every day. That stuff grows wild. I don't care for the leaves, but the bread they make with the ground-up root is great."

Sam nodded. About what she expected.

Brad dug into his food.

"I want to go with Mom and Jan," Hal said. "Dad doesn't want to go."

"Why not?" Todd asked. Sam knew he was thinking about going soon.

"He doesn't really believe in this new world." Hal grimaced. "I've told him you were there, Sam, but he thinks I'm making it up. He's never been the same since you took his councillorship away from him. That's all he'd ever known."

"I know," Sam said, already missing Hal. "What about your parents, Todd?"

"Mother will go when Dad goes, but he won't talk about it. I can go and start setting up land parcels and rules over there, after I see what's going on."

"Okay, Todd, I'll put you on the list."

"Brad, you think there's any way to make a cart for Jan?" Hal asked. "She's too heavy to carry and her chair won't go up that trail."

"Ah," Brad wiped his beard. "Let me think about it. We'd need wider wheels, for one thing."

"Let him rest tonight," Sam said.

•   •   •

In the morning, Sam thought about what she was going to have to do that day: more interviews, more damage assessment, more soothing ruffled feathers. At least Brad was back. One good thing for the day.

Requests to go dropped off. People continued to arrive from the west with very few possessions and wanted immediate shelter and food. Susan's relocating department was putting some in the places people who had gone through had left empty, but that wasn't nearly enough.

Kirk came to Sam's office. "Do you have a moment?"

She looked up. "Oh, hi, Kirk. What's up?"

"That thing in the sky I told you about earlier? It's growing and masking some distant stars. I still can't tell what it is. Some sort of nebula, but they don't usually grow that fast."

"Oh, no. You think it's not natural?

"Yes. Maybe this person on the other world can check it out."

"Okay, let me make a note. By the way, when do you want to go?"

"Will it be like last time?"

"No. You'll go up to a cavern, step into the room, and wake up on the other world. You'll be up and walking in a few minutes."

"Are any of the constellations in their sky like the ones in ours?"

"I have no idea." Sam shrugged. "Ask Brad. He was in the Space Corps."

"*Ya*, I will. Thanks." Kirk left.

Later, Brad told her he thought the two solar systems weren't too far apart as space goes. There was a place in the sky where constellations looked vaguely similar.

At least we can watch it coming.

On her midday break, as Sam rocked in her chair on her porch, she considered what Kirk had told her. Her farseeing told her it was part, if not all, the menace, but no details of what it was and how it would affect her world and Peace.

What good is this ability if it won't give me details?

Sam shivered. Although she could see sunlight on the tops of the trees, it was cool on the shady porch. Then she noticed the river seemed low. They hadn't had any rain lately, but she had seen black clouds over the mountains.

So why was the river low?

She sighed. Something else to check on.

Sam forgot about it until late meal when Brad said, "The river's down."

"Oh. That's right, I saw it at midday."

"We need to send someone up to check on it." Brad picked up his spork.

"Do we have anyone to spare?"

"Not really." Brad took a bite of his stew.

"Something else," Sam said. *As if there wasn't enough already.* "Too many people who don't belong are wandering around up here, getting into things. Could we post a sentry or something?"

"Yeah, I've noticed that. I guess it's time to set up a security department. I know a fellow, Leonard, who was in security in City. I'll talk to him and set something up. A sentry at the bottom of the mesa trail would be good. I guess just having a few security people around isn't working too well."

"Well, no one has much, so there's not much to steal. A few attacks here and there when someone gets really angry at someone else. Anyway, let's allow only people who work up here or have official business to be up here on the mesa. If they're real insistent, have the sentry call me. He can have Maxee's comm, she left it with me."

"Sounds good."

Late that afternoon, Evelyn showed up at Sam's office.

"What brings you here?" Sam smiled.

"Bad news, I'm afraid." Evelyn leaned on the table. "An elderly man had a heart attack on the trail and died before the people with him could get him to a clinic. I suggest we have everyone have a physical before they go. At least, a basic look-over. Especially older people."

Sam put her head in her hands.

"Oh, crap," Arlene said. "So if they don't pass the physical, they have to stay here whether they want to go or not."

"Something else for people to complain about." Sam sighed and looked up. "Okay, we'll set it up. Do you want them to come to you?"

"Yes, and these three other clinics." Evelyn laid a paper with the clinics' names on the table. "Sorry to make more work for you." She straightened up. "Oh yes. I was treating a paper maker for a bad cut, and he said they're having trouble finding good leaves to make paper with."

Sam groaned again. *No more, please, no more.*

"I know. I'm glad I don't have your job." Evelyn smiled. "Has Brad come up with a way to get Jan up to the Gate?"

"He's working on it. We'll let you know in a few days."

"Good. I'd like us to go soon, to get things set up over there. A new group of medics showed up yesterday and they can have my clinic when we leave. They brought a lot of supplies."

"Good. We'll get right on this."

Evelyn left and Sam closed her eyes. "Arlene, I don't know how much more of this I can take."

"We'll make it, all of us." Arlene patted Sam's shoulder.

I wonder, Sam thought.

41

OTHER / PEACE

S OMEWHERE IN SPACE, BETTAH WORRIED. Pilot Hetch was not following orders. Her people were searching for others who were becoming Watchers. It wasn't necessary to eliminate all of that race. Hetch believed pilots were top gods. Bettah might have to disable him.

•   •   •

One morning at breakfast, Papa Allen suggested they go down to the beach for the day.

"Yes," cried Mick.

"I'll get Janni, she needs a break," Marisa said.

Janni *heard* them as she prepared for the day. *I don't have time*, she thought, but when Papa came to get her, she was willing to go. She told Willie, but he couldn't go, had a project with someone.

As they approached the beach, Janni saw dark clouds along the horizon, but didn't think much of them. By midday, the clouds were halfway up the sky, and a breeze blew in from the sea. The salty sea smell grew strong.

After they ate, Papa said, "I think we'd better get home now."

"Oh, Papa," Steve whined.

"You don't want to get blown away, now do you?"

A stronger gust hit, blowing over an empty bag, and the quines splashed out of the water.

'Go now,' Qione sent.

Marisa looked at her. "Okay. Janni, help me pack."

They mounted their quines, who'd been dancing around, and took off at a trot.

So much for a break.

As they reached the line of trees, the wind blew harder and clouds covered the sun. The three adults sent a message to the clan that a storm was approaching, and to get things under cover.

By the time they reached the plaza and dismounted, rain poured down and the wind howled. People ran for home and Janni hurried to her house. As she waited for Willie, she made sure all the windows were covered and they had plenty of water and food.

A few hours later, Willie came home drenched. "I've never seen rain like this, with so much wind," he said, stripping his wet clothes.

After he put on dry garments, he hugged her.

"There were only a few clouds along the southeast horizon this morning," she said. "It came really fast."

They ate, and huddled on the couch, listening to the rain pound on the roof and the wind shake the house. The storm continued all night and most of the next day. People kept in touch by mind Talent. Sometime during the night Janni was awakened by a loud crash on the roof.

"I'll check it out in the morning," Willie muttered.

Janni inspected the ceilings throughout the house for leaks. She found none and returned to bed.

•   •   •

In the morning, Glori *called*. 'A tree fell through our roof and it's leaking. I've got a couple of tubs under it.'

'Same here,' Janni *replied*, 'but I haven't seen any leaks.'

A message from Granlyn said there was a tree down on their roof. She *sent*, 'Bedroom okay, keeping Larry in there.'

'A tree fell and is blocking our front door,' Mama *sent*.

Janni worried about newcomers who didn't have houses yet. Did people take them in?

Gramma Perri *said* she put the latest group in the meeting hall. 'For the others, up north, we'll just have to wait and see how they fared.'

Later, Janni learned that two groups of newcomers on the beach hid in the trees. One wanted to go back, but the others talked her out of it. The signs had been knocked down and Grampa Charley sent a couple of people to go down and replace them. The paths were muddy and hard to find in places, still covered with water. Trees and branches were down all over the place.

'This place smells like a swamp,' Mama *sent.* She had experienced a swamp on Roroy's world.

The quines were safe, huddled together under their umbrella of trees. Grampa Charley went up and found the new people had not been hit as hard. Their few buildings still stood. People in tents didn't fare as well, but no one had anything more than scrapes and bruises.

The rain stopped about mid-afternoon, but it was still breezy. Willie went out, but Janni didn't want to leave her cozy little nest, afraid of what she might find. Now she understood how Sam felt. This was too much for her on top of everything else. She dozed and felt the loneliness of space.

Willie woke her when he slammed in through the front door. "I pulled that branch away from the house. The windowsill got bashed, and we'll have to replace it, but other than that, our house is okay." Willie pulled his cloak off and dropped it on the floor. "There's a tree down on the front corner of Brian's place."

"Yeah, I know. Glori told me." Janni picked up his cloak and hung it on a hook.

"You two."

"I can't help we were born at the same time." Janni opened the front door, peered out, and closed it quickly.

"Come on, let's go next door." Willie took her hand.

"Okay." Janni *sent* that they were coming.

Glori opened the door as they approached. Janni winced when she saw the tree inside. The top of the tree sat in the big chair in the front corner, surrounded by tubs and containers, under a large hole in the roof.

"Hey," said Brian. He was studying the tree, dancing between tubs. "I don't know how we're going to get this out of here."

"Hmm," said Willie.

Janni followed Glori back to the kitchen area. "Have you been outside yet?" Glori asked.

"Only to come here. It's awful. The ground all covered with twigs, leaves, and seed pods. Broken trees everywhere. At least the quines are all right. I talked to Qilla earlier. They all huddled in the middle of their grove of trees, where they are so entangled nothing blew down."

"That's good. Brian's scatterbrain mama just huddled in the bed and his papa only had a half loaf of bread for supper and nothing much this morning." Glori leaned against a bit of wall in the corner. "Have you talked to Granlyn?"

"Yes. She and Grampa are okay. Two trees fell toward each other and are propping each other up over their house. Mama said they've got a tree across their front door, but otherwise fine. Stevie kept wanting to go out and play in the rain and Papa had to keep dragging him back from the door."

"My family's okay. How are you on food? I meant to collect some more yesterday morning, but never got around to it."

"I've got enough for tonight and the morning." Janni twisted her hands. "I hope the store house is okay."

"Grama Mindy says it looks okay."

'Janni, come here,' she *heard* from Mama. "Mama's calling. Gotta go. Later." Janni told Willie, who grunted, and went out into the mess.

There was so much tree litter on the ground it was hard to tell where the paths were. A big branch had broken off one of Mama's trees and lay across the front doorway. Papa was hacking at branches with the old saw. Janni went around to the side window. Mama had the shutters open and stood there waiting inside.

They hugged through the window. "Do you want me to send Willie over to help Papa?"

"Does he have a better saw?"

Janni thought so. She *called* Willie and he came after a few minutes. She watched from outside and Mama from inside until they had enough cut off that they could drag the thing away.

"I want to see the plaza," Mama said.

Steve ran out and jumped into the branches.

"Watch him, Allen."

Mick wandered out and looked around.

The plaza was covered with water. The little wall around it kept it from draining.

"Need to redo drainage," Mama said aloud and *sent* to Grampa Charley.

Janni could always tell when someone was *sending*, but not usually the words.

They walked around on the narrow paths between the plaza and the flowerbeds. Most of the plants had been pushed down on their faces.

The buildings on the high side away from the river, including the clinic, were dry, but the kitchen and science lab were flooded. Susan and her mother appeared, along with a few other women.

"Oh, my Oneness," Susan said. One of the others spouted a mild curse word. "Okay, ladies, let's get the mops."

They swept the water out, leaving mud on the floor and cabinet bottoms that had to be cleaned up before the kitchen could be used. The food had not been touched, it was all in containers and up on shelves. Susan assigned Janni a cabinet to clean. Water dribbled out when she opened the door. Janni put the pots and pans up on the counter and wiped out the cabinet, then scrubbed the floor and mopped the area in front. After that, she had to wash the pots and pans and put them back.

And that was only the beginning. Janni looked around. Someone would have to redo the drainage of the Plaza, and all the outsides of the buildings needed to be washed down and the insides cleaned up. Two of the plaza tables had been damaged and had to be mended.

Carlos and Vern appeared and asked if there was anything they could do for shelter.

"All the tents are soaked, and some torn where branches fell on them," Carlos said.

Vern's arm was wrapped in a bloody bandage. "Just a scratch from a falling tree. Our medic said I should have one of your medics look at it."

Janni took them to the clinic. Medic Anne and an assistant were busy dealing with injuries. "You'll have to take your turn," she said. She was working on old Freddie, who had fallen off his roof trying to remove a large branch and banged himself up beautifully.

Janni helped with a boy who had torn up his hand.

When Medic Anne got to Vern's arm, she sucked in her breath. Almost the length of his forearm, the gash was deep as well. The sides had been pulled together with a few stitches of some coarse thread, but still gaped. She painted the wound with numbgoo and sewed it up with finer thread. After she wrapped it up and got him a sling, she asked, "What kind of medic was that, to do such a poor job. Don't you have any finer thread?"

"Yes," Carlos said, "but the only medics we have here now are fairly new at the job and they were too rattled to find the finer thread. I'm hoping one of our head medics gets here soon, we've had injuries too."

Medic Anne nodded. "Have her check it in a week and if it looks sufficiently healed, take the stitches out. If it starts looking red and swollen, come back here, we have preparations that can deal with infections. If your head medic hasn't come, and there are any questions, come back and see me."

"Thank you," Vern said. "What is that pain stuff?"

"An old Bramite recipe. They were people Granlyn and them lived with before we came here. Fortunately, the plants grow here."

The two men left.

"Do you need any help, Aunt Anne?" Janni asked.

"Maybe. The last thing I need is having to treat them, too."

"I know, but we can't not help them. I wish Sam would come back."

A woman came in with a child holding a bleeding arm.

"Excuse me," Medic Anne said, and turned to her new patient.

Janni left for home. In the growing darkness, a cold wind teased her.

•　　　•　　　•

That night, Janni's being leaves her body and drifts in space. Bubbles of solar systems surround her as she hangs in the nothingness. One after another, the bubbles come to her. The primitive worlds will not be touched so she leaves them alone. On another world, she finds a woman and two young children adrift on a raft where a ship has sunk. She manages to rescue them and send them to Peace. The rest of the people occupy three large cities and the land around them. Unable to contact them with her mind, she creates a message with debris on a nearby beach. She hopes they can read it.

Janni seeks the Otherness, but first puts a block on her awareness so they can't perceive her. She touches them with a sliver of her being. The thing she 'saw' before is a ship containing beings who have Talent. Apparently, the Watchers are preparing them also. Two main beings appear to have a difference of opinion. They are not human, but they have emotions like her.

They want to destroy the humans so they can become Watchers.

42

PEACE

Back in her body, Janni fought terror.

Is their Talent stronger than ours? If they have spaceships, they are lot farther along in technology than we are.

Janni's mind went in spirals. Sam's people, the storm, and now this certainty. Not to mention Willie and all the everyday stuff. She wanted to find a cave and pull it in after her. But she had to tell Granlyn and the others.

Janni opened her eyes to find it was almost midday. The woman and her children. She *reached* for Mama. Marisa had gone down to meet them. The woman was in such a state of terror she could not move. Mama had *called* Kelly, Dottie's nine-year-old daughter, to come down. A bubbly, outgoing child, she could talk her papa into anything. Perhaps she could talk to the children. The girl was her age.

Janni sat up and saw Granlyn sitting by the bed. She couldn't speak.

"Hello, Janni. I understand you brought some more people."

She nodded. "They were stranded in the sea," she managed to say.

"Of course, you had to save them. Especially the children." Granlyn smiled. "Marisa says the little girl is talking to our Kelly. Charley and Will have gone down to carry them if necessary."

Will was Willie and Brian's papa.

"Are you ready to get up?"

"Granlyn, I touched the Other. They aren't human, but they have Talent and are trained to be Watchers, like us. And they want to kill us all, so we don't become Watchers first."

"Oh, my Oneness. You are sure of this?" Granlyn sat up straight.

"Yes. I never believed before, but now ..." She blinked tears back. Terror entwined her being.

Granlyn put her hand on Janni's arm. "Be calm. We will find a way." She paused and looked up. "It seems that every generation has to deal with an increasingly worse problem to save our people. Perhaps the only way to break this cycle is for you to not have any children at all."

That sounded great, but when the old woman said that, Janni realized she did want children. Someday.

"What do we do now?"

"First, write down every last thing you can remember of this experience. If you can, let Sam know she needs to come through as soon as possible for a meeting with us. Do you know, do they just kill humans, or do they wipe out whole worlds?"

Janni *heard* her thought; 'Here I am talking about wiping out worlds and, when I was Janni's age, I only knew spaceships like the *Enterprise* in *Star Trek* — and those weren't real.'

"I believe they only destroy humans. On the planet with the one survivor I sent to Sam's world, there were still animals in the forest and only the places where humans lived were destroyed."

"Good." Granlyn patted her again, sighed, and rose. "I need to get back to Larry."

"How's he doing?"

"As well as can be expected. If I could only remember our childhood adventures."

Janni swung her legs over the side of the bed and stood. "Hasn't he told you about them?"

"Yes, but it's not the same. Rest up, get something to eat, and we'll see you at supper at Marisa's."

"Okay." She tottered out to the outhouse. At least she didn't have to take care of this all by herself. A thought came. Granlyn had told her once about a song called Yesterday by some bug group on Earth that she thought of when she had trouble coping.

If I could only go back quite a few yesterdays …

Back in the house, slumped in a big chair, Janni *called* Mama again. Kelly had got the girl to talk to her mama and they were coming up to Mama's place. She wanted Janni to come over in about a half hour. Janni still felt as if she'd spent all yesterday rolling logs up the slope. After picking up Willie's clothes, she headed for Mama's.

Mama greeted her and said, "This is Gwendolyn."

A tiny woman with very pale hair, not much taller than Mick, sat in a big chair holding a small boy. Kelly and a little blonde girl sat on the couch. Dottie lounged in another chair.

"Hello. Welcome to Freedom. We don't bite." Janni smiled at Gwendolyn.

She returned a half smile.

"This is my daughter, Janni," Mama said.

"She's the smartest," Kelly said. "This is Jeanie."

"Hello, Jeanie." Janni smiled at the little girl.

Marisa brought a chair from the table for Janni.

'Do they understand us?' Janni *asked* Mama in her mind.

'They're learning, we're giving them our words in their minds.'

"This Davie," Gwen said in a high-pitched, child-like voice, patting the boy on his head.

He stared at them with wide brown eyes.

"Hello, Davie." Janni took a breath. *What are we going to do with them?*

"They will stay with us for right now," Mama said. "Gwen and Jeanie will have your room, and the boy will bunk with Steve."

"Where are the boys?"

"Out helping with the harvest."

"Boy, will they be surprised when they get home. Or did you tell them?"

"No, I haven't told them, but I did let Allen know. He'll bring extra food when he comes home." Marisa glanced at the kitchen.

"Okay. What have you found out, Kelly?"

"They were on a big ship with more than twice as many people as we have here, and water started coming in and it sank. Gwen and many others jumped off and she found this piece of wood floating and she and her kids got on it. Two darks and no food."

"What about the people on that world?"

"Not as many as before. Cities not crowded, lot of babies die. That's all I got,"

"That's fine, Kelly, you did well." Dottie stood. "We need to go now. We'll see you in the morning." The two left.

Janni took Dottie's chair and leaned back. Although she was glad she was able to save them, especially the children, it was one more problem to add to the list.

Will we have to find a place for them here, or could Sam's people take them in? Let someone else answer that. I need to rest.

Jeanie said, "Kelly nice."

"Good. I hope you two become friends." Janni closed her eyes.

Mama brought out some needlework. There was always something in progress. Gwen watched as Mama sewed up a split seam on a tunic.

"I do," Gwen said.

"There's plenty here," Mama said. "Always something to mend; boys do go through clothes."

Gwen nodded. Janni *sensed* her relaxing a little. Mama gave her a shirt to mend, and she did quite well.

Janni dug out an old picture book someone had brought from Old Earth and sat beside Jeanie, showing her the pictures and saying the words. Janni figured she'd be the one teaching them Standard. Davie slipped out of his mother's lap and sat beside her. They were deep in the book when Steve ran in.

He stopped short. "Who're they?"

"Steve, these are our guests, whom Janni rescued from another world." Marisa introduced them.

"Oh, hi." Steve took after Papa, with the straight brown hair and eyes. He had twice as much energy as Janni ever had.

Finally, Papa and Mick came home and welcomed the newcomers.

At dinner, Gwen and Davie ate well, but Jeanie just picked at her food.

"Don't you like it?" Janni asked, making a yummy sound.

The girl shrugged. Gwen said something Janni didn't catch, and the girl picked up her spork.

Willie, who'd come at Marisa's command, ate quickly and ignored everyone except Janni. The boys asked questions and Gwen kept shaking her head as an answer.

Janni and Willie left after she helped her mother clean up.

"Why do you keep bringing these odd people?" Willie asked.

"I have to, they'd die if I didn't. But they're Mama's problem now."

"Good. You don't need any more responsibilities."

43

PEACE

A FEW DAYS LATER, the community kitchen was shining clean and the tables mended. Several families wanted to eat at the plaza just to get away from their houses. After Granlyn sent an invitation via Maxee for Sam's people to come down, Uncle Artie found his grandfather, Old Art, dead in his cubby hole in the science building.

Gramma Perri and her sister-in-law, Medic Anne decided they should go ahead with the meal. People had to eat. None of Old Art's generation attended.

The Arts sat with Gramma Perri and her group. Janni and Willie sat at the next table with other young couples, and she could hear their conversation.

"I never really knew him," Uncle Artie said.

"I know," Big Art stroked his beard. "He only interacted with me as an apprentice, not a son, after Mama went."

"I still regret I couldn't save her," Gramma Perri said.

"It wasn't your fault."

"I know, but ..."

Janni lost the thread. She'd only seen Old Art once, when she was about seven and she talked Willie into sneaking into the science building. She remembered the old man roaring at them to get out.

Most of the new citizens sat together but a few ate with Janni's group, such as Carlos and Vern. Behind her. Janni heard Mary, Big Art's sister, mutter about people taking their supplies.

Her daughter, Nancy, said loudly, "Why are they here anyway? Wasn't their world good enough for them?"

Others joined in and Grampa Charley had to finally quiet things down.

"Sorry about that," he said to Carlos. "We older members remember living with the Bramites and their reactions to our evolving Talent."

"Don't worry, we'll stay out of your way. Unfortunately, we have to come through your place to get to ours."

"We've marked a pathway for your people and encourage you to stay within your boundaries. I realize your people are probably not happy about moving, I've been through two, and maybe you are curious about us. We caught someone peeking into Janni's house."

"She was walking in the front door." Janni said. "Are we going to have to put locks on our doors?"

"Sorry about that, sweetie, but there's not enough of us to be everywhere at once."

"I took care of her, Grampa." Janni smirked. "I put the thought in her mind that if she wasn't careful, someone would put her back through the Gate to another world."

"You could do that?" Vern asked, wide-eyed.

"Oh yes." she said. "You'd be surprised what we can do with our Talent."

"Janni," Grampa said sternly.

"Okay." She rolled her eyes. "Is anyone going back soon? I want to see Mayor Sam again, to discuss things."

"I think Gus is, he wants the rest of his stuff." Vern took a bite of his bread.

"Ask him to ask Sam to come through for a short visit, a few days."

"Yes," said Grampa.

"You don't want to go there?" Carlos asked.

"I need to be here, so I can ask others about things if I need to."

•   •   •

The next day, Granlyn called a meeting of the three young women.

"You have had time to get used to your new responsibilities. Storm cleanup went well. Now I will assign you your first adult duties."

The three looked at each other but didn't speak.

"Janni, you are now first assistant to Marisa in education. That means you are responsible for the smooth running of the school whenever Marisa is unable to handle an event. Get with her on what your new duties will be."

"Yes, Granlyn." Janni closed her eyes. *Not that I need anything else to do.*

"Glori, you are now first assistant to Perri in needlework. You, too, need to get with Perri to discuss your duties in case she is unable to do them.

Glori nodded.

"Leona, you are now first assistant to Beth in childcare. You need to figure out some new projects for the children. Like the others, you need to get with Beth about your new role."

"Yes, Mama."

"This is part of you becoming adults and moving away from childhood, learning to take on adult responsibilities." Granlyn closed her eyes for a moment. "When your children grow up, it'll be Perri who welcomes them into adulthood."

"No," Janni said. *Granlyn has always been there …*

"Yes, Janni. I am training Perri to be my assistant. I won't be around forever, you know."

44

STARVIEW / PEACE

Sam was not surprised when Gus returned and gave her Janni's message. Gus said he wanted to go back in a couple of days. Sam, Arlene, and Brad had to sit down and plan duties so Sam could leave for a few days. Kirk wanted to go with them.

The three left on a cool, overcast day. Gus scuffled along in the dry leaves, and Kirk looked around at everything. Two people asked them what was happening before they reached the bridge.

"Haven't you heard? We're moving to a new world," Sam said, annoyed. "Go sign up at the information booth at the foot of the mesa."

They looked at her blankly.

"Go on. They'll tell you all about it."

Sam and the men continued on. "I can't believe there are people who don't know about it," she muttered. Then to Gus, "How is the new place coming along over there?"

"Not bad for such a massive project. The main buildings are going up, and houses laid out. We need more builders."

"A lot of people have gone through. Can't you use them?"

"Most have to be trained. Wastes time of good builders."

"Okay, I'll see if I can get more builders to go through, when I get back." *If I get back.*

They walked to the bridge in silence. After they started up along the river, Sam asked, "What do you think of the new place? Do you have a name for it?"

"Not bad. Not enough trees close by. Don't want to use the ones along the river."

"I know."

They trudged on up the trail. Sam tried a few more times to make conversation, but Gus was not one for chitchat. Kirk didn't say anything.

At the Gate, Sam asked, "Do you want to camp here and go in the morning, or go now?"

"Might as well go now," Gus said.

They entered the Gate.

•   •   •

When Sam came to, she saw Janni, Qilla, and another quine waiting in the glade.

"Good, you came," Janni said.

Sam sat up. This wasn't as bad as the other time. She looked around at the trees, and when she saw the giant tree, her eyes widened.

"That's where the Gate is," Janni said. "Inside the tree. We'll go when you're ready. You get to ride this time. This is Qiatta." The quine nodded. "Miss Sam will ride you. I didn't know you were bringing someone else, or I'd brought a quine for you."

"This is Kirk, our astronomer," Sam said. "He's the one you sent to our world."

"Oh," Janni said. "I hope you didn't mind. All your cities were burned out."

"I saw one. I'm fine now. Thank you." Kirk hefted his bundle.

"That's okay. You ride, Kirk, I'll walk." Gus eyed the quines from a distance.

"Are you sure?" Kirk asked.

"Yes." Gus looked around.

"You can put your bags in my panier," Janni said.

Sam shakily got to her feet. "Hello, Qiatta." She held out a hand and the quine sniffed it.

Janni mounted Qilla, and Qiatta knelt so Sam could get on. The other quine followed suit and Kirk mounted.

"This like animal I used to ride," he said.

As the quine stood, Sam felt a thrill of something totally new and exciting through the haze of her awakening. When she started down the path to the beach, Sam held on to the quine's neck hair with a tight grip. She and the quine seemed to grow together. She remembered the blue green sky and was amazed at the beach and the sea.

"Nice, isn't it?"

Janni and Qilla stopped, as did the others, Gus a little distance away.

"It's gorgeous." Sam patted Qiatta. She hoped that here on Peace she would get a better picture of the coming menace. At least, it felt stronger here.

"Very nice," Kirk said. "Good boy." He patted his quine's neck.

The quines trotted down to the water and Gus walked along on the hard, damp sand. They stopped at the first stream where they rested and ate. Sam took in the bushes and trees above the beach, and the low green islands out in the deep blue sea. The air was unlike any on her home planet.

She breathed deeply of it as they moved along. She sat back and let the quine carry her. Although tired from the long day she'd already had, she had no desire to stop and camp yet. Occasionally she dozed, as did Kirk. Gus plodded along like an automation.

Yes, this was much better than Cityworld.

She hadn't realized how much her world had deteriorated. Most of the people wouldn't believe her if she tried to tell them that.

Kirk talked about the sea and the sky. "Must look at stars tonight."

Gus trudged along without a word, keeping his eyes on the trees inland.

They reached the halfway camp just before dark. Sam had carried the food for both of them, in Qiatta's paniers. Gus trudged up to the trees and collapsed.

After the others ate, Kirk unpacked and set up his telescope, even though he could barely keep his eyes open. Sam curled up into her blanket and fell asleep.

•   •   •

In the morning, Janni had to wake them. "I know your time is different, but we need to get going."

Sam pulled herself up and rubbed her eyes. She wanted to just lie here by the sea all morning and relish the salty sea aroma. Her hand picked up a handful of sand and she felt the softness of it as it trickled through her fingers.

As they ate, Janni talked. "Granlyn wanted you to come so we can discuss with you how to handle your people when they go through our clanhome," Janni said.

"Are you having problems?" Sam asked.

"We have put up signs, but your people don't always follow them." Janni didn't look at Sam.

"Sorry to hear that. We have meetings and paper lists of rules and inspectors who check them out and tests them. I don't know what more I can do."

"Well, we'll talk about it when we meet. You can rest tomorrow after we get home. You can stay with Mama in my old room. We'll find someplace for Kirk and Gus."

The group left as the sun was rising and they met a trio from the clan shortly after they reached the end of the trees. Janni had *called* her mama when Sam, Kirk, and Gus showed up.

Marisa, Grampa Charley, and Susan, on quines, had brought an extra for Gus. They all persuaded him to ride.

"Glad to see you," Marisa said.

"Glad to be back. This beach is marvelous." Sam grinned. "And Qiatta."

The quine jerked her head up.

"How long will you be staying?"

"Only a few days. After we figure out what we're doing here, I'll have to go back and reeducate my people."

My people? Who am I kidding?

•   •   •

After they reached the plaza and let the quines trot off, a tall, gray-haired man greeted them. Marisa introduced the three newcomers.

"Bill, can you let Kirk and Gus bunk with you tonight? We're having a general meeting tomorrow morning, and we want Gus to be there. Save him from going up to his place and coming down in the morning."

"Sure," Bill said. Sam thought he looked a lot like Janni's papa. The three men left.

Marisa and Janni took Sam to Marisa's house.

"You'll stay here," the older woman said. "Now, you'll probably want to rest. Janni, tasks?"

"Yes, Mama." She stomped off.

Marisa showed Sam her room and the outhouse. "I have to go back to work. Do whatever you want. Feel free to read a book. We'll have supper here."

Sam settled down with The Secret Garden. She thought she would like to have a garden like that.

Later, Janni and Willie showed up with two loaves of bread.

"Gwen likes her new little house," Janni told her mother. "She's good with the little children. Someone I rescued from another world," she added to Sam. "She's in childcare."

Willie headed for the couch. "Hi, Willie," Sam said. He waved a hand.

Janni went back to the kitchen where Marisa was chopping carrots and squash.

"Oh, good, you brought bread. I haven't had time to make any."

"Me either. Glori made these."

A few minutes later, Allen, Steve, and Mick came home and soon they all sat down to eat.

"Are you going to bring anybody my age soon?" Mick asked.

"Probably." Sam selected a slice of bread. Dark and heavy, the bread was also tasty.

They talked about the two colonies.

"If you find someone doing something really bad, send them back to us." Sam took a bite of mixed veggies.

"I told one woman we'd send her through the Gate to another world, not necessarily yours. That scared her." Janni grinned.

"Janni, we do not use our Talent like that." Marisa said.

"Oh, Mama."

"Do you mind if I ask how your talent works?" Sam asked.

"We don't know exactly how it works," Marisa said. "It just is. Granlyn didn't find hers until she was in her twenties and away from

Earth. Gramma Perri had the mindlink from an early age, but didn't find her teleportation Talent until she was sixteen. I developed mine early."

"Can you turn it off?"

"No. Unfortunately. There are times I wish we could." Marisa picked up her cup. "Do you have any special food on your world?"

"There's one plant that has a fat root that we can grind up and make bread with, when the regular grains aren't available." Sam wrinkled her lip cloth.

After the meal, Sam offered to help clean up, but Marisa told her to go sit down and look at a book.

"I gotta go home," Willie said, and left.

"It would be much easier if they were all like her," Sam heard Marisa say. She felt her face grow warm.

45

PEACE

IN THE MORNING, Sam, Marisa, and Allen collected Janni and Glori and headed to the meeting hall, joining Granlyn and Grampa on the way. He walked slowly with a pair of walking sticks, a smile on his face. The boys had gone to work in the fields.

"He doesn't get out much anymore," Granlyn said to Sam.

At the hall, they met up with Granli and Grampa Bay, Gramma Perri and Grampa Charley, Uncle Peter, Uncle Artie, and the rest of the clan. After greetings, everyone went inside and settled down in circles of chairs, one circle inside another. Grampa Bay sat to one side.

"He can't shut out the noise of our minds the way we can," Janni whispered to Sam.

Gus and Bill sat next to Sam in the front row. Kirk was out exploring.

"Welcome everyone," Grampa Charley boomed out. "We are meeting here to discuss and plan how to manage Sam's people joining us on this world. We want this to be a pleasant experience for all involved, and I hope we can live together peacefully and enhance each other's communities. Granlyn?"

The old woman stood. "Let us welcome Mayor Samanda Lar of Starview, on Cityworld."

Sam stood and bowed her head.

"This woman has the responsibility of moving her people from their world to ours, after moving them from their dying City to their current location. We need to help her the best we can." Granlyn nodded at Sam, who sat. "I know that some people are concerned about the fact they will outnumber us, and about having enough food until their crops come in. We do have plenty of loovah, and I have suggested we cut down on eating eggs so we will have more chickens. Sam?"

"We have a supply of food and plants we are bringing. If we are allowed some loovah root, we can make our own bread." Sam smiled. "We don't want to take anything unless it's absolutely necessary for our survival."

"I understand," Granlyn said. "I will see that you get your own loovah plants. They will multiply quickly. We need to set up rules for your people so they don't intrude on us, and you may make your own rules."

"Excuse me," Grampa Charley said. "What kind of government setup do you have?"

Sam was perplexed. She'd never thought of how to explain it. "Well, I'm the mayor, the head person. I have assistants, most of whom are heads of departments, like Gus and his wife are heads of construction and Doug who came here earlier is the head of the waterworks. Each neighborhood has a leader who is supposed to report any problems to my assistants."

"Supposed to?" asked Marisa.

Sam nodded. "Only about half of them do regularly, and my partner, Hal, has to go around and talk to them and report back to me or Arlene, my second in command."

"I see," Granlyn said.

"What do you have in the way of science labs?" Artie asked. Big Art had refused to go to the meeting.

Sam stopped and thought. She hadn't expected to be quizzed on Starview. "There's the science workshop which does all sorts of things, such as making sure the local plants are edible and what combinations work best for us. The medics have a shop where they work on things to make medical care better. There's the mechanics shop where they make tools and things like pipes for water. We have an astronomer, Kirk, who came here with us. He wants to see your sky. He says there's some kind of cloudiness in one part of our sky, and it's growing."

"Where?" Grampa Charley asked.

"Well," Sam had to stop and think, "if I was on my world facing south, it would be up there." She pointed her left hand away from her body and about two-thirds of the way to straight up.

"How does that tell us where it is from our world?" Allen asked.

"That's what Kirk is going to try to find out."

"Did you ever see such a thing when you were out in space, Janni?" Granlyn asked.

"I don't know. I couldn't tell what direction it was from here, anyway."

"What about your childcare and schooling?" Granli asked.

"We have childcare centers for when the parents are working. The grandmothers and young girls run them. We teach them our history on Cityworld and about Old Earth. And about the Volen, who gave us City nine hundred years ago and took it away ten years ago." Sam looked around.

"Volen," said Granlyn. "Sounds like our Watchers."

A buzz in the crowd.

"Janni, tell us about this threat you found."

She did. "They're aliens who are also becoming Watchers."

"What's the timeline on this? How fast do I have to get my people through?" Sam asked. She sensed that this was part, but only a part, of the menace.

"I really don't know. They seem to be going around in circles, and we're on the other side, but I don't know how long it will take them to get here. Is there a problem?"

Sam looked at Gus.

"We can't build houses fast enough," he said. "We can't keep up with all the people coming though now. There's not even enough tents to house them, and some are sleeping in the meeting hall."

"You can slow down, but that may mean that fewer get through." Janni shook her head. "I really don't know how long it will take the Other to get here."

"We have to carry everything we want to bring, and it's uphill from the valley to the Gate," Sam said.

"You have no carts?"

"No. We could build the cart part, but no one has figured out a way to make wheels."

"Make wide skis," Grampa Larry said. "Boards about a foot wide, two of them side by side, and put the cart body on them. Make the bottoms as smooth as you can and pull them along like that. Measure the door to the Gate and make the carts a little narrower. When you go through, you'll need two persons in the Gate room so they can pull the cart out on the other side. Leave the carts in the glade and we'll loan you a big, quine drawn cart to put your belonging in. Then whoever goes back can take a cart though."

Sam stored that in her memory. "Thank you. We'll do that. Some of the alien races on our world are humanoid. Do you think this threat will affect them?"

"How much like you are they?" Granlyn asked.

"With the Ambaak, the only noticeable difference is some facial features. The other two groups have darker skin but look similar. Another looks like an animal, so I'm not worried about them."

"From what you described, Janni," Grampa Larry looked at her, "these other beings that threaten us, don't have observable sense organs, so we don't know how they perceive us. It may not be visual. Could be sound or smell or some other sense we don't know anything about."

Sam sighed. "The other species sound like us, but all smell different. What do we do about that?"

People looked at each other.

Grampa Bay spoke from his corner. "I suggest we set up a more defined corridor for Samanda's people as close to the big river as possible. Have it marked off every few meters. And lead straight over from the bridge. Perhaps fences as necessary."

"Good idea, Papa," Grampa Charley said. "Sam, if you could hold up your people for a few days, that would help."

"Okay." *Now I must tell them to stay in the corridor. Oh, well.*

"Another thing," Gramma Perri said. "We will need a list of your people who we can work with, in communicating between the colonies. You, of course. Although you do not have the receivers for mind communication, we can put the thought in your mind to come to us."

"Oh." Sam was nonplussed. *If they could get into our minds ...*

"Don't worry, we have strict rules about going into other people's minds without their permission. So if someone does, let us know immediately." Granlyn touched her silver curls.

"Quines," Marisa said. "Now that we have more quines than people, can we let some of them go up there?"

"If they want to. Sam, would you like to have quines available?"

Sam's eyes lit up. "Sure, it would make it easier to get down here when you want to see me."

"You talk to them, Marisa," Gramma Perri said.

Grampa Larry stood. "Anyone else have any comments or questions?"

"Are their kids going to go to school with us?" an adolescent boy asked.

"No, they'll have their own schools up in their colony. Their place will be quite separate from ours."

"Oh." The boy slumped back into his chair.

Sam began to feel surrounded, hemmed in. All these people who could see what she was thinking.

Please, no more questions.

She clamped her teeth on her lower lip to keep from screaming.

"Okay, that's it for now. If anyone has any questions or suggestions, see Charley or Perri." Grampa Larry picked up his walking sticks.

People rose and milled around. Sam ran out, down to the little river, and hugged a tree. Shaking, and with her head against the tree trunk, all she could think of was going home.

Something cold touched her hand. She yelped and jumped away from the tree.

46

PEACE

"SORRY," ROROY SAID. Beast looked at her and made a little sad sound. "We didn't mean to scare you."

Sam caught her breath and yanked herself under control. "It's all right." She patted Beast.

"I know, sometimes you have to get away from them. Even if they say they won't go into your mind, you can't help thinking about it, and after a while it gets to you."

Roroy led her to a nearby bench. The river gurgled and sent a watery aroma their way.

"You know." Sam sat.

"Elli, my mate, Grampa Larry and I are the only ones who don't have mind Talent." He sat at the other end of the bench, leaving a space between them, and Beast hunkered on his haunches nearby.

"You understand."

"Yes. What have they told you about me?"

Sam put her arms around her knees. "Only that Marisa brought you here from another world. Don't you have any desire to go back?"

"No. There is nothing there for me. When I left, only family was old father. I stayed here because of Marisa. She saved me from a dull, useless life. My father rules a small kingdom and wanted me to give him grandsons. My brother was meant to, but he died." Roroy stared at the river.

"And your mother?" Sam thought of her mother, who'd left for her home world when Sam and Brad were five, and Aunt Linda, Todd's mother, who had tried to replace her.

"She died when I very young."

"I lost my mother when I was young. So there's no one to mourn your father when he dies?"

"He had retainers." Roroy paused. "Marisa and I were mated for a while, but I was not able to give her children. I left for a while and let her choose another mate. Better for her to have one of her own kind. Janni is special to me."

Sam didn't know what to say. She had a feeling he had waited a long time to find someone to talk to.

"My Elli had both parents on Earth, and wanted to get away from them. She is my angel; I am complete with her." He twisted his hands together.

"I'm glad you found someone to share your life with," Sam finally said. "You and Elli and Beast are welcome to come up to our community any time."

Roroy bowed his head. "Thank you. How is it coming?"

"Slowly. Some people work very hard, but others don't. We need more people, but only one, if that, out of each group is willing to work. They do work because it's the only way they get food, but don't always do a good job."

"I can come and help. I have built houses."

Sam dropped her hands. "Would you? If they don't object."

"They won't." Roroy looked up at the sky across the river. The sun was high.

"Ask for Glenda. She will know where she needs you the most."

He rose and nodded. "Thank you." He and Beast strode off downriver.

Sam sat there and watched the water. It was comforting to find someone else who was not of the clan. She felt that most of the people were good people, she just couldn't accept that they were able to read minds. But she and her people would have to live with them, at least as neighbors. The menace hovered in the background.

Sam headed back to the plaza and sat on a wooden bench. A young woman led a line of little children out of the schoolhouse. Sam thought of all the young ones they didn't have and prayed that the Clan procedure on birth control would work.

Hungry, she went to Marisa's, but no one was there. She wandered back to the plaza and found Gus, Kirk, and Charley. "We're going up to your place," Charley said. "Want to come?"

"Sure. Can I get something to eat?"

He got her a piece of bread, and they took off for the quines. Qione selected a group for them to ride and take up.

As they approached the new place near the end of the day, Sam saw Maxee sitting by a tree, with little Deki arranging twigs nearby, and stopped.

Maxee looked up and squealed. "Sammie! Are here for good?"

"No, just a visit. How are you and the kubs?"

Before Maxee could answer, the other three kubs piled out of the trees and chorused welcome.

"Come see." Maxee showed Sam her new home.

Sam thought it was too small and dark, but Maxee said, "My nice home. Little caves for kubs, place for food. I sleep on cozy seat."

"Kind of dark, isn't it?"

"Too bright out. You go see Glenda?"

"Yes."

"Tell her we fine."

"Okay." Sam remounted Qiatta and headed on up.

A meeting house and three other buildings had been built around a large open area. Beyond them, along the river, stood a line of houses. Away from the river, parallel, were a few half-built houses and a group of tents. Sam found Glenda in the meeting hall. It had offices along one side.

"Well, hello there," Glenda said. "I didn't expect you to come yet."

"Only visiting. How are things going?"

"So-so. The people who came to work, work hard. The others complain about not having a house, but don't want to help build one."

"Sounds like when we moved out of City."

"Yep. By the way, it is possible to slow down the rate people are coming through?"

"Why?"

"We can't keep up with them. At least half don't want to work, and I have to keep repeating: no work, no house. No food. That's a problem, too. Some people have no idea how much a week's worth of food is."

"I'm not surprised. Gus also said you can't keep up with the newcomers." Sam looked around for him.

"He's already out in the field. It was great to see him back."

"I can imagine," Sam said, thinking of Brad. "Anyway, Janni said to not let anyone through for a few days, so you'll have a break."

Glenda nodded. "I've saved some places along the river for you to choose where you want your house. Come look."

Sam followed her over to the line of trees. There was plenty of space between them and the first row of houses.

"There's a small river that flows into the big one further up, so we're planning crops there." Glenda stopped at a place where only a single line of widely spaced trees separated the land from the water. "Here's one."

Sam looked at the area. It was big enough for a small house, and there were bushes at each end with red flowers. She moved between two trees and watched the river. It was so wide she couldn't imagine how they could build a bridge across it. There seemed to be three or four different streams in it. Much louder that the one in Starview; indoors, it would be a soothing sound.

"Yes," she said, turning to Glenda. "I like this. I want my house here."

"I thought you'd like it. I'll mark it on the map and put Hal's next door."

"And Brad and Emily's on the other side." Sam grinned. She caught a glimpse of mountains through the trees on the far side of the river. "Can you build it higher, up off the ground?"

"Let me talk to Gus about that."

Sam wandered around and visited the people who were there. She found Doug up by the smaller river, planning the waterworks.

"See here by the corner, we can cut off a waterway and put the waterwheel there. We'll have to shore it up, but we can do that." Doug smiled. "We can dig out a holding area, so even if the river gets low, we'll still have water."

"Very good." Sam pushed her hair back. "I'm glad to see someone doing something."

She returned to the hall and found Kirk. "Have you had a chance to look at the sky here?" she asked.

"Ja. Can't tell where nova is."

"Okay. Keep looking." Sam tracked down Glenda. "Looks pretty good what I've seen so far."

"We're trying. Come eat." Sam followed her to a table in the rear.

Sam gazed around at the bare wood walls. "You need pictures on your walls."

"I've put up a few in my office." Glenda took a drink of water. "I'm waiting for some of the artistic people to come and do something with this place."

"What is this bread?"

"That's made from loovah root. At least we have plenty of that."

After the meal, they sat and discussed the new community.

"What do you need most?" Sam asked.

"Everything." Glenda grinned. "No, really. What we need most is people who will work like Jay."

"Have you met Roroy and his big black beast?"

"I saw him once. Why?" She fingered a dark spot on her collarbone.

"He volunteered to come and work up here. He says he has built houses. He's big and strong." Sam looked around at the barebones place.

"Good. Every pair of hands will help. See if you can get more of the builder people. Have you seen Addie lately?"

"Yes," Sam said. "She's on the list. I'll move her up, and a couple others I know of." Addie had worked on Sam's house in Starview.

"Thank you. Are you staying here or going back down tonight?" Glenda wadded her lip cloth.

"It's almost dark. Do you have a place I can sleep?"

"Sure."

Glenda showed Sam a little room in the back corner of the hall just big enough to hold a bed and tiny table. A door next to it led to an outhouse built onto the back of the building. Next to it was a washroom.

The bed was harder than her bed at home, but not enough to bother Sam. She was glad to see the new community coming along so well, but her reaction to being in a large group of Marisa's people dismayed her. She'd have to keep her meetings with them to a minimum.

Then there was the menace. Sam was sure now that whatever was going to happen would occur here on Peace, and somehow Marisa's people's Talent would protect them. She was peeved that there were still no details, and wondered when, or if, she should tell Marisa about her farseeing.

•   •   •

In the morning, Sam breakfasted with Glenda and Gus and a few others. Afterward, she collected a list of requests from them and said, "I need to get back to Starview. Guess I better get going. I want to visit with Maxee for a little bit. Great to see you again. Keep up the good work." Sam stood.

They said their goodbyes and Sam rode down to Maxee's place.

"You go back?" Maxee asked.

"I have to. It's good to see you. We miss you. How are the kubs?"

"They love it here. Always climbing trees. These here better."

"So what do you do with yourself?"

"Go up help Glenda, give kubs lessons."

"Good. You're keeping busy. What do you think of our new place so far?"

"Can be lot better than Starview if done right. People are lazy. Brax learning to be helper."

Sam noticed the kub was almost as big as Maxee and smiled. "Very good and tell him I said so."

They talked some more, about what was happening in Starview and in the new community.

"We need to make a name for it. You have any ideas?"

Maxee stretched her ears out to the side with her hands and let them plop back. "I found word in City I think is good. Haven."

"Haven. Yes, that sounds nice. We'll do it. Next time you go up, tell Glenda."

"Iss." Maxee bounced on her bottom.

"Well, I need to get going."

"Come back soon."

"Okay. Take care."

Sam had no idea when she would be back, and the menace was beginning to creep out from the back of her mind.

47

PEACE

S AM HEADED BACK TO FREEDOM. At the first house, Qiatta stopped and knelt.

"I guess this is where I get off," Sam said, dismounting. "Thanks, Qiatta."

The quine nodded and trotted off to her trees.

Sam arrived at Marisa's house just before supper. Allen and the boys appeared shortly after she did.

"Welcome back," Marisa said. "I'll set a place for you. How are things going up there?"

"Making progress, but as Glenda says, 'it takes time to build a house.'"

"Oh, yes. I remember when Roroy and I built ours. It seemed to take forever, always one more thing."

Sam ate and Marisa returned to her kitchen.

Janni came in a little later with Willie.

"Oh, there you are. How was it up there?"

"Glenda's frustrated. People don't want to do hard work like building houses. I told her Roroy volunteered to come up and help us with our building."

"Isn't he the best? I think he works harder than anyone else, except maybe Grampa Charley. What do you want to do after supper?"

"Rest and go home in the morning. Can I get a ride, or will I have to walk to the Gate?"

"We'll arrange a ride. I'll have to see who can go with you. Gus and Kirk are staying here, right?"

"Yes."

Sam lay on Janni's old bed and thought about what she had learned. These people could be trusted, but her people would have to be wary of spending too much time with them. If they kept their communities separate, they could easily coexist. If. There were always troublemakers.

Again, she felt the menace more strongly here, but there was still no definition.

·   ·   ·

After breakfast, Allen fetched his quine and Qiatta. "Thanks so much for your hospitality," Sam said. "I will do my best to see that my people are well-behaved."

Marisa nodded. "Travel mercies."

Sam and Allen rode away.

"We do not let people ride alone outside of the community," Allen said. "We, meaning us humans and the quines. Once, not long after we'd got to Harmony, I was still a kid, I tried to go off on my own. Bay followed me and brought me back and told me why they never let anyone go off by themselves."

He paused as they reached the bridge over the little river. "He said a Bramite boy went off by himself up into the hills, fell and broke both legs and hurt his head. It took two days with all of us searching to find him. He was still alive, barely, and the medics did what they could, but his legs never healed right and he had to use a stick to walk."

Sam nodded. "We have that rule too. No one goes up to the cavern where the Gate is by themselves."

Although Allen had a touch of grey in his brown hair, he had the spirit of a much younger man. His wide mouth was always set in a smile, and Sam could tell he adored Marisa and their children.

They rode in companionable silence.

Sam was glad to get away from the clan. One or two was not a problem, but when several hovered around and she was aware of more not too far away, it became oppressive. She felt a reluctance to leave this world. *Deja vu.* Like leaving cramped stuffy City for the valley, knowing she would have to go back because it was her duty.

At the halfway camp, Allen asked, "What do you think of this world?"

"It's lovely. It certainly lives up to its name." *And doesn't talk to me like Cityworld.* She decided to ask a question she'd been wondering about. "So many of your people look so much alike. Are you all related?"

"Yes." Allen grinned. "Most of us except Roroy and Elli. The rest of us, except Grampa Larry — he's Granlyn's cousin on her mother's side — are descended from Granlyn's paternal grandparents. We consider ourselves a clan. Granli is my big sister and Bill my big brother."

"I wondered. You look so much like him."

"Yeah, we take after our father. Back on Earth, he was a veterinarian and anti-science like the people who ran the country back then.

"Vet– what?"

"Animal doctor."

"Oh." Sam leaned back on her elbows on the sand by the campfire.

"What do you know about Earth?" Allen asked.

"Not a lot. We came from there. They had countries who were always fighting each other. They had a lot of technology we've lost over the years because the Volen did everything for us. Earth people had gods they prayed to. We have Oneness which is everything and everyone. I don't know where it came from."

"We have it too. Granlyn and Grampa Larry found it when they were escaping the Bramite world."

"They must have had some adventures." Sam found it very interesting to hear how these people had come to this world.

Allen told her how they escaped from Earth and more of his adventures.

•   •   •

The next day, Sam soaked in as much of the beach and surroundings as she could. The closer to the Gate she got, the more uneasy she felt.

At the Gate, she decided to go on through. She wouldn't be able to sleep if she camped there.

"I'm going to go through now," Sam said. "Thanks for your company. Bye, Qiatta." She patted the quine.

"Okay. Have a good trip home." Allen and the two quines headed for the beach.

Sam walked into the Gate and pushed the button.

48

STARVIEW

SAM CAME TO IN THE CAVERN. Home. She sat up and shook her head. When her mind cleared, she became aware of how alone she felt. She rose and left the cavern. Outside, early afternoon sunbeams striped the trees, and creatures made noises in the forest. Woodsy aroma and the dull blue sky told her she was home.

Thoughts of her ex flowed into her mind. She realized she had not thought of him at all on Peace.

When I go for good, I'll leave him here.

Although she'd already had a long day, she wasn't ready to sleep. *Brad,* she thought and pulled out her comm.

"Yeah," Brad answered.

"That's no way to greet your sister."

"Sam, you're back."

"On my way down." She stepped onto the trail.

"Thank Oneness."

Sam stopped. "What? Why?"

"I'll tell you when you get here. I can't send anyone to meet you. Keep your comm on."

Oh, no, now what?

Sam walked faster. After she tripped twice, she slowed down. When she reached the bridge, it was almost dark, and she was starving. It had been a long time since she had eaten.

"Hi," said Lucy, stepping out of the shadows. "Come rest and eat."

"How ..."

"Brad called and told me to meet you." Lucy took Sam's arm and led her over the bridge.

"No, I have to get home. Brad said ..." She tried to release her arm, but was overcome by fatigue and went along.

At Lucy's, just beyond the end of the bridge, Sam collapsed on the couch and stared at the yellow walls. So close, but she couldn't walk another step.

Lucy brought her a bowl of beans and veggies, with a couple slices of bread. "Eat."

Sam ate the food and slumped over in sleep.

When she woke, lying on the couch with a blanket over her, bright light poured in through the window.

"Good morning," Lucy said, sitting in a chair across from her, doing needlework.

"Oh," Sam said. She sat up, pushed her hands through her hair, and looked around at pictures of brightly colored flowers on the walls. "Oh, hi, Lucy."

Lucy nodded. Sam hurried out the back to the outhouse. When she came out, she saw the sun high in the sky.

"Oh, my."

Back inside the house, she said, "Thank you. I need to get going. Brad ..."

"I called him last night to let him know you were here. Before you run off, you need to eat something."

Sam wanted to leave, but her stomach had other ideas, so she ate some bread. She hurried over the bridge and ran into Brad. In his hug, she relaxed.

"So, what's going on?" she asked as they started back to the mesa.

"We had another earthquake. A good five block's worth of the cliff behind City fell in. It took parts of Far and Mid east with it."

"Oh no. Liia ..."

"She's all right. Her people are mostly all right. They'd stayed away from the cliff edge. They'll be at the turn in the river in a few days. We've got all sorts of people coming this way. The reservoir was destroyed, so there's no way to cross the river except up here at the bridge."

"Oh no."

Sam remembered walking along the reservoir above City with Hal on their first trip to Ambaak. It had been easy to step down from there to the roof and to her old apartment.

Across the bridge, where the trail turned along the river, a pair of young men sat on a wooden bench. Brad waved at them, and they waved back.

"They are the sentries to keep people from running up to the Gate," Brad explained. "We decided to not let anyone go until you got back."

A group of people were camped a little further along.

A young man called out, "Miss Sam! When can we go?"

"Are any of you builders or willing to build houses?"

Three men and a young woman stood. "We are," she said.

"Addie, how are you?"

She walked over to her. Addie had helped Sam rebuild her house when the original builders put it too close to the edge of the mesa.

"Anxious to get going. We've been here three days. I want to try for a baby."

"Okay." Sam counted.

One day at Haven, one day from there to camp, one day from there through the Gate and to Lucy's. That makes three days; they can go.

"Gus and Glenda desperately need more builders." She turned to the group. "Anyone else want to go build houses? Don't think you can go and get out of it. They'll put you to work."

Another couple stepped forward.

Sam checked their bags. "Good, you're prepared. Follow the signs and stay out of the other colony. There are signs and people will direct you. Good luck. You may go now. Just you six."

The group trotted off.

Others rose, and one fellow yelled, "Hey, I've been here longer."

"Are you a builder?"

"Farmer."

The others clamored around, demanding to go too.

"Okay. Farmers can build houses, too, especially if they want one of their own. You can all go, but only six can go through at a time, and you'll have to wait for at least a couple hours after the previous group or it won't work. Take your time, it's a stiff hike."

They all rushed off.

"No more today or tomorrow," Sam told the sentries. They nodded.

Sam and Brad moved on. She saw people wandering around between the rows of apartment buildings and wondered what they were doing.

They ran into Susan, Sam's friend. Sam noted the circles under her eyes and thought, *Another one overworked.* "How are you? Haven't seen you for a while."

"Busy. No one wants to settle down." Susan wrinkled her nose. "When this is over, I'm retiring to sit on a porch and watch the world go by. Even be nice to have the company of a comfortable old man."

"Susan, you?"

Sam knew that, after the boy who was going to marry her chose another at the last minute, Susan had sworn off men.

"That was a long time ago."

"Do you have someone in mind?"

Susan shook her head. "Have you heard? Linda and I've set up her caff so that they ask people they don't know where they're from, and if not from here, give them food and send them to a certain corner where my people ask them what they do, assign them jobs, and put them on a list. But we don't know whether they do their jobs or even if the names they give us are their real names." She smiled wryly with her triangular mouth.

The three of them walked around to the base of the mesa trail. A very large young man greeted them.

"I keep the riffraff out," he said. "But you can go up."

"Thanks," Susan said wryly.

Three people stood around Sam's office door. "Miss Sam, we need ..."

Sam blocked out the rest. She was tired and just wanted to sit. Arlene emerged and shooed them away.

Sam dropped into her chair. When she saw the piles of papers and oddments on her table, she wanted to go home and curl up in her bed.

"What is all this?"

"Requests. Demands. Lists. Welcome back." Arlene smiled.

"Anything I need to see right now?" Susan asked.

Arlene handed her a few papers.

"Okay. See you at meal." Susan left.

Sam put her head in her hands. "Tell me."

"Did Brad tell you about the earthquake?"

"Yes. Everything looks okay up here. I didn't see any obvious damage down below."

"No, but we sure felt it. Did he tell you how he and Hal flew west to check the damage? Whole cliffs fell into City."

Sam nodded. "I figured he must have flown out there."

"He told Far and Middle West that, if they wanted to stay, they'd have to go over the bridge at Far and rebuild on the north side of the river. No one was in any shape to make decisions. He said he'd go back in a week."

A young man with long, blond hair poked his head in. "Excuse me, some people are climbing up the back side."

"Tell security," Arlene said. "Three offices down."

"Okay." He left.

Arlene rolled her eyes. "All the time, interruptions. Where was I? Oh, yes. Brad told the others to build over by the river. Why Far wanted to build by the cliff overlooking the wreckage of City, I'll never know. About a third of their town dropped along with the cliff. So a lot of people are coming this way."

She took a sip of water. "They're all going to North Valley because there's no way to cross the river. The reservoir where you crossed is gone and Brad said there's a really wild waterfall there now."

"It was pretty big last time I saw it before we left." Sam rubbed her forehead. "What's North Valley doing?"

"They're sending the newcomers through and over the bridge."

"That's who those people were I saw wandering around."

"Yes. Now, this stack is requests for items we don't have or can't make. This one is for items we have a few of and take time to make, and we're rationing them to the ones who need them the most. These are all the applications to go to the new world. Over here are lists of new people. Oh, by the way, Evelyn wants to see you."

"Did she say why?"

"No, but it's important."

"I bet she wants to check me out again. Okay, I'll go."

As she stood, a young woman appeared.

"I have some free time, Miss Arlene. Is there something I can help you with? Oh, hi, Miss Sam."

"Yes. Come on in."

As Sam trudged over to Evelyn's clinic, she hoped the medic wouldn't find anything bad. She couldn't afford to miss any work.

49

STARVIEW

"**T**ELL EVELYN I'M HERE," Sam said to the woman at the front desk.

"Go on in."

"Oh, hi, Sam. Have a seat."

Evelyn and Jan were smearing a salve on a boy's red back. "I told you to keep your tunic on."

"I was hot," the boy, almost a man, mumbled.

"Now you're even hotter," Evelyn said caustically.

"Hi, Sam," Jan said, from her wheeled chair on the other side of the boy's bed.

"Hi, Jan. How are you doing?"

"Ready to go if we can figure out how."

"I have an idea." Sam remembered what Grampa Larry had said. She called Brad, who showed up about the time the two women were finished.

The boy left, after being admonished about leaving his tunic on.

"Sunburn," Evelyn said. "Hello, Brad. What's up?"

"Brad, would Jan's wheeled chair work on the trail?" Sam asked.

"I doubt it. It's too bumpy and there's that one place where we have to go single file."

"What if we made a narrow box and put it on wide boards so the box would slide on them? Take the wheels off the chair and put them in the box with Jan. We'll pad it, of course," Sam added to Jan.

"I certainly hope so." Jan made a face.

"Do you think it would work?" Evelyn asked, eyes wide.

"Let me make some measurements and see what I can find out." Brad smiled at Jan.

Evelyn heaved a sigh of relief. "I've been so worried about how we were going to get her up there. That was one of the two things I wanted to see you about, Sam. Jan, get the blood pressure tool."

Sam's blood pressure and pulse were slightly lower than last time, but not enough to satisfy Evelyn.

Jan listened to Sam breathing. "Sounds good," she said.

"So you want to go soon?" Sam asked.

"Yes."

"Okay. As soon as Brad makes you a cart, you can go. Who'll run this place?"

"That group I told you about. They're coming in later to take a look at the place."

"Good. Do I pass?"

"Yes." Mother and daughter smiled. "Thank you both," Evelyn added.

Sam and Brad left.

"Where'd you get that idea?" Brad asked.

"Grampa Larry on Peace."

Brad nodded. "Probably have to have one man pull and another push. See you around."

He trotted toward the construction office, and Sam returned to her own office.

That evening, as she sat on her porch, listening to the river burble along and watching the cloud shadows on the mountains, Sam wondered again whether she was doing the right thing for her people, moving them to Janni's world. A strong aftershock gave her the answer: Yes. This was something she definitely had to do. Even if they didn't all go.

•   •   •

The next day, Sam was back at work, dealing with multiple problems.

After three days of dealing with people who wanted replacements for items damaged in the quake, people who wanted to go to Peace, but were not prepared; and people who didn't know what they wanted, passed. Sam welcomed the call from Brad to come to Evelyn's clinic and see what he'd done.

By the side of the clinic sat a long cart just wide enough for Jan. Two strong ropes attached at the front corners joined at a round wooden handle. Wide, pointed runners poked out from underneath the front. A padded section awaited Jan, and the rear held her chair, bag, and a few other things.

Hal was there. "I want to go with them," he said. "I'll come back."

"Has Jan tried it out?"

"Yes."

"Yes, it will fit in the Gate," Brad said.

Evelyn came out.

"When can you be ready?" Sam asked.

"In a couple of days."

"Okay, I'll put you down for day after tomorrow."

•   •   •

Two days later, Sam, Hal, and Brad went down to Evelyn's clinic. She and Jan were both packed and ready, along with Hal and Jan's father, Dirk. He had been a councilor in City and had no real job in Starview, working as a man of all trades. Todd was there, also.

"Are you going, too?" Sam asked.

"Yes. I need to scope out the situation and see what I need to do. I'll come back with Hal."

"Okay." The menace continued to hover in the background. *At least, Brad would still be here.*

Jan's brother and father got her settled in the box cart. Hal gave Sam a big hug, and he and Todd picked up the ropes. They pulled, and the cart moved easily.

Sam and Brad accompanied them to the bridge. The cart moved smoothly along the leaf covered path. At the bridge, Sam and Brad wished them well.

"Call us on the comm in the cavern," Sam said, "so we know you got there."

"I'll get them settled and come back." Hal grinned.

"Check with Marisa or Janni for messages," Sam said, muffled in his hug.

"Will do."

They separated and Hal's group started up the trail.

Sam and Brad trudged back to the mesa. The cool breeze caused her to shiver. Now she had something else to worry about. The menace hovered in the background, maddeningly unclear. Normally by this time, she would have a good idea of what it was and could start preparing for it.

Sam had begun foreseeing events a few months after she'd moved to Starview. At first, she was startled by it, but quickly grew used to it. Pivotal events like dangers or major changes in weather. Brad also had the ability. He figured they'd got it from their mother, born on another world, and the Volen had masked it until they left.

50

PEACE

J ANNI, WILLIE, AND SEVERAL OTHERS marked off the corridor for Sam's people, and put up wooden slat fences along the quine area and in back of the houses nearest the way. Marisa would know when people came through, and station someone at the bridge and at the northward turn to guide them. The guide would give each citizen a loaf of bread and a loovah plant.

It seemed to work well at first. Janni struggled to ignore Sam's people and focus on Willie and the clan. She and Willie spent many evenings with Glori and Brian.

When the men complained about the girls not getting pregnant, Janni said, "We can't until we know that our children won't have any more Talent than us."

One day, Marisa asked Janni to go to the bridge. An unusual arrangement of people was coming up. Janni watched a pair of men pull some kind of contrivance up the slope. Someone was sitting in it. *Why couldn't she walk?*

A man and woman trudged along behind. The sun was brushing the tops of the trees along the big river when they arrived and stopped. A young woman sat in the cart, which was on wide boards.

"Hi, I'm Janni," she said, eying the cart. "You can't walk?"

"No, I have no feet," the girl in the cart said. "I'm Jan, short for Janice." She giggled.

"I won't forget your name." Janni grinned and turned to the others. The tall man looked familiar, but she couldn't place him.

"I'm Todd," he said. "This is Evelyn, a head medic, her husband, Dirk, her daughter, Jan, and her son, Hal, Sam's good friend."

"Are you her friend, too?"

"Sam and Brad and I grew up together after their mother left."

"Oh." She'd have to find out about that later. "What is your specialty?"

"I'm in legal. I will be doing surveying, marking off exact boundaries of each plot of land and writing up deeds to show who owns each one."

Janni didn't understand why that was necessary, but maybe it was because there were so many of them.

"Hal?" He had beautiful brown eyes.

"I'll check out everything and make lists of what is needed, what needs to be done, any problems and so forth, and report back to Sam." He smiled.

I see why Sam likes him.

"Okay, there's a corridor marked off. Just follow the signs, across to the trees and north. That's the big river in those trees." She pointed west. "Welcome to Peace."

"Thank you," Evelyn said. "How far is it?"

"You'll want to camp after you get past Freedom, then it will be most of the next day."

Evelyn sighed.

"We'll make it, Mother," Jan said. "I like this world."

"Easier to pull her up this hill than the one on our world," Hal said.

"Yes, it was easier to walk, even in sand." Evelyn smiled.

"Good luck." Janni watched them maneuver the cart over the bridge and move on.

Since no one else was coming, Janni took a shortcut through the village to the quines' enclave and asked Qione to select three of her people. "There's three men and two women. I'll take them up to the camp. One needs to pull a small cart."

Qione nodded and sorted out a crowd of volunteers. 'Only for females,' she sent.

Janni and the quines met the group as they left the corridor and looked for a place to camp.

"Over here," Janni called. They turned and Evelyn gasped. "These are quines. You women will ride them tomorrow." One quine sniffed Evelyn and the other snuffled Jan's hair.

"Oooh," Jan exclaimed, wiggling in her seat. "How do we get on them?"

"They will kneel. Talk to them. They understand our language and you will hear them in your minds. They will take care of themselves tonight and in the morning, just tell them when you are ready to go. One will pull the cart with all your bags and stuff. They know the way. Just enjoy the ride. If you need to stop, just tell them so."

"Thank you so much," Evelyn said, eyes gleaming.

"Just head straight up along the river and you'll find the new place. Do you have any food?

"Yes. Another lady gave us each a loaf of bread and a plant to take up to our new home." Evelyn smiled.

"Okay. I'll come up in a few days and see how you're doing. Take care."

"Thanks again," Hal said as Janni trotted off back to Freedom. She found Marisa at Granlyn's and told them about the newcomers.

"Good, they have a real medic now," Mama said. "Tell Artie or Big Art about those skids, I'm sure they'll be interested."

"They sound like they're taking this seriously," Granlyn said. "That's a relief."

"Who are they to create deeds to property on our world," Grampa Larry grumbled, crumpling a nose cloth in his lap.

"We don't need the whole world. It's like on Earth, each town and city had their own space and their own property deeds," said Granlyn.

"Until some countries tried to take part or all of others."

"All right, Larry. That's ancient history. Don't you have some tasks, Janni?"

"Yes, Granlyn."

She ran to the plaza kitchen to sort food. These people also seemed very pleasant, but maybe Sam was only sending the nice people first. She had missed the group that had come after the four builders. A few at a time were no problem, but when there would be a mass of people up there, that bothered her.

She believed Sam when she said they would leave the clan alone, but what would happen when someone else took over? The only defense the clan had was their Talent.

Janni and Glori arranged to have dinner for the four of them at Glori's house. Janni brought a loaf of bread. As usual, the main topic of conversation was the new people. Janni was both glad and uneasy. The Other and the Watcher haunted her.

Brian enthused about how well the crops were doing this year.

"We'll need all the food we can get." Janni grabbed her fork.

•   •   •

The next dawn, Janni's being floats in space. Something has changed, but it takes her few moments to determine what it is. Something is missing. No, changed. The Other — where is it? A gray mist passes over her and when it is gone, she is somewhere else.

Where am I?

No humans. Searches for Peace — she's at a solar system of many worlds, not her Peace. Countless aliens live in small groups in savannahs, there are areas of many fruit trees, along oceans and rivers. A number of different worlds are called Peace in whatever language the population uses. But she can't find hers.

She tries Earth, and finds a very warm world where the natives live in burrows in the ground. Several others, but again not hers. Another common name, in whatever speech. Cityworld brings her nothing. She tries to think of other worlds in the Earth system.

There's Harmony, but she has no idea where it is in relation to Peace.

Janni's self is lost in space. And then she changes.

She focuses on her body and finds her way home.

•   •   •

Janni, the young woman, woke.

"You were out again," Willie said. In daylight, he hovered over her.

"Yes. I'm here now." Whoever she was now. She felt as if she were still out of her body, watching it rise and react.

"Janni, are you all right?" Willie asked.

"Of course. Give me a moment."

"Gotta go." He kissed her and left.

Janni went out to the outhouse. *Why am I like this?* Back in the house, she puttered around, nibbled on some bread, pulled the coverlet up over the bed. She had no desire to leave her house and tried to figure out what was going on in her head.

She could think logically about her world: all her learned knowledge was there, although a bit skewed. People now. No trouble recognizing or dealing with Willie. But others, she wasn't so sure.

She could find nothing new added to herself, but that didn't mean it wasn't there. Overall, she felt like she was in a state of duality, in her body and also out of it. Inside, she felt muddled; outside she saw everything clearly, down to the tiniest detail. And she could move things by just thinking about it. Janni shivered.

A rap on the door and Marisa barged in. "Where have you been? You're supposed to have been at work hours ago."

"Mama," Janni said, and stopped. There was nothing she could say.

"Janni," Marisa said, staring at her. "Are you all right?"

Janni felt her touch her mind. "Do I look different?"

"No, but there's something about you ..."

"Yes."

"Did you go out? What happened?"

"I don't know. I got lost and couldn't find my way back. Do you know how many worlds named Peace there are?"

"Oh, my dear." Marisa drew her into a hug. "But you did find your way home."

"Yes. After discovering any number of Earths, I finally homed in on my body."

"That's good. I think we need to go see Granlyn."

Janni still felt reluctant to leave her house but went with Marisa.

"Looks like they found you," Granlyn said after they explained what happened.

"How come you accept it, but Gramma Perri doesn't?"

"I always knew of other worlds; Dad always had stories to tell when he returned from being away. Larry and I thought they were neat stories, but Beth, my sister, stopped listening to them after she reached about ten or so. I don't know where she got her skepticism; neither Mom nor Dad had any.

"I don't remember the stories. I never did get my childhood memories back after the Watchers took them away when they sent me to Adam's world. After being sent to several other worlds, nothing much fazed me." Granlyn smiled.

"Perri spent most of her life on one world, until we moved here, and by then her daughter was grown. She remembers what it was like, living with the Bramites."

"What are we going to do?" Mama asked.

"I have no idea."

"Are you up to going to work, Janni?"

"I guess so." She didn't really want to, but she didn't want to sit around her house all day either.

Janni went to the craft house, where she counted and sorted tunics by size. They had plenty, many of the boys and men were constantly wearing theirs out and there's only so many times a tunic or pair of pants can be mended.

Gradually the out-of-the-body effect faded, although Janni still felt not quite right.

Like there was another version of her in the background, watching. Or someone or something watching. Was she changing?

No, I can't be.

She pushed the thought away.

51

PEACE

HAL AND TODD HELPED EVELYN AND JAN onto their quines. When hers stood up, Jan gasped.

"Wonderful," she said, as the quine took a few steps. "Something else I don't need feet for."

"Yes," Evelyn agreed. "You men don't mind walking?"

"No, Mother," Hal said, walking between the quines.

The day was bright and sunny. They took rest and food stops. The men carried Jan into the bushes so she could relieve herself.

As the sun was setting, they saw someone ahead who waved. E darted away, and soon a tall woman with dark hair appeared and they pulled up beside her.

"Hello and welcome. I'm Glenda," the woman said. "What is that contraption?" She pointed to the cart.

They had broken down the wheeled chair and the parts stuck out of the back of the cart.

Hal explained, and Glenda showed them where they could camp. "We should have a house ready for you soon."

Evelyn and Glenda watched as the men put the chair together and lifted Jan down and into it.

"I don't have any feet. I lost them in an accident when I was little," she said.

"Oh, my. But you had no trouble riding."

"No. I used my knees and hands to hold on."

"Did you bring any food?" Glenda asked.

"Yes," Evelyn bent over and rubbed her knees.

"Come, I'll show you the sanitary facilities and where we eat." Glenda had seen the girl in the chair, but had never met her. She hoped she wasn't a complainer.

They followed Glenda as she showed them around.

"I'd like to see the clinic," Evelyn said, after Jan was settled in a comfortable chair in the meeting hall.

Gus took the men to see the ongoing construction.

"Sure. Over here." *Thank goodness we have a real medic.*

Evelyn took a quick look around the clinic. It was empty, but there was a sign on the door that said, 'at evening meal'. "Not bad for a start."

"We plan to build a bigger one later, but first we've got to get people into houses."

"Of course."

They went to eat and met the others. Glenda found one of the young medics and introduced her to Evelyn.

"Tomorrow morning, I want you to show me what you have. I brought more supplies, bandages and stuff." Evelyn smiled at the girl.

"Oh, good. We're almost out of a lot of things and I hate to ask the clan."

•　　　•　　　•

In the morning, Glenda showed Evelyn around, and asked her what she would like to have in the permanent building.

"We'll have to get with Zilla, the director of medicine, to see what she wants. I would like to see what the clan has at their clinic."

"I think we can arrange that." Glenda smiled. This woman knew what she was doing.

52

STARVIEW

O N THE WAY BACK TO HER OFFICE, Sam ran into a woman from food service.

"Sam, I've been trying to get a hold of you. We're trying to figure out how to break down and take the caffs through and still feed people here. And we need to know: how big is this Gate? We have some of the grain carts from City."

"Well, six people can go through at a time. You need to get with Brad for actual measurements. I can see where that could be a problem, especially with all the new people from the west." *Not mine.* "I was thinking, over there we should go to having kitchens in every house, like the clan. We can keep one big kitchen and a few small caffs. The food people could show the others how to cook."

"Okay, I'll tell June. Thanks." She ran off.

At her office, Sam told Arlene about the caff's problem and personal kitchens.

"Hm. That's an idea." Arlene pulled her ear.

"And we should have storehouses where we can put food and clothing and tools where people can go get what they need."

"We'd have to have some kind of signout system, and limits on how much of any one item any one household could take." Arlene tapped her comm.

"The caff workers could be the monitors."

"Right."

Sam thought. "Have June make a list of what she needs to keep a caff going, and if she can divide them into two groups: one to go and one to stay. What equipment and supplies can be carried, and what can be pulled on some kind of sled."

Arlene nodded. "Oh, yes. George wants to see you. Something to do with moving."

"Couldn't you help him?"

"He wanted you because you've seen and used the Gate."

"Okay."

She went to find George, the head of the science department. He and an assistant were taking inventory

"You wanted to see me?"

He looked up. "Yes. How much room will I have for my labs over there?"

"As much as you want." Sam smiled at his assistant, who was scribbling as fast as she could.

"Are you sure?" he asked.

"Yes. They are building all the official buildings in one area, around a plaza, and they've left plenty of space between them and the first row of houses."

George raised his eyebrows. "I'll start planning my layout."

"When do you want to go over?"

"Not for a while. Perhaps someone can take my plans when I have them ready?"

"No problem."

He also wanted to know the size of the Gate.

After Sam told him, she left.

Next on her list was Zilla, the director of medicine. She didn't want to go yet, but she was working on a plan to slowly close clinics and move their people to Peace.

"Good," Sam said. "This is a real juggling act, isn't it?"

"And you have to deal with everything. What's it like over there?"

"Plenty of room. We won't be all crammed in like we are here."

Sam headed back to her office.

At least some people are preparing for their move.

•   •   •

Two days of emptiness. Maxee, Hal, and Todd gone to Peace; and Brad gone up to the gate with four groups of three young couples. He wanted to recheck his measurements. He took his nine-year-old son, Del, with him. Sam buried herself in her work.

At home in the evenings, she tried to keep busy. Worn out, she sat on her porch and stared at the river. It was still low, the men who had gone up were only able to remove part of the blockage. They said the overflow was making a new river down to North Valley. Then she looked up at the stars.

Which one of those is Peace's? Where is the menace coming from? What is that fuzziness over there?

•   •   •

The next day, after Brad called to let her know they were on their way home, Sam met them at the bridge.

"Aunt Sam," Del exclaimed. "We had a great time. I even saw a brown animal in the trees. And we found a place where we could go down to the river and I saw a fish."

Brad shook his head slightly and gave her a hug. "They all went through, but Gate noise sounded a little funny the last time. I scribbled a note and put it through." He tousled his son's hair. "I guess this was his walkabout. Anything new down here?"

They started back.

"No. Only minor attempts at repairs, and more people coming in from the west. At least George and Zilla are preparing their departments for the move."

53

PEACE

ON PEACE, THE FIRST GROUPS WAITED for the last one. Time passed, longer than the periods between the previous groups. "Where are they?" one of the girls asked.

Finally, one fellow opened the door to the room. It was empty. "No," several of the girls said.

•　　　•　　　•

In Freedom, Janni *sensed* their distress and told Uncle Artie. He and Big Art left for the Gate.

They met the first two groups at the halfway camp.

"What happened?" Big Art asked.

"The last group of six never came out," a tall boy with long light hair tied behind his head said.

"How long did you wait?"

"Hours. There's still one group back there waiting for them."

"Okay. You go on to the community in the morning." Uncle Artie *called* Marisa and told her what had happened.

The Arts rested for a few hours and took off in the night. The moon gave them some light. The others slept.

•　　　•　　　•

Janni was with Marisa when Uncle Artie *called* the next day.

'We tested the Gate,' he *sent*. 'Someone had definitely entered on Cityworld, but they never came out here. I've shut down the Gate and we'll stay here and work on it.'

"Oh, no," Marisa said.

'Where are they?' Janni asked. The thought came: *They're gone.*

"Unknown. We'll stay here until we figure it out; I shut it down so it won't work from the other end. You may want to go down and meet the other groups."

Janni groaned. The Otherness was still there, when she thought about it. But this ... If the Gate quit working, what were they going to do?

"Artie will fix it," Marisa said, soothing her daughter.

"What if he can't?"

"We'll worry about it then. Now what were we doing?"

•　　　•　　　•

The next morning, Janni and Marisa rode down to the beach with extra quines. Soon three couples appeared, exhausted.

"Welcome to Peace," Janni said. The quines were already in the sea.

"Don't be scared," Marisa said. "These are quines, a people in their own right. They let us ride them. Let's sit up here on the grass. I'm Marisa and this is my daughter Janni," She pointed up the hill. "Our home is up there, but you can ride from here if you wish."

"Water," one of the boys croaked.

They got him and the others water. "Why didn't you get water out of the streams? It's perfectly good."

After gulping down a large cupful, another boy said, "We were afraid to."

"Didn't Sam tell you it was okay?" Janni asked.

"She said so many things, I don't remember."

"I told him," his mate said. "His mind was on us getting home afterward."

"So you were paying more attention to your hormones than what would save your lives," Marisa said.

"We knew it was okay, and tried to tell the men, but they wouldn't listen. Jane, Sandy, and I drank some when they weren't looking."

"Kari," her mate said.

"I told you not to drink all the water so soon."

"All right, you two." Marisa patted her hair. "Are you up to moving along?"

"Can we really ride those things?"

"Yes."

"Mama, look, someone else is coming." Janni pointed down the beach.

Another group of six approached.

Janni stood and did her spiel. "Do you need anything?"

"No, thank you, we're fine. The water in those streams is much better than what we get at home," one of the girls said.

The first three girls said, "I told you so."

Their men grimaced.

"Did you have any trouble coming through the Gate?" Marisa asked.

"No, except it just knocked us for a loop. but we recovered quickly," one fellow said. "The only thing is, the last group never showed up. We met Big Art last night and he said they were going up to fix it."

"Yes, we know. Did you know the other group very well?" Janni asked.

"Not really. Just acquaintances."

The sun was setting. "Do you want to go on, or stay here for the night?" Marisa asked.

"I can't move another inch," one gal said.

"Okay, we'll camp here. Qione," Marisa called.

'What?' Janni heard the quine *send* to her mother.

"Come here. I need my things."

The quine trotted up and Marisa unloaded blankets and food. "We'll set up here."

"We have our own food," the man from the second group said.

"Have some bread anyway." Marisa handed out a loaf to each group.

•   •   •

In the morning, people were packing up when the third group showed up.

"Qione, can you get some more of your people down here for these youngsters?" Marisa asked. The quine nodded.

The third group lay down on the grass while everyone waited for the new quines. The ones there splashed back into the water.

Janni sat down by Kari. "How are things in Starview?"

"A mess. We've had more earthquakes and everyone coming in from the west. Some can't decide whether to repair the places or just live there until they go."

"Oh dear. Was anyone hurt?"

"I heard that part of Far West caved in onto the ruins of City."

"Oh, no." *We have to get those people over here.*

Presently a herd of quines galloped down the slope to the sea.

"What are those?" someone from the third group asked.

"Quines." Marisa stood. "We'll let them splash a little bit. They love the water."

Finally, she signaled, and Qione ushered the other quines out of the water and arranged riders.

Bags in the panniers, everyone seated on a quine, Marisa asked, "Everyone ready?"

A chorus of "Yes," "I guess so," and "What do I do now?" rang out.

"Let's go." Janni led the way on Qilla. Marisa and Qione brought up the rear.

These young people are not like Sam, Janni thought as she rode along. *The girls just wanted to have their birth control removed so they could have babies. Are these people going to be scared of anything new? Are we going to have to show them how to do things? I hope Glenda and the others up there can straighten them out.*

Qilla walked at a sedate pace so the newcomers could get used to riding. Janni wanted to gallop and fought impatience. At the bridge, Roroy waved them over it. Janni looked around for Beast but didn't see him.

Just as well. These people would be scared out of their britches.

At the corner where they turned north, Susan handed every couple a loaf of bread.

"Is this all?" she asked Marisa.

"Yes. Come see me when you're done." To the newcomers, she said, "Don't eat it all at once. Unless you have your own food, this is all you'll get 'til tomorrow when you get to your new home."

The group moved on, riding in pairs along the corridor and up to the camp, where Qione stopped, as did the rest of the quines.

"This is as far as we go." Marisa dismounted, followed by Janni.

"Can we keep the quines?" someone asked.

"What do you think, Qione?"

Qione communicated with the other quines. For the first time, Janni could understand what the quine was saying. *No!* she screamed in her mind.

"Yes, you may. You all stick together. When you get up there and get off, the quines will come home." Marisa said.

'They may stay there,' Qione *sent.* 'Our place is getting too crowded.'

"Fine," Marisa said. Qione and Qilla left. "We will leave you here. If you have any problems up there, go to Glenda. How many of you girls want your birth control removed?"

All nine young women raised their hands.

"Our medic is creating a schedule. I'll let Glenda know when it is time for each of you to come down to Freedom for the procedure. It may not be right away. Be patient."

"Thank you," Kari said.

"Remember, straight up along the trees along the river. Take care."

Janni and Marisa left to walk home.

"What do you think of that group?" Marisa asked.

"I hope they stay up there." Still shaken by her new ability, Janni was unable to say more.

She had to get rid of Talents, but how?

54

STARVIEW

S AM TOOK STOCK. Aftershocks had made everyone nervous. Some people said why bother doing anything. People climbed trees for the high fruit, and fell out, breaking bones. Zilla said they'd seen more broken bones in the last month than they had in the last two years. The caff people had to put the bread behind the counter — too many citizens were taking three or four loaves. No way to contact Marisa or Janni. Sam was being ground down by having to keep track of who's over there, what services are over there, and what is still here.

Sam checked the lists of the citizenry, marking the people who'd gone to Peace. She had another list of the heads of departments and others she worked with. She had to keep track of who was where and make substitutions when necessary. In addition to the everyday stuff.

The next day, she sent up four more groups. Later, she got a call from one of them, the Gate was closed.

"What?"

"The door to the room won't open."

Now what? she thought. "Stay there tonight and try in the morning. Do you have enough food for another day?"

"Maybe."

"If you think you do, and if you want to, stay there and try again later in the day. If you try early afternoon and it doesn't work, you should be able to get to the bridge by dark and stay in North Valley."

"Okay."

Sam sat back in her chair on her porch. *Why was the Gate closed? Did Janni not want any more people to come through, or did the Gate break down? What were they supposed to do if the Gate quit working? I don't need this at all.*

She called Brad and told him what she'd heard.

"What are we going to do?"

"Wait and see if they can fix it. I'll go up in a few days and see if it's working. Don't worry, sis, we'll find a way."

"The eternal optimist," Sam said, smiling. "I hope you're right."

•   •   •

The next morning, she told everyone no one else was to go for the time being. Arlene groaned.

"Is this ever going to end? Are we ever going to have a settled life? I think I'll retire with you."

"Who would take your place?" Sam asked.

"Carolyn, my first assistant. She can do it all and has the energy of the young. Who will replace you?"

"I'm thinking of Hal. He'll hand everything to other people and sit and make plans."

When the travelers returned, one said, "We tried the next day and still nothing happened."

"Okay." Sam shook her head.

"If we haven't heard anything, I'll go up and check out the Gate day after tomorrow," Brad said. "I've got too much to do tomorrow."

"All right." Sam shook her head again."

Her phone beeped.

"Hello, Liia here."

"Liia, how are you? Or I should say, where are you?"

"We're north of the big bend in the river. There's a little one comes down out of the hills. We're camping there for a while."

"Good."

"Sam, I'm so tired. I've lost half the people I saved from City. I don't know where we're going. I don't know what to do."

Sam's heart clenched. "Hang in there. How's Giil and Jone and the children? How are you on food?"

"Giil's with me. Jone, Jim, and Betty are in the group behind us. Jim has a mate and she's with child. They'll be here in a couple of days. We have food for about a week."

"Good. How far along is she?"

"Only a few months."

"Okay." *At least she wouldn't have to worry about that for a while.* "Our north valley is just east of there. I'll get someone to come talk with you. I'm on the other side of the river and it would take me two or three days to get there. Would you be interested in moving to another world where you would have plenty of room for your people?"

"How would we get there?"

"Through a Gate between worlds. I'll explain later, if you're interested."

"Is it like this one?"

"Yes. Mostly wide open; mountains a lot farther away."

"Let me think."

"Sure. I'll try to get over there soon. Take care."

Only a quarter of her people. Sounds like us.

Sam went to her office and called Lucy. "There's a new group, from the Ambaak sector, just west of the west end of your valley. The leader is Liia. Could you send someone over to welcome them to Starview? You're a lot closer than I am."

"Certainly. I'll keep you updated."

Nothing unusually disruptive happened the next day. Brad came by and told Sam, "I'm going up early in the morning, before breakfast. I'll take a food bar."

"Fine. Call me when you get there." Sam smiled at him.

"Yes, sis."

•   •   •

Next day, late morning, Sam got a call from Brad. "Hal's back. He and a young couple just came through and appear to be fine. He brought a note from Janni that said the Gate is working now and to start sending people though again."

Sam was glad he was back, but terrified at the thought something might have gone wrong.

"So the Gate is working?"

"Apparently. We're on our way home. See you soon."

As she ended the call, Sam heaved a sigh. *Could we really trust the Gate? What other choice do we have?*

She went back to her duties with mixed emotions. Happy because Hal was back, worried about the Gate, unhappy there was still no more information about the menace.

•   •   •

At the cavern, Brad asked the couple, "Any problems?"

Hal went off on his own.

"No. That place is nice, but I don't like living in a tent. We'll go back when they have houses ready."

"The idea was for everyone to help build their own houses. If you don't know how, you'll be taught."

"You're not going to make us go back, are you?"

"No. How are you on food?" Brad asked.

"We ate the last of it last night. Do you have any? We're hungry."

"What did you expect to eat tonight and tomorrow? It'll take most of the day for you to get home."

"Oh. Jerry said there'd be food here." He looked around.

"Jerry who? How did he know? What did Mayor Sam tell you? Did she say there would be food here in the cavern?"

"Um, no, but ..."

"Has this Jerry been to one of the travel classes?"

"I don't think so, but ..."

"I see. You trusted someone who had not even been to a class, instead of the mayor who knows everything about travel." Brad sighed. He pulled out a loaf of bread. "Here. This will have to last you 'til we get home. I'm going to camp outside. You two do what you like."

He left them standing there, clutching their bags, the boy clutching the bread, the girl crying.

After finding a suitable place to camp, he called Sam.

•   •   •

Sam finished her most necessary tasks in midafternoon and headed up the river trail. Long shadows stretched in front of her. At the bridge, she met Brad and Hal, and slipped into Hal's arms.

"I've missed you," she said.

"Me, too." Hal let her go. "Next time, we both go."

"Yes. I thought you said there was another couple."

"They're coming." Brad indicated the upward trail. "They didn't want to go as fast as we did. I suggest, since it's almost dark and we'll be bombarded with questions, that we go see Lucy and see if she or someone can put us up for the night."

"Good idea," Hal said. "Sam and I will go. You wait here for the others."

Brad nodded.

At Lucy's, Sam introduced Hal. "He's a special friend."

"Welcome. What do you need?"

"Shelter for the night for us, Brad, and another couple."

"Oh." She looked nonplussed.

"We can sleep out if you can loan us a couple blankets. The others all have theirs."

"No, no. We'll find a way. Come on in."

Sam *called* Arlene to tell her where she was, and that Hal was back. "Don't send any tomorrow, I need to talk to Hal about what's going on over there."

Sam and Hal slept on the boys' beds, Brad on the couch.

"The boys love to sleep on the floor; they do that a lot," Lucy said. She took the couple next door.

•   •   •

In the morning, as Sam and the others crossed the bridge, she met a pair going up. "Where are you going?" Sam asked.

"To the other world." They were young and obviously in love. Both dark blond, the girl had wispy bangs and the boy's hair covered his ears.

"Who said you could go? Where's your bags of possessions and food? Have you taken the orientation class?" Sam demanded.

They looked puzzled. "We'll get food there," the boy said.

"Where? Do you have any idea how long it will take you to get there?"

"A day?" the boy asked.

"More like three or four. It'll take the rest of the day to get to the Gate. Do you know where it is?'

"They said follow the signs."

The girl's mouth drooped.

"It will take you the rest of today to get to the Gate. You must camp overnight, you'll need the rest, and after you go through, at least two days to get to Freedom and another day up to our place."

"Oh," said the boy.

The girl looked like she was about to cry.

"Come on back with us and we'll get you signed up for a class," Sam said, smiling. "Don't worry, you'll get there."

Once they moved ahead of the two, Brad asked if he'd missed anything.

"George caught Del snooping around in his lab."

"That kid of mine is one big pot of curiosity. I'll talk to him."

"I think George already did."

"I'm going on home. Emily thinks she's pregnant again."

"That's nice."

Sam had never wanted children after what her ex-husband had done to her. For some reason no one could explain, Emily's birth control had stopped working when they came to Starview. Brad thought it might have been caused by the fall she took when she was leaving City. Their four children had few playmates. In a few cases, a woman left with a new baby before her birth control was turned back on, and so was able to have more.

55

OTHER

OUT IN SPACE, BETTAH WORRIED. One third of Groupleader, she stretched her long body and settled in her couch. Hetch, another third, was not performing as he should. Nooch, the third party to the Group, observed. As Torgs, they were only supposed to be looking for the others the Watchers had selected as possible replacements. She did not understand why Hetch chose to destroy that race.

They and their crewmates had acquired this ship by controlling the minds of those who used it before. They needed it as they had no ships of their own. After conforming it to accommodate their long bodies and sense of viewing, they learned how to use it. Unfortunately, the master pilot died before they could retrieve all ship information.

Bettah growled. She wanted to become a watcher, get rid of this cumbersome body. A long body in a hard shell, short legs and arms, brain mostly inside body because the head got too big to come out. Fortunately, her sense organ was on the tip so she could view both sight and sound as one.

Hetch could not totally control the ship, determine where it was going. Ship would continue life support as needed, but only accepted certain commands from the new pilot. Accelerating to a faster speed was not one of them. The Groupleader's data processor could not interface with Ship.

They and their people, the chosen ones, had been kicked out of their world by the havenots, and now lived on Ship, traveling aimlessly. Until they found a world with the other race. Hetch had found weapons and destroyed them. Unnecessarily, Bettah thought. She didn't even know whether they were the ones who had the talent.

How could they determine who had it, and contact them?

56

PEACE

Uncle Artie *called* Grampa Charley from the Gate. 'I believe I have it fixed.'

'Believe?' said Janni, who also *heard* it.

'Nothing is guaranteed. Do you want to send someone to try it out?'

'Not me.' Janni shook her head.

'I'll ask Marisa,' Charley *said*.

'No,' Marisa *said*. 'I'll ask if someone from Haven wants to. Did you find the missing group?'

"No sign. They're gone, their molecules spread out in space."

"Oh, no." *More losses.*

Later, when Sam heard about it, she groaned, marked them off the list, and notified whoever had been left behind.

When Marisa checked with Glenda, the latter said Hal wanted to return. She also heard that a young woman who had just undergone the removal of her birth control wanted to go back. Hal and the girl and her mate were given quines and sent off. Artie welcomed them and sent them through.

"I hate not knowing whether it worked." Janni said.

"Artie said it worked fine. Now, back to your tasks."

"Yes, Mama."

Janni felt lost. She could not orient herself, doing her tasks as she had always done them, but in a fog of uncertainty. Outside of herself, she watched, corrected mistakes, and waited. She enjoyed being with Willie in bed, but the fog dulled her attention to her eggs, and one slipped by and found a sperm.

She wanted to go out to space, but could not. Something out there prevented her from going.

She threw herself into her work, coming home exhausted, throwing food into the stew pot for supper with a loaf of bread.

"Come on, Janni, you're wearing yourself out," Willie said one day. "Where's my Janni?"

She felt a wave of sympathy for him. He'd expected to have a loving mate, and instead had been saddled with a distant, dreamy lover who fell asleep in his arms every night.

Janni went to him, took his face in her hands and kissed him. "Let's go see what happens."

•   •   •

Janni woke to a feeling of happiness. For a moment. Then the duality came over her, as if she were splitting into to two people. Her natural self and ... Watcher?

"No," she cried and jumped out of bed. If Willie said anything, she didn't hear it. She ran out to the outhouse, then ran north without a single coherent thought in her head. As if she could outrun the Watchers. She ran until she collapsed, and lay sobbing.

Allen, who had just left his house, reached her first. Qilla galloped up right behind him. He picked her up and held her to him. Qilla nosed her head and made little moaning sounds. Others came, human and quine.

Janni was aware of them in a basic way as she fought the urge to become Watcher.

"Janni," Willie cried, stumbling down beside her.

She felt her papa's body, Qilla's nose, Willie's hands. She heard people talking, quines huffing; smelled Papa's scent, Qilla's hair, Willie. She held on to them, pulled, grasped, felt the earth under her legs and feet. Slowly Janni drew back into herself.

She quieted and opened her eyes. "Papa," she said. "Willie." She took his hand.

"Janni," Mama cried, dropping down beside Papa.

He moved one arm from Janni to Marisa. "She'll be all right," Papa said.

Gramma Perri huffed up. "What happened?"

Janni sat up and looked around. She was surrounded by her people, human and quine. This is where she belonged. She closed her eyes and took a deep breath.

"I'm starting to become Watcher."

"No," Mama moaned.

"I felt it too," Glori said, pushing through the crowd.

"Can you stop it?" Gramma Perri asked.

"I did this time."

A voice from up north said in her mind, 'Shut mindlink.'

"Maxee?" Janni looked toward the north.

A tiny figure stood far in the distance.

"Yes," Glori said, reaching over Marisa to take Janni's hand. "I heard that. Close down your Talent, as much as you can."

Janni brought in boundaries of mindlink, closing out quines and older generations except her grandparents and Granlyn. Then she closed out others except for her immediate family. These she tucked into an easily accessible place in her mind where she could reach them quickly when needed. The link with Glori was the only one she could not hide, although she was able to damp it down some.

Janni drew a deep breath and climbed to her feet, *sensing* a few people testing her. She looked around at everyone.

"I'm okay now. Sorry, Qilla." She hugged the quine's neck. "Call Glori. She'll let me know."

Janni pulled her shoulders back and marched back down to her house, Glori and her family with her.

"Go on," Allen called to the others. "We'll be all right." The quines trotted away, and people hurried down the hill.

A new sense of freedom stole over her. She was aware of Glori, but none of the others. But the freedom was accompanied by aloneness.

Why couldn't we all turn off our Talents? she thought, then realized that no one else, except maybe Glori, was able to do so.

Willie held her hand as if he'd never let her go.
"I'm not going anywhere," she said.
"Damn right you're not."
That night he tied her to the bed again. She hid her giggles.

•   •   •

In the dawn, Janni goes out into space. It is different. She can see each solar system and their worlds without having to go into each bubble.

'No,' she sends. 'Watcher, wherever you are, I'm not becoming one of you. Leave us alone. The Other want to be, let them.'

No response.

There are fewer human colonies this time.

The Other touches her, gently. Janni sends her message again.

•   •   •

Back at home, Janni remained out of her body, although connected.

57

STARVIEW

HAL'S GROUP RETURNED and went their separate ways. He checked in at Sam's office and told her about the missing group.

Sam held her head in her hands. "Give me the names and I'll mark the list and notify relatives."

Hall rubbed her back. "Brad and I think it's okay to start sending people through again."

"In the morning. Too late now."

That night, Sam dreamed of the old Ambaak place with all the plants and flowers. She was on the hill above, looking down at the green roof, when something screamed out of the sky and turned the place into a charred, smoking mess.

She woke up screaming, "No, no!"

As she realized it was only a dream, someone pounded on her door and burst it open.

Hal grabbed her and held her tightly. "Sam, honey."

"Dream," Sam mumbled, gasping.

"Okay, you're safe now," Hal murmured, patting her back. "What was it?"

"Ambaak, destroyed." She couldn't say more, just clung to him, shaking.

Brad charged in. "What happened?" He lit a lantern.

"Bad dream," Hal said as Brad approached.

"About Ambaak?" Brad asked.

Sam looked up at him. "You too?"

Brad sat next to her on the bed and patted her shoulder. "Can't remember details, but it was bad."

"Oh." Sam's thoughts began to coalesce. "Hal?"

"No. Just something uncomfortable."

"Oh, dear ..."

Before Sam could go any further, a timid knock on the door interrupted them.

Maxee stuck her head in. "I come in?"

"Sure," Sam and Brad said.

Maxee tiptoed in with her kubs. She carried the youngest and Haki clung to her.

"Sammie, bad thing. Ambaak destroyed."

"You dreamed it too?" Sam asked. *How could this be happening*?

"Iss. Kubs too. Scared." Maxee collapsed into the big chair and Haki and Toki climbed in along with her. Brax leaned next to her.

"So it wasn't just a dream, it was a warning," Sam said, drawing comfort from her friends.

"Of what?" Hal asked.

"We need to get Liia's people over to Peace, too."

"Oh, crud," Brad said. "Do you have any idea how many people they have?"

"Not really. Less than we have. I'll talk to her tomorrow."

"This morning," Hal said. "Look." The windows were beginning to lighten.

"Okay, this morning."

"Have her get a group to go through so they can see what's it's like," Brad said. "Where are they now?"

"Liia and her group are just west of north valley. They'll have to go through that way." Sam sighed. *Something else, no end in sight.*

"You all right now?" Hal asked.

"I think so." Sam was still shaking. "Thanks, you two."

Brad rose. "I better go tell Emily what happened. She was mumbling in her sleep. See you later." He kissed Sam's hair and left. Hal followed.

"I stay?" Maxee asked. "Please?"

Sam had never seen the Klocti so shaken.

"Of course. Scary, wasn't it?"

Sam rose and went to the back window. The river meandered through darkness at the foot of the mesa. She couldn't hear it.

"I never have dream like that," Maxee said. "Never remember dreams."

Sam turned. "I hardly ever remember mine, either."

The kubs were asleep in her lap, Brax on the floor with head on Maxee's knee. Maxee yawned widely.

Sam lay down on her bed.

•   •   •

Sam didn't have a chance to call Liia until late morning. The image of the blackened inside courtyard wouldn't stay tucked away.

"How are you doing over there?"

"Waiting to find out where to go. Where we are is not good place for us."

"You will be going to the new world." Sam paused. "I had a dream last night, a warning. Your people are not safe here either. We have to figure out how to work you into the schedule. Brad suggested you pick a few people, and we'll send them through so they can see the place and come back and report to you."

"Have you been there?"

"Yes, and it's wonderful. Not mountains like here, but a very big river. And plenty of room for all of us. Peace has a gorgeous beach free to all. And a moon, a satellite you can see in the sky."

"A moon? We had two on our home world: one large, and one you could barely see. How do we get there?"

"There's a Gate in a cavern up the river path. It links the two worlds. Step into ours, everything goes black, then you wake up on theirs."

"Ah. So how many?"

"The Gate can hold up to six. I suggest two couples with knowledge of the land."

"This dream, you are sure?"

"Yes. Both Hal and Brad had the same dream, and none of us usually remembers dreams."

"I will talk with Giil, and we will decide. Thank you for telling me."

•   •   •

That afternoon, someone reported to her office that an older man from the west had held up a couple with his knife and demanded their food.

"Did they give it to him?" Sam asked.

"Yes. The gal drew a picture of him." He thrust out a scrawled drawing.

Arlene took it. "Have one of Hal's boys go around and find out who he is. Then we'll bring him in."

"Crime," Sam said. "I can't believe it. Are we going to have to have a regular security force?"

"Heavens, I hope not." Arlene picked up a piece of paper.

They caught him, took his knife, one from a caff he'd sharpened somehow, and locked him up. Sam told June no more knives.

When Hal showed up to see how she was doing, Sam asked him, "Hal, would you be interested in being our next leader? After we get over there?"

"Me? I don't know. I hadn't thought about it. Why?"

"Because I've had it. I'm ready to quit, and this is a very good opportunity." Sam leaned into him. "I've been telling people, but no one believes me. So what do you think?"

"I don't know. I'll have to think about it."

"You'd be good at it. You're good at delegating tasks. You'll have to find your own assistants; Arlene is retiring too."

"Oh, she is, is she? So you two are in this together." He grinned.

Sam's heart flipflopped. It always did, ever since the first time she met him. She had no desire for conventional marriage after the disaster of her first. Hal was gay and had lost his lover in the avalanche as they left City for the last time. She didn't care to know how he took care of his needs. He was a cuddly friend.

A thought popped into her mind. "Hey, what about ships at Starport?' Sam asked.

"Yeah, they have ships, but it would cost a lot more credits than we have to rent one."

"Well, forget that."

"Let's get to work," Arlene said.

Sam, Hal, and Arlene updated lists, and sent people through. Occasionally some returned, and she interviewed them about what was going on over there. They usually brought messages from Janni and Marisa. Work was progressing on the new place.

The weather cooled, and only the loovah, the root vegetables, and the nut trees kept producing. Brief rains kept the river half full.

58

PEACE

J ANNI WATCHED AS PEOPLE STREAMED UP through the corridor to Haven, Sam's place. Her mind was clearer, and she was getting better at pushing the duality away. Every day was a new adventure; she never knew any more what was going to happen. She was learning the ins and outs of the school system and finding things she thought should be changed.

She and Marisa rode up occasionally to check with Glenda and bring food. Roroy was staying up there, helping build housing.

Janni didn't quite understand the relationship between her mother and Roroy. She knew they had mated, then he left, allowing her to mate with Papa so she could have children. She sensed that Roroy still cared for her a lot, but Mama had Papa now, so why did she need Roroy?

Roroy was nice, but he never showed emotion. He was always pleasant and helpful, but quite reserved and would not answer questions about himself.

"I have put that world away. My only home is here," he would say.

Back in the clan home, Janni heard mutterings about the other people and food. Older children would run and watch the newcomers as they went by. In her classes, Janni would explain that they were people from a dying world who were coming here through the Gate and building a new town up north.

"How come they're so pale?"

"They always live indoors and don't go out much, so they don't get tanned like we do."

"There's a lot of them. How many more?"

"Their place had a lot more people than we do."

For Janni, the terror remained in the background, and duality shoved back as much as possible. She dutifully performed her tasks, feeling out of place.

•   •   •

One morning, Janni's being finally returns to space. All is as it was before. She checks around. No, there are the Others, in a ship of sorts. Rounded and longish, with a lumpy tail, odd bumps and warts decorate its exterior. Unable to distinguish color, she can only note it is dark.

Hiding her talent, she pokes inside. Several aliens awake, many in sleep. Like the first, long and round with a hump for a head. Their minds are totally alien, all she can find are references to Watchers and changing. She withdraws, but not before something designated as Bettah touches her for a brief moment.

Janni drifts in space, waiting, unaware. The Watcher does not come. Presently, her body draws her back.

•   •   •

When Janni woke, it was midmorning. Gramma Perri sat in a nearby chair, watching her.

"Gramma?" she whispered.

"Janni! You're awake." Gramma came to her bed. "We were so worried. What happened?"

Janni closed her eyes and tried to remember. The ship, the things inside. Watchers. It didn't make sense.

"Janni?"

She opened her eyes. "Gramma, there's a ship." Hesitated. "Things inside." Paused. "They know Watchers."

"Watchers."

"Something else, I can't remember." Janni closed her eyes. It was too much trouble to move.

Finally, her bladder got her up. When she returned from the outhouse, she dropped heavily onto the couch and leaned back. "So hard," she said, not knowing what she meant. The duality of being outside and looking at herself was back.

"Will you be all right now?" Gramma Perri asked.

"I think so."

"I have some things I need to do. I'll let Marisa know you're awake." She left.

Janni leaned back and closed her eyes.

Why does my body feel so tired when it stays here and rests? It's as if the connection between my mind and my body has gotten all stretched out. How long am I going to be able to keep going out like that?

Maybe being a housewife and mother wouldn't be so bad after all. *Ooops.* Quickly she checked — yes, she had conceived. *Oh murbles. Now what? Mama will know, but do I have to tell anyone else yet? Glori will figure it out soon enough. If I tell Willie, he'll have it all over the clan by supper time.*

She decided to wait and see.

A little later, Marisa came by and sat on the couch next to her. She touched Janni's mind. "Janni, are you pregnant? Why didn't you tell me?"

Janni rolled her eyes. "Yes, Mama. I just realized."

"Oh, my dear. You really shouldn't go out in space anymore."

"Why? My body doesn't go, it just lies here."

"I know, but there might be some connection." Mama scratched her head.

"Mama, I was out this morning," Janni pointed out.

"Did you know you were pregnant before?"

"No." She wished Mama would shut up so she could think.

"How are you feeling?"

"Like I was run over by a herd of quines."

"They wouldn't do that." Mama picked at the arm of the couch

"I know, but that's what I feel like."

Janni felt Mama studying her and closed her eyes.

"This is not good, losing a day of your services to the clan every time you go out."

"I know." Janni looked at the drawings on the wall at the end of the couch. She turned back to her mother. "Mama, I saw the others, in a ship. They have four arms and two legs, but no head. Just a hump on the top of their bodies."

"How can they not have a head?"

"I don't know. Maybe I can draw it. There's paper and drawing pen over there in the drawer." She pointed to a small wooden cabinet by the door.

Marisa fetched them and Janni drew what she remembered.

"I couldn't reach their brains, too different, but I did catch the word, 'Watchers'."

"Watchers?"

"I'm sure that's what I heard."

"Oh, dear. Is there some way you can tell them that we do not want to be Watchers?"

"I've been trying to, but they won't listen." Janni said.

Willie burst in. "Good, you're up. What's going on?" He gathered her in a hug. "Don't do this again."

"Calm down, Willie," Marisa said. "She's okay."

"If I wake first, I'm always scared she won't wake. I can't live like this. I want a mate that'll be there when I want her." Willie let Janni go and sat beside her as Marisa rose.

"I suppose you want lunch," Marisa said.

"Mama." Janni began.

"It's all right, I'll take care of it. What have you got?" She bustled over to the kitchen.

After lunch and the others left, Janni puttered around, unable to focus on anything. She couldn't accept that she was pregnant, so pushed that to the back of her mind. Finally, a thought coalesced. She needed a way to communicate to the Other that her people were not interested in becoming Watchers and wanted to stop changing. The Other was apparently not getting her messages.

That night she dreamed of holding a young, deformed child whose essence kept leaving her body. 'It's all right, Mama. I only need this body until I can grow up and have my own baby.'

Janni woke up screaming, "No!"

Willie took her into her arms. "What is it?"

"A bad dream." She burrowed her face into his chest.

"Musta been really bad. You're shaking. You want to tell?" He rubbed the back of her head.

"Our child was deformed. One leg, no hands, face a mess." She couldn't tell him what the child had said. She couldn't tell him about the terror that enveloped her.

"Just a dream. Our child will be just fine."

Janni wanted to believe that, but the terror wouldn't let her.

Willie let her go and went back to sleep. Janni lay there staring at the ceiling. The dream was more than just a dream. In spite of what her mother had told her, she was not the last generation to move toward becoming Watchers. Her daughter would become more Watcher than human. She couldn't tell exactly what would happen, but felt it would be a big change.

Now she had to fight for both of them. Her hands fisted up against her chest.

This she had to keep to herself for now. And tell the watcher voice next time she went out. Her dream went into her private place in her mind, that no one, not even Glori could touch.

•   •   •

At the craft hall, Glori asked, "What happened? I can see something's bothering you."

"Nothing." Janni sat and pulled out her loom.

"Nothing, my left eyeball. Come on, tell. If you don't, I'll look."

"You can't." Janni tied a yellow thread to her loom.

"You know you can't keep anything from me." Glori grinned at her.

Janni gave in. Glori could go on all day. "I had a dream about my baby."

"Baby? No, you didn't."

"With all this stuff going on I sorta lost track of things."

"Okay. What kind of dream?" Glori threaded a needle.

"Bad. She only had one leg and no hands."

"Oh, how awful."

Before Janni could answer, Glori added, "Granlyn wants you. Now. You need a break."

"I just got here." But Janni put her quilt square away and trotted off to Granlyn's.

"I hear you're pregnant," the old woman said as Janni stepped up on the porch.

"Yes, Granlyn."

"Why now? I thought you were going to wait."

"Um, I guess I lost track of things. He's so impetuous."

"That's no excuse. You can always take care of it later."

"I know, but ..."

"Never mind. We'll just have to deal with it."

"How?"

"First, go over to the clinic and have Anne check you out. Then do what she advises and take care of yourself."

"Yes, Granlyn."

"Have you been feeling all right?"

"Yes, Granlyn. I'm fine."

"No, you're not, but I see there's nothing I can do to help. Feel free to come talk whenever you want."

"Okay. Bye."

Janni went to the clinic, and Medic Anne said everything looked fine. "Just keep an eye on your embryo and let me know if you see anything that bothers you. But you'll be fine. Enjoy your pregnancy."

"Oh, really. Not from what I've heard."

"Every woman has her own story. I enjoyed mine. There's nothing like the feeling of a new little person growing inside you. Go talk to the others if you want."

Janni did and found Medic Anne was right. She also discovered that the women in Mama's generation had fewer episodes of morning sickness and other problems than the ones in older generations.

Sam's people continued to pour through, of which Janni was constantly aware, and she took her turn at the checkpoints. One young man tried to go up along the little river instead of over to the big river after he crossed the bridge. Janni had to *call* Chad III, who was the closest, to shepherd the man back.

"What are you hiding up there?" the young man demanded.

"Our homes, which are private." Janni said.

"I want to see how you live."

"Ask Glenda when you get up to your place. Uncle Chad, can you go with him to make sure he doesn't get lost?"

"Sure." His craggy face carried a white moustache.

The two men left.

59

STARVIEW

A COUPLE WHO RETURNED brought Sam a message from Kirk. 'I see darkness in sky, still can't tell what is. May be danger. I keep watch.'

Sam's futureseeing told her it was a threat, with no details.

Before she could get back to work, Liia called. "We will go when you say. My people said it was very good place, much better than here."

"Good. We'll fit your group in our schedule. When do you want to go?"

"When all others gone. I must see that my people will go."

"Of course. Talk to you later."

Sam and Arlene refigured the schedule to include groups of Ambaak people. While they were working on that, an errand boy brought a list of citizens from North Valley who'd gone up to the Gate. Sam had left gaps in the schedule for Lucy to plug her people in to go. Sam had to update her list from that.

A group arrived from Far West and the next one east to tell Sam that some people in the far west were staying, no matter what. They didn't need Starview and they didn't believe the nonsense about a danger coming from the sky.

"That's their problem," said Brad, who happened to be at her office.

"I know," said a middle-aged woman. "I'm just letting you know so you can mark them off."

"Thank you. When do you want to go?" Sam twiddled her stylus.

"Not for a few days. We need to rest. Is there food?"

"Yes, if you like loovah bread."

The Noreg had kept the last of the grain harvest. Every loovah plant grew a circle of new ones around it. When the outer ones were big enough, the inner one was harvested. One loovah plant could produce at least six loaves of bread. The caffs still had some regular flour, but knew there wouldn't be any more until next harvest. They were using it faster than usual because of the extra people and having to provide it for the travelers.

People were building carts on runners and taking more stuff.

One day at late meal, Brad said, "I guess I'll have to leave my little ship here. It's too big to go through the Gate, and I can't tell where Peace is from here."

"Is there any way you can find out through Spaceport?"

"We'd have to have a much better knowledge of Peace. Their sun seems very much like ours, but we'd need to know what other worlds are in that system. Then we'd need a star chart of their sky and compare it to ours. And, of course, how far away it is. If it's too far, forget it."

"Could you take it apart, take the sections through and reassemble it there?"

"No. I don't have the proper tools. And I don't know whether their sun could fuel it the way ours does. The Volen may have made it star specific. But it would be nice to have it over there."

"Maybe you'll think of something." Sam picked up her spork.

The next day, Arlene told Sam she'd heard one caff in the central valley closed down and their people were coming east, pulling their tools and food on a couple of boxcarts on runners.

Two days later, when they heard the caff group had reached the hills on the west side of the turn of the river, Brad flew Sam over to meet them.

The places to the west were half empty, they said. Sam showed them where to set up by the headland just before Starview.

"People from the west can stop here to eat before they get to Starview." Sam said.

Their leader nodded. They showered her with questions about the other world.

"When will you need us to go through?"

"Probably in a couple weeks. How many of you are there? I'll have to schedule several trips for all of you and your stuff."

Good, Sam thought. *We need another group of caff people over there.* "We're thinking of going to the system the clan has, of everyone fixing their own meals. We'd keep a couple of caffs for when a group wants to eat together. What do you think?"

"What would our people do?"

"At first, teach everyone how to cook. Maybe set up a cooking school. You'll have new foods to play with. Don't worry, you'll be doing your caff until enough people get to cooking on their own. I'll have to learn too."

"Okay." She shrugged.

Sam had a thought. "Will you be able to take plants, too?"

"We're planning on it."

"Good."

People dribbled in from the west until another earthquake knocked down more buildings, then the trickle became a stream.

The quake shook Sam, and her farseeing told her to get out of there.

"We're all right here; this mesa is solid rock." Brad said.

"Yeah, but down below isn't, and we've got so many damaged buildings no one knows whether we should try to rebuild them or tear them down. People are living in them because they have nowhere else to go. And we're sending them through as fast as we can, and I keep my fingers crossed that nothing else goes wrong."

"Okay, Sam. We'll hang in there together."

That night, Sam dreamed every citizen was yelling at her, when can we go, do we have to go, why can't we go back to City, and closing in around her.

Her yelp woke her up. For once, she wished Hal was here with her.

Sam sat and shook until she was able to pull herself together. She could see the trees out her windows, so she got up, dressed, and sat out in the chair on the porch. She could still feel the sense of being surrounded. The sounds and aromas of the river and the trees soothed her a little, but the pressure of the future would not go away.

When it was time, she rose and started for the caff.

One of the legal people stopped her. "Did you feel the earthquake? What are we going to do now?"

"I don't deal with questions before breakfast." Sam pushed by her and hurried on.

At the caff, she only took toast and a wakeup drink.

"You look worried," Hal said as she sat down. "Bad night sleep?"

"Bad dream," she muttered. She didn't feel like talking.

"You gotta eat more than that," Brad said.

"I'm okay." Her hand shook as she picked up her mug.

"It'll go away once you get into your work routine." Brad rose.

"My rut." Sam set the mug down.

Brad returned with a bowl of mash. "Here, eat."

"Thanks." Sam nibbled at her toast, took a few bites of mash. She felt a little better, being with her two special men.

Hal told funny stories about councilors in City. By the time she and Brad left for the office, Sam felt almost cheerful.

Until they were accosted by one of the clerks on her way to work. "Sam, Sam, the river is disappearing!" she shouted.

"What?" Sam and Brad said together.

They ran out to the east edge of the mesa. The water was down to a third its usual level.

"Not again," Sam said.

"Something's blocking it upstream," Brad said. "I'll get a crew and go up."

"Take your comm."

"Of course. I'll call you when I find the problem." He took off running back to the meeting hall.

Sam followed more slowly, her gut in a knot.

This can't be happening. We can't lose our river, our only source of water. Oneness, help us.

She stopped and looked back at her house. *If Maxee were only here.* If she could only go home and curl up into a ball and forget everything. If she could be on Peace, somewhere out in the trees by the river, by herself.

She turned and headed for her office.

Brad ran up to her with two other young men. "I'm going to see Gus and collect some tools, then go. Tell Emily and the kids, please. I have no idea how long it will take."

"Be careful," Sam said to his back.

At her office, she told Arlene what was going on.

"I thought I heard something about that." Arlene said.

"Tell everyone who comes or calls, we're taking care of it and we'll let everyone know when it's fixed. Have people fill the rain barrels using their buckets." Sam closed her eyes and leaned back.

Arlene patted her shoulder. "I will." The comm beeped. Arlene answered.

Hal trotted in. "I heard." He squatted down beside Sam's chair, put his arms around her, and laid his forehead on her head.

Sam soaked in his warmth and caring. She wondered how many groups she could send through in a day.

What about at night? It wasn't night there.

She knew the Gate needed breaks to recharge, but how long did it need?

Two groups could camp in the cavern and two more outside. Some could stay at the outlook, too. What about food and water?

"Thanks, Hal. Brad will call me when he finds something." Sam looked at the blue-gray oblong with an inset black button on her desk.

"Staring at your comm won't make it beep any quicker," Hal said. He kissed her forehead and stood.

"I know."

"Okay, I'll see you at midday meal." He gave Sam a squeeze and left.

Little did she know it would her last meal there for some time.

60

STARVIEW

THAT AFTERNOON, AFTER SAM AND ARLENE had gone through several stacks of requests and sorted them into piles, another strong tremor hit, sending papers all over the office.

"Oh, no," Sam cried, and put her head down on her arms on the table. The suffocating feeling returned.

"Oh, squiddy," Arlene snarled at the same time. "Are you all right?"

"I don't know." Sam lifted her head, picked up two pieces of paper on the table, set them at one side, and put her head back down.

Arlene went to the door and stuck her head out. "Viv, come here please."

A young girl appeared. "My stuff is all over the place."

"I know. I need you to help pick up papers and sort them out. You start over there and I'll take this corner."

They went to work, and Sam gathered the papers still on the table. The words didn't make any sense, so she stacked them by the design of the letters. One of the lab people came by; they had a mess, needed people to help clean up.

"Everybody's got messes. Find your own help." Arlene picked up another handful of odds and ends.

"Well," he huffed and left.

Arlene closed the office door. "Be prepared for a mob scene."

"No," Sam said, the dream returning. She gathered her papers in one big stack.

Arlene brought three stacks back to her end of the table and took Viv's. "Thanks, Viv. You can go back to your mess now."

The girl left and two people pushed in at the door. "Our whole building collapsed. What do we do?"

"Go out and wait," Arlene, a good-sized woman, swept them back out.

Three more were waiting.

"Miss Sam, we need help," one said.

"No. Go away." Sam cringed. Her heart pounded and she had to suck in a big breath.

Arlene shooed them out.

Sam heard people out in the hall, raised voices claimed they were here first, their problem was worse, they needed help right now.

"No!" Sam put her hands over her ears. She hadn't felt this close to falling apart since her ex-husband had killed her father.

Arlene closed the door and stood with her back to it. "Call security."

Sam picked up the comm with a shaking hand and punched in the code. "Sam. My office is being besieged. Get me out of here." She dropped the comm and began to sob. "I can't do this anymore, I can't do this anymore."

Arlene went to Sam. With one arm around her, Arlene picked up the comm with the other and called Hal. "Sam needs you."

Hal came running and shoving through the crowd and took Sam into his arms. "I'm here, cuddles."

"I can't do it anymore," she cried. "Get me out of here."

Try to hold it together until we get out of here.

Arlene and Hal held Sam on either side and opened the door. People shoved and yelled.

"No," Sam screamed. "Stop it! Go away!"

They stumbled through the crowd, pushing and swatting at the citizens, and out the hall door. People followed. Several hefty young men showed up from Security and held back the mob. The three trudged over to Sam's house where she dropped on the bed, still sobbing and gasping.

Sam tried to hold onto reality, but the pain was too much.

"Thanks, Arlene," Hal said. "When you hear from Brad, tell him to get back soonest."

Arlene was in tears herself. She sat in one of the table chairs and put her head in her hands. "I'm not going back there until that mob is gone."

Hal sat on the bed and rubbed Sam's shoulders and back. "Get it out, get it all out."

Sam's sobs soon subsided, and she fell asleep.

"Take care of her, Hal," Arlene said as she wiped her eyes, rose, and left.

Sam heard her in the dimness of sleep and became aware of Hal's arms around her. Memory of her hysteria came back, and she moaned. Hal squeezed her and brushed the hair back from her face.

Sam dropped back into sleep.

"Better?" Hal asked when she awoke.

Sam searched for her self and found it. She wanted nothing more than to lie there in his arms. Nothing else mattered. She heard Hal murmuring, but words slid right by.

Slowly, she rose out of her daze. "I think I'm here."

Hal let her go and sat up. "I hope so."

Sam pulled herself up and sat beside him. "I can't believe I did that."

"You did."

"In front of half the colony."

"Yup. Let's go sit out on the porch."

They settled together in the wide chair. "You're staying right here until late meal." Hal waved his hand.

The thought of the others staring at her brought a lump to her throat. "I'm not going."

"Okay. We'll bring you some food. And you are taking tomorrow off."

"Hal," she said, with a half-smile. *He's so good to me.*

She looked out over the river, less than half as wide as it used to be.

"Could we build a bridge up here while it's so low?"

"That's an idea. I'll talk to construction, see what they have to say."

Sam leaned against him and let her mind wander. If she could just stay here forever and not see anyone except Hal and Brad …

And then she saw the menace to come. The Others Janni saw would attack them on every world. They'd only be safe on Peace, where Marisa's people could protect them with their Talent. She didn't know how that would work, but it was the only way her people would be safe. If she could get them there in time. Sam shivered and moaned.

Hal held her tightly.

When Brad returned, the spell was broken. He charged in yelling, "Sammie."

"Hey, Brad." Sam stood just in time to reach his muddy hug.

"When I called, Arlene answered and said you'd gone home sick and for me to come as soon as I could. She said Hal was with you, so that helped. What happened?"

"Too much and I snapped. Crying and saying I can't do this anymore."

"Don't scare me like that. Next time do it when I'm around."

Sam saw the anguish fade in his eyes. "I don't do it when you're around."

"You all right now? Oh geez, I got mud all over you."

"It'll wash off." Sam went into the washroom, peeled off her tunic, threw it into the laundry basket, washed her face and arms, and put on a clean top. She came out and sat with them.

"We have to get everyone to Peace," Brad said.

Sam felt him shaking. "You saw it too?"

"Yes. Not clearly."

"How can we move people any faster? The Gate can only take so many at a time, and it needs to recharge every so often."

"I know. As for the river, another huge boulder had rolled down into the riverbed where it narrows, just above the bridge. We couldn't budge it, but we were able to dig out the riverbank to increase the flow. I couldn't tell how much more will flow through." Brad crossed his legs and took a big breath. Some of the water is flowing down into North Valley."

Sam tried not to think about river problems. She tried not to think about anything at all. She shivered at what might happen next.

61

PEACE

J ANNI COULD NOT ENJOY THE NEW LIFE WITHIN HER. Although she knew it was real, she couldn't accept its realness. She was too worried about the Other and the Watchers. The last time Sam had been there, Janni had *seen* that she knew about the threat, but Janni was hesitant to ask her about it.

She did her tasks, and took her turn greeting the newcomers, but it was all just going through the motions. Internally, she kept fighting the duality.

Even with Willie, she didn't feel alive. One night, as they lay in bed, he asked. "Are you pregnant?"

"I think so," she said. "I'll know for sure in a few days." She didn't feel like doing anything; she'd been feeling like that all day. The fun of life was gone.

•　　•　　•

Two days later, Janni's being is out in space. This time danger is clearer. She probes and quickly draws back. A mind power. She pulls back into herself. *Did they notice her?* She only used the narrowest tendril of her Talent, but she did access something.

The Other, a creature with a mind, but no head. Janni collapses herself into a tight ball. She is right. The Other are becoming Watchers and want to get rid of her people. Only one of the three of them shows desire to kill. If she could talk to one of the others ...

Janni finds another human colony, just too late. The ruins are still smoldering. She finds a woman and her child, hiding. She zaps them to Peace. She groans as if punched in the gut by Beast.

Now at Cityworld, she sends a message to Sam via the feline alien. 'Send more through, day and night.'

She leaves quickly and returns to her body.

•　　　•　　　•

Janni was supposed to pick carrots with Glori, but when she did not show up, Glori *reached* for her and found nothing. Scared, she dropped her basket, ran to Janni's house, and tried to wake her, with no luck. She *called* Marisa, who came, but the two of them couldn't wake her. Marisa *called* Gramma Perri and Granlyn.

"She's hiding from something," Marisa said. "We all need to go into her and let her know she is safe here."

They joined and *eased* into Janni's mind.

Suddenly, she blinked and opened her eyes. All that she had in her mind about the danger *passed* to Glori and Marisa. Gramma Perri and Granlyn just *received* the feeling of danger.

"Janni," Marisa said, still holding her hand. Janni looked at her mother.

"Danger," she managed to get out.

Marisa looked at Glori, who nodded and said, "We got it."

Janni closed her eyes, trying not to think of what she had accessed.

"We're supposed to be pulling carrots," Glori said.

Janni produced a little snort.

"I know this is important," Gramma Perri said, "but we still need carrots."

Marisa took Janni's pulse and listened to her breathe. "She sounds okay."

Granlyn nodded.

"It is real," Gramma Perri said.

"Yes." Granlyn nodded. "We'll need to plan for it. Do a trial run, perhaps. I will call a meeting for tonight."

Janni heaved a great sigh, opened her eyes, moved her hands. The light was midday bright. "Oh. How late is it?"

"Late morning." Marisa said. "How do you feel?"

"Okay. Did you find the woman and child I sent here?"

"Yes. She and her baby are being taken care of at the clinic. They were burned. When they heal, we'll fit her in somewhere. However, I don't want you going out there anymore. It's not good for you, especially now."

"Mama. I can't stop. You know that." Janni sat up and leaned back against the wall.

"But it's going to kill you."

"I don't think so," Granlyn said. "She's a tough gal, and there's nothing she can do about it. I'll tell Charley to call a general meeting. We need one even without this."

"Okay." Marisa sighed.

Janni rose, dressed, and staggered through the day.

•   •   •

At the meeting, Granlyn first asked about problems involving the new people. They were forced to put a person on the east/west path where it crossed the north/south path from the clan to the sea. Most of them cooperated, but there were a few who wanted to see the clan village and had to be led past the place so they wouldn't leave the path.

One of the women complained that her house backed on the trail, and she had to keep her rear window closed and shaded all the time, because those people peeked in.

"Nothing we can do about it. Keep your chin up," Granlyn said.

Next, Granlyn brought up the news about the danger. She had Janni explain exactly what she had experienced. Janni watched most of the older folk shake their heads. She sluffed it off; they had the least Talent anyway.

Marisa asked, "Has any one of you had any of your Talents reflect any kind of force?"

People looked at each other, puzzled. One hand went up.

"I have," Leona, Granlyn's younger daughter, said.

"Tell us."

"I only have the mind talent, but sometimes it bends at the edges. Especially with Curtis. I can repeat words back without actually thinking them." Curtis was her twin.

"Papa?" Marisa asked Grampa Charley. "What do you think?"

"I think we should do some testing."

The clan accepted that, especially the young people who foresaw a new group of friends.

Janni watched from outside her body as she and the others talked.

That night the dreams began. Dreams of a red world with gray bushes and a dark blue sky. Dreams of long, six-limbed creatures with no heads. Dreams of a longing for escape from their land.

When Janni woke, the dreams stayed with her. Always in the corners of her eyes, she saw red and gray. She plodded through her days, doing whatever was asked of her, but feeling no joy. Every time she had a moment to sit and think, she tried to figure a way to convince the Watcher-voice to turn off her clan's Talents.

The Other, she understood, wanted to be Watchers. She needed to find a way to communicate with them, to tell them her people did not want to be Watchers.

Janni felt like she was two people. One was the girl she'd always been, doing her allotted tasks and enjoying the company of her family, friends, and Willie. The other, the stranger who went out to space and dealt with the Other, was someone she didn't know well yet. Some who kept interfering with the real Janni.

When she went to the storehouse to collect some food, she ran into Marisa.

"Oh, there you are," she said.

"Hi, Mama. I went to help Anne, but she was on watch at the corner. I seem to be getting behind on everything, either because I'm on watch or whoever I'm supposed to work with is."

"I know. Granlyn was called in to watch a couple of babies in childcare because Betsy was sent to the kitchen to help Mindy because her helper was at the crossroads. People are getting sloppy and we're getting behind on a lot of things. We just don't have enough people."

Janni picked out several squash and Marisa made her put one back. "Save some for the others. We're also getting short on everything."

"Maybe we could get a few of Sam's people to help out."

"That's an idea, but I'm afraid the elders, other than Granlyn, wouldn't agree."

62

STARVIEW

A T LATE MEAL, BRAD AND HAL WENT TO THE CAFF. Sam sat and watched the sun set downriver, comfortable in her cocoon. The only thing she missed was Maxee's presence. She would have liked to be in Peace, but the trip there was too much to consider right then. She tried to pretend the menace wasn't there. It didn't work. A sheen of terror glowered in the background.

The men returned with a small bowl of stew and a slice of bread for her. Sam rose, went inside to her table and ate, not really aware of what she was eating.

"We ate there," Hal said. "Everyone was asking about you."

"Nothing bad," Brad added. "I told them you had work overload and had to rest."

"Understatement of the year," Sam said, thinking of the menace.

The men looked at each other. "Sam, I have things I should have done this afternoon I need to do." Hal took her hand. "I'll be back in the morning unless you want me to come back for the night."

"Okay. Thanks for being there."

"I'll stay for a while." Brad grinned.

They talked until Sam yawned, then Brad put her to bed. "I'm right next door if you need anything."

•   •   •

The next day, Sam began her morning routine before the previous day's events came to mind. She felt more like herself but had no desire to go to work.

This house needs a good cleaning.

First meal. Sam's stomach growled. She checked to see if she had any food tucked away and found one piece of stale bread. Before she could decide whether to go to the caff or not, Hal appeared.

"Good morning, how are you?" He hugged her.

"Feeling better." Sam decided she wasn't ready to face other people. "Would you mind going to the caff and getting me something to eat?"

"I was just going to ask you if you were up to going."

"Not yet."

When he returned, he sat with her while she ate, talking about what he wanted to do at the new place. Sam noticed he avoided work topics.

After he left, Sam spent the day alone at her house, except when Brad or Hal dropped by. Arlene showed up at midday.

"Much better. How are you?" The two sat at the table.

"Okay. I slept in half the morning and missed first meal. I'll go to the office later. The boys taking care of you?"

"Oh, yes. Hal's been here twice and Brad three times."

"Good. Take your time and don't come back until you're ready." Arlene looked around. "Your house looks neat and tidy."

"That's what I've been doing this morning. I haven't had much time lately for housekeeping."

"I know the feeling." Arlene rose. "I'm going to grab something to eat and see what's going on. See you later."

"Thanks for coming."

Sam spent the afternoon making lists and sitting on her porch. A faint foreboding haunted her. The river was a little higher, but not much. She felt World didn't want them here at all. She wouldn't worry about Starview anymore; just focus on the new place. Haven.

She would miss her porch, the gurgling of the river, the whispering of the trees, the distant mountains.

I'll have a new place on another river. A river with high banks that can't flood.

When Hal came at late mealtime, she was ready to go with him to the caff.

A helper let them in a back way, and they slipped into their seats in a corner. Brad and Emily were already there, and Arlene showed up shortly thereafter.

After greetings, Hal went to get their food.

"How are you doing?" Arlene asked Sam.

"Better." Sam glanced up.

People were staring at her. She felt uncomfortable, but safe, surrounded by her kinfolk.

Hal returned with food.

"What's the matter with this bread?" Sam asked. Darker than normal, and lumpy, she wasn't sure she wanted to eat it.

One of the serving women came over. "Glad to see you up, Miss Sam. Anything I can get you?"

"What's with this bread?"

"The last batch of flour had bits of bugs in it. It tested fine, and the bread too, so we're using it. Can't afford to discard any useful food."

"Okay," Sam said. "We do what we have to do."

A few other people came over during the meal to welcome her back. No one mentioned why she had to leave. She smiled and nodded at them. Her food tasted good, even the bread.

"We got the requests taken care of and some of the other stuff," Arlene said. "Carolyn is doing a great job teaching people about going to the new place."

"Good. Maxee thought of a name for it. Haven. What do you all think?"

"I like it." Arlene took a bite of stew.

"Nice," Hal added. The others agreed.

"I can't wait to see it," Emily said.

"Does anyone have any idea how many more are going to go?" Arlene asked.

"Not me." Sam grimaced.

"At the rate we're going, it'll take most of the rest of the year," Arlene said. "If everyone goes. We've been seeing people from the west settling in here as if they're going to stay."

"I would like to set up a system of my people going to every neighborhood and checking who wants to go, who's iffy, and who doesn't. Then we'll have an idea of how many more to expect." Hal waved his bread around.

"Sounds good to me," Sam said. "Go ahead."

The others concurred.

"How's things with you, Emily?" Sam asked. "Haven't seen you for a while."

Emily's round face shone with the beauty of motherhood.

"Chaotic. Del and Felicia can't wait to go, the little ones aren't sure what's going on and I have to keep reassuring them. And now there's another one coming. Going through the Gate won't hurt it, will it?"

"No, Marisa's mother went through several times while she was carrying Marisa and there have been no problems."

"Oh, good. They've all been so healthy so far. I just wish there were more children their age to play with."

"Well, maybe we can set up something with the clan's children."

After the meal, Emily left to collect her youngsters, and the rest went with Sam to her house.

"Are you coming in tomorrow?" Arlene asked.

"Yes. Can you start on your project tomorrow, Hal?"

"Sure. We'll have security people permanently stationed around the hall, in addition to the ones stationed at the foot of the mesa."

All but Hal left, and they had a cuddle.

The next morning, Sam went to her office and all the stress came back.

63

STARVIEW

SAM AND ARLENE HAD SET UP A SYSTEM with a master list of those who wanted to go through. One check after they passed the course, another when Sam gave them paper instructions, and third when Arlene or one of her people checked them to make sure they carried sufficient belongings and food.

Hal reported that only about a third of the neighborhoods he'd talked to so far wanted to leave.

"Did you explain why we need to leave?" Sam asked, fiddling with papers on her table.

Hal leaned against the office doorway. "Sure. They don't believe me; say we're just trying to get rid of them."

"Let them stay," Arlene said. "They have their little group beliefs and ignore what anyone outside says. Let them learn the hard way. Keep going, Hal."

All the people we lost who wouldn't leave City, and now a lot more who won't leave Starview. Sam sighed. *And they'll die if not protected.*

Once the system had been set up, it seemed to be working fine. There were no more problems with the Gate. A few came back, mostly for more belongings.

As Hal canvassed more neighborhoods, he found some where most of the people wanted to go. Every day, the list grew longer.

Todd returned, to advise his father of progress and to pack up more of the legal papers.

At Sam's office, he told her, "It's a big mess over there. People camping everywhere, not enough food, people moving into houses as soon as the roof is on, before they're finished."

"How is the clan taking it?" Sam asked.

"The younger generations are being helpful to some extent; the older people don't seem to be happy with us at all. Now that we've got families with children going through, we have to keep an eye on the youngsters. They keep wanting to see the clan's village."

"I'm not surprised," Sam said.

"After I go over some things with Dad, I'm going back and start writing up deeds. I've made a partial plot map showing who lives where and will add to it as more come through. Gus and I are assigning people plots where they can build their houses." He paused. "Some are just building little one-room shacks. Gus says they'll have to tear them down later and build real houses."

"I suppose the shack people all want to eat at the caffs."

"Yes. There's two now, and not enough people to run them properly — let alone start showing people how to use their kitchens."

•　　•　　•

Zilla called Sam to come to her clinic. There, Sam found Laurel and her daughter, Allie, about ten, and two little boys playing in a corner piled with bags. A large, greenish-gray patch lined the little girl's right forearm.

"I've never seen anything like it," Zilla said.

Laurel held the girl's other hand.

"It itches," Allie tried to pull her hand away from her mother.

Oh crud. Something else to deal with. Sam asked, "How did you get it?"

"Playing."

"There's a new kind of bush that grew this year," Laurel said. "In Midwest. The girls were playing with the flowers." She pulled a dark purple, long cup-shaped blossom wrapped in a large leaf out of her bag and laid it on a table. "I'm a medic, you know, but I had no idea what to do. I thought of the salve we use for sunburns, but we're all out of it. So I thought I'd bring her to you."

Zilla peered at the flower. "Must be something on it that creates a reaction in us. Does it hurt at all?"

Allie shook her head. "Just itches."

"We'll try the salve first." Zilla got out the big green jar. "Lay your arm on the table," she told the little girl. She dipped a clean cloth into the jar of salve and gently wiped the goop onto the child's arm. "Does that feel any better?"

Allie shrugged.

"I see the bags," Sam said. "Have you come here to go through?"

"Not right away." Laurel looked down at her twisting hands. "I want to be sure Allie is well first. If you need any help, I'm available."

"Not here, but there's another clinic that could use you. How long have you been practicing?" Zilla asked.

"About twelve years. I was pregnant with Allie when we left City."

"Did you tell people to leave that bush alone? Is it the only one?" Sam asked.

"Of course I did. One of the builders put up a fence around it. It's the only one I've seen."

"Okay. I'll get Hal to go out and see if there are any others. That wouldn't be contagious, would it?" Sam asked Zilla.

"Shouldn't be. Any better now?"

"A little." Allie put a tiny smile on her face.

"Good. I'm going to wrap it up. I want you to stay here for now. If you want to rest, I have a couple empty beds."

Sam rose. "I need to get back to work. I'll get someone to look for a place where you and your children can stay, Laurel."

"Thank you," Laurel said.

Sam left.

It better be just a single case and nothing more.

She wondered what else was going to happen. At least Zilla could handle this one.

Later, as Sam headed to the caff for late meal, Zilla called her. "Good and bad news. The salve seems to be working. The skin thing is contagious, by touch. Both boys touched it and have small patches, so I'm treating them, too."

"Oh, no," Sam said.

"Don't worry about finding a place for them to stay. I want them to stay here where I can watch them. I'll put them in the private room. Laurel agreed, though the children aren't very happy about it."

"Good. Keep me posted."

"Will do. The boys think it's a game."

"Watch them. We don't want this to get out."

"I know. Later."

Sam heaved a big sigh. She'd just lost her appetite.

"Hey, what's up, sis?" Brad asked, catching up to her.

"Oh, hi, Brad. You won't believe this."

"What?" He patted her shoulder.

"We now have an infectious skin disease. Zilla's treating it and keeping the affected family sequestered in her clinic, but it's scary."

"Contagious? How?"

"Only by touch, as far as we know now."

"That's easy to contain." Brad held the caff door for her.

"As long as those two little boys don't get out."

"Right. I know what escape artists little boys can be."

They collected food and went to their table.

•   •   •

Two days later, Zilla called Sam.

"We have a problem. One of the boys got out and spread the rash to two others. I've conscripted three apartments next door for their families. I'm running out of salve and the plants are out of season. I need a team of people to look for similar plants."

"Oh, great. I've got three people here just hanging around. I'll send them over."

"Thanks, Sam."

"Okay you three," Sam said. "Go see Zilla at the main clinic. She's got something for you to do."

The boys started complaining, but the girl said, "Come on. It'll pass the time."

Sam told Arlene, "They can't go through until they're healed. If it spreads ..."

"Let Zilla take care of it. It's her job. Here comes another group."

•　　　•　　　•

The days rushed by. Most of Liia's people had gone through. Sam noticed there were many people who had not left. Hal told her everyone wanted to stay.

"We can't make them go," he said. "Just let them know the Gate will stay open, if they decided to go later."

"You're right," Sam said. "How long are they going to live here?"

"That's their problem."

64

PEACE

EVERY WEEK, JANNI WENT OUT TO SPACE, and every week she sent messages to Other and the Watcher voice. Other did not respond, and Watcher said they're not ready or we'll see.

Janni became more aware of the new life within her. Kaylyn. The name just came to her. When she told Glori at the craft hall, the other woman nodded.

"Mine's going to be Adam," Glori said. "The original Adam was Brian's great-grandfather. Papa Will wanted it, and it's fine with us."

"Have you told Granlyn?"

Glori looked away. "She knows I'm pregnant, but we haven't told her the name yet. I hope you don't mind."

"I don't," Janni said, "But I think Willie was thinking about it."

"Uh oh."

"Don't worry about it, she's a girl anyway." Janni picked up a quilt square. "When I go out, I want you to go with me. I have to tell these whoever they are to leave us alone."

Glori grimaced. "Brian doesn't like it."

"If he says anything, tell him it's for the life of his son."

"You're serious."

"Yes. You didn't see that burned out world. I did."

"Okay. When?"

"Day after tomorrow."

•   •   •

Janni and Glori find their beings linked in space. The first thing Janni notices is a faint haze in the direction she believes Peace's sun hangs.

'What is that?' Glori asked.

'I have no idea.'

Janni searches for the Other and finds herself at Sam's world. The purple-blue swirls are quite obvious from here. She *reaches* for them, but senses nothing. She and Glori go into the solar system globe and approach Starview.

'This is Starview — Sam's community.'

'So many people.'

They watch the mesa by the river in the center, all the long brown buildings along the valleys, all the people moving here and there.

'It's not going to work, there's too many,' Glori *sends.*

'Yes, it will. It has to.' Janni cannot image leaving people here to die. 'Look there.'

A line of people climbed up the mountainside along a river.

Glori shakes her being and they are out in space. 'I'll have to think about that.'

Janni searches again and finds the Other. She and Glori combine and send a tendril with a message, no Watcher. They are aware of a three-part being, only one part who wants to kill. Can the other two parts hold him?

The voice comes. 'You are becoming Watcher well.'

'No, I don't want to be a Watcher. My friend doesn't want to be a Watcher. My clan don't want to be Watchers. These Others do. Let them be Watchers and let us go.' Janni pleaded.

'They are not ready yet.'

'When will they be? They're trying to kill us.' Janni sent fear and pathos to the voice.

'We will see.' The voice left.

'What was all that about?' Glori asked, in Janni's space.

'Later.'

A sting and back to their bodies.

•   •   •

Janni woke to bright light. Gramma Perri sat watching her. "Late again," the older woman said.

"I can't help it."

Janni remembered the colors in space and looked for them when she went out, but saw only the blue green sky. Maybe she could see them at night. She did her stint at school. Mama had given the children tasks to do while they waited.

Then she went to Granlyn's. The old woman welcomed her. "Anything new?"

"Glori and I went out. We contacted the Other and told them we didn't want to be Watchers. I don't know whether they understood. But there's something else, broad colors in space. I can't see it here, maybe at night."

Grampa Larry hobbled out and sank into his chair. "Or maybe we can only see it from the other side of the world. What did it look like?"

"Swirls of purples and blues with white dots here and there."

"Sounds like a nova. Coming this way?"

"I can't tell."

•   •   •

Next time she goes to space, she tells the voice, 'What good will it do you if you make us Watchers and the others kill us before we're ready.'

A pause.

'They won't.'

'I just saw another colony wiped out.'

'Why would you not want to be Watchers?' The stars swirled about her.

'We like our bodies, our physical senses, being with others.'

Why couldn't this being, this entity see?

The voice left without replying.

Janni sought out the Other and sent her message again.

•   •   •

Two days later, Janni *heard* a ruckus and a call to the north side of clanhome. She hurried up with several others. A group of adolescent boys had come down from Haven and were yelling for the clanspeople to give them food and supplies.

"Barrier up,' Janni and Marisa *sent* to their people.

They lined up, spaced apart, newcomers filling in the spaces. Many of the men were in the crop fields or working up in Haven, so the group was mostly women and boys.

"You don't scare us," one of the Haven boys called.

"Reflect," called Janni.

The people closed their eyes and together sent the words back.

Grampa Charley arrived on his quine. "Go home," he yelled. "There's nothing here for you."

One boy threw a rock at him and missed. Janni picked up the boy and threw him back.

"Get them," another boy screamed.

They surged forward only to run into an invisible wall.

"Net," Marisa yelled, and they were unable to move.

"Go get Glenda," Marisa told Janni.

The girl hopped on Qilla, and they galloped up to Haven.

"A bunch of your boys came down and tried to attack us," Janni gasped out.

"No," Glenda said, standing up. "Where are they?"

"We have them under control, but you need to get them back up here. We had to use our Talent."

Glenda nodded and yelled, "Gus!"

"What's the fuss?"

"Boys went down the hill. We have to go get them. Janni says her people have them under control."

"I knew it wasn't going to last." He trotted out and, in a few minutes, had collected a half dozen tall young men.

They all headed back down.

"Take them away," Grampa Charley demanded, waving his arms. "We will not tolerate this. One at a time."

Janni had never seen him so angry.

One of Haven's men approached a boy sitting hunched over. Janni *took the net off* and *released* him. The man grasped his arm and moved to the next boy. Janni *released* him and the man used his other hand, turned, and started up the hill, dragging the boys. Soon they all were gone.

Glenda approached Gramma Perri. "I am so sorry this happened. I'll make sure this doesn't happen again. I know this must be difficult for you, having our people constantly streaming by. If there's anything we can do to help, please let us know."

"We do not blame you," Gramma Perri replied. "The parents must control the children. As you have seen, we are not helpless. Especially with these young ones."

She patted Janni and smiled. "How are things going up there?"

"Rough. We do appreciate you letting your men help build our houses. It will be better when everyone has a home."

Gramma Perri nodded. "We have little work here right now. This keeps them busy. We all must work to have food, clothing, and other supplies. That's our rule."

"Good rule. Wish we could enforce it, but we have too many people. I'd best be getting back. Thank you again." Glenda nodded and followed the men back up the hill.

65

STARVIEW / PEACE

FINALLY THE TIME CAME. Everyone who wanted to go to Peace had left except Sam's group. One of Arlene's assistants who was several months pregnant was staying to oversee the people who remained.

Sam made sure Martha understood how to get to and through the Gate if she decided to come later. "Keep an eye on the sky. If it gets a funny color, stay inside. Could be dangerous."

"Okay. I can't walk up that trail now anyway. I'll take care of things as best I can," she told Sam and Arlene.

One medic was staying and had some supplies.

They piled everything into one last cart. Sam looked around at the meeting hall and her office, with bare walls, her pictures packed. At her house, she sat on her porch one last time.

If I could only take that view with me.

Brad arrived. "Time to go, sis. We're waiting."

"Okay." Sam sighed, rose, picked up her bags.

Hal came in and the two men carried out her chair and heaved it on top of the cart. Sam looked around her little house one more time, stepped out the door, and didn't look back.

They met Arlene and Todd at the top of the mesa trail.

Martha was there and said, "Take care. Maybe I'll see you again someday."

The three men wrestled the cart down the trail and stopped to rest at the bottom.

"At least this was downhill," Hal said.

"Don't remind us." Todd picked up the cart handle. They moved on. The cart slid easily on the flat land.

Sadness, anticipation, and worry fought in Sam's mind. She ignored the people who watched them leave. She couldn't take responsibility for those who refused to use their brains and senses. The river was still low and moved sluggishly. Woodsy and flowery aromas tickled her nose and she inhaled deeply.

I hope I can remember all this.

At the bridge, Lucy and her family waited with their bags, along with Liia and Giil.

"Jone and the others went through yesterday," Liia said. "I'm ready to go."

Sam led the group up the trail, with Todd and Brad pulling the cart behind. Later in the afternoon, Sam and Lucy went ahead and located the cavern. Lucy chose to camp inside. Sam went back outside as the sun set, to wait for the others at the main trail.

"Okay, we're leaving," she said to World. "Leave the others alone." She sensed an acknowledgement.

Lucy's boys trotted up, followed by their dad, Brad, and Hal.

"Do you have a lightstick?" Brad asked. "I gave them mine, but it's not working too well."

"Let me look." Sam fished in her bag. "Hi, Liia, good to see you. How are the youngsters?"

"Growing up. Wait until you see them." She widened her lips.

"Thanks," Brad took the lightstick and trotted back down.

"I hope they get up here soon." Sam settled down beside Liia. They had a lot to catch up on.

Presently, the three men lurched into the cavern and dropped to the ground.

"The cart's outside," Todd huffed. "We had to dump a couple tables and cabinets to get it up."

"It's flat over there except for the last bit, and we'll have help there," Sam said. "We'll camp here and go in the morning."

Sam curled in her blankets. The sadness of leaving her old home blended with the anticipation of reaching her new home. The menace was close, but still undefined. She had, at least partially, accomplished her goal and would have a new life on the new world. She decided to give up always worrying about things.

•   •   •

Liia and Giil went through first with Lucy and her family, while the men got the cart into the cavern. Then Todd's parents and another pair. It took a while to get the cart maneuvered into the Gate room. Hal and Todd went with the cart, and Sam, Arlene, and Brad last.

When Sam came to, she saw the others scattered around the glade and the cart on its side, belongings strewed everywhere.

"Welcome to Peace. I'm Janni, your guide."

"Hi, Janni." Sam looked around and found the girl by her side.

"This is Glori, my sister in birth," Janni said, indicating a dark girl with a narrow face.

"What?" Lucy asked.

"We were born at the same time to different mothers."

Sam saw the quines at the stream. "You brought rides."

"Yes. What happened to your cart?"

"I don't know," Brad said. "It was upright when the blackness came, but like this when we woke up. You've met Todd. This is Arlene, our most important assistant. Lucy and Darrell and their boys."

"This is Liia and Giil, the Ambaak leaders," Sam added. "There may be a few coming through later. One woman wanted to wait until after she had her baby. And people do change their minds."

"Nice to meet you." Janni and Glori stood. "Are you all ready to go?"

Murmurs of *yesses* and *I-guess-sos*.

"Qilla," Janni called. One of the quines turned and looked at her. "We're ready to go."

The quine tossed her head and led the others over. Qiatta nuzzled Sam's hair as the woman patted her. They turned out to be one short, so Lucy's boys rode together on one, bouncing and pointing at various items. The men put what they could in the panniers and turned the cart over to cover the rest of the load.

"I called home and some people will come with a cart and collect the rest of your things." Janni mounted her quine. "Let the quines lead the way. Hold on to the neck hair if you need to; just don't pull hard. Okay, Qilla."

The quine moved down along the stream and the others followed.

The newcomers *ooh*ed and *aah*ed at the beach and the sky, and the quines headed for the water.

Sam sat on her quine and watched.

Home at last. The thought came unbidden.

Next to her, Janni said, "How can you stand to leave those other people back there?"

"I have no choice. They refuse to come. We can't carry them. I hate it, but I don't know what to do about it. One group says there is no other world and we're just trying to get rid of them."

"Oh, my." Janni looked around. "Qilla, we need to get going."

The quine bellowed and the others turned to her, then followed her along the water's edge.

Sam looked around at her new world and breathed deeply. Brad rode on the water side, Hal behind because his quine wouldn't leave the water. Hal had agreed to take over the mayorship, so, for the first time in years, Sam was able to fully relax.

It grew dark, so they camped at a stream. The next morning, when they reached the halfway camp, several people with quines waited for them. Sam also saw a narrow cart with wheels. Marisa, Allen, and one of Marisa's brothers greeted them.

"So you're here at last," Marisa said to Sam.

"Yes. I hated to leave, but there were some things I was glad to leave behind."

The men and two extra quines headed for the Gate with the cart. "We'll see if we can repair your cart," Allen said. "If not, at least we'll know what we need and can send someone up later to get it."

"Okay," Sam said. She wasn't going to worry about it.

Sam and the others headed for the colonies. Shortly after they passed the end of the trees, Sam saw a group of people up the slope. Liia and Giil stopped.

"That must be our place," Liia said. "We wanted it close to the forest and the sea."

"Not too close. We've had a couple of big storms that blew the water up the slope," Marisa said.

"The hill slants more here, it might not be too bad." Sam shrugged.

"Thanks, we'll tell the others," Liia said.

"See you around," Sam said. "Do you still have your phone?"

"Yes. Do you think it'll work here?"

"We can try it and find out."

A young man carrying an infant, followed by two young women, ran down to them.

"Hi, Uncle Brad," he said. "My son, Brad."

"Jimmy?" Brad asked.

"You can call me Jim now. Here's Siila, my wife." She was a pretty, adolescent girl. "And Betty. You remember Uncle Brad."

"Oh, yes. I love this place. No earthquakes."

"You're all grown up." Sam smiled.

Brad had saved Jim and Betty as children in the downfall of City and left them with childless Jone and Liia. Betty was almost as tall as Sam, nicely filled out, and her brown hair tied back. She still wore her mother's locket. A wide smile covered her face.

"We need to get going," Marisa said.

"I'll come visit one of these days," Brad said.

"Me too," Sam added as they left. "Have to call you gramps now." Sam smirked at Brad.

"Quiet, woman."

At the bridge over the little river, Lucy, her family, Todd's parents, the others, and Arlene went on up to Haven, and Sam and her men continued with Janni to the plaza.

Granlyn and Grampa Larry sat at one of the tables in high back chairs.

Granlyn rose and embraced Sam. "Welcome home."

"Thank you." Sam bent over and hugged Grampa.

Granlyn sat. "Welcome all of you. We are having a community feast here tonight. I've invited Glenda and several of the others to come down and join us. I'm afraid a few of the older folk might not be too happy about that, but tough. We have made arrangements for you to stay here tonight and go up to your place tomorrow. Do you want to rest now or talk?"

"I'm not tired," Sam said. "I'd just as soon sit here and take this all in." The buildings and the trees glowed in the western sunlight.

"Thank you," Todd added. "We'll stay. It's very nice here."

Sam smiled inwardly at Brad's scowl.

Granlyn nodded. "Sit down. Samanda, since you and I are the heads of our clans, we need to get some rules straight."

"Actually, I've retired. Hal is the big boss now." Sam grinned and Hal shook his finger at her. "But I'll listen."

"First, I need a list of your people who may contact my clan. Any others with questions or needs can go through them. You four, Glenda, and who else?"

"Arlene, she's my second in command, or rather Hal's, Zilla, the director of the medical clinics, George, the head of our science workshop, and Doug, our watermaster. He'll need to get with someone to build a waterwheel."

"What about food?"

"That will be June, who runs the big caff. We're putting kitchens in the houses."

"That's ten. That should be sufficient." Granlyn waved at an older woman crossing the plaza. "Now to our rules. Number One. No one is to come here unless invited, and you ten are. Make sure your young ones understand this. We've already had problems with a group of your adolescent boys.

"Two. Stay out of our crop fields. We will help you with food when necessary; we don't want anyone to go hungry. Three, leave the quines alone. They will let you know if they don't want you around.

"And of course, help anyone who's hurt, no matter who they are. If one of your people is caught breaking a rule they will be punished. Punishment depends on the offense. Just remember, we can see into their minds if we choose to."

"Fine," Sam said. "Your people should stay away from Haven, also."

"Haven?" Granlyn said, and looked at Larry. They shared a chuckle.

"Yes, that's the name we picked. What's so funny?"

"That's the name of the town we grew up in on Earth." Granlyn smiled. "It's all right, you can use it."

Sam's heart dropped back to normal. "You, Perri and Charley, Marisa and Allen, and Janni can come up any time. I know you won't use your mind talent unless you have to, but some don't believe that."

"Sam is right." Hal grinned at her. "We don't need people messing with our places and crops."

"What about Liia and her people?" Sam asked.

"I have talked to them and they agreed to the same rules." Granlyn pushed herself up from the table and helped Grampa Larry to his feet. "We are going to go rest in the clinic. Janni, show them where they'll sleep."

"Sam, you can stay with Mama, and one of you men on her couch. The other two can have my and Gloria's couches. They're long enough.

•　　　•　　　•

At the banquet, Sam greeted Glenda and the others from Haven. "Where's Maxee?"

"She decided not to come. Too many people who don't know her and her kubs."

"Okay. I'll go see her tomorrow."

Glori, one of the servers, greeted Sam warmly. "So, it's over. All your people are here."

"Not all. Many decided not to come, but some may change their minds if it gets too bad over there. A few women are waiting until they have their babies, so there will be a few more show up after a while." Sam grinned at the girl.

Jan rode a quine down and Hal carried her to a seat. Sam heard grumbles and ignored them.

Sam felt more relaxed and happier than she had in a long time. She enjoyed the food and the company. Later, at Marisa's, Sam and Marisa talked for a long time. Finally, Sam told her about her farseeing and the coming menaces.

"All I know now is they'll be coming from the sky, so I'd suggest people get under cover. I don't know exactly when, but it will be soon. We will have some warning, again I can't see what. When I know more, I'll let you know."

"Oh, my Oneness," Marisa said. "To see the future. That's one thing we don't have. Thank you for telling me. We will have to let everyone know."

"There's some discoloration in space, which might be one of them. Another might be Janni's Other. We'll just have to all be on the alert."

"Yes. I'll tell Janni and Glori tonight." Marisa looked around and twisted her hands. "We'll talk again in the morning. You look like you're ready for bed."

"Yes, it's been a long day. Good night."

In bed, Sam thought of her farseeing. She knew now the menace — no, menaces — would come from the sky, but still couldn't tell exactly what they were.

66

PEACE

THE NEXT DAY SAM'S GROUP WENT UP TO HAVEN. Sam found her house, but there was no porch or window on the side overlooking the river. After she and Glenda got that straightened out, she and Hal held a meeting of everyone in the meeting hall and plaza, where she introduced Hal as the next mayor and Carolyn, his assistant.

"Arlene and I are retiring," Sam announced. "I will help out wherever needed and I will be one of your contacts for the clan. The others are Brad, Todd, Hal, Arlene, Zilla, George, Glenda and June. If you have any questions or problems regarding the clan, please bring your concerns to one of us and we will contact Marisa or Perri. Now, I heard about what happened to the boys," she added, and explained the rules. "The clan will have no compunction in enforcing them. Be warned."

Then she left and visited with Maxee.

"I'm here for good," Sam said, sitting beside the Klocti. The kubs played around her. "I can't believe how many refused to come."

"No brains. I want see your house."

"You will. It's not finished yet. How are you doing?"

"Fine. Wonderful place. Teaching little ones."

"Good."

They chatted for a while.

Finally, Sam said, "I need to get back. I'll see you tomorrow."

"Iss." Maxee bounced up and down on her bottom.

During the next few days, Sam explored the place while Hal set up his mayor's office.

•   •   •

One day, Evelyn and Jan met Sam.

"This is for you," Jan said, handing Sam a large flat package.

Sam opened it and gasped. It was the view from her window in Starview stitched in colorful detail on a white cloth and framed with strips of dark wood.

"How in City did you do this?"

"Maxee drew it and helped me pick colors. I had to do something, you were the only one, except Hal, that would do anything for us."

Evelyn nodded weepily in the background.

Sam was stunned. No one had ever made anything like this for her. It must have taken Jan months.

"Thank you so much," Sam said, tears in her eyes. "I will treasure this forever." She reached over and hugged Jan.

67

PEACE

IN THE DAWN, JANNI'S BEING IS OUT IN SPACE. She calls the Watcher voice, but it does not respond. A small colony on another world has been trashed. Janni expands through the galaxy and finds the Other. Again, she tells them her people do not want to be Watchers.

There is an ugly purple bruise in space. As Janni tries to understand what it is, the voice comes. 'Get all inside structures or beneath trees. Use shield for all. A tail of nova will pass over your world.'

'When?'

'In two of your days.'

'How long?'

'Sky may change.'

'All of the other colony is on Peace. Now can you stop our Talent?'

The voice is gone.

Janni returns to her body.

•   •   •

When Janni woke, the memory hit her like a sledgehammer.

Must tell Granlyn. Why can't I think? No, must tell everybody.

She *sent* to everyone, 'I have received a message from Watchers that a wave from space is coming through and we must all stay indoors tomorrow, or we'll be fried. This is for real. I have seen other worlds that have been destroyed.'

She was barraged with calls and shut down her mind.

"It's true, Willie," she told him as she prepared breakfast. Marisa, Gramma Perri, and several others showed up at her door.

"Mama, Gramma, I was out this morning and saw a darkness in space coming this way. The Watcher voice told me, so it has to be true. You know they can't lie."

"Is this the others?"

"No, something different." Janni put Willie's plate down in front of him and ate off hers in the kitchen.

"It's true," Glori said, bursting in. "I know it in my bones."

"I feel it too," said her mother, Susan, right behind her. "Think, Marisa."

Marisa closed her eyes. "You're right, but how do we convince the others?"

"I'll put the fear of it in their minds."

"Janni, no. You know we don't meddle with other people's minds, even if you can."

"Not even to save their lives?"

"Oh Janni, what am I going to do with you?"

'She's right,' Granlyn *sent* to the other women's minds. 'She's grown up now and is using her Talent to save her people.'

"What about the outhouse?" Susan asked.

"Get chamber pots."

"Okay."

Willie jumped up and left. "Gotta get to work."

"I need to tell Sam and Hal, and the Ambaak group."

Janni ran over to the quines and she and Qilla headed north. She found Sam and Hal meeting with Gus and Glenda.

"I just found out there's a massive danger coming here, and you need to keep all your people indoors tomorrow. Some kind of space wave. A Watcher told me, and they do not lie."

"So that's what it is," Sam said. "Yes, I see it now. What can we do about it?"

"It'll only affect people and things out of doors."

"Are you sure?" Hal asked.

"Yes!" she almost screamed. "Sam, I need you to come with me to warn the other group. You know them better than anyone."

"I can't, I have to go tell Maxee. Brad knows them just as well."

Janni and Brad headed out cross country. The creatures happily waded across the little river. When they reached the farms on the outskirts of the community, they slowed to a walk. The pair followed the road through the neatly laid-out community to the square in the center of town.

Brad asked for Liia, and they met with her and Giil.

Janni told them what she knew. "I know you don't have many houses yet, but you can hide in the forest."

"Brad?" Liia asked.

"She's right. It's true. Take cover." He smiled.

Janni was on pins and needles the rest of the day. She could not concentrate on any task. Her thoughts roamed wildly through her head; her outside self was barely there.

A tongue of purple appeared in the northeast sky and the day grew dark.

'Shields up, everyone,' Janni and Marisa *sent* after supper.

The purple sky showed only a faint light where the sun should be.

"Go to your houses and stay inside."

Janni huddled with Willie in her house, constantly linked with Glori. The whole clan linked and shielded. Even the naysayers couldn't deny the sky.

Sam and Hal stayed in her house, now with a porch overlooking the river. She couldn't believe this was happening after all she'd been through. Although the sky was not visible, the river had a purplish tint. At least she wasn't alone. Brad had Emily and the kids, and most of the other loners were with other loners.

In Newamb, Liia and Giil huddled in one of the few completed buildings. Most of their people had gone to the forest. She hoped the clan girl was right about the forest being safe. Oh, if she could only have a quiet life again.

No one slept much.

The next day crept by. Old Maria and Granli dropped out of the Talent force. And, shortly after, Old Chad. Janni, and Glori strengthened their Talents to replace them. Granlyn was holding her own, but Janni didn't know how much longer she could hang on.

Janni arranged for each person to take breaks, one at a time, to eat and rest. Since Grampa Larry was unable to participate, he took care of Granlyn. Roroy notified each person when to take his or her break. He and Elli also tended to youngsters as needed.

The purple lessened as the world turned away at night. The second morning it was gone. Most slept through the day and night.

'Are we safe now?' Maxee *asked* Janni.

'I hope so.'

But the clan wasn't.

•   •   •

Janni woke midafternoon. Willie snored beside her. She rose and left the house. Outside, the sky was clear. She turned around and felt the Other. It was too close if she could sense it from the planet.

"Glori," she shrieked and ran to her house.

"What?" Glori mumbled, half awake.

"The Other. It's here. It's going to attack us. Connect all the Talent."

"Calm down."

"No, there's no time."

Janni began linking with others, Willie and her family first. Glori followed. When all were linked, the two created a shield to cover all three communities.

Janni not only felt the impact of the beam as it slid off the shield and took out a large chunk of land to the northeast, she also *sensed* the one called Bettah destroy the killer and, in the process, their threesome.

The women clutched each other. "There's an old saying," Glori said, "that troubles come in threes. What's next?"

"No. We've had enough."

But Janni knew she still had to deal with the Watcher. They stood together for a moment, Janni not quite believing the threat was gone. She turned and the two wandered down to the plaza. An atmosphere of closure and peace surrounded the women. The silence was eerie. Usually there were a lot of people coming and going.

Janni heard a baby cry. "We've got to go help," she said as she took off in the direction of the sound.

She located him and woke his mother so she could feed him. Then she and Glori went around and checked for children awakening and tended to them.

Janni felt the duality strongly. Part of her watched the two making the rounds, part of her felt the aftermath atmosphere and the feel of the food and the children. Always in the back of her mind lurked the Watcher.

How could she get it to take their Talents away?

68

PEACE

WHEN SAM WOKE, she couldn't tell whether it was dawn or dusk. A cloud of smoke hung over the northeast.

"Well, we're still here," Hal said, sitting up and hugging her.

"Yes. Let's see how the others fared."

They went out and found others gathering in the plaza. Someone noticed the smoke.

"Fire not good," Roroy said. "We will go check it."

"Thank you," Sam said. "Glenda, check everyone. I need to go see Maxee, she can call the clan."

"Okay. Two more days lost." Glenda put on a small smile.

The quines refused to come out from under the trees, so Sam walked. She met Maxee and her young coming to the community.

"Sammie, you all right?"

"Yes, you?'

"Iss. Kubs scared." The four-year-old clung to her, the baby in her arms.

"It's over now. I need you to contact Janni, let her know we're okay and find out how they are and if they need anything."

"Okee." Maxee sat down and closed her eyes.

Sam pulled out her phone and called Liia. She hadn't known whether it would work here, but they'd tested it and it did.

"Sam," Liia said breathlessly. "Are you well?"

"We're fine. Maxee is trying to contact Janni. You?"

"The forest worked. Our ears still ring from the noise. All is well here." Liia gulped. "I thought this was going to be a peaceful world."

"Me too. I'll tell Maxee." Sam touched the Klocti's arm. "Liia's group is all right."

Maxee nodded.

"Okay, take care. I'll call you when I can come over."

"Good."

After Maxee finished communicating with Janni, she gathered up her bags and the kubs, and accompanied Sam back to Haven, to Sam's house.

Inside, Maxee looked around. "Nice. Can see river." She went over to Jan's stitchery. "Jan did real good."

"Yes, it's gorgeous. She said you drew the outline."

"I draw good."

"Yes, you do. You can stay here if you wish."

"Okee."

That night the stars dazzled.

After things settled down, Sam and Hal sat in her house looking through the trees at the rushing river. Jan's picture hung on the wall near the window.

"At least, we still have each other," she said, leaning into him. "And I'm going to enjoy my life here."

The menace and her ex were gone.

69

PEACE

WHEN JANNI GOT THE CALL FROM MAXEE, relief washed over her. So their shield did work over all three communities. Most people were up by dinner time and wandering around. Everyone seemed to be all right. Gramma Perri corralled a few other women to fix supper at the plaza.

Marisa called *Janni* to her. "You and I and Miss Sam will work together to make sure our communities get along with each other. You and Beverly will be the contacts for your generation."

Janni nodded. "I'll talk to each of their women who want their birth control removed. But I still have to deal with the Watcher."

•　　•　　•

Janni sent her being out that night. 'All right, the Other and the menace are gone. Now can we have our normal human lives back,' she *yells*. She *senses* Watchers surrounding her.

'With other gone, must have you.'

'Why do we need Watchers anyway? What makes you better than us?' She *pushes* back at their presence.

'Many races need overseers.'

'Why?' She *pushes* harder.

'Destroy selves, others if not guided.'

'We don't need to be guided. We're doing all right as we are.' She *twists* them. Something bends. She doesn't need Talents any longer.

'You are. Others not.'

'So let them live the way they want.' One section of her being is free.

'Cannot.'

'Who appointed you as rulers?' She *twists* another way and *senses* something give.

'We one of first intelligent races.' They do not fight back. 'We not live much longer. Is much to teach you.'

'Forget it. If you're dying, then perhaps the rest of us don't need Watchers anymore.'

She *pushes* them away and *surrounds* them. They begin to shrink.

'No,' comes faintly.

The Watchers disappear. Not just from where Janni is, but from the universe. A great peace steals over her as she returns to her body for the final time.

•　　•　　•

In the morning, Janni went to visit Granlyn and Grampa Larry and found them both still in bed.

"Why aren't you up? Are you unwell?"

"No," Granlyn said. "We can't handle any more of this. We've had enough."

Janni went to her side. "Granlyn, there's lots more to see and do. Don't leave me."

Granlyn sat up, Janni beside her in a hug. "I never expected all this when I was your age. I figured I'd teach younger children, get married and have a family, go traveling. Well, I have, but not the way I visualized. This has been a vast adventure with Larry by my side.

"Four lovely children. Not surprised by twins, my mother and Larry's father were twins. Seven wonderful grandchildren and I've lost count of great grandchildren, of which you were the first. I can no longer teach, and I've finished traveling, farther than I could have ever imaged. What more is there?"

"Don't you want to see my child?" Janni asked, grinning. "She won't go into space."

"She …?"

"Yes. She will be Kaylyn."

Granlyn closed her eyes. "Yes," she whispered.

Janni welcomed the mantle of womanhood as she allowed it to slip around her.

ABOUT THE AUTHOR

Lorna Hopkins Keith was born in Hollywood, California, earned a B.A. in Mathematics, and has been writing since her teens. Fascinated by both numbers and words, she is also a musician, photographer, and puzzler.

Lorna has self-published a science fiction trilogy, attended many science fiction conventions and writing workshops, and has read science fiction most of her life.

She grew up in California, lived in Colorado, and moved to Florida with her physical therapist husband, where they live by a lake with a chatty calico cat.

ALSO BY THE AUTHOR

CITYFALL

After Samanda Lar destroys her ex-husband, the Volen hand her the mission of saving the people of City and establishing their new home.

Available from Water Dragon Publishing in
hardcover, trade paperback, and digital editions
waterdragonpublishing.com